KILLER SMILE

KILLER SMILE
LISA SCOTTOLINE

DOUBLEDAY LARGE PRINT HOME LIBRARY EDITION

HarperCollins*Publishers*

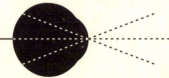

This Large Print Book carries the
Seal of Approval of N.A.V.H.

In memory of my father,
Frank Joseph Scottoline,

and my grandparents,
Giuseppe and Mary Scottoline

A woman is like a tea bag. You never know how strong she is until she's in hot water.

—ELEANOR ROOSEVELT

ONE

"Rosato & Associates," Mary DiNunzio said into the receiver, then kicked herself for answering the phone. The caller was Premenstrual Tom, a man who wanted to sue the Philadelphia Police Department, the United States Congress, and a local cantaloupe. He'd been calling the office at all hours, and Mary felt sorry for him. He was obviously off his meds and had reached one of the few lawyers in the city who wouldn't sue fruit.

"This is Mr. Thomas Cott!" he shouted. "Who's this?"

"I'm Mary DiNunzio. We spoke yesterday—"

"Get me Ms. Benedetta Rosato!"

"Ms. Rosato is gone for the day, sir." Mary checked her watch. 10:16 P.M. Everyone had gone home hours ago, and until now, the offices had been blessedly quiet. "The office is closed."

"Then what are *you* doing there, Ms. Mary DiNunzio?"

Good question, Mr. Thomas Cott. Mary was working late again, reading until her brown eyes turned red and her contacts dried to the crispness of breakfast cereal. Documents blanketed the conference table like a legal snowstorm, and her compact figure had been curled into the swivel chair for so long she felt like a meatball. "Mr. Cott, I'll take a message and tell Bennie—"

"I refuse to leave any more messages! Get Ms. Benedetta Rosato on the line! I demand to know why she won't represent me! She specializes in constitutional rights, it says so on the computer!"

"The computer?"

"In the library! The website, *your* website! It says it right there! That's false advertising! What about *my* constitutional rights? They don't matter? *I* don't matter?"

"Mr. Cott, no lawyer can take every case," Mary answered, then hesitated. Bennie had told the associates not to engage Premenstrual Tom, but if she could explain it to him, maybe he'd stop calling. "I think Bennie told you she didn't think your case could prevail in court. She's practiced constitutional law for a long time and has excellent judgment, so—"

"All those judges are in on it! All of them are crooked, every single one of them! City Hall is a pit of conspiracy and corruption! They're all in the mayor's pocket!"

"Mr. Cott, the judges in City Hall aren't crooked, and your case would be in federal court anyway—"

"You're not fooling me, either of you! Put Ms. Benedetta Rosato on the telephone right now! I know she's there! She must be, she's not at home!"

Mary blinked. "How do you know she's—"

"I went to her house! I knocked on her door, I waited for her to answer! The windows were dark!"

Mary stiffened. "How did you get her address?"

"It's in the phone book, I looked it up! What do you think I am, *incapable*? I may not have a fancy law degree, but I am not *incapable*, MS. MARY DiNUNZIO!"

Mary suddenly stopped feeling sorry for him. He was shouting louder now, almost screaming.

"I SAID, get MS. BENEDETTA ROSATO on this telephone RIGHT NOW! I KNOW she's right there with you!"

"Mr. Cott, if you'll just—"

"DON'T LIE TO ME! Don't you DARE LIE TO ME!"

"Mr. Cott, I'm not—"

"I'll come down there, you LYING WHORE! I'll come down there and SHOOT—"

Mary hung up, shaken. The conference room fell abruptly silent. The air felt charged. It took her a moment to process what had just happened. Okay, Premenstrual Tom had morphed into Psychotic Tom, and it wasn't funny anymore. Bennie was at an ACLU dinner, but it would be ending soon. She could be going home. Mary had to warn her. She reached for the phone to call the boss's cell.

Rring, rrriiinng! The phone rang underneath Mary's hand, jarring her. *Rrrriiinng!* She gritted her teeth and let it ring twice more so voicemail would pick up. She should never have engaged Premenstrual Tom. When would she learn? Her good-girl reflexes—Help Out, Be Nice, Tell the Truth—sucked in the practice of law.

Mary pushed the button for her direct phone line and called Bennie, but there was no answer. She left a detailed message, then hung up, uneasy. She'd call her back in five minutes to make sure the boss had gotten the message.

Mary eased back in her swivel chair, wishing suddenly that she weren't alone in the office. She eyed the doorway to the conference room, surprised to find the threshold dark. Who turned out the lights in the reception area? Maybe the cleaning people, when they'd left.

I'll come down there and shoot

Mary eyed the phone, daring it to ring again. She didn't leave it off the hook because the drill was to record threatening messages for evidence, in case the office had to go for a restraining order, like with Premenstrual Fred. Mary wondered fleetingly if she could find a career that didn't attract garden-variety homicidal rage or bad television commercials.

She told herself to get over it. Premenstrual Tom had been blowing off steam, and there was a security desk in the lobby

of the building. The guard wouldn't let anybody upstairs without calling her first, especially after business hours, and nowadays
you couldn't get past the desk without a driver's license and a mortgage note.

She got back to work, tucking a dark
blonde tendril into its loose French twist,
and picking up the document she'd been
reading. It was a letter dated December 17,
1941, from the provost marshal general's
office, a federal agency that no longer existed. Its type was grainy because it was
a Xerox copy of a photocopy of a carbon
copy, and on another night, Mary would
have gotten a charge out of its vintage.
Everybody in the office called her case the
History Channel, but she loved the History
Channel. Mary loved mostly everything on
cable except The Actor's Studio, which she
wouldn't watch at gunpoint. But she didn't
want to think about gunpoint right now.

Mary scribbled USELESS on a Post-it,
stuck it on the letter, and set it in the USE-
LESS stack in front of her. She ignored how
tall the USELESS stack was getting because it would be USELESS. Documents
surrounded her and sat packed in boxes
along the side wall of the conference room.

Somewhere in these papers was the file for a man named Amadeo Brandolini. Amadeo had emigrated from Italy to Philadelphia, where he'd married, had a son, and built up a small fishing business. When World War II broke out, he was arrested by the FBI and imprisoned along with ten thousand other Italian-Americans, under an act better known for authorizing the internment of the Japanese. Amadeo lost everything and eventually committed suicide in the camp. His son's estate had hired Mary to sue for reparations, and she couldn't help but mourn him. Very few shows on the History Channel had happy endings, which was why everybody watched Fox.

Rring! The phone rang, and Mary jumped. It had to be Premenstrual Tom calling back, because she had told Bennie to call her on her cell and she didn't *have* anybody else to call her, which was why she was working late. Perhaps these things were related, but Mary was in no mood for introspection. She tensed all over. *Rrriiinng! Rrriiinng!*

Finally the ringing stopped. The conference room fell silent again. Mary waited for the silence to seem more like friendly-silence and less like scary-silence, but that wasn't

happening. The reception area was still dark.
She tried to relax but couldn't. She glanced
over her shoulder even though she was
thirty-two stories up. It was dark outside,
and in the onyx mirror of the windows, she
saw the sparkling new conference room, a
messy table dotted with Styrofoam coffee
cups, and a Drama Queen with a law degree.

I'll come down there and shoot

Mary turned back, picked up the phone,
and pressed in Bennie's cell number. Again
there was no answer, so she left another
warning, slightly more hysterical. She hung
up and checked her watch again. 10:36. It
was late. She didn't want to sit here while he
called back again. She couldn't concentrate
anyway. Time to go. She got out of the chair,
stuffed her briefcase with documents,
grabbed her purse, and left the conference
room.

Leather chairs and a matching couch
loomed in the darkened reception area, and
Mary scooted past the terrifying furniture for
the elevator, which didn't come fast
enough. Once inside, she breathed a little
easier, and when the elevator reached the
lobby, she stepped off and glanced around,

her pulse slowing to normal. The fake-marble lobby was bright and empty, except for a fake-granite security desk manned by a guard too sleepy for her comfort level. Bobby Troncello, an amateur boxer Mary knew from the neighborhood, undoubtedly dozing over the sports page.

"Wake up, Bobby," she said, making a beeline for the desk. She set her briefcase on its glistening surface and peeked over the edge. "We got trouble."

"What do you mean?" Bobby looked up, edging the maroon cap he hated over his thick eyebrows. His brown eyes were glassy-wet, his nose wide and dotted with large pores, and his mouth a slash that was usually swollen from the gym. The *Daily News* lay open on his desk, tabloid-size, its pages cut in a soft zigzag fringe, and a can of Coke warmed beside an oily white wrapper from a cheesesteak dinner. Only the end of the long hoagie roll remained, with a brownish knob like an elbow.

"I just got a phone call from a very angry man named Tom Cott. I don't know what he looks like, but he threatened to come here tonight and shoot me."

"Uh-oh." Bobby's forehead knit unhappily.

"You're supposed to tell me not to worry."

"Don't worry, Mare. Bennie already told us to watch out for this Cott guy. Nobody gets upstairs, you know that. He comes in my lobby, I'll take care of him myself. I wouldn't let anybody hurt my homegirl."

Mary smiled, almost reassured. "He went to Bennie's house tonight. He said he looked her up in the phone book. I called her and left a message warning her, but I'm worried."

"About *Rosato*? I'd worry about *him*." Bobby laughed, rising to stretch arms that strained against the seams of his maroon blazer. His lapels parted as he reached up, releasing a heady combination of Drakkar Noir and fried onions. "If that knucklehead tussles with her, she'll kick his ass from here to Broad Street."

"But he said he'd shoot me, or us. I think." Mary couldn't remember much Premenstrual Tom had said after *shoot*, and his calling her a whore bothered her more than it should have, especially when it was part of a death threat in general. "What if he has a gun? What if he goes to Bennie's house with a gun?"

"So what? Rosato carries concealed."

Bobby snorted. "She'd bust a cap in him before he could find his pants pocket."

Strangely, I feel worse. "Is this your best stuff, Bobby?"

"Don't worry, everything's fine. You been workin' too hard, night after night. Lemme get you a cab." Bobby grabbed Mary's briefcase, walked around the security desk, and looped an aromatic arm around her shoulder. "By the way, what did you decide about my friend Jimmy? You gonna let me hook you up?"

Mary hid her dismay. Bobby had been trying to fix her up with his fellow boxers, a continuous loop of Joeys, Billys, and a stray Pooch. Lately, everybody was playing matchmaker, as if they'd all decided Mary wasn't allowed to be a Young Widow anymore. She hadn't known there was an official cutoff.

"I told you about Jimmy. We went to Bishop Neumann together, he's a real nice guy. Works his dad's plumbing business, got a nice car. Season tickets to the Eagles. *Club level*, Mare."

"Thanks, but I don't think so."

"You sure?" Bobby led her to the polished brass door, opened it for her, and gentled her outside onto the sidewalk. The night air felt crisp, and there was almost no traffic at this hour. Rosato & Associates had moved to nicer offices uptown since they started doing class action work, and the ritzy new location made it easier to get cabs. Bobby hailed one almost instantly. "Come on, Mare, whyn't you give Jimmy a shot?"

Mary smiled. "Give him a shot? You're a poet."

"You gotta get back in the saddle, girl." Bobby opened the cab door with a wink.

Yowza. "Another time, thanks." Mary tucked herself inside the backseat of the cab, waved good-bye to Bobby, and gave her address to the cabbie, a bald, older man. He merely nodded in response, strangely taciturn for a Philadelphia cabdriver, and for a minute she thought he didn't speak English, but his ID card read John Tucker. They lurched off, rattling through the dark, empty streets of the city, and the cab took on an oddly hollow feel in the interior. Or maybe it was just too clean inside. The black carpet reeked of strawberry spray, the vinyl seat shone with Armor All, and the seat belt actually worked. It was all too topsy-turvy for Philly, and Mary felt disoriented.

"You keep your cab very clean," she said pleasantly, but he didn't answer. Maybe he hadn't heard.

"This cab is so neat!" she said, louder, but he still didn't say anything, so she let it go and slipped lower in the seat, glancing out the window as they barreled up Walnut past a darkened Burberry's and Kiehl's. A few businesspeople walked down the street, the men with ties loosened, the women with purses swinging. A raggedy homeless man shouted from the corner of Eighteenth and Walnut, reminding Mary of Premenstrual Tom. She reached in her purse, retrieved her cell, and pressed redial for Bennie. Again the boss didn't answer, and she left another message. She flipped the phone closed and watched the rearview mirror for the cabbie's reaction. He said nothing, but his gaze shifted hard-eyed to the right. They traveled in silence to her neighborhood, and he swung the cab more roughly than neces-sary onto her street. Mary felt unaccount-ably as if she'd wronged him, so when they pulled up in front of her house, she handed him a ten-dollar bill on a six-dollar fare.

"Keep the change," she said, but he only nodded again. She opened the door, gathered her belongings, and had barely climbed out of the cab before the cabbie hit the gas and sped off, leaving her alone at the curb.

I'll come down there and shoot

The voice echoed in Mary's head, and then it struck her: Premenstrual Tom could have looked up where she lived. He knew her name; she was in the phone book, too. The realization startled her, then she wondered why she hadn't thought of it before. He could be here, on her street. Watching her. Right now. With a gun.

Her gaze swept the street, a skinny alley lined with small brick trinities. Its one streetlight, at the far end of the street, wasn't bright enough to reassure her. Some of her neighbors had mounted lights beside their front doors, but they cast little illumination except on their own front stoops. The sidewalks were vacant. Everybody was inside. A few city trees planted at curbside rustled in the breeze, and Mary sized them up with suspicion. Their trunks looked too thin for someone to hide behind, but Premenstrual

Tom could be skinny. If he wasn't retaining water.

I'll come down there and shoot

Mary felt a panicky urge to get in her house. Her front light was off, and she hurried up the front stoop in the dark, shoving a hand into her purse for her keys. She could hear the sounds of an argument coming from two doors down; the Mendozas, who never fought. Odd; everything seemed strange tonight. Was it a full moon or what? She was fumbling with her key ring when the phone began ringing inside her house. She slid in her key, twisted the lock, and hurried inside, running through her darkened living room for the phone. "Hello," she answered, and it was Bennie, laughing.

"You don't listen, DiNunzio. I *told* you guys not to talk to him."

"I thought I could help. I just got in. Where are you?" Mary had never been so relieved to hear that it was her boss on the phone. Actually she had *never* been relieved to hear that her boss was on the phone, but that didn't mean she wanted her dead.

"I'm at home, safe and sound."

"Is Premenstrual Tom there?"

"Of course not. Thanks for worrying about

me, though. Remind me at evaluation time."
Bennie laughed again, and Mary guessed
she'd enjoyed the ACLU dinner, evidently
celebrating her First Amendment right to
chocolate martinis.

"Bennie, I think you should be taking this
more seriously."

"Relax, child. There's nothing to worry
about with him. He's all talk."

"How do you know he's all talk? You don't
know that."

"I know that."

"A hundred percent?" Mary didn't add
that she was a little worried for herself, too.
Or that Premenstrual Tom had called her a
name that hurt her feelings when he threatened to kill her. "He's such a creep!"

"Absolutely, he is. It's a given that he's a
creep, but that doesn't end the inquiry."

Almost convinced, Mary flopped down on
her couch, flicked on the glazed lamp on the
end table, and kicked off her pumps. The
shoes went skidding across the nubby
Berber, and the left one landed heel-up near
the front door. She glanced idly in its direction, then frowned. A skinny strip of light
shone from the threshold underneath her

front door. Had she not closed the front door behind her?

"Trust me, child," Bennie was saying. "I defended murder cases forever. There's the creeps you worry about and the creeps you don't. I'll tell you which is which."

Mary watched her door. Was it open? Where were her house keys? Her hand was empty, she didn't have them. She must have left them in the front door!

"The creeps you worry about are the ones who *don't* threaten you first. Believe me, *they're* the dangerous ones. They're the ones who don't broadcast it, or give any warning at all."

Mary's front door edged open. She went rigid. Was it a breeze? Or was someone out there? *Opening her front door?*

"The dangerous ones, the truly murderous ones, lie in wait. And then, when the moment's right, they *strike*."

"Yikes!" Mary blurted out, dropping the phone and bolting for the door. She darted across the room, wrenched her keys from the lock, and slammed the door shut with both hands. *Good. Yes. Phew.* She laughed with giddy relief. She twisted the deadbolt knob to lock the door and inserted the brass chain for the slide lock. Then she turned to go back to the phone, which was when she saw it.

A shadow of a man, flitting past the shutters that covered her front window.

Mary froze. Then he was gone. She listened. She didn't hear the sound of footsteps, but then again, the walls of her house were too thick. Maybe she should open the door and see?

OF COURSE NOT! ARE YOU NUTS? She hurried back to the phone and couldn't hide her panic.

"Bennie," she said, out of breath. "The weirdest thing just happened! A man just ran past my front window!"

"What did he look like?"

"Like a shadow!"

"Stay calm. Was there anybody out there when you came in?"

"No."

"And you said you just got in."

"Right."

Bennie chuckled. "Then there's nobody out there now."

"But I saw him!"

"A shadow. A shadow's not a man, DiNunzio."

"What if it was Premenstrual Tom? He looked up where you live, he could have looked up where I live. He's not *incapable*."

"Oh, he gave you the 'incapable' speech, too." Bennie laughed. "You're getting carried away. It's nighttime, there are shadows. You're a little spooked is all."

A little?

"Now, are you okay or do I have to come over there?"

No! "Yes!"

"Good, go to bed. I'll deal with our new best friend in the morning. Leave it to me, and thanks again for the call. Good night, kiddo."

"Good night," Mary said, but she hung up worried. Had she seen a man at the window? Had he opened the door? Had she been imagining it? Was it Premenstrual Tom? She rose uncertainly and padded barefoot to the window. The shutters were unhooked in the center, and she peeked out of the tiny opening between them. She could see only a cross section of her street; a sliver of red brick from the house opposite hers, a strip of flat asphalt roofline, and a slice of the black sky. Clouds rendered even heaven opaque, hiding the stars and keeping the moon a secret.

Mary stayed at the window, wondering. It seemed unlikely that Premenstrual Tom could be out there, but it wasn't impossible. There were dangerous people in this city; she knew because one of them had taken her husband's life. They had been married only two years, and Mike had been killed while he was riding his bicycle on the West River Drive, intentionally struck by a car. That his murderer had eventually been caught gave Mary no comfort. She was a lawyer still trying to understand the meaning of justice. She understood completely the meaning of loss.

She hooked the shutter closed, turned away from the front window, and switched off the light.

Plunging herself into a familiar blackness.

TWO

"Go away," Mary said without looking up. She was in her usual spot in the conference room, having spent another full day reading government documents. She still hadn't found Amadeo's file and she had three billion documents to go. Many lawyers would have balked at the task, but not Mary. She grew up in South Philly, where she'd learned to pop her gum, wear high heels, and work overtime. One of these skills would prove useful in life. Guess which.

"Come on, you need a break," called a voice from the threshold. Judy Carrier, fellow associate and best friend. "Let's go, it's time for dinner!"

Mary finished reading her document and

went on to the next. Only 2,999,999,999 to go. *If I never eat again, I can be finished by menopause. Yippee!*

"It's almost seven o'clock. Aren't you hungry? I'm starving."

"That's because you move around too much. Sit still. Work." Mary knew it was futile, even as she said it. Judy Carrier was from Northern California, where she climbed mountains for fun. Mary couldn't relate. Once she saw a photo of Judy's family wearing waist belts, ropes, and clips, and she thought they all worked for Comcast Cable.

"Let's go to the sushi place across the street. I hear that superhot guy from Dechert goes there, his name is Nicastro. Louis Nicastro." Judy brightened. "He must be Italian, like you!"

"Then we belong together. Register us at Bloomingdale's."

"Also if we go now, we can be back when Premenstrual Tom calls. Boo!" Judy had been ragging Mary all day and had even left a box of Midol on her desk.

"That's very supportive. Now go away. Let me work. Leave."

"Thanks. Don't mind if I do." Judy walked

into the conference room and plopped into a swivel chair.

Mary looked up, vaguely annoyed. Judy was pretty in a wide-open, all-American way, with round, bright blue eyes, a small, straight nose, and an easy, optimistic grin. Her chin-length hair had been dyed most recently the canary of legal pads, which Mary hoped was coincidental. And in contrast to Mary's stiff navy suit, Judy wore a tie-dyed T-shirt, baggy jeans, and yellow clogs that looked like bananas for the feet. The total effect was Business Casual meets Cirque du Soleil, but Mary didn't say so. Best friends know when to shut up. "So you just gonna sit there and stare at me?"

"I want you bad."

"Weirdo."

"When can we eat?"

"After I find Amadeo's file." Mary held up the paper she'd been reading. "These are inventory sheets of property and bank accounts from other internees. If I find his inventory sheets, I'll know what happened to his boats."

"What's the difference?"

"If I can trace what happened to his boats, I can get his estate reimbursed for their loss.

All the money he had he put into that business and it was lost when he was interned. You read the *Korematsu* case, you know the great dissent by Brennan. That's the justice part."

"True, except that the dissenters in *Korematsu* were Murphy and Jackson. You and Bennie always get that wrong. Brennan wasn't even on the Court at the time." Judy smiled. "And justice can wait until after dinner."

Mary knew Judy was kidding, at least about justice. An honors graduate of Boalt Hall, editor in chief of the *Law Review*, and a former law clerk to the Chief Judge of the Ninth Circuit Court of Appeals, Judy Carrier had legal credentials that enabled her to correct everybody in the office, and far surpassing others who dyed their hair with Jell-O.

"Wait a minute," Judy said, frowning at the documents scattered over the conference table. "You must have read these documents at the National Archives when you Xeroxed them. Did you see Brandolini's file then?"

"No, but I'm double-checking. I could have missed it. It has to be here." Mary skimmed the next document and sent up a silent prayer to St. Jude, Patron Saint of Lost Causes and Document Productions.

"*You* miss it?" Judy's eyes flared in blue disbelief. "You never miss anything. You're the most careful girl I know."

"Except for the dissenters in *Korematsu*. Besides, I couldn't concentrate when I was Xeroxing. I had to find the right files and I could only use the copy machine for five minutes at a time. They had so many rules, between the declassification stickers and the Identicards and the one-folder-at-a-time." Mary didn't add that she'd gotten distracted by just being at the National Archives. The College Park building was sleek, modern, and beautiful, a fitting edifice for the documented history of her country. She'd loved every minute of her research there, down to the cheery red pencils they gave you for free and the sign that read THIS IS YOUR HERITAGE!

"Mare, you're wasting your time."

"My time is officially worthless. This case is pro bono, remember?" Mary finished reading the letter, which was USELESS, too. She reached for a Post-it, slapped it on the letter, and instead of USELESS, scribbled THIS SUCKS. For variety.

"Okay. Fine. You force me to Plan B." Judy produced an almond Hershey bar from her jeans and unwrapped the tinfoil. She took a huge first bite, ignoring the perforations around the chocolate rectangles. Judy didn't like to be told what to do, even by candy.

"Don't get chocolate on my files," Mary said, but Judy was already chomping a coveted almond and soon would begin excavating all of them, saving for last the nutless chocolate remnants. It was one of her saturated fat fetishes. "Jude, I mean it, with the chocolate." Mary set her letter aside and scribbled THIS SUCKS, TOO on a Post-it. "Don't touch anything."

"Hey, what's this?" Judy picked up a sheaf of papers, which Mary grabbed back.

"Please! They're Amadeo's personal papers." Mary set the stack safely on her side of the table, but when she looked up, Judy was picking up something else. "Stop! That's an original, too!"

"An original what?"

"It's his alien registration booklet." Mary

grabbed it back, relieved to see it wasn't chocolate-covered. A pink booklet, it measured slightly larger than her palm and its faded paper cover was as soft as her old Catechism manual. It bore a round purple stamp dated MAR 6, 1941. "Amadeo had to register as an enemy of the country, even though his son fought for us in the same war. I can't believe that my country did this to its own people, to Amadeo. It's not the American way."

"Amadeo wasn't an American."

"He was too. He lived here for thirty years. He offered up his only son to the war, to fight for the country. If that isn't an American, what is?"

"But he wasn't a citizen, was he?"

"You're being legalistic."

"I'm a lawyer. What do you expect? Don't get your thong in a bunch."

"I don't wear thongs. What kind of girl wants people to think she doesn't wear underwear?" Mary sounded crazy even to herself, and Judy was looking at her like she was nuts. "All I'm saying is that I'm Catholic, okay? I *welcome* visible panty lines."

Judy put up a hand. "You're hungry, that's

why you're so cranky. So let's go walk my dog, then eat."

Mary returned to the booklet. The caption read, United States Department of Justice and under it, Certificate of Identification. There was an inky, rolled-out fingerprint on the left, and on the right, a black-and-white photo of Amadeo Brandolini, who was movie-star handsome. His eyes were dark under a strong forehead, his full mouth formed an easy smile, and his thick black hair glistened, evidently pomaded for his meeting with his adopted government. Mary held up the photo. "Doesn't Amadeo look like George Clooney?"

Judy squinted at the thumbnail-size photo. "No, freak, he looks nothing like George Clooney."

"He does, too. Exactly."

"You're getting bizarre. It's like you have a crush on him or something."

"Don't be ridiculous." Mary's gaze shifted to the right page of the booklet, which recorded that Brandolini was five seven and only 155 pounds. Under Distinctive Marks, someone had written *scar on forehead left side*. It said that he was born on August 30, 1903, in Ascoli-Piceno and had resided at

4933 Thompson Street in Philadelphia. Under Length of Residence in United States, someone had written *32 years*. Mary shook her head. Thirty-two years in this country, but he'd never applied for citizenship because he couldn't read and write. It would be his undoing.

"Where did you get that registration book? That wasn't at the National Archives, was it?"

"No, it was in his son Tony's personal effects. I got it from the lawyer for the estate, Frank Cavuto." Mary looked at the last page of the booklet. On the line that read Signature of Holder was scrawled a scratchy *X*. Next to it, someone had written *his mark*. Mary couldn't stop looking at that *X*. The unknown.

"Girls!" came a shout from the door, startling them both. It was Bennie Rosato towering in the threshold, her thick blonde hair piled into an unruly topknot. She wore jeans and a Fairmount Boat Club sweatshirt and hoisted a heavy handbag, trial bag, and black suitcase. She didn't look at all hungover to Mary, which was only one of her superpowers. "I gotta go to New York, I got called to trial in Preston on Monday. I'll be two weeks, tops. Can you tykes hold the fort?"

"Is a raise involved?" Judy asked with a smile, but Mary didn't have the guts, especially since Bennie carried concealed.

"That's almost funny, Carrier. Now. DiNunzio." The boss fixed her intense blue eyes on Mary. "I left two of my cases on your desk. They both have depositions this week. Take one and defend the other. Thanks."

"Sure. Yes. Fine." *Eeeeek!* "What about Premenstrual Tom? I heard he called again today."

"I didn't take the call, and you'd better not take any more while I'm away. He didn't come to my house last night, did he? He didn't come to the office today, did he? See? He'll go away, they always do."

Premenstrual Fred didn't. "What about that man, at my window?" Mary asked. She'd slept lousy last night and couldn't shake her bad mood. Even Conan O'Brien hadn't helped, when he did his little hip dance.

"That man was a shadow." Bennie shook her head. "Now tell me what's new in Alcor and Reitman. I heard they were getting active."

"No, they're quiet right now." *Because I'm ignoring them.*

"I don't want you spending all your time on Brandolini, I told you that. We're just recovering from last year, so this isn't the time to let down." Bennie's eyes narrowed. "Bill some time, ladies. Clients who pay deserve justice, too."

"Got it. Right." Mary set the papers down, and Bennie kicked the back of Judy's chair with a worn running shoe.

"Carrier, I almost forgot. I left the Neely Electric file on your desk, you'll see the notes on it. I need a summary judgment motion drafted and emailed to me by the end of the week. Tell me that's not a problem."

Judy laughed.

"Excellent. All right, I got a train to catch. I told Marshall to call me if we hear from Premenstrual Tom, and I'll stay on top of it. DiNunzio, don't forget about your other cases. And Carrier, don't pierce anything else. Bye, kids." Bennie rapped the threshold smartly, then disappeared. The associates remained silent until they heard the *ping* of the elevator that carried her away, then they burst into chatter.

"Don't pierce anything *else*?" Mary leaned

forward. "What does she mean by *that*? And why does she know before me?"

"Tell you on the way to dinner." Judy leapt to her bananas and rounded the table, where she grabbed Mary by the sleeve of her jacket and hoisted her to her pumps. "Now, girl! Out! You're coming to dinner with me."

"No, stop! I hate sushi!" Mary tried to stay rooted, but it was USELESS. She was a fireplug, but Judy was a Sequoia.

"We're not having sushi." Judy tugged Mary toward the conference room door. "I have a better idea."

"Better than piercing whatever?"

"Yes!" Judy yanked Mary to the elevator, got her downstairs, and stuffed her into a cab. Only then did Judy reveal where they were going.

And what she had pierced.

THREE

Mercer Street was a typical side street in South Philly, only one-Ford wide and lined with attached rowhouses of red brick, each a squat two stories. Every rowhouse had two windows on the second floor, and on the first, a bay window that generally displayed a plastic statue of the Virgin Mary and a miniature flag of Italy, the United States, or the Philadelphia Eagles. There were minor variations in the front doors, but everybody owned a screen door that displayed a scrollwork initial. On Mercer Street, the scrollwork initial was usually D. When Mary was young, she thought the D stood for Door, then her family got one and she realized it stood for DiNunzio, D'Orazio,

DiTizio, D'Agostino, DeMarco, DiAngeli, D'Amato, DeCecco, Della Cava, and finally, Dunphy. Whose wife was a DaTuno.

Mary and Judy climbed the front stoop of her parents' house and were just about to open the screen door when a gleaming black Escalade barreled down the narrow street. Nobody drove like that down Mercer, and Mary turned in annoyance, just in time to get a glimpse of the driver. He wore a black shirt and was burly, with his head slightly down and his cheeks pitted with acne scars. She was about to holler at him for driving too fast when Judy yanked her inside.

Familiar odors of fresh basil, homemade tomato sauce, and lemon Pine-Sol filled the tiny kitchen, and crackling palm fronds and dog-eared Mass cards remained stuck behind an ancient cast-iron switchplate. Colorized photos of Pope John, Jesus Christ, and JFK were still taped to the wall with yellowed off-brand tape, and the slop basket sat tucked in its customary corner of the white porcelain sink. Nothing would ever change in the DiNunzio house, which was still mourning the demise of the Latin Mass. Mary missed the Latin Mass, too, al-

though when Mike was murdered, she realized that she and God didn't speak the
same language anyway.

"Maria, Maria!" Vita DiNunzio gave her
daughter a hug, wrapping herself around
Mary's waist in the kitchen, but her embrace
didn't feel as strong as it always did. Her
grip was loose, and her arms as delicate as
the wings of a wren. She seemed thinner,
and the softness in her back had vanished.
She was wearing her favorite flowered
housedress, but it hung on newly knobby
shoulders.

"Ma, you okay?" Mary hugged her closer,
burying her face in her mother's stiff pink-
gray hair, teased like cotton candy to hide
her bald spot. Her coif smelled wonderfully
of dried oregano and Aqua Net, but reached
only as high as Mary's chin. Three weeks
ago, it had reached to her nose. When did
her mother shrink? *Can* you afford to shrink
if you're only four eleven? Mary broke their
clinch. "Ma, really, are you okay?"

"So pretty, my Maria," she purred, her
round brown eyes smiling behind her impossibly thick glasses. Her nose was strong
and smile soft, and she patted Mary's arm
with fingerpads pasty from pilled flour. "It's

so nice, you come viz," she said. Born in
Italy, she usually dropped her last syllables,
unwittingly proving they were superfluous.
But Mary noticed that she hadn't answered
the question.

"Ma, I'm serious, did you . . . lose
weight?" Mary didn't want to say *evaporate*.

"No, no, no, a little."

"How much? Maybe you're doing too
much, taking care of Gabrielle?" Her mother
had been baby-sitting part-time, helping out
the receptionist from Rosato & Associates.
Mary had thought it was renewing her en-
ergy, but maybe she'd been wrong. "Ma?"

"I'm fine, fine. Sit." Her pasty hand slid
down Mary's arm and she led her to the
kitchen table. Her mother had been making
gnocchi, and sifted flour dusted the
Formica table, covering stains and knife
marks Mary knew by heart. Homemade
pasta dough lay in long, skinny ropes, covered with the soft indentures of her mother's
fingers. Later her mother would cut the
fresh dough into tiny pillows, then pinch
each pillow in two, roll it with her fingertips,
and send it skidding across the floured
table with a *shhhppp*. Mary eased into the
padded chair, and her mother looked hap-

pily down at her. "You have coff'. You and Jud'. I put onna pot."

"Ma, I want to know why you're so skinny." Mary couldn't hide her dismay. Here, in the House of Things That Stayed the Same, something had *changed*. The most important thing.

"MRS. D, I'M STARVING!" Judy shouted. She would get away with it because Mary's parents adored her. Also because she got away with everything, even with bringing her golden retriever here for a visit. Mercifully small for a golden, Penny went everywhere with Judy and had better manners. "Help me, Mrs. D! I need food. Feed me!"

"Jud', Jud'!" Laughing, Mary's mother fluttered over to Judy and gave her a big hug, while Penny lapped water noisily from a chipped bowl that Mary's father had set on the linoleum floor. Her father was all-business now, having greeted Mary at the door with a hug that crushed her cheek to his white shirt, stiff with baked-in spray-starch. Although Matty DiNunzio had long ago retired as a tile setter, he always wore his short-sleeved shirt, black Bermuda shorts, and his hearing aid when Mary came home. He also loved seeing Judy, who was now hamming it up:

"Mrs. D, Mary wouldn't go out to eat with me and you know why? Because she's *working too hard*!"

"Maria," her mother said, waving a gnarled index finger. "Maria, I tella you, no work so hard! I tella you and Bennie! She no listen? *You* no listen?"

"I listened, she listened, we all listened." Mary felt vaguely as if she had just conjugated something. "Don't start, Ma. It's for Amadeo Brandolini, and there's a lot to be done."

"BUT FIRST WE EAT!" Judy said, hugging her mother again. "How can I help, Mrs. D?"

"No, no, you sit! Sit!" her mother replied, waving her off as she always did, because the kitchen was her exclusive territory and offers to help were construed as insults. "Sit!"

"Talked me into it." Judy took a seat across from Mary. Meanwhile, Penny, who had finished drinking, ran a dripping pink tongue over her chops and trotted over to the kitchen table, her black nose in the air, undoubtedly sniffing for Aquanet.

"Okay, I make gnocchi for you, and coff'!" her mother said.

Mary scrutinized her mother as she picked up a plate of gnocchi layered with waxed paper for freezing, carried it to the counter, and set it down. Her mother seemed to move nimbly enough as she filled the dented spaghetti pot with water, took it to the burner, and twisted the knob to HI for the flame. Mary had to find out what was going on, but she needed a secret plan. Italian mothers had force fields that deflected the fears of their children, even when their children reached thirty years old. Actually, the force field got older, too.

"Ma," Mary began, talking to her mother's flowered back, "so what's the matter with Mrs. DiGiuseppe? I saw her outside and hardly recognized her."

"She's got the cancer," her father interrupted. He evidently didn't understand about the force field and the secret plan. He scuffed in black slippers to the cabinet and retrieved two cups and saucers, which he brought to the table and clunked down in front of Mary and Judy. Mary straightened her cup in the chipped saucer, happily mismatched, and took another shot.

"What kind of cancer, Ma?"

"Liver," her father interrupted again, but he missed the dirty look Mary shot him. He turned around and headed for the silver-ware drawer, retrieved two forks and two spoons, then brought them to the table. "How she suffered, with the chemo. It's a sin."

"She looks so thin, Ma." Mary would need Kryptonite to crack this force field. Or her father would have to shut up. "She even looks shorter. Smaller. What could make her shrink, Ma?"

"It happens when you get older," her father said, coming to the table with two dishes. Mary caught his eye with a mean-ingful glare, and he met her gaze, his milky brown and a little sad behind his bifocals. And then she knew. Her father wasn't being dumb, he was playing dumb. He was hiding something.

"Dad?" Mary said, involuntarily, but he waved her off.

"Nothing to worry about."

"For real?" Mary's heart lodged some-where in her throat. They both knew they weren't talking about Mrs. DiGiuseppe.

"Not now," he said firmly, easing into his seat at the tiny round table.

Mary's gaze shifted to her mother at the stove, where she was shaking salt into the gnocchi water and stirring it with her wooden spoon. Then she turned on the burners under the pot of gravy and the old-fashioned coffeepot they had used forever. It a few minutes, everything would boil, bubble, and percolate, and Mary would pretend everything was all right, at least for the time being. On the sidelines, a mystified Judy looked from Mary to her father, staying silent. She had been around the DiNunzios long enough to know that English was their second language and their first was Meaningful Eye Contact.

"So how's Angie?" Mary asked, about her sister. A former nun, Angie had gone on a mission in Tajikistan, teaching English and helping build homes for poor people. Because of Angie's life and works, the entire DiNunzio family had an E-ZPass to heaven. The girl took pro bono to a new level, and Mary couldn't help but miss her. "You hear anything lately?"

"Not since last month," her father answered. "Tell us about Brandolini's case. They been askin' at church."

"I haven't gotten anywhere. I haven't even found his file yet." Mary filled him in against the throaty gurgling of the coffee, and in the next moment, its aroma scented the already fragrant kitchen. And just when the room was too small to fit even one more smell, the tomato sauce started to bubble.

"Brandolini was sent to a camp in *Montana*?" Her father's eyes widened. The DiNunzios never left the house, much less traveled, and their only summer vacations had been to Bellevue Avenue, in an Atlantic City that no longer existed. "Montana? *That* where they shipped him? Why?"

"I don't know, not without the file, anyway. There were forty-something internment camps around the country, and I haven't figured out the reason for who went where."

"But *Montana*!" Her father smacked his bald head, as if she'd said Pluto. "That's *way* out. That's *cowboy* country!"

"They packed the internees on trains, and when they got to Missoula, they called it *bella vista*."

"Beautiful sight," her father translated, undoubtedly for Judy's benefit.

"Right, because there were mountains and all. Or at least that's the propaganda the government was putting out." Mary had researched Fort Missoula, read a book about its history, and pieced together what she could from the other internee files. "Most of the Italian internees at Fort Missoula were from cruise ships that were at sea when war broke out. Some had been waiters at the Italy Pavilion at the World's Fair in New York. Amadeo was one of the ones from Philly."

"How did they keep the records?" Her father was a smart man, albeit uneducated. Mary, who had graduated from the University of Pennsylvania and its law school, didn't think she'd ever be as smart. In fact, lately she'd considered asking for a refund.

"I think they were kept at Fort Missoula, and when the camps were opened and the internees released, the files ended up in the National Archives."

"So maybe not all the files made it."

Mary shrugged. The coffee was done. She wanted to get it herself, but that was against the rules. Her father was already on his slippers, fetching the pot and bearing it back to the table. Simultaneously, her mother reached over and turned off the burner, one of the smoothest moves in their kitchen dance. Mariano and Vita DiNunzio had been married forever, and it showed.

"Maybe his file got taken out, because he died in the camp." Her father poured hot coffee into Judy's cup in a glistening brown arc. She thanked him and dumped in three spoons of sugar, followed with the light cream that was always on the table after dinner, next to a plastic napkin dispenser of the Praying Hands. "Maybe it got sent somewhere when he died and didn't end up in the same place as the others. Did anybody else die in the camp?"

"From my research, three other Italian internees, all of natural causes. None by suicide except for Amadeo." Behind her, Mary heard the hiss of fresh gnocchi hitting the boiling water and the gurgling of the gravy in the pot next to it, bubbling its heady brew of ripe tomatoes, extra virgin olive oil, and bits of chicken cooked until it melted off the bone. As delicious as she knew the meal would be, none of it tempted her. Between her mother and Amadeo, she was too bummed to be hungry. "I'm double-checking the files for references to him. Maybe that will lead me to whatever happened to his boats and business."

"Poor guy." Her father poured Mary's coffee, and she thanked him. "So what else is new, girls?"

"Mary has another date coming up," Judy chirped. "With a lawyer, a friend of Anne's."

"That's nice," her father said, before Mary could start whining. "It is about time, you know, Mare? If Anna likes this young man, you should give him a chance." Her father returned to the stove with the coffeepot, and as soon as he turned his back, Mary flipped Judy the bird. Judy flashed her an L for loser. They were really good friends.

"I am, Pop. I will." Mary nodded. She knew when she was beat. Her parents had loved Mike as much as she did, but lately even they were trying to fix her up, most recently with an accountant who lived with his mother on Ritner Street. Her father returned to the table and eased into his chair, his movements stiffer than before the subject of Mike came up. Behind him, her mother was pouring cooked gnocchi into the colander, then shaking it to drain off the excess water. *Slap, slap, slap.* Steam billowed out of the sink. Nobody said anything, letting the empty moment pass.

"Is ready!" Mary's mother turned from the counter with a steaming plate of gnocchi, then picked up a metal ladle and poured gravy in a tomatoey ring on top. Everyone brightened at the sight of the meal, and her mother bore it to the table and set it in front of Judy with pride. "Alla fresh for Jud'! Cheese onna table!"

"Thank you, Mrs. D!" Judy said, grabbing her tablespoon and digging into the hot gnocchi. She would burn her mouth, but nobody warned her because she wouldn't listen anyway. In the next minute, her mother was setting a plate in front of Mary.

"This looks great, Ma," she said. Her mother looked so happy that Mary swore she'd eat, hungry or not. "Thanks."

"Okay!" Her mother stroked her back, then segued into scratching it like she always did. It made Mary feel like a treasured kitten, and she looked down at her gnocchi, speared a forkful, and ate, causing third-degree burns to the roof of her mouth. Her mother kept scratching her back. "Maria, you pray to Saint Anthony for the paper?"

"Paper?"

"Brandolini. You look for his paper." Her mother made an arthritic circle in the air, and Mary understood. She hadn't realized her mother had been listening to the conversation, but she should have known better. In addition to force fields, Italian mothers had sonar.

"You mean Amadeo's file."

"*Sì.* You pray to Saint Anthony to find?"

"Well, yes," Mary admitted, breathing gnocchi fire. She'd learned the prayer in grade school: *Saint Anthony, Saint Anthony, please come around. For something is lost and cannot be found.* To be on the safe side, she had prayed to Saint Jude, too, because she wasn't sure who had jurisdiction.

"Then, they take," her mother said, with typical finality.

"Who takes what?" Mary reached for her cup and tried to cool her mouth with scorching coffee.

"Somebody. *They* take his paper." Her mother frowned deeply. "Brandolini's paper. Somebody *take* it!"

"You think somebody *took* his file?"

"*Sì.* They want nobody to see. So somebody, they *take*." Her mother snatched the steam that curled upward from the plate of gnocchi, and when she opened her palm, the steam had vanished. Mary was surprised by her mother's cool hand tricks, but not her suspicion. Vita DiNunzio was always vigilant to the Devil At Work, especially in law firms.

"I doubt it, Ma."

"This, I feel. This, I *know!*"

"Nobody took the file, Veet," her father said wearily, his forehead creased all the way to his liver-spotted scalp. "Don't jump to conclusions. The government loses more papers than it hides."

But Judy had stopped eating, and her azure eyes glinted with doubt. "It's a toss-up, Mr. D. I'd believe that somebody would deep-six the file of a suicide in federal custody. It's a no-brainer. There was liability there. Maybe they were afraid of getting sued. After all, that's exactly what's happening, with Mary on the case."

"Nah." Matty DiNunzio shook his head. "I lived through that time, kiddo. Suing woulda been the last thing on anybody's mind, then. People didn't sue each other like they do now. And the government, who would sue them? Especially during the war."

"It's not completely impossible, Pop,"

Mary said, thinking out loud. "Amadeo's suicide had to be an embarrassment for the camp and for the government. Hell, for a long time they tried to keep the entire Italian internment a secret."

Vita DiNunzio wagged a crooked finger. "Maria, this I feel, something *evil*! You pray and you no find? Then somebody *take*!"

And Mary, who had never before put that kind of faith in Saint Anthony, couldn't say that her mother was mistaken.

FOUR

Mary eyed her latest blind date, one Jason Pagonis, as he read his menu. He was tall, cool, and reasonably handsome, with close-cropped black hair and brown eyes behind hip little glasses. His smile was pleasant and his manner friendly. He was her age, apparently healthy, with good teeth. He wore a black sport jacket over a black T-shirt, with jeans. In short, there was nothing wrong with him. Mary would have to work hard to find something.

"So what are you having?" Jason asked, looking up unexpectedly.

Mary reddened. "Don't know. What's good here?"

"Everything. I love this place. It's owned

by Masaharu Morimoto, one of the Iron Chefs. You've heard of them."

"Sure." Mary nodded. Her mother was an Iron Chef.

"I love the design elements here. The aesthetic. It's interesting, isn't it?"

"I guess." Mary glanced around. She had never seen a restaurant like this except on *The Jetsons*. The tables and chairs were sculpted of transparent Lucite and lit from within with colored lights, so they actually glowed. Not only that, but the hue of the tables and chairs changed constantly, so at the moment, Mary's chair was blue, turning her butt blue, too. Two minutes ago her butt was green, having segued from a bright yellow. Mary wasn't sure it was a good look for her.

"The restaurant has an incredible website, too."

"I bet." Mary was suspicious of restaurants with websites. In fairness, she was suspicious in general, tonight. She'd worked the whole day, read approximately 129,373 documents, and still Saint Anthony hadn't found Amadeo's file. Could it really have been taken by the government? And was it behind this stupid decor, too?

"For an appetizer, I'd start with the shira ae."

"I always do."

Jason looked up. "You've eaten here?"

"No, I was joking around."

"Oh." Jason shot her a mercy smile, and Mary vowed instantly to stop joking around. Joking Around evinced a Bad Attitude, and she would fall prey to everyone's claim that she Just Wasn't Trying.

Jason was saying, "Shira ae is asparagus with sesame oil."

"Mmm." *Barf*. "What's a good entrée?"

"The ishi yaki burl bop."

Mary wondered what language Jason was speaking. She squinted at the menu but couldn't read it in the orange haze emanating from the table. "What is whatever you said?"

"It's yellowtail on rice, and it's great. And for dessert, I'd have the togarashi."

Mary blinked.

"Japanese sweet potato cake."

"Great. I like cake. Cake, I understand. Cake is great." Mary closed her menu, and Jason closed his.

"Great."

Now that everything was great, Mary wanted to leave, but she knew she was expected to Make Conversation. "So you went to Stanford Law, with Anne."

"Yes, how is she?"

"She's on vacation, in St. Bart's." Having just opened the subject of her fellow associate, Mary realized that she had to close it right away. Anne Murphy was the hottest girl ever to earn a J.D. degree. No guy who was thinking of Anne would want to be in a multi-colored restaurant with anyone else. Mary tried to think of something else to say. "You were on Law Review, right?"

"Yeah, until I quit to spend more time with my band."

Mary blinked. The only thing cooler than making Law Review was quitting Law Review. "You had a band? What kind of band?"

"Beginner Foo Fighters. I still play a little, with a pickup band. On a good day, we sound like Wilco."

"Wilco?"

"Spoon?"

"Got one, thanks," Mary said, but when she peered at the table setting through a now-yellow cloud, only chopsticks were there. "Oh, I guess I don't have one."

"No. Spoon is an indie rock group. Like Flaming Lips, ever heard of them?"

"No." Mary didn't know what he was talking about and found her thoughts straying back to Amadeo. Where was his file? Then she stopped her train of thought. It's not a hot date if you find yourself fantasizing about work during it. She was pretty sure it was supposed to be the other way around.

"How about Vertical Horizon?"

"Huh? No." Mary was worrying that she would never find anything of Amadeo's, that there was nothing he had left behind. Why did it bother her so much? Then she knew. Because it made it seem like Amadeo didn't matter, and he did. Everybody did. Mike mattered, even though he was gone. She loved him still. She had learned a long time ago that you don't stop loving somebody just because they die.

"What kind of music do you like, Mary?"

Huh?

"Do you like music?"

"Sure."

"What kind?"

Mary was too preoccupied to think of the right answer, so she told the truth. "Sinatra," she said, and she could see *Check, please* flutter behind Jason's eyes.

"*Frank* Sinatra?"

The question was so absurd, Mary didn't know what to say.

"I heard Frank Sinatra sing a duet with Bono, and it was great. Bono is great, don't you think?"

Bono wishes he were Sinatra.

"I heard there was a mural of Frank Sinatra, somewhere in town."

"There is, at Broad and Reed." Finally, something Mary knew about. "It's almost seven stories tall. It's a painting of that photo where he has his jacket slung over his shoulder and his hat is tilted. It's really amazing."

"I don't know that photo."

"Oh." *Great.* Maybe it wasn't a good time for Mary to mention she was the only member of the Sinatra Social Society under age sixty-five, now that Yolanda had passed.

They fell silent.

Mary said, "Mario Lanza is on a mural, too, at Broad and Dickinson."

"Mario Lanza? Who's he?"

Ouch. Mary felt stupid for knowing, which seemed somehow ironic. "Mario Lanza was a great tenor and he was born in Philadelphia." She didn't add that Mario Lanza was her mother's favorite. Or that Vita played his classic "Be My Love" on a continuous loop every Sunday, after Mass. These were colorful details Jason Pagonis would never hear. He was missing the best parts of the conversation. "They even have a new museum to him, on Montrose."

"Montrose, where's that?"

"In South Philly."

"I've never heard of him," Jason said, his tone surprised. "When did he sing? Or perform?"

"In the forties."

"The *nineteen* forties?"

Again, Mary didn't know what to say. *Yes, Frank Sinatra.*

"That was a long time ago."

That's what makes it classic. Mary broke into a sweat. She couldn't relax. She needed a drink but she didn't drink, especially not Japanese sake, which tasted like warm balsamic and came in ceramic thimbles too small for Italian noses.

"So." Jason cleared his throat. "Anne tells me you're working on a really interesting case. Wanna tell me what it's about?"

No. "Sure. It's to get reparations for a man who was interned during World War II and committed suicide."

Jason's eyes flared. Suicide didn't get guys hot, and Mary tried to recover.

"I went to the National Archives and saw all these documents that were typed on real typewriters. The documents are from 1941—"

Jason laughed softly.

"What?" Mary asked, interrupting herself, which had to be a first.

"You have an old soul."

"I do?"

"Listen to yourself." Jason paused. "You love old things. Old music. The past."

Is that bad? Mary wanted to ask, but she couldn't because her throat constricted. She felt tense and, suddenly, sad. Sad that she was here with Jason, and sad that since Mike had died, she didn't belong with anyone. She had stopped fitting in anywhere. She wasn't a member even of her own generation; somehow she felt older and younger at the same time.

Mary thought unaccountably of the Venn diagrams she had studied in grade school, and how they overlapped. But she didn't overlap anybody, anymore. She remained in her own circle, and she couldn't seem to change that, turn it around, or make it better in any way. All she knew was that she wished with every cell of her being that she could go home, take out her contacts, and lie down.

"You two ready to order?" asked the waitress, appearing at the illuminated table.

FIVE

WORLD WAR II ROOM, read a paper that Mary had taped to the conference room door, and she and Judy had spent all Sunday searching the remaining documents from the National Archives for Amadeo's file. By nightfall, twenty cardboard boxes full of USELESS documents lined the wall, and at dead center of the table rested a single white memorandum.

"We found something!" Mary said, leaning over the document.

"One lousy page? St. Anthony slacked off." Judy sank into a swivel chair, crossing her legs in jeans and a striped tank top. Cirque du Soleil meets the Freedom of Information Act.

"No, he didn't. You wouldn't let me pray while we were looking, and that's the only way his prayer works."

"He's picky."

"He's a *saint*."

Judy sniffed. "I'm still mad at you for not marrying Jason. Anne said he was really nice."

"Let her date him." Mary picked up the document, feeling a tingle of excitement. Not only that History Channel thing, but what her mother had said. A new suspicion that there was a reason Amadeo's file had gone missing. She reread the document for the tenth time:

CONFIDENTIAL
MEMORANDUM BY THOMAS
WILLIAM GENTILE, Pvt.
4433366698.

On March 22, 1942, the undersigned monitored a conversation between MR. JOSEPH GIORNO, GIORNO & LOCARO, Columbus & South Broad Streets, Phila., Pa., and Internee AMADEO BRANDOLINI,

ISN 3-31-I-129-C1, at Area "B" of this Internment camp.

MR. GIORNO took out a Mass card and asked permission to show it to SUBJECT. MR. GIORNO then informed SUBJECT that his wife Theresa died when she fell down the stairs at home. MR. GIORNO informed SUBJECT that his son, PVT. ANTHONY BRANDOLINI, had been so informed by mail. MR. GIORNO explained that they hadn't told SUBJECT of the death earlier because this was the soonest he could make the trip.

Mary felt a spike of anger. She couldn't imagine Amadeo hearing such awful news this way, and she wanted to know more about Joe Giorno. The name of his law firm was Giorno & Locaro, which must have been an earlier incarnation of Giorno & Cavuto, the firm that represented Amadeo's son, Tony. The address was the same, too. The lawyer for Tony's estate was Frank Cavuto, and he had brought her the case because he knew her from the neighborhood.

MR. GIORNO then asked SUB-
JECT how they should dispose of
the house and the car. MR. GIORNO
said that the car contained four gal-
lons of gas, which should increase its
value. SUBJECT rubbed his hands,
then started to cry. MR. GIORNO
said, "Don't do that." SUBJECT'S
nose ran as well, and the scene was
unpleasant.

Per request, a copy of this memorandum was forwarded to Director,
Military Intelligence Division, and
Director, Federal Bureau of Investigation.

Signed, Pvt. THOMAS WILLIAM
GENTILE, Pvt. 4433366698.

The memorandum ended there. The bottom of the page bore no number, so it was
probably the first and last page of the
memo. It raised more questions than it answered, and Mary's thoughts churned.
"Judy, don't you wonder why they monitored Brandolini's conversation?"

"No, I'm too tired."

"In the individual files, only a few had
memos of monitored conversations, and

they were of internees the government actually believed were dangerous, like that guy who ran a fascist newspaper. Why would the FBI care about a fisherman from Philly?"

"Let's call it a day, Mare." Judy smoothed her bangs back but they popped forward again.

"Why did they keep the FBI informed? It says 'per request.'" Mary couldn't stop looking at the document. Oddly, she'd found it among correspondence from the camp commander's office about coffee rations, milk orders, and laundry schedules, the quotidian business of running an internment camp during a world war. "Aren't you curious why this page was stuck in the correspondence file?"

"You'll figure it out. We're tired. Very tired." Judy patted Penny, who had curled into a neighboring swivel chair and fallen asleep. Dogs were allowed up on the furniture at Rosato & Associates, which was the sort of thing that happened at an all-woman law firm. That, and the refrigerator was full of Lean Cuisine.

"And think about what we learned from the files of the internees who died in the camps." Mary reached for the three files of deceased internees and stacked them in front of her on the table. "Each one has a death certificate and burial arrangements. These files are thicker than the others, that's why I noticed them. So where is Amadeo's death certificate?"

"What a good doggie you are," Judy cooed to the drowsy retriever.

"Like you said, it's a big deal when someone commits suicide in federal custody." Mary opened up the second and third folders and laid them side by side with the first. On the top of each was a letter that read LEGATION OF SWITZERLAND. "All three of these files are the same. When an internee dies, a letter gets written to Geneva informing them of the death. So where's Amadeo's letter?"

"Don't know." Judy stroked the dog's smooth head. "Maybe Penny knows. My smart Penny—"

"Amadeo would still be covered by the Geneva Convention, he was a prisoner of war." Mary was freewheeling here. International law wasn't her forte. Unfortunately, she lacked a forte, which was part of the rationale behind that college refund business.

"Such a good doggie." Judy petted the dog, whose tongue had slipped from her mouth in a stupor common to golden retrievers and crack addicts.

"Also, the internees who died in the camps were buried locally. I found a file of one other internee who died at Fort Missoula, and he was buried in the Catholic cemetery in Missoula. He died of colitis, and his file had a death certificate. So where is Amadeo's death certificate?" Mary shuffled through the file again, then realized something. "I wonder where Amadeo's buried. I don't even know. I never thought about that before. If he committed suicide, they might not let him be buried in a Catholic cemetery."

"I love you, Penny."

"All this time, I've been concentrating on his business. What happened to his body? Is it in Missoula or Philly?"

"I love you, yes I do." Judy lapsed into a continuous loop of *pretty dog, smart dog, good dog*, and soon Mary would have to barf.

"His son was in the army when he died, so he couldn't have had the body sent back, and his wife was already gone. Amadeo had no other family in the area, and I have no idea if his wife's parents were still alive. But still, would his in-laws send for a body all the way across the country, during war-time? When their daughter was already dead? I doubt it. It had to be expensive, and a pain in the ass. What do you think, Jude?"

Mary looked over but Judy was resting her forehead against Penny's while she baby talked to her, the two of them floating on a cloud of girl-and-dog love. Mary checked her watch. Almost ten o'clock. Maybe it was time to go home. "Okay, you two, you win."

"Woohoo!" Judy got out of the chair and stretched. So did Penny, climbing out of the chair and extending her forelegs until they lined up almost even, which made Mary smile.

"Thanks for helping, Jude. I couldn't have done it without you."

"Of course you couldn't." Judy finished stretching, lowering her arms and rubbing her slim tummy. "I'm the one who found the memo."

"Lucky."

"Ingrate."

"Freak."

"Geek," Judy said, and the women continued to trade pleasantries as they gathered their bags, papers, briefcases, and back-packs, then walked to the elevator, with Penny trotting behind them, her tail wag-ging.

Mary hit the button for the elevator, in-wardly elated. The memo was safe in her briefcase, and though it raised more ques-tions than it answered, she couldn't wait to get it home.

With her secret stash.

SIX

At her apartment, Mary downed a bowl of Special K, slipped into an oversized McNabb jersey, and piled her hair on top of her head in a Pebbles ponytail. It was almost midnight but she felt oddly energized, sitting cross-legged on her puffy blue comforter with her newfound FBI memo and Amadeo's personal effects spread out in front of her. She had gotten them from Frank Cavuto, the estate's lawyer, who'd gotten them from Amadeo's son, Tony. She had seen the effects a hundred times, but the FBI memo had got her blood going, and she looked at Amadeo's things with new eyes.

On her left sat three photographs. The first

was of Amadeo, bending over in a fishing boat and evidently doing something to one of the nets that lay in ropey piles on the deck of his boat. Mary squinted but couldn't see what he was doing. Repairing the net? The deck? Either way, he focused intently on his task and didn't smile for the camera. It told her that he wasn't a vain man; he was a little shy. Mike had been like that. She set the photo down on the bed.

The next photo was a wedding portrait of Amadeo and his wife, Theresa. He stood stiff as a toy soldier with his bride, and Theresa's dark eyes shone behind the gauzy veil. Her hair curled to her shoulders, and her dress was frilly in an appealing, old-fashioned way. Mary found herself drawn back to Amadeo. His eyes, brown-black but so animated, had been joyful on his wedding day. Again, it reminded her of Mike, on their wedding day. He had teared up at the altar, and his frat brothers had never let him forget it. Mary smiled at the memory, then remembered something Judy had said, in her office:

It's like you have a crush on him or something.

Mary set the photo down. The next was of

Theresa and Amadeo holding a baby boy with dense, black curls; their son, Tony. The end of the photo was tattered, as if it had been torn from a booklet. Mary turned it over to read JULY 4, penciled in a woman's flowing hand. There was no notation of what year the photo had been taken, but if the baby was Tony, it had to be around 1920; Tony grew to be old enough to enlist when World War II came around. But in the happier times of the picture, they were all dressed up to celebrate the birth of their new country. Mary couldn't ignore the irony, as bitter on her tongue as broccoli rabe.

She set the photos next to the last item, a flimsy black wallet with a cheap fake brass snap. It was made of black plastic and inside were three clear photo compartments, now cloudy with age. She flipped to the first, which held a black-and-white picture of a woman's face, cut out in the shape of a circle. Mary slid it out and flipped it over, the paper thin and pulpy in her hands. The writing on the back was printed Italian, cut off where the circle was, but the name was visible. *Francesca Saverio.* Mother Frances Xavier Cabrini, patron saint of immigrants. Mary should have recognized her. Cabrini's face was typically framed by a black veil and graced with a sweetly melancholic smile; her story was that she was a quiet, withdrawn child. Her symbol was a boat. It made sense that Amadeo, an immigrant and a sailor, would have adopted Cabrini as his patron. And if his suicide was any indication, he had been the melancholy type, too.

Mary went to the next envelope, which contained a lock of dark hair pressed within the dusty plastic. It had been snipped crudely and curled into a question mark about an inch long. She pried open the envelope and caught the lock as it came sliding into her hand. It felt soft, fine, and seemed to have almost no weight in her palm. She prodded the strands with an index finger, as if the lock were something alive, then held it under her bedside lamp, watching the filaments catch the light. The hair wasn't as black as it looked in the envelope, but was a deep brown, shot through with russet highlights. Whose hair was it? Amadeo's son's? His wife's? Mary held the hair to the heads in each photo, like a fright wig. Funny, but not good detective work.

Mary fingered the lock. Amadeo's effects

only reinforced her sense of him. He was a simple man whose world was small, yet perfect. Wife Theresa. Son Tony. Growing business. Three boats. He had his family and his fishing. Love and work. Rich by any standard, even Freud's. She opened the billfold in the wallet, where money would be kept.

A thick stack of white papers nestled inside, and she slid them out. They were five pieces of scrap paper, and on each were a series of drawings. The drawings were of a circle of some sort, with a tiny bump on the side. Each page had several different views of the circle, drawn with a crude pencil. There was no writing on it, not even in Italian. The circle drawing was repeated at least twenty times. Was that obsessive? Not really. When Mary doodled, she'd usually draw the same things over and over; her name, a pair of large eyes, or for some reason, a ballet slipper. But she wondered about it, with Amadeo. Was it an early sign of depression? And why did he keep it in his wallet?

For no reason, she held the papers up to the lamp, so the light shone through. There was no watermark or secret inks. It told her nothing more, which was the problem with things you do for no reason. But they were drawings of Amadeo's, Mary felt sure. It was the only tangible thing she had seen—apart from his *X* mark on the registration card—that had actually come from him. That he had touched.

She found herself closing her hand around the paper, then opening it again. She thought of her mother in the kitchen, playing hand tricks with the steam. She couldn't help but feel that she was closer to Amadeo, connected to him, and she admitted to herself that Judy had been right. It was as if she had a crush on Amadeo, not because he reminded her of George Clooney, but because he reminded her of Mike. She didn't know if Mike had gotten justice and she didn't know if Amadeo could either, but the confused tangle in her heart told her she had to try. She slid the papers back in the billfold, closed the wallet, and snapped it shut. Then she gathered the photos, set them neatly back in her briefcase, and switched off the light.

Mary lay back in bed alone, as she had almost every night since Mike had died, except for one love affair that hadn't worked out. She had changed apartments, hit thirty, and still didn't own a house. She didn't even have a cat anymore and had grown used to being on her own, kept company at night by Jay Leno, HBO, the Discovery Channel, Lifetime, or at last resort, Paid Programming. She had grown so accustomed to being on her own that it didn't feel lonely anymore. It was just the state of things. Her friends would send her on blind dates, and she would go because it was easier than resisting, but being alone wasn't so terrible. She was a single girl, and it felt like enough. Especially with cable.

Her room was dark except for the orange rectangle glowing from the Westclox and a white slice of the moon, so bright it shone through an opening in the curtain. She tried to ignore it but couldn't, so she climbed out of bed and trundled to the window. She pulled the curtain closed just as she saw a dark Escalade leave a parking space across the street and drive away.

Mary blinked. Which one of her neighbors had an Escalade? None that she knew of. It looked like the same car she'd seen the other day, on Mercer Street. What was go-

ing on? She couldn't decide if she was being paranoid.

*The dangerous ones, the truly murderous
ones, lie in wait. And then, when the moment's right, they strike.*

Mary tried to banish the voice, but
couldn't. She returned to bed and climbed
under the comforter, her body stiff with a
bad feeling.

The bad feeling was fear.

SEVEN

First thing Monday morning, Mary stopped by Frank Cavuto's law office to take him the FBI memo that she, Judy, and Saint Anthony had found. She sat across his desk in a slippery leather chair, waiting for him to finish reading it. Frank's shave was so fresh she could smell the minty Gillette on his softening cheeks, and he wore a three-piece pinstriped suit, because lawyers still dressed up for work in South Philly. Down here, they were proud to wear ties. A tie meant you were a high school grad.

"Interesting document, huh?" Mary asked, but Frank merely held up an index finger as his large, brown eyes darted across the page. His head was pitched slightly back to see through his black-rimmed reading glasses, and she wondered what was taking so long. The document was all of two paragraphs.

She looked impatiently around the office, which was overstuffed, downscale, and even dirty, like most of the solo practitioners in South Philly. They made good money doing wills, contracts, and the occasional slip-and-fall in the produce aisle, but you'd never know it from their offices. The walls were covered with thin wood paneling, a backdrop for diplomas from a Catholic university and law school, mounted in a precut frame from CVS. In the self-promotion department, there were certificates from the Knights of Columbus, the Masons, Kiwanis Club, and framed thank-yous from the Boys' Club, PAL, and the ASPCA, this last telegraphing that Frank was a soft touch. Puppies don't hire lawyers.

Next to that hung group photos of the girls' softball team he'd sponsored over the years, posed in red jerseys on the weathered bleachers of Palumbo Field. A nine-year-old Mary DiNunzio grinned from the third row of one of them, next to her old best friend, Marti Funnell, her face partially obscured by a dust-covered corn plant that struggled for air behind Frank's desk. The desk itself was of dark veneer, cluttered with correspondence, manila files, and white curls of adding machine tape. There wasn't a single law book in the office. In South Philly, you didn't need books if you wore a tie.

Frank set down the document and slid his glasses off, folding the eyepieces together with the faintest *click*. "Now, what did you say?"

"The FBI monitored Amadeo in the internment camp. Surprising, huh?"

"I guess so, sure."

"The memo says that Joe Giorno met with Amadeo to tell him about his wife's death. Did Joe represent Amadeo?"

"I think so."

Mary blinked. "You didn't mention that when you hired me. You told me that you represented his son, Tony, but not that Joe represented Amadeo."

"I didn't remember, or I didn't think it mattered. My firm represents the family, going back. So what?" Frank shrugged, which got Mary thinking that although she had known him a long time, she didn't know him that well.

"How was Joe connected with your firm?"

"Joe founded it. It was Giorno & Locaro, then it became Giorno & Cavuto." Frank eased back in his chair, leaving his glasses and the memo on the desk. "Joe was the one who picked this building, bought it bargain-basement, which was key. The man was legend. He owned lotsa property down here, and he could see how important the office location would be, you know."

"Of course." Mary did know. The law firm of Giorno & Cavuto owned the prominent corner of Broad and Columbus Streets, in a limestone Victorian that marked the start of the Italian neighborhood. Its turn-of-the-century turret looked like a lighthouse, especially to South Philadelphians who had never seen one. "How well did you know Joe?"

"Not that well. I'm old, but not that old." Frank smiled. He was about fifty-five, with a surplus of thick black hair, coarse as a boar bristle and not at all tamed by tap water. Crow's feet appeared whenever he smiled, which was as frequently as a city councilman, and his eyes were ringed with dark, almost tubercular, circles. "Joe was a smart man, an okay lawyer. But cheap! Cheapest man on the planet."

"How so?"

"I come in, I hadda redo all the plumbing and the electric. Fresh coat a paint, all three floors. New water heater, new toilets, the old ones use too much water. This place hadn't been touched in years." Frank gestured around the office, and his pinky ring glinted in the faint sunlight from a sooty window. Traffic was picking up on Broad Street, making noise and casting shadows on the pane. "What are you gonna do? People are people."

Mary couldn't help but smile. Everyone in South Philly said things like this, which passed for content. She should have countered with, *Ain't it the truth,* but said instead: "Well, when I found the memo, I started to wonder. Why would Joe go all the way to Montana to tell Amadeo about Theresa's death? It's a long way to travel, especially in wartime. It must have cost a lot, for a cheap guy."

"Joe would have charged the client, no doubt." Frank paused. "I don't know why he went, maybe just to be nice."

"He doesn't sound that nice, in the memo." Mary hadn't been able to sleep last night, thinking about it and the Escalade. "I mean, to go and tell Amadeo, Your wife's dead. Get over it."

"Maybe he went because he was Theresa's executor, I don't know."

"Was he? Did Theresa have a will?"

"I don't know."

Mary shook her head, puzzled. "It's your firm, Frank. If she was a client, wouldn't you know it? If your founder were her executor, wouldn't you know?"

"Depends. When did she die?"

"In 1942, right after Amadeo was sent to the camp. Tony was at the front."

"This is 1942 we're talking, Mare? *Psh!*" Frank waved his hand. "If there was a will, no way do I have that will anymore. I checked the will vault before, but we don't keep the wills that old. There's no point to it."

This would be the point, Mary wanted to say, but didn't. She knew it cost money to archive legal files and solo practitioners like Frank didn't have the resources of Rosato & Associates.

"Just like Brandolini's old business files, it's all gone. I only joined the firm in 1985.

To me, 1980 is archives. And 1943 is nowhere." Frank shook his head, clucking. "When Joe left in 1981, he took his files with him. That's how they did it, him and Locaro. Split the clients and the files, went their separate ways. That was in 1981. Joe musta had the files for Theresa and Amadeo, but who knows where they are now. She died of cancer, right?"

"No, like it says in the memo, she fell down the stairs in her house. I guess she broke her neck."

"It's a sin." Frank was still clucking. "Poor Tony, that cancer's no picnic either. That's what got him. You knew that, right? At least he went quick."

Mary thought of her mother, then shooed it away. "Did you go to Tony's funeral? Where was he buried?"

"Of course I went." Frank checked his watch, a heavy fake-gold Timex, but Mary knew it wasn't even nine o'clock. He shook it back into place on his wrist and gave a little cough, *hough-hough*. "He's at Our Lady of Angels."

Everybody in the neighborhood was buried there, but not Mike. Mike wasn't there, by her choice. "Is Amadeo there?"

"No. Theresa is. Not him."

Mary made a mental note. It meant that Amadeo was probably buried in Montana, like the other internee had been.

"Come to think of it, I doubt they had a will. They didn't have much money, that much I know." Frank chuckled. "Amadeo used to pay Joe with crabs he caught down Wildwood. They ran all over the office, the way crabs do. You know."

"Okay, so we don't know if they had a will and we don't know why Joe went to Montana. You know what else I don't get?"

"What, Mare?"

"I don't get why Tony, when he needed a lawyer to do a will, would come to you and not Joe. Joe was the family lawyer, but when Tony needed a lawyer to trace his father's property, he came to you."

"Joe was retired by then. Besides, I'm twice the lawyer that Joe was, believe me. But I won't speak ill, may he rest." Frank crossed himself.

"Did Joe have any partners who might know where the file or a will could be?"

"No. Joe went solo, then retired. We went over this before. Things change, Mare."

"So I hear." Mary didn't add, *and it totally*

sucks. She kept thinking that lately all she did was chase missing files. "Will you double-check for a file? The house on Nutt Street, I don't know if they owned or rented, and the bank accounts I can't find, either personal or Amadeo's business. There used to be a Girard Bank near them on Nutt, my father remembers it. That was the closest branch of any bank to their house, and probably where they banked."

"There you go."

"But Girard got bought by Mellon and that branch got closed, and nobody at Mellon could find records of Amadeo or Theresa Brandolini. It was before computer records, too. All ink and paper."

"I'm impressed, Mare. You're doing your homework."

Mary sighed. Doing-your-homework was her middle name. She had to make up for her lack-of-forte.

Frank checked his watch again. It was only two minutes later. "You say you didn't find any of his business records at the Library of Congress?"

"National Archives, and no."

Frank handed Mary the FBI memo. "Win some, lose some."

Not me, she wanted to say. *Not this, anyway.* She put the memo back into her briefcase, then retrieved Amadeo's black wallet, which she'd put in a Baggie for safekeeping. She opened the billfold, slid out the thick packet of scrap drawings, and handed it to Frank. "Last question. Do you remember these drawings? They were in the wallet in the box of stuff you gave me from Tony, when you hired me."

"I don't remember the stuff in the box." Frank barely glanced at the drawings before he pushed them and the wallet back.

"It was only last year. You gave it to me after Tony died."

"Mare, gimme a break here. I didn't look in the box." Frank leaned over the desk, hunching his shoulders at the seams, where the pinstripes matched. "You know the number of people who come in my office with a cigar box? A shoe box? A little wrinkly paper bag from Passyunk Avenue? You know the *crap* these people have, that they save for decades? You think I look at that?" Frank's voice grew louder with exasperation, but Mary was used to being exasperating. It was the double-checking that put people over the top.

"Do you know if the box was from before Amadeo went to the camp or after?"

"I don't know. Tony gave it to me. Said it was all his father's things. That's all I know. Sue me!"

Mary looked at the drawings. The crude pencil lines. The circles. "I think Amadeo drew it and I think it meant something to him. What do you think?"

"I think I have to get to work. Now." Frank cleared his throat. "I gotta earn a buck."

"Just a minute more. Do you know what they're drawings of?" Mary pointed to one view of the circle.

"No."

"They look like something, don't they?"

"No, they don't."

"How can you tell without your reading glasses?"

"Oh, for Christ's sake." Frank picked up his glasses, slipped them on, and thumbed through the drawings. Mary eyed him. Was he just antsy or was it something about the drawings? He seemed more testy than before she'd shown them.

"You can see, he drew it several times. It looks like a circle, doesn't it?"

"No, it's a doodle, so what? He's drawing

the same cockamamie thing over and over."
Frank's glare challenged her over the rims of
his glasses. "So this is it. The end of the
line."

"Okay, I'll let you get to work." Mary
picked up the drawings, folded them, and
slipped them back in the wallet, then into
the Baggie. "Thanks for your time."

"No, I meant the end of the line with
Brandolini. It's time to give it up, Mare."
Frank rose, pulling up his belt so that the
change jingled in his pants. "You tried to get
reparations for the estate, but you couldn't.
There's no shame in it. You even went to
Washington and all."

"I'm not giving up, Frank," Mary said, surprised.

"I'm sorry I sent you on a wild goose
chase. The boats, the business. It's time to
end the case and cut your losses."

"It's no loss. I'm enjoying it, and I'll find
something sooner or later. You know me, I
never give up. Remember the game against
Vecchia's Auto? Seventh inning?"

If Frank remembered, it didn't show. "It's
my fault, I shouldn't a started it. I wanted to
fill Tony's last wish. Justice for his father and
all that, and you know how it is, with the

neighborhood all worked up. I'll tell 'em it's over, tell 'em to call it a day. They have to let go of the past. You know?"

But this time, Mary didn't know. "You can't really blame them. And the past is always present." She'd never heard herself say something so deep. Was she getting smarter?

"So we'll hold a big party, all the *circolo,* to thank you for fighting the good fight." Frank continued as if he hadn't heard her, and a professional note sounded in his voice. "That retainer we gave you must be almost out by now, so I'm telling you to let it go."

"You're *firing* me?" Mary felt her jaw drop, and Frank looked down at her. He was taller than she thought, so she stood up, brief-case in hand. He was still taller than she thought.

"Not firing, just telling you to quit."

"I don't want to quit."

"The *circolo* is my client and we can't pay you anymore. The money Tony left for the suit is all gone."

"You haven't been paying me. I've worked this case *pro bono* for a month now."

"That okay with Rosato?" Frank laughed uncomfortably, and Mary felt an ember of suspicion flare within her chest. *Why would he want to fire a lawyer who was working for free?* She put on her game face.

"That'll be my lookout. You'll double-check about those files for me?"

"Ain't gonna happen, Mare." Frank had already sat back down, but Mary wasn't buying. If he was hiding something, he was even a worse actor than her father. Frank wanted her off the case, and something smelled fishier than Jersey crabs. Mary couldn't believe it, not from Frank. He used to treat the softball team to cherry water ice from a stand on Wolf Street, scooped into pleated paper cups with a flat spoon. Evidently, that was then. She set her jaw, picked up her briefcase, purse, and a white box of pastry she'd got at Isgro's, then managed a same-old-Mary smile.

"Frank, you check on those files for me, or I'm telling my mother on you!"

"You *wouldn't*!" he said, with a dry laugh, and Mary left the office.

With the sound of his laughter echoing behind her.

EIGHT

Mary waited at the bus stop outside Frank's building. There were more than a few buses traveling Broad Street at this hour, and she would normally grab one and be at work in no time. But this morning, traffic was bumper to bumper, stop and go, and she spotted the C bus five blocks away. Waiting for it gave her time to sort out her thoughts. Frank wanted her off the case. Why?

HONK! Mary started at the horn blast from a Yukon SUV, the driver tailgating a battered Toyota wagon. Traffic was slowing to a complete stop, the cars at the end of the street catching up with the front like an urban inchworm, coming to a standstill that stretched into several minutes. Stoplights blinked red and green with no forward progress. Mary eyed the traffic for the Escalade. It wasn't in sight. Good.

It was sunny, cool, and clear, good weather for a city with four seasons: fall, winter, spring, and humidity. She decided to hoof it. Her briefcase wasn't heavy today and neither was the pastry. Philly was so small she could be uptown in twenty minutes, and at this rate maybe even beat the C bus. She headed north, passing people in fresh shirts and pressed pants, carrying newspapers and covered cups of coffee to jobs in the nail parlors, funeral homes, and dry cleaners that lined Broad. A waitress in a black-and-white uniform walked by on her way to the Broad Street Diner, and there were no ties on the street except for her bow tie.

Mary reached the corner and crossed on the red with everybody else, since traffic wasn't going anywhere. Another block went by before she knew it. Traffic chugged ahead, and she glanced over her shoulder. The C was only three blocks away now, getting closer, plowing cars out of the bus lane. Mary used to be able to beat the C in high school, except when it cheated, like now.

Then she did a double-take. There was a black Escalade in the far lane.

She watched the Escalade stop in traffic and stalled to get a look at the driver. She walked slowly, her heart thumping, and swung her pastry box, which would be the acting-casual part. Then the traffic moved on, she slowed her pace almost to a stop, and in one more block she got a glimpse of the Escalade driver—and a dash of coral lipstick. Same car, different driver. She exhaled with relief. She was being paranoid. Maybe she was wrong. Maybe last night was nothing, too.

She picked up the pace and in no time reached the next corner, then stopped at the corner and looked up at the traffic light. It was red, next to the sign that read NUTT STREET. Amadeo's street. He and Theresa had lived in a house on Nutt, six blocks down, to the east. Mary didn't move when the light turned green and the covered cups crossed the street. It was only a short walk. The C bus rolled to a stop that belched hydrocarbons and emitted a hydraulic *screech*. The bus doors snapped open, letting riders on, but Mary wasn't among them.

She took a right onto Nutt. She couldn't
remember the last time she'd been east of
Broad Street, but she knew it didn't used to
look like this. Many of the rowhomes were
shells, their front doors boarded up and
nailed fast against the urban version of a
hurricane. Rusted tin sheets covered
punched-out windows, graffiti marred the
red-brick facades, and discarded trash lay
strewn on the pavement. It made Mary feel
sick inside. City Hall was only ten minutes
away on foot. How could this happen? By
the third block, she had a terrible feeling in
the pit of her stomach, and the feeling
wasn't I-Hate-Change. It was a bad enough
feeling to have passed I-Hate-Change three
feelings ago. It was what loss felt like. Just
plain loss.

Two teenage boys slumped toward her on
the street, oversize T-shirts flapping like
flags, hands shoved into the droopy drawers of the Hilfiger generation, and superwide
pant legs overflowing identical Iverson's. The
boys were Asian, their jet hair spiky and
gelled, and as they drew closer Mary could
hear them speaking to each other in another
language. When they reached her, they
looked her up and down, this white lawyer

bearing a stiff briefcase and a pastry box. They sniffed at her best navy suit and her matching pumps, gritty with pavement dirt. When they had passed her completely, they burst into laughter. She was the foreigner on this block.

Nutt Street, which Mary knew used to be solidly Italian, was evidently Asian now. She passed a corner store with a sign of bright yellow plastic, bearing what she guessed were Korean characters, and on the corner across from it sat a wig store, featuring platinum wigs on featureless Styrofoam heads, behind hand-lettered signs in Korean characters. Mary fought a politically incorrect urge to miss the Italian bakeries and grocery stores that used to anchor the street-corners, then realized the obvious: Asians were the new immigrants, coming over for the same reason as her own ancestors. For the same reason as Amadeo. That was the part of change that stayed the same. And in the next minute, she found herself standing across from 630 Nutt Street.

Amadeo's house. She examined the house from the opposite side of the street. It sat in the middle of the north side, illuminated by the morning sun. It stood two stories tall, and the bay window in front was covered by tattered sheers. The two windows on the second-floor bedroom had venetian blinds with slats missing. The brick facade needed repointing, its mortar crumbling like sugar, and black paint blistered off the front door, which showed two deadbolts above the regular door lock. A spongy black rubber mat sat on the front stoop.

Go inside, something told Mary.

NINE

Mary stood on the welcome mat, and an older Asian woman peeked from behind the peeling black door, blinking against the sun shining in her face. The woman's aged hand fluttered to a thin housedress of incongruously cheery red checks, and Mary introduced herself, then said, "I was wondering if I could come in for a minute, to see the house. I know someone who used to live here a long time ago."

"Come, come," the woman said softly, with a thick accent. Her onyx hair had dulled to steel gray at the temples and was scissored unevenly in a short, homemade haircut. Her dark eyes were hooded, and the parentheses from her nose to her lips deeply fissured. Still her small mouth curved into a remarkably kind smile as she bowed slightly, opening the door wide. "Come."

"Thank you so much." Mary crossed the threshold, feeling intrusive, but not intrusive enough to back out again. *Amadeo's house.* "I just wanted to look around, if you wouldn't mind."

"Come, come," the woman repeated, then closed the front door and locked the two deadbolts.

Mary glanced around. The living room was about twenty by fifteen feet, a skinny rectangle roughly the dimensions of her parents' rowhouse. The layout would be the same, too; living room, dining room, and kitchen strung out in a line, like beads on a rosary. A staircase to the second floor sat along the east wall; it must have been the stairs where Theresa had fallen to her death. Mary suppressed the twinge of sadness and looked away. The living room was neat, clean, and simply furnished with an old couch, two velour side chairs, and an oak coffee table. Wafting from the kitchen were familiar odors of strong coffee and scrambled eggs, but there the similarities between this house and her parents' ended.

The living room ceiling sagged in the center, and the thick plaster walls had cracked, with jagged lines running down the walls like bolts of lightning. The wallpaper was a faded gold floral, its colors bleached by the room's southern exposure. Mary flashed on what Frank had said about his office: *This place hadn't been touched in years.* Ironically, it made it easy to visualize the way the house had been when Amadeo and Theresa had lived here.

Mary gestured toward the dining room. "May I go in there, too?"

"Yes, yes," the woman answered, soft as a whisper.

"Thank you." Mary couldn't deny the tingle inside her. She could just imagine Amadeo's compact but powerful form crossing into the dining room. It was another skinny rectangle, but it wasn't being used as a dining room. Against the wall where Mary's parents had their dining room table was a single bed, its worn chenille coverlet neatly tucked in on all four sides. A cardboard box served as a nightstand for a yellow lamp and plastic alarm clock. Mary's heart went out to the woman, who touched her elbow.

"Come, come," the woman whispered, leading Mary on as eagerly as a realtor.

They went into the kitchen, which was dilapidated. Brown water spots stained dingy ceiling squares, and the linoleum floor tiles had been ripped out, revealing a grimy subfloor and sticky brown glue squeezed out in serpentine lines. A plastic table sat in the middle of the room, accompanied by only one chair, a red plastic stool. Even so, Mary could picture Amadeo sitting at a different table, wearing a fresh white T-shirt, sipping a tiny cup of espresso and talking to Theresa as she stood at the stove. Mary could almost feel his presence.

"Come, come," the woman said, motioning Mary excitedly to the back door, covered with black security bars. She followed, and the old woman pressed open the rickety back door, revealing the backyard.

Mary gasped at the sight. Suspended over the backyard hung a network of weathered ropes, strung together in an elaborate crisscross pattern, making a ceiling of twine diamonds. Laundry hung from the rope canopy on old-fashioned wooden clothespins; thin white socks, floppy panties, blouses in different patterns, pajamas, and a series of cotton hand towels. It was the most unusual clothesline Mary had ever seen.

"Wonderful!" she said. The woman nodded happily and shuffled to the side of the backyard. A rusted metal crank Mary hadn't seen before had been screwed to the fence, and the woman turned the handle.

Suddenly, shirts, undies, and black socks moved over their heads, traveling this way and that on the old ropes, following a map only they understood, directed by a series of pulleys. Water sprinkled from the moving canopy, and Mary couldn't help but applaud. The old woman laughed and sped her cranking, making the laundry go fast, then fly. Droplets sprayed everywhere, and the clothes zipped back and forth in all directions. It wasn't laundry, it was magic, and the old woman laughed in delight. Mary did, too. And then it hit her.

The ropes. She watched the whirring laundry and the whizzing ropes, blinking at the droplets that sprinkled her cheeks. The pattern wasn't diamonds, but squares. It didn't look like a canopy, it was more like a net. Like a fisherman's net. Remade, restrung, and redesigned on pulleys to make a wonderful clothesline. Was it possible? From so long ago? It looked old enough, considering the thinness of the weathered ropes and the rust caking the metal crank.

Suddenly Mary wasn't laughing. How many people had owned the house since Amadeo? It couldn't be that many. People down here didn't get off the couch, much less move from their family home. Mary's parents were typical of South Philly; the house she had grown up in on Mercer was the very house in which her mother had grown up. Even if the house had changed hands a bunch of times, who would cut down a contraption like this? It was useful, unique, and fun. *Amadeo made this for Theresa.* Mary knew it; she felt it *inside*. She was about to ask the old woman when a shout came from the door.

The cranking stopped abruptly, the laundry came to a halt, and Mary turned. A young man of about twenty-five, his dark hair disheveled from sleep, stood in the doorway shouting in Korean at the woman, who cowered in the corner. He was lean and bare-chested in low-slung gym shorts, but he was oblivious to his own nakedness. His angry glare turned on Mary.

"What are you doing with my mother?" he demanded. "You woke me up!"

"I'm so sorry, really sorry. Really sorry." Mary was on an apology roll. Hey, maybe she did have a forte. "I just wanted to see the house and ask a few questions about a former owner, named—"

"Oh, you're the one!" The young man threw up his hands. "They were asking have you been here! You know that jerk with the zits?"

Mary felt a chill. Jerk with the zits. The Escalade driver. "No, not at all. My name is—"

"I don't care, I need my sleep, I work all night. Get out of here!" The young man faced his mother and began yelling again, but Mary couldn't shake that chill. What was going on? And what about the clothesline? The laundry still dripped from its merry trip.

"I'm sorry, I'll leave right now," Mary said again. "I just need to know if you made this clothesline."

"No!"

"How long have you lived here?"

"Seventeen years, eighteen, none of your business. Listen, I worked all night. I have to go back to bed. Leave now. Go!"

"Was the clothesline here when you got here?"

"Leave, I said! You want me to call the cops?" the man shouted, then turned on his mother.

"Wait, stop!" Mary interrupted, raising a palm. She couldn't stand him treating his mother that way. *Her* mother would have beat him senseless with a wooden spoon. "Calm down. Please. I'm sorry, and I'm leaving." She turned toward the door, then had a second thought. She pivoted on her pumps, bowed to the older woman, and handed her the box of pastry. "Please take this, with my thanks. You're very kind."

The woman accepted the box and bowed back, with a shaky smile.

"What's in the box?" the young man demanded.

"*Sfogliatelle*," Mary answered, and because he hadn't translated his language, she didn't translate hers. "If that guy with the zits comes back, tell your mother not to let him in."

"Why?"

"He's dangerous," Mary said, without knowing why.

TEN

Philadelphia's City Hall was under renovations that hadn't yet reached Room 154, the Registrar of Deeds. Dingy tan linoleum with blue streaks covered the floor, lights in the vaulted ceiling hung by a twisted wire, and rosy brown marble ran partway up walls that needed fresh blue paint. Mary sat with the rest of the citizenry in a bank of padded chairs, waiting to be called to the counter, where boxy computer monitors stood in various states of swivelhood. Deed clerks helped people at the counter, and chatter filled the room, interrupted by the ringing of phones, the squeak of the heavy door, and an office radio tuned to Power 99. Eminem and 50 Cent.

Mary fingered the thin pink slip bearing number 82, then glanced up at the deli-style NOW SERVING sign. Its red numbers blinked 81. She should have gone straight to work, but she couldn't help but take a quick detour after what she'd seen at Nutt Street. She wanted to know if that clothesline was Amadeo's.

"Eighty-two! Number eighty-two, please!" a deed clerk called out, and Mary went to the counter. The clerk was a well-built black man, with bright brown eyes and a ready smile. "How can I help you?"

"I need to trace the chain of title to a house."

"No problem, let's get the plot number," the clerk said, turning the monitor toward him with a strong hand. Mary gave him the address, and he called it up on the bright screen and wrote a number on a pad. "How far back you want to go? Last year, year before?"

"I need to know from around 1900 to the present."

The clerk arched an eyebrow. "Most people, they want a copy of the current deed."

They're the sane ones. "This is a research thing."

"Leave your driver's license," the clerk said, and soon after Mary produced it, he returned with a jacket of microfilm no bigger than an index card, containing two rows of tiny black and white windows, preserved in plastic and bound at both ends. He pointed to the far corner of the room. "Viewers are over there. Turn off the light when you're finished, please."

"Thanks," Mary said and hurried past the counter to the microfilm viewers. There were two, large blackish boxes, each bearing a proudly oversize label that read EYE-COM 3000, which had probably sounded futuristic thirty years ago. She dropped her stuff on an empty chair next to her, switched on the light, and slid the microfilm into the grimiest viewer tray in existence. It took her three tries, wiggling the sticky handle back and forth, until she got something besides blinding light on the screen. Then she turned a gummy little dial to focus and zoomed in on the first deed in the top row.

THIS INDENTURE, read modern, matter-of-fact letters that Mary translated as Deed, made *this 19th day of December, 1986.* She skimmed to the name of grantor, *LEE SAM* to the grantee, *MI-JA YUN.* So it was the most recent deed, and Mi-Ja Yun had to be the older Korean woman's name. Mary read the property description, just to make sure, and it was the right house. The sale price came next: *sixty thousand and two hundred and thirty dollars and no cents*.

Mary moved the tray to the right to move the screen image left, hoping it would be the second most recent deed. It was, and she sharpened the focus. *This Indenture*, began the first line again, and the date of the deed was November 2, 1962. She skimmed along to double-check the grantor, *LI-PAK*, to the grantee, *LEE SAM*, and the sale price was thirty-two thousand dollars. Two owners down.

Mary moved the tray to view the next deed, and its letters came up, slightly more old-fashioned, in Gothic font. *This Indenture,* it began, and it was made April 18, 1952. She read across to the grantor, *JOSEPH and ANGELA LOPO*, and to the grantee, *LI-PAK*. The sale price was eighteen thousand dollars. Mary considered it; only three different owners, so far so good. She was getting closer to the time Amadeo owned it, going back. If there weren't many more owners, it made it more likely that the laundry line was his. She hadn't thought it would be this easy. Fun with double-checking!

The next deed popped onto the screen, positively curlicue in its THIS INDENTURE opening, and the date of the transfer was November 28, 1946. Close, but no cigars. She read quickly to the grantor, JAMES and MARIA GIANCARLO, to the grantee, JOSEPH and ANGELA LOPO, the asking price was twelve thousand dollars. Fourth owner. Amadeo's had to be next. With only four owners, that clothesline could have easily been his, still intact. And the next deed would tell her what had happened to his house after he died. A ghostly white square appeared on the screen, and Mary turned the knob to focus the image.

MORTGAGE BANK OF PHILADELPHIA read old-fashioned letters, and underneath it, JAMES and MARIA GIANCARLO. So the house had been bought at foreclosure, and the date on the papers was August 18, 1942. Mary paused. A month after Amadeo had died, his house had been sold at a sheriff's sale. She skimmed to the price; *five thousand, six hundred and twenty dollars.* She couldn't help but feel a weight in her chest and moved the tray one document over.

THIS INDENTURE read self-important letters, and the date of the deed was June 3, 1940. Mary skimmed ahead to see the grantor, and her heart stopped. JOSEPH GIORNO. She reread it, just to be sure. Joe Giorno, Amadeo's lawyer? Founder of Giorno & Locaro, later Giorno & Cavuto, had sold Amadeo his house? She checked the grantee, and there it was: AMADEO and THERESA BRANDOLINI. The price of the house was *nine hundred and eighty-two dollars*.

Mary read it again, shaking her head. Why hadn't Frank mentioned this, either? Did he know? She went to the next deed, to see how Giorno had gotten the house in the first place. THIS INDENTURE, began the deed, and her eyes widened. The date of the deed was April 2, 1940—less than two months before Giorno had sold the house to Amadeo. The grantee was indeed JOSEPH GIORNO, and the grantor was one GAETANO CELLI, a name that meant nothing to Mary. But her gaze slipped to the purchase price: *Two thousand and twenty-three dollars and no cents.*

Mary went back and checked the previous deed. She had remembered right. The purchase price for the Celli-Giorno deed was *more* than the Giorno-Brandolini deed—in other words, Joe Giorno had sold the house to Amadeo at a huge loss. She considered it. Why in the world would anybody buy a house for two grand, only to sell it two months later for *half the price*? Mary didn't get it, especially since Giorno was allegedly one of the cheapest men on the planet. And it wasn't as if history had intervened to affect housing prices; Pearl Harbor wouldn't happen until December 7, 1941. This case kept getting stranger and stranger. Mary switched off the viewer, gathered her microfilm and money for copies, and packed up her bags.

She had to get to work.

ELEVEN

A troubled Mary charged off the elevator into the firm's reception area, which looked friendlier than it had the night the furniture was trying to kill her. Chairs covered in taupe cloth curved around a buttery leather couch, on which clients who didn't look psychotic read magazines. Marshall Trow, the firm's receptionist, was seated at the reception desk wearing a pink cotton sweater with a tan skirt. Her brown hair, which she used to weave into a hippie braid, had been cut and shaped since Rosato & Associates had moved uptown and become a good hair office.

"Where have you been all morning?" Marshall asked, her voice low.

"Did we hear from Premenstrual Tom?"

"Only four times today."

Mary tensed. "So what did you do?"

"What I'm supposed to do, record the messages."

"Shouldn't we be going for a restraining order? Or buying bazookas?"

"Peace. Judy's working on a TRO, with Bennie supervising from afar." Marshall handed her the morning mail and a slew of yellow phone messages. "That man on the couch is a reporter from the *Philly News*. He's been waiting for you since nine o'clock."

"For me?" Mary took the messages, puzzled. She had never been interviewed in her life, and something else was pressing on her mind. It was Marshall's infant daughter that her mother had been baby-sitting. "Marsh, did you notice my mother getting thin?"

"Actually, yes." Marshall's smooth forehead creased. "I mentioned it to her last week. She said it was nothing. Why?"

"Tell you later." Mary couldn't say more because the reporter was already getting off the couch and crossing to her. He struck her as incredibly good-looking, with dark eyes and a confident grin, dressed in khaki slacks and a soft blue work shirt.

"Jim MacIntire," he said when he arrived, smiling and shaking her hand. "You must be Mary DiNunzio. Do you have a sec to talk to me? It's about Amadeo Brandolini."

"Amadeo? How do you know about Amadeo?" Mary asked, surprised. Nobody else knew about Amadeo, especially nobody this hot.

"I'd like to write a feature about him, maybe shed some light on his plight. Shine a spotlight on him and history, so to speak."

"Before you answer, Mary," Marshall interrupted, pretending to consult an appointment book, "I did tell Mr. MacIntire that you had a deposition in half an hour, and you might need the time to prepare."

Huh? Marshall was giving her an out, because Mary didn't have a dep. She probably needed permission to be interviewed. Still, Bennie wasn't around, and she was intrigued.

"I'll finish before the dep," she said and led the reporter to her office, where he settled into one of the new navy cloth chairs opposite her desk. Mary glanced self-consciously around, relieved to see the place remained in order. Telephone and stacked correspondence on the right, accordion files and closed laptop on the left, clean space in the middle. Bookshelves lined the far wall, full of dust-free law casebooks, the Federal Rules, and two bound volumes of the University of Pennsylvania Law Review with her name pompously embossed in gold. On the near wall hung a pastel patchwork quilt, the girl part of the girl lawyer thing.

Mary went around the desk, set down her bag and briefcase, and took her seat. "So how did you find out about Amadeo Brandolini?" she asked. *DiNunzio on the case. Cross-examination our specialty.*

"My barber, Joe Antonelli, mentioned it to me."

"Uncle Joey!" Mary felt a rush of familiarity. So the reporter was a guy with an Uncle Joey haircut. The Executive, unless she missed her guess.

"Joe's been cutting my hair for three years. He's a great guy."

"He sure is." *Except he chews with his mouth open, but what are you gonna do? People are people.*

"He's very proud of you. Your job here and your accomplishments. You're the star of the family. The neighborhood!" MacIntire grinned. "He didn't say he was your uncle, though."

"He isn't, technically. I have about three hundred eighty-two aunts and uncles in South Philly, all of them fake. In fact, I have two fake Uncle Joeys, but you're talking about Skinny Uncle Joey as opposed to Fat Uncle Joey, because he's the barber, if you follow."

MacIntire laughed. "You have a terrific sense of humor, Mary."

"I do?" *I mean, I do.*

"Sure you do. I love a woman with a sense of humor. I think it takes real intelligence to be funny."

"Intelligence?" *Duh.*

"You also have terrific eyes, too, but I bet everyone tells you that."

Everyone. "I mean, they're just brown. One on each side."

The reporter laughed again. "By the way, you don't mind if we record this."

"Of course not." Mary wasn't on tape any-where except her answering machine, but she tried not to let it show. The reporter was already reaching into his knapsack, a black Jansport, and extracting a silvery tape recorder, which he set between them on her desk.

"Cool. You know, I Googled you before I came over today. Got your bio on the firm's site. The photo doesn't do you justice."

"Thanks." Mary knew she was being flattered, but it was about time. She found herself wondering if he was married. He didn't wear a ring and he was so good-looking. Not that she was attracted.

"Okay, let's get started." MacIntire looked up eagerly, and she noticed that the light from the window brought out the dense espresso of his eyes. "Why don't we start by you telling me everything you know about Amadeo Brandolini. How did you come to get interested in him? I'm fascinated."

"Okay," Mary began, warming to being fascinating. Besides, it was fun to talk about Amadeo to someone who actually wanted to listen and who also happened to be totally handsome. The reporter told her his nickname was Mac, and she found herself telling Mac about the FBI memo from the National Archives and the circle drawings. He asked such good questions that she ended up telling him about the clothesline and the gift house, too, and by the end of their conversation, she had decided that Mac's eyes were more French roast than espresso. They'd such a great time that she couldn't help but wonder if he was going to ask her out.

"Well, thanks so much," Mac said, switching off the tape recorder. The little red light went out, and he slipped the tape recorder back into the Jansport. "I have the making of an incredible story, thanks to you."

"Really?" *Are you going to ask me out?*

"I called for a photographer to get a picture. He should be in the waiting room right now. That's cool with you, isn't it?"

"Now? Okay. Sure." Mary figured she looked okay, and her eyes were terrific, both of them.

"Sweet. So you know what's going to happen next, don't you?" Mac rose with a smile and zipped his backpack closed.

Mary flushed. *You're going to ask me out?* "No, what?" she asked, suddenly dry-mouthed.

"There is only one logical next step in your investigation."

"My investigation?" Mary repeated, then held her tongue while Mac told her something that wasn't asking her out at all and was so unexpected that for a minute she couldn't speak. Then all she could say was, "Really, you think?"

"Of course. Why not? Don't think about it, just do it. Keep me posted if you find out anything more." Mac hoisted his heavy backpack onto his shoulder and went to the door, which was when Mary realized he had forgotten to ask her out.

"Wait a minute!" she blurted out. It was her heart talking.

"What? I'm kind of on a schedule. I have another assignment."

Mary blinked, mortified. He wasn't even thinking of asking her out. She considered asking him out, but she had never done that in her life and was sure it qualified as a venial sin. She felt suddenly like a fool. "Uh, what about the photographer?"

"I don't stay for that. I told him what I wanted. Smile pretty. *Ciao.*"

"Bye." Mary let him go, and told her heart to shut up.

Mary and Judy sat side by side on one of the wooden benches that ringed Rittenhouse Square. The air was cool and sweet and the sky clear, so the park was packed with businesspeople having lunch. They filled the benches and sat on the concrete wall bordering the Square, men eating with their ties tossed over their shoulders and women balancing salads on purses in their laps, a lineup of Etienne Aigner tables. Everybody was enjoying the Spring day, except Mary.

"What do you think, Jude?" She leaned over, keeping her voice low so no one else could hear. "Why would the guy with the zits go to Amadeo's? Why would Frank fire me? And why would Giorno sell a house to Amadeo at a loss?"

"Marshall told me that the reporter was really hot," Judy said, between mouthfuls. She looked almost normal in a jean skirt, a white T-shirt, and brown Dansko sandals. Her hair was combed smooth and its ersatz filaments caught the sunlight. She bit off an unladylike chunk of her hoagie while Mary poked at a scoop of tuna salad on anemic iceberg. Eating in the park was Judy's favorite thing, but to Mary it was camping.

"What about what I'm saying? Aren't you a little worried about me? What if I'm being followed?"

"Did he ask you out?"

Gulp. "Don't be ridiculous. It was business. I think he's married anyway."

"Remember, you have a blind date tonight with my friend Paul. Give him a chance."

"I'm not going, and what about what I'm saying? The Escalade and all. Aren't you worried?"

"You're not weaseling out of this date again. You've canceled on him twice." Judy eyed her over the hoagie. "Now, how much did you tell the reporter? You might need damage control."

"Basically, I told him everything about Amadeo," Mary answered, but she was already wondering why she had told Mac so much. She felt pathetic. She slumped on the bench, watching a young man pass their bench. He was walking a puppy with a paintbrush tail that flopped back and forth.

"Did you tell him about the clothesline?"

"Yes."

"What about the circle drawings?"

"Well, yes. He didn't know what they were."

"You *showed* him?"

"I thought he might have an idea about them."

"They're just doodles, like Cavuto said." Judy had seen them and didn't know what they were, either. "You didn't tell him about the hair, did you?"

"Uh, yes."

Judy moaned. "Did you ask to see his story before he files it? You're supposed to."

"Not really." Mary's appetite vanished. She closed the Styrofoam lid of her salad and put it back in the bag, to be stowed in the office refrigerator until she could throw it away untouched, three days from now. She couldn't bring herself to waste food, at least not on time. "I know it might have been dumb, but I guess I just wanted to talk about Amadeo. It wouldn't be the worst thing if he got a little attention. He deserves it."

"He *deserves* it?" Judy set down her hoagie, shifted around, and faced Mary directly. "Mare, I understand that you went through hell when Mike was killed, but frankly, I think you're getting a little nuts. Ever since Premenstrual Tom called, you're like a freak."

"You getting the TRO, right?" Mary asked, and Judy waved her off.

"Completely missing the point here. Let's

review. The Escalade is a very popular car. Files from 1942 *should* be gone. Lots of big guys have zits, and you don't know that *your* big guy with zits was the one who went to the Korean lady's house."

"He asked about me!"

"He asked about someone, that's all. Or maybe he's interested in you and Brandolini. After all, a reporter got interested in you and Brandolini, and he's not a killer. Jeez, at any given moment, three of your uncles are blabbing about you."

"But what about the deed business?"

"Maybe Giorno did Brandolini a favor and took it out in fees. It's not inconceivable that a lawyer would do that for a client, especially in that day and age. Maybe Giorno wanted to help him out. You said he owned a lot of property in South Philly."

"What about Frank firing me?"

"Maybe he's sick and tired of hearing about Brandolini all the time!" Judy shot back, so sharply that a man on the bench opposite them looked up from his roast beef special.

Mary felt stung. She didn't say anything for a minute.

"Sorry." Judy sighed, then leaned over, her forehead knit with worry. "Mare, usually I'm with you, but I have to tell you, you're losing it. Going to Brandolini's house, and the way you said you felt in his house. You're running around with *human hair* in your briefcase! That's creepy!"

"It's part of the case file. It's in my desk now."

"Next thing you know, you'll be holding a séance." Judy wrinkled her upturned nose, and Mary flushed, defensive. Not that she hadn't thought of it, last night when she couldn't sleep. Judy continued, "You're too immersed in this case, too immersed in the past. In old people and ghosts. Let it go, will you? That's why I'm pushing the blind date." Judy's voice softened, almost to a whisper. "You *are* going out with Paul, girl. You have a lot in common. You'll like each other. You need to *move on*."

Mary shook her head, hurt. She knew that Amadeo had gotten bound up with Mike and somehow it was all of a piece. But she couldn't move on, not yet. She didn't know how and, now, she didn't want to.

"Don't look like that." Judy's blue eyes narrowed. "You know, even if what you're saying is true, about the Escalade and all, it's even a greater reason to get out of this case. Because you could be in danger, and for what? Are you keeping an innocent man from jail? Catching a murderer? That, I'd understand. But this? I helped you find that FBI memo because I thought that it would end all this, but I'm sorry I did. On balance, it's just not worth it."

"But Amadeo—"

"Is dead! He's dead and gone. Nothing you do can change that or bring him back. Nothing you do now can bring anybody back." Judy's fair skin colored with emotion, and Mary knew who she was talking about.

I wish this feeling would go away, she thought, but didn't say.

"And you're working on Brandolini all the time, not your other cases. Did you get ready for those deps, for Bennie? Alcor and Reitman?"

"I'll get to it." Mary watched as a young mother approached, holding a toddler by its tiny hand. The baby wobbled along in blue overalls and new white sneakers, practicing his steps. "You think she'll be mad?"

"Are you kidding?" Judy's voice regained its familiarity, and they were on safer ground now, complaining about the boss. Judy was feeling good enough to eat her vegetables and opened a crinkly black bag of Yukon potato chips, to which she was currently addicted. "She won't like it that you talked to the reporter, either. You didn't have her permission and you know how she feels about the press."

Mary shook her head. "Half the time she yells at me to assert myself, and the rest of the time she yells at me to ask permission."

"Women."

Mary looked away. The baby took a wiggly step forward, chest out, arms loose in the air, then stopped and swayed before plopping down on his cushioned bottom. He burst into a two-tooth smile. Mary said, "You know what that reporter said to me?"

"What?" Judy managed to get a large potato chip into her mouth, sideways like a pizza into a Tuscan oven. It wasn't pretty.

"He said I should go to Montana. See Fort Missoula, the internment camp. It still stands, as a museum."

"*You?*" Judy's cheeks bulged like a giant squirrel's, her blue eyes wide. "Go to *Montana*?"

"Yes, me. Of course, me, go to Montana."

Mary felt miffed, even though she'd had the exact same reaction. "I can find Amadeo's grave."

"But Montana! It's just so not *you*."

"Why isn't it me, Jude?" Mary really wanted to know, because she agreed and wondered why.

"I don't see you in big sky country. You're so totally Philadelphia. You went to college in Philadelphia, you went to law school in Philadelphia, you grew up here and you've lived here all your life. It's like your dad said the other night at dinner, remember?"

Mary remembered. *Cowboy country. Pluto.*

"Do you even know where Montana is?"

"Somewhere to the left." Mary watched the baby, almost in front of their bench now, holding on to his mother's hand. He made cute little grunting noises from the effort, *eah eah eah*. He couldn't have been more than eleven months old, but he wanted to walk so badly. You could see it.

"Montana is directly under western Canada, Calgary, and it borders Idaho and Wyoming. Glacier National Park is there. It's a beautiful state. Mountains, plains, great

trout fishing, deer, elk, moose, and antelope. Have you ever seen an antelope?"

"Sure. Looks like a dog with horns. Don't
you tire of being my straight man?"

Judy smiled. "Montana's great. You'd love
it. I've fly-fished near Butte with my dad and
hiked there, in the West, with my sisters and
brother."

"Show off."

"I didn't say you couldn't go. Go."

"It's a free country."

"Clearly."

"I have the money, I can buy an airplane
ticket." In fact, Mary had never even been
on an airplane, which was the first of three
secrets she kept from the world. The second was that she couldn't swim. She fell
silent, watching the baby take its wobbly
steps. It passed right in front of them, tot-
tering by. *Eah eah eah.*

Judy was watching the baby, too. "Mare?"

"What?"

"Did you pay the baby to walk by us, just
now?"

Mary burst into laughter, and Judy
laughed with her, which was when they became best friends again. "Isn't it funny how
things happen like that? Sometimes you're

thinking about something and then something like that happens, and they seem to connect? Like you hear a song. As if someone's sending you a sign."

"You've lost it, Mare."

"Things like that are happening to me lately. Signs."

"No, they're not. It's spring, time for new babies and little lambs to walk around. They're not signs, they're just coincidences."

"Maybe," Mary said, but she didn't think she was wrong, or that lambs had anything to do with it.

"You know, if you want to go to Montana, you absolutely should go. Maybe out there you'll find whatever you're looking for, and then you'll be done with the case. Get Brandolini out of your system. Go. You can do it." Judy paused. "Tell you what. If you decide to go, I'll cover your desk and take Bennie's depositions."

"You will?" Mary looked over, and Judy was herself again, grinning crookedly.

"So, you gonna go?"

"I don't know." *Airplanes. Pluto. Montana scares me.*

"Of course, if I take those deps for you, you'll have to do something for me in return."

"What?" Mary asked, but she already knew the answer.

TWELVE

Mary spent the afternoon following up on the internee files that she and Judy had found, double-checking for references to Amadeo, and being ambivalent about going to Montana. She didn't bother to run home, shower, and change for her blind date, not only because she was Definitely Not Trying, but also because somebody could have been following her, which was an excellent excuse.

She took a cab from the office to Dmitri's, a Greek restaurant in Olde City, which she liked on sight. Three rows of tables filled the small, unpretentious room, and an open grill was located behind a counter in the dining area, filling the air with the fresh smells of broiling fish and greens sizzling in olive oil. The tables were cozy, the dishware heavy-weight, and every place setting had a spoon. Mary felt comfortable immediately and not only because nobody was colorizing her butt. She peeked over the top of her menu at her date.

His name was Paul Reston. His brown hair was wavy, and his eyes smallish behind fairly nondescript horn-rims. He had a straight nose and a full mouth that gave his face an appealing, if not wildly handsome, look, and he was dressed in a tweed jacket over a white oxford shirt. She forgot what kind of pants he had on, but he was the Dockers type. Paul seemed more down-to-earth than her last blind date, which meant that she would have a harder time finding fault with him. Mary knew she could succeed, if she just put her mind to it.

"Would you mind if I made a suggestion for an entrée?" Paul asked, looking over the top of his menu, and Mary smiled inwardly. If the scene felt familiar, it was. All of her blind dates started this way, then had the same middle and end, as predictable as a dialogue in high school French. *Où est la bibliothèque?*

"What would you suggest?" *Là-bas, près de la gare.*

"Everything's good, the bluefish especially. I'd start with the avocado salad."

"Okay, sounds good." Mary closed the menu and set it down on the tiny table, beside a flickering votive candle. Now if Paul would just order, they could eat and get out of here, go home to separate beds, then get up and go to work the next day.

"You seem in a hurry."

Oops. "Sorry."

"You don't have to apologize."

"Sorry." *It's my forte.*

Paul set down his menu. "Judy tells me you're her best friend."

"Guilty."

Paul smiled. "Judy and I grew up together."

"Judy's still growing up."

Paul laughed. His laugh sounded masculine and deep, and it wasn't a charity laugh either. He was her age, but he seemed more mature than she was, which wasn't difficult. He could probably swim, too. "She's worried about you."

"I didn't realize you two were that friendly."

"We're not, she's just that worried, and she was trying to make excuses for why you keep canceling on me."

"Sorry." Oh, oh. Bad to worse. *Où est la salle de bain?*

"She said she had to put a gun to your head to go out tonight, that you made some kind of deal."

True. Mary also had to agree to baby-sit Penny next weekend. She was a lousy negotiator. "It's not personal, obviously. I'm just busy at work, on this case."

"She also said you're not allowed to talk about whatever that case is, and I'm supposed to get your mind off it and talk about my job." Paul smiled. "She thinks you're becoming dangerously obsessed."

Mary flushed. "I come with a lot of directions, it seems." *Wait'll I get her. I'll pierce her myself*. "Okay. What do you do?"

"I teach engineering."

"Interesting." Actually, Mary didn't even know what it was, not specifically. She was an English major, which meant all she could do was compare and contrast. "Where do you teach?"

"I started in September at Penn."

"My alma mater! You're a professor there?"

"Yes. I am Professor Reston." Paul nodded in a courtly way, and Mary laughed.

"In the conservatory, with a wrench."

"Everyone says that."

"Sorry."

"That's three times you've apologized."

Mary hated that he kept count. Couldn't he let her apologize in peace? The relationship was doomed. "Do you like teaching?"

"Very much. It's a challenge. The kids are smart, able, energetic. I like it."

"Great. It's good to like your job." Mary hadn't liked hers, until Amadeo. But she wasn't supposed to talk about that. "How do you like Philly? You have to say you love it."

"I do love it." Paul smiled. "It's hard to get to know people, but I'm getting there. This dinner is a good start. A great start."

Mary felt her face redden. Paul was making her job of hating him harder. Inconsiderate man. "Where do you live?"

"A few blocks from here, in Bella Vista."

"Nice." Bella Vista, in addition to being the immigrants' name for Fort Missoula, was also a neighborhood near Olde City, but she couldn't tell Paul about this coincidence because she wasn't allowed to talk about work. Or suicide.

"It's a rental with an option to buy, and if I get tenure, I'll go for it. Real estate is a helluva lot cheaper here than the Bay Area."

"Jeez, your own house. That's great." Mary felt happy for him. She was working toward a house, too. But when you bought a house, people always said the same thing: "Owning a house is a lot of responsibility."

"That's okay. I like responsibility."

Mary smiled. So did she. Then she realized that, so far, she hadn't thought at all about Mike.

Paul looked at her.

Mary looked back at him. She sipped some water, impossibly cold. The candlelight flickered. An animated man at a nearby table burst into laughter. She felt suddenly fresh out of conversation.

"Okay, I give up, tell me about your case," Paul said, with a smile.

"It's just a case, sort of historical, but it seems a little sketchy, the way it's unfolding."

"Judy said you're way too involved with it.

She says you're showing an unusual interest in laundry and worshipping dead hair."

"It's just the file!"

"Tell me about it. I'll keep an open mind."
Paul cocked his head, and Mary felt a tug in
her chest. He was a nice man. He even had
a nice voice, soft and deep. He was a good
listener, better than the reporter, who just
wanted his story. Paul didn't seem to want
anything from her, nor could he. It would
take 38,270 more dates before she slept
with him, and even then she wouldn't enjoy
it. Enjoying it belonged to Mike.

"Well, I don't know where to start." Mary
didn't want to say the wrong thing. It was
fast becoming her new forte, and since she
wasn't allowed to apologize, she felt dis-
armed. She needed a replacement forte.

"Tell me about the hair."

"It's hair I found in an old wallet, that's all.
My client's wallet. He passed away in
1942."

"So your client is dead?"

"Well, technically, his estate is my client,
but I guess I think of him as my client."

"I see," Paul said, without apparent judgment. "Whose hair is it? Is it his?"

"I doubt it, but I don't know. The hair thing

isn't as wacky as it sounds. Lots of people, traditional people like immigrants, carry hair with them or keep it somewhere. It's a family thing, an old-time thing. It's not that weird."

"Like when you save some hair from a kid's first haircut?"

"Yes, exactly."

"My mother did that for me. She showed it to me last time I visited, at Christmas. She even saved my baby teeth in an old envelope. They were disgusting, hollow with brown edges on the top." Paul laughed, and so did Mary. Still, she felt uneasy. Old teeth and dead hair didn't seem like good dinner conversation, though he wasn't barfing yet. She decided to shift gears.

"And there were drawings in his wallet, too. Judy thinks he just liked to draw or doodle, but I think they mean something."

"Why?"

"Because people don't save doodles, and he saved these. He carried them around in his wallet, with the hair, a saint's picture, and some photos that meant a lot to him. He didn't have a lot of possessions and he was a simple man. He kept the drawings in the billfold section, where money would be. So I think they were important."

"Okay, I'm with you there." Paul nodded. "I put important papers in my billfold all the time. Bank deposit slips, ATM slips, store receipts."

"Me, too," Mary said, encouraged. "And also they're not just doodles. When I showed them to the lawyer who hired me, he got a little agitated. Nervous."

"So what are the drawings of?"

"I don't know. A reporter I know had no idea, either."

"What do they look like?" Paul leaned slightly forward on his seat. It was too dark to see clearly, but behind his glasses, his eyes seemed to sharpen. Mary couldn't discern his eye color, but she thought it might be blue. Smart blue.

"I don't know. They look like a circle, with things on it. Different views of the same circle, over and over."

"Do you have the drawings with you?"

"No."

"Just the hair?"

"I don't have the hair with me!" Mary yelped, but Paul's sly smile told her he was Joking Around. Okay, she officially liked him. "I could draw the circles from memory, though."

"Be my guest, and I'll order for us." Paul extracted a ballpoint from inside his jacket, passed it to Mary over the table, and flagged the waitress. She took the pen, opened her napkin, and began to draw a lame version of Amadeo's circles. When the waitress arrived, Paul ordered them both avocado salads and grilled bluefish.

"This is what one looks like." Mary finished her drawing and handed him the floppy napkin. Paul held it up by both sides, squinting in the votive candle, then lowered it to reveal an unhappy professor.

"I have no idea what this is."

Mary took the napkin and assessed her handiwork with a frown. Her drawing looked like a pepperoni pizza. "I didn't draw it well enough."

"Where did you say the drawings are?"

"At my office."

"So why don't we have dinner and go see them?"

Mary blinked. "Really?"

"Why not?"

Mary's hopes soared. "I have a better idea. How hungry are you?"

"Not very."

"Me, neither. So let's go see the drawings and *then* have dinner. Would you mind?"

Paul laughed. "Now I see what Judy meant," he said, shaking his head, but Mary was already signaling to the waitress.

It took them only fifteen minutes in a cab to get uptown, and Mary held on to the hand strap as the cab lurched and swerved. No one seemed to be following them, but the Escalade driver couldn't have kept up anyway. Her knee, thigh, and arm touched Paul's about 9,274 times, and when they pulled up in front of her office building, she could have sworn the cabbie was trying to marry them off. They entered the building, signed in with the guard, and took the elevator upstairs.

The gleaming doors slid open, and Mary stepped off the elevator.

And stood stunned at the awful sight.

THIRTEEN

"My God," Mary said, uncomprehending as she surveyed the scene.

The reception area of Rosato & Associates had been completely destroyed. The new leather couch had been slashed and its white stuffing yanked out, and the matching side chairs had been upended, their cushions sliced open. The glass top of the coffee table was broken in the center, and magazines had been thrown on the floor. Marshall's desk had been overturned, and her correspondence, pencils, pens, and other stuff strewn on the rug. The desk drawers hung open, their contents spilled. Her chair lay on its side, and someone had even crushed her baby's picture, shattering its glass. Amid the debris lay the green metal box they used for petty cash, open and empty. What else had been stolen?

"Let's get out of here," Paul whispered. "They could still be inside." He took Mary's arm and turned to the elevators, but she wasn't leaving.

"No, call 911. Call security, too. The number's taped to the reception desk. I'll be right back." Mary hurried from the reception area, stricken. She and Judy had told Bennie they'd hold the fort. Now they'd been burglarized. She had to know what else had been taken. The office was full of new laptops, fancy flat-screen monitors, fax and copier machines, even color TVs.

"No, wait!" Paul shouted, but Mary hurried to the conference room, where her heart sank.

Her WORLD WAR II ROOM sign had been torn down, and the umpteen cardboard boxes had been torn open and dumped. Documents from the National Archives lay all over the carpet, many of them ripped in two. Her notes, pens, legal pads, and old coffee cups from the conference room table had been whisked onto the rug, and the phone had been yanked from the socket, taking with it a chunk of new drywall. Somebody had evidently hurled a chair at one of the large framed Eakins prints behind the table, cracking it in a jagged network. The chair lay on its side in a shower of glass shards, next to a new thirteen-inch Sony TV that had been smashed, its gray casing split. Mary was appalled and confounded by the sight. It made sense that they stole petty cash, but why take the time to trash the place? It looked like they'd been enraged.

Premenstrual Tom. Could it be him? How had he gotten upstairs in the first place? She flashed on the scene downstairs at the security desk. Bobby hadn't been on duty tonight, and a new guard had signed them in. When Mary had asked him his name, he'd said he hadn't gotten his name tag yet. What was going on? What other damage had been done? She ran down the corridor to the offices.

"No! Mary! Wait!" Paul called, hurrying after her. "Mary! Stop!"

Mary reached Judy's office, the first one off the hall, marked by the sliding nameplate JUDITH CARRIER. Her heart in her throat, she peeked inside, then got good news. No damage! She looked around with relief. Judy's desk, chairs, books, and papers were the same clutter as usual. Maybe the reception area and conference room had been the only places vandalized.

"Mary!" Paul shouted behind her, but Mary darted to the next office off the hall.

ANNE MURPHY read the nameplate, and the office was pristine! Maybe whoever had destroyed the reception area hadn't come back this far. Even Anne's laptop sat in the middle of her desk, undisturbed. Hope surged in Mary's chest. Maybe hers and Bennie's offices would be fine? She rushed down the hall to Bennie's office, larger than those of the associates, and looked inside.

Amazing! Nothing had been disturbed. Bennie's desk and shelves were all in order; nothing in the office had been torn or broken. Mary felt elated. Okay, at least they'd have something good to report when they called Bennie with the news. It boded well for the state of Mary's office, which was one past Bennie's down the hall. She hurried past her nameplate to her door. But she freaked when she looked inside.

It was a nightmare. Everything had been swept off her desk: phone, legal pads,

Dictaphone, pencils, papers, and a Swingline stapler lay all over the floor. Her desk drawers had been yanked open, turned upside down on the carpet, their contents dumped. Pencils, rows of staples, an old Great Lash mascara tube, scissors, and loose change lay everywhere. Her bookshelves had been wrenched from their metal brackets, and her law books, case reporters, and family photos covered the carpet. The accordion files she kept in alphabetical order on the credenza had been pulled off and emptied onto the floor. Confidential papers, trial exhibits, charts, depositions, and correspondence lay in a huge heap of messy paper.

"Yes, I'm still with you, dispatch," Paul was saying into his cell phone, catching up with Mary on the threshold.

Amadeo's file. She squatted on the rug like a madwoman and tore through the heap of files, folders, and papers on the floor. She had put the circle drawings, the wallet, and the FBI memo in the file, and stacked it with the other active cases on the credenza. Where was the file? She checked the empty accordions for each case. Brenneman Industries. Alcor. Reitman. She tore through the accordions twice, double-checking. Amadeo's file was missing. It was gone.

"Hello? Hello, security?" Paul barked into his cell, then he closed the phone. "That gives me no confidence. No answer at the security desk."

Mary wasn't completely surprised. She bent over the debris of her files and wanted to cry. Could Amadeo's file really be gone? She could never get that wallet back. She hadn't made a copy of the FBI memo. The hair might still be in its Baggie in her desk, but who needed hair? Which other files were missing? She tried to remember her other active cases but she was too upset. Amadeo's photos were gone, too. She hadn't even scanned them. Then she remembered. She hadn't seen her laptop on her desk.

Mary looked around frantically for her laptop. It was nowhere in sight. Maybe it had been buried somewhere. She turned around and rummaged through the papers and files on the floor near her desk. Her laptop wasn't among them. No! That laptop contained all of her work for the past three years, including tons of notes she had taken at the National Archives. Mary felt sick, deflating on the floor. Her thoughts returned to Amadeo's file. The circle drawings. She couldn't show them to anybody else now, much less Paul. She looked miserably at him as he slid his cell phone back into his tweedy pocket, extended a hand, and helped her up.

"Think of it this way, Mary," he said, pulling her to her feet. "At least you weren't here when they broke in."

"I wish I had been, I could have done something." Mary rose on weak knees. "The drawings I wanted to show you are gone now."

"I'm just glad you're safe," Paul said softly. Then he raised his arms and gentled her into an embrace that gave her surprisingly little comfort.

Mary, Paul, and now Judy stood in the firm's trashed reception area with a tall African-American cop, Officer DeLawrence Rafter. Officer Rafter was slim-hipped and muscular, with a demeanor so professional it calmed Mary down just to be around him. Almost. He slid an Incident Report pad from his back pocket and a bitten-off Bic from his breast pocket.

"Now, Ms. DiNunzio, you wanna tell me what happened here?" Officer Rafter asked, and Mary could hardly wait until he had the pen ready to spill her guts.

"I don't know who did this, or why, but I have a few ideas." She was thinking out loud, trying to sort out what had happened. "It seems to me that I'm sort of the target of this break-in, since mine was the only office ransacked, and apparently my case file and laptop were the only things they took. I was the only one using the conference room, too, and it was my sign that was on the door."

"Correction." Officer Rafter raised his pen. "The receptionist's desk was ransacked, too, and petty cash was stolen."

"Okay, right." Mary reminded herself not to jump to conclusions, but it was so hard and she was Italian. "At first I thought the guy who did it might be Premenstrual Tom, who's been calling the office."

"*Who?*" Officer Rafter stopped her with a half-smile, and Paul arched a professorial eyebrow, leaning against the side wall with his arms folded. Mary didn't think she'd be seeing him again. First dates were not improved by major felonies. If she wanted to see Paul again, she'd have to serve a subpoena.

"The man's name is Tom Cott. He's a psychotic who threatened to kill me the other night."

"Threatened to kill you?" Officer Rafter repeated in disbelief, and Mary noticed Paul's eyes widen behind his glasses. *Okay, they are blue. Incredulous blue.*

"We're in the process of getting a TRO against him," Judy interjected, her usually carefree face showing signs of strain. She had rushed to the office as soon as Mary had called, wearing an Old Navy sweatshirt and threadbare jeans. They had called Bennie's cell phone together and left her a message. "But frankly, I'm not sure it's Premenstrual Tom at all. He threatened Mary, but this break-in took planning, especially since the new security guard appears to be in on it. Also we can't explain why Premenstrual Tom would go after the Brandolini file."

"I agree, it's not likely that it's him," Mary told the cop.

"Plus, lots of premenstrual men hate us," Judy added.

"I see." Rafter made a note on his pad,

and Mary was dying to know what it said.
THESE BROADS ARE NUTS.

"Lately," Mary continued, "I've noticed
that a black Escalade has been around me,
sort of following me. First it was on my parents' street when I went over for dinner, and
then I saw it outside my house. I don't know
if it's connected to this, but it may be."

"Are you serious?" Officer Rafter frowned
under the shiny patent bill of his cap. "Did
you get a look at the driver, either time?"

"The first time, I did. He was a burly guy
with zits."

"What race, how old, wearing what?"

"He was white, wearing a black shirt,
about thirty years old, maybe thirty-five. He
was big and thick, like a linebacker. I don't
remember much else."

Officer Rafter nodded. "What about the
second time? Same guy?"

"I didn't see him, but the Escalade was
parked outside of my house."

"Did you get a license plate, either time?"

"No."

"So you don't know for a fact that it was
the same Escalade."

"They were both black, and I heard that
a big guy with zits went to visit the house

of the guy the file's about, Amadeo Brandolini."

"Can you slow down a minute?" Rafter
asked, writing on his pad.

"Sure. I'm thinking that this break-in
tonight has to do with a case I'm working
on, about a man named Amadeo Brandolini.
That's the file that was taken, and I haven't
double-checked, but as far as I can tell, his
is the only file that was taken. There was
even a reporter here today, Jim MacIntire,
asking about Amadeo." Mary met Judy's
eye and she sensed their collective imagination was running wild. *Did that reporter
have anything to do with this?* Mary re-
solved to call Skinny Uncle Joey and see if
Mac was legit.

But Officer Rafter, who didn't read minds,
looked at her with concern. "Ms. DiNunzio,
if you truly have reason to believe you're being followed, I can't deal with that here. You
need to come down to the precinct house
and make a report. There are stalking laws
on the books."

"Maybe I will," Mary said, but she had
been through that before and knew it would
be USELESS.

"Now, you told me there was usually

about a hundred dollars in petty cash. What was the value of your laptop?"

"The office paid two grand for it three years ago, which means it's worth thirty-five dollars today." Mary managed a smile. "It's what's in it that had value to me, the work I did on the case."

"What was the value of the case file that was stolen?" Officer Rafter asked, his pen poised over the white pad.

"I thought it was priceless. It contained a wallet and original photos and drawings."

"How much money was in the wallet?"

"None."

Officer Rafter made a note. "You said something about drawings. What were the drawings of? Were they, like, art?"

"No." Mary's thoughts raced ahead. Besides her and Judy, the only people who had seen the drawings, or even knew they existed, were Frank Cavuto and Mac the reporter. She made a mental note.

"Now, was this client, Mr. Brandolini, an artist or something?"

"No."

"Then his drawings didn't have any value."

"I guess not." It was hard for Mary to concede.

"How about the photos?'

"No. Family photos."

Officer Rafter flipped the pad closed. "All right, well, that about covers it. We'll follow up on the security guard issue and we'll be canvassing the block for witnesses. We'll search Dumpsters in the neighborhood and let you know what turns up, if anything."

"Can't I do anything? I really want that file back."

"Thanks for the offer, but I gotta tell you, I'm not overly optimistic. The only thing a witness would see is somebody walking around with an accordion file and a laptop, in the business district. It's not like they're running down Walnut with a boosted plasma screen."

"I understand," Mary said, disappointed just the same.

"However, if I were you, Ms. DiNunzio, I'd get myself a TRO and file a report about this fellow, then think seriously about taking a vacation."

Mary snorted. "A vacation? The last thing I want to do is take a vacation. This case is heating up, big-time."

"It would be good to make yourself scarce, right about now. Get out of town for a while. I know that's not the party line, but I like to be practical. If someone's harassing you, go away." Officer Rafter slipped the pad into his back pocket and returned the pen to his breast pocket. "I'm finished, and you're all free to go. I'll join my partner downstairs."

"Great, thanks," Mary said, and Judy thanked him, too.

"Let me know if you discover that anything else has been taken." Officer Rafter moved toward the elevator door. "My partner inventoried everything on the walkthrough, but you never know."

"Sure, thanks again for coming."

"You're welcome." The cop grabbed the elevator, and when the doors slid closed, Mary met Paul's eye with a final sigh.

"Well, professor," she said. "I guess we'd better get you out of here. You've had enough excitement for one night."

"It was interesting," Paul answered, with a smile. He unfolded his arms and turned to Judy. "You told me she was . . . different."

Judy laughed. "You academics gotta shake it up once in a while."

"True." Paul smiled and turned back to

Mary. "But we never did have dinner. Can I get a rain check?"

Mary blushed, surprised. "Sure."

"Okay, then. I do have an early class in the morning. Quantum mechanics."

"Yikes. Can't be sleepy for whatever that is."

"See ya, Paul." Judy gestured to Mary. "Walk him to the elevator, girl. It's the least you can do."

"Of course," Mary said, but she wasn't counting on that good-night kiss. She didn't even want one. Nothing like a B & E to kill the mood. She was just about to walk him out when the phone rang from beneath the mess in the reception area, and Mary turned on her heel. She looked at Judy. Judy looked at her. They both knew who was calling. Things were about to go from bad to worse.

A minute later, Paul had walked himself to the elevator and Mary was on the phone telling Bennie what had happened to her law firm, between apologies. "I'm sorry, I'm so sorry. The reception area looks like—"

"Are you *nuts,* DiNunzio? I don't care about the reception area!" The boss was shouting so loud Mary had to hold the phone away from her head. "I care about you! I care about Carrier! I don't like the sound of any of this!"

"Bennie, I know, I'm sorry." Mary had told her everything except for the newspaper part, and now didn't seem like an opportune moment. The boss had screamed at her before, but never like this. She must really care a lot. "I didn't realize that—"

"No, *I* didn't realize that you were *in danger*! That a *car* was following you? I can't believe Premenstrual Tom's behind this, but Carrier will deal with him right away. Nothing is worth your getting hurt! Or her!"

"Bennie, honestly, I don't think I'm in any real danger." Mary heard the words coming out of her mouth and even she wasn't sure she believed them. "I mean, if somebody wanted to hurt me tonight, they could have come to the restaurant."

"And tomorrow they will. Or the next day. Did you tell the cops you were being followed? What did they say?"

"They said I could fill out a report—"

"That's a waste of time! I want you safe and I can't come down there until the trial's over. You have to protect yourself, DiNunzio, until I get back. First thing, shut up about everything. Don't talk to anyone you don't know. Don't tell anyone about Brandolini or any of your other cases."

Would that include blind dates and major metropolitan newspapers?

"Second, you have to get out of town."

"That's what the cop said, but I have so much work to do."

"No case is as important as your safety! Get out of town!"

Then it hit Mary. *Get out of town? Get out of town!*

"Take a vacation until I get back and can deal with whatever's going on!"

"I can't, Bennie." Mary couldn't seem too eager or the boss would get suspicious. "I have to take that dep for you in Reitman tomorrow, remember?"

Judy's ears lifted like Penny's.

"No, you can't take that dep," Bennie was saying. "Why can't Judy do it?"

"I think she can—" Mary started to say, just as Judy caught on, frowning deeply. "She says fine, no worries, she can take the dep for me."

"Excellent! Let her do it. You get yourself a plane ticket. Go to Miami. Get out of town for a week."

"Bennie, if you really think I should, I guess I could go away for a while."

"Call the office when you get there. As soon as you get there, you hear?"

"No, Bennie wait!" Judy yelled, grabbing the phone, but Mary wrenched it back.

"Sure, right, bye!" she said quickly, then pressed down the hook with a well-timed index finger, coming nose to nose with her best friend.

"Oh no you didn't!" Judy said.

"You said you'd take the Reitman dep before. Now you have permission. What's the problem?" Mary asked, but she knew the answer. She could see it in the fear in Judy's face.

"The difference is that I believe you now, about Brandolini. Something really is going on here. What happened tonight couldn't be any clearer. Whoever they are, they want you off the case." Judy's mouth went grim, but Mary's went grimmer.

"Then I don't have a choice. Somebody wants me off the case, then I want on. I want to know what they could possibly be hiding. I owe it to Amadeo."

Judy met Mary's gaze. "I can call Bennie

back, you know. I can bust you. Tell her the whole thing. Then she won't let you go."

"Would you really do that?" Mary asked.

The two lawyers had a Girl Standoff over the telephone.

And Mary swallowed, waiting for Judy's answer.

FOURTEEN

Fort Missoula was a quaint edifice of soft red brick topped with a red tile roof, which was situated on a preserve on the fringe of Missoula, Montana. Mary scanned the remarkable surrounding landscape. The Sapphire Mountains soared to the left, forested with green trees that seemed to glow in the bright sun. The Bitterroot Range lay to her right, its jagged peaks poking holes in the proverbial big sky, which sheltered the scene like the Marist-blue cloak of the Virgin. Cool air wafted across the verdant valley, smelling sweet and pure, and acres of green grass stretched like nature's own carpet to Mary's loafers. *Bella vista,* she thought, realizing the nickname wasn't government propaganda after all. She was glad she'd braved the airplane ride to get here, not to mention Northwest's trail mix.

She approached the fort's front door, passing a flapping American flag that made her feel like a schoolgirl on a field trip. It thrilled her to be here, walking where Amadeo had walked, seeing what he had seen. She felt the same tingle she'd gotten from his wallet, that he was *with* her somehow. On the way to the entrance, she walked past five old log houses and passed a sign: THE WESTERN MONTANA GHOST TOWN PRESERVATION SOCIETY.

So many ghosts here. One of them, Amadeo.

It sped Mary's step through the grass. Dew soaked her shoes and the cuffs of her khaki pants, which she'd coupled with a navy blazer and white T-shirt for this out-of-town phase of her investigation. She hadn't had much luck with the in-town phase yesterday, leaving messages for Frank Cavuto and the reporter, Jim MacIntire, during her layover. Neither man had returned her call.

She entered the museum and found herself in a tiny entrance room with low ceilings, waiting while her eyes adjusted to the darker interior. The museum was small and contained not a single soul. There was a cashier's desk but no cashier, so Mary put five dollars in a donation basket. Beyond the desk was a gift shop stocked with Missoula T-shirts, Montana calendars, and something called Moose Drool Soap, which she passed up in favor of a room that read HEATH EXHIBITS in stenciled black letters. Again, nobody was inside, but black-and-white photos of the camp buildings lined the walls, showing the conditions as they had been in internment days. Mary went to the first panel and drooled like a moose.

The panel displayed group photos of the internees, and she scanned the grainy and unfocused pictures for Amadeo. He wasn't there. She went to the next panel, then the next, and ended up spending an hour in the exhibit, watching a documentary and eyeing every still photo futilely. Still she couldn't shake that tingle and she needed answers. She left the room and went in search of a human being. Happily, a cashier with soft gray hair had returned to her post by the museum door, and she looked up when Mary approached.

"Did you enjoy your tour?" she asked, pleasantly. She wore small silver earrings with a long denim dress, and stood behind a glass counter covered with color post-cards, a dishwasher safe Fort Missoula mug, and a stack of BITTERROOT MEM-ORIES jigsaw puzzles.

"Yes, thanks, but I have a question. I'm doing some research on an internee. He died here, by suicide, and I was curious where he was buried."

"Oh, my." The cashier flushed. "Wouldn't you know it? You asked me the one question I don't know."

"I'm sorry."

"No, I'm sorry," the cashier replied, and Mary fell in love with her instantly. They could have apology wars. Guess who would win. "I'm sorry to say, I don't know that. The only cemetery on the grounds is for officers at the fort. But there's another man who helps out here as a handyman, and he may be able to tell you for sure. He wasn't a bor-der guard, but he worked in the motor pool at the camp, as a mechanic."

"Really?" Mary couldn't hide her surprise. She didn't want to say, *And he's still alive?* "What do you mean by border guard?"

"The Immigration Service ran this camp during the war, so the guards were technically border guards. As I say, Mr. Milton was a mechanic, but he might know the answer to your question. Let's go find him."

"Not often we find someone so interested in the camp as you," Mr. Milton said, smiling shakily as they stood together in the gift shop. His eyelids were hooded, and his jowls soft with perhaps eighty years of smiles. He was tall and lanky in baggy pants and a red flannel shirt that smelled pleas- antly of cherry pipe tobacco, and Mary liked his manner immediately. Truth to tell, she *was* partial to older people. They knew everything.

"I'm very pleased to meet you," Mary said. His hand felt cool and papery in hers, but his calloused grip was still strong, and she fought the feeling that she was shaking hands with history. "I'm just doing some re- search on an Italian internee who was from Philadelphia. There were a few internees from Philly, and the man's name was Amadeo Brandolini. Does that sound familiar?"

"No, no. Wait, hold on." Mr. Milton paused, putting a clubby index finger to dry lips. He shook his head after a minute, and Mary respected him for double-checking.

"No, it doesn't ring a bell. I knew some of the internees, but not many. I kept the Jeeps running and the officers' cars, that was my job. But the internees I met, they were a nice group of fellas. Played the music, in the little orchestra, the ones from the ship."

The cruise ships. One was *Il Conte Biancamano,* Mary knew from her reading.

"Got bocce going and soccer, in the field out back. Sang operas, put on shows. They were lively."

Mary had seen the photos at the exhibit and in books. The internment camp had sounded like summer camp at times, at least for the Italians. Except for Amadeo, especially after he'd learned Theresa had died. "This internee, Amadeo Brandolini, he committed suicide."

"Suicide!" Mr. Milton startled, then nodded. "I do recall that now. Not him, but I do recall that. A suicide. That was big news here."

"I would think so."

"Yes, and my memory is very good." Mr. Milton nodded, with a faint hint of pride. "There was only the one suicide here. Everybody knew about it. One of the internees, an Eye-talian, he did himself in."

"What did you know about it? About him? I'd like to see his grave, if I could. I'm guessing he'd be in a Catholic cemetery but for the fact he committed suicide."

"No, let me think. This isn't my bailiwick, either. I think the internees who died here are buried at the city cemetery in Missoula."

No.

Mary blinked. *Who said that?* "Excuse me? Did you say the city cemetery?"

"Yes."

Then who said no? She must have. "There must be a Catholic cemetery in Missoula."

"There is," Mr. Milton answered. "Out on Turner Road. I guess that's a possibility, too." He paused. "You know, I remember, about that suicide. How he killed himself, and where. It was big news. Big news."

"What happened?"

"I'll show you, if you like."

"*Show* me?"

"I'll take you there."

Mary felt her heart begin to pound. "When can you go?"

"Anytime. That's the pleasure of being retired, dear."

"How does right now sound?"

Mr. Milton grinned.

FIFTEEN

Mary found an empty space in the con-
gested parking lot and got out of the rented
Toyota, looking around in disappointment.
They were only a ten-minute drive up
Reserve Street from the camp, but the
Sapphires and Bitterroots had been replaced by the Staples and the McDonald's.
Cars and trucks drove back and forth, and
shoppers laden with plastic bags tugged
daisy chains of children to minivans. Mary
couldn't see the connection between this
bustling strip mall and Amadeo's suicide.

"This is the place," Mr. Milton said, emerg-
ing from the car. At that moment, a stiff
breeze whipped across the lot, ruffling his
sparse gray hair. He stood up, leaning

against the hood on his side. "My, windy to-day, isn't it?"

"Yes," Mary said, only because he actually seemed to be waiting for her agreement.

"This is the old Mullan Road. It was built by Captain John Mullan in 1859, 1860. Went all the way from Fort Benton to Walla Walla. This land here, all around us, used to be sugar beet fields." Mr. Milton gestured with a sweeping hand, his shirtsleeves flapping like plaid sails. "Sugar beets as far as the eye could see, and then some."

"This used to be all beet fields?" Mary looked around, skeptical. Businesses anchored all four corners of the busy intersection of Mullan and Route 93; a Conoco gas station, a SuperWalMart, another strip mall, and a liquor store. On the horizon stood a gray-and-red Costco. "How far? Far as the Costco?"

"Farther. Sugar beet fields for twenty miles, all the way to Frenchtown."

"I've seen the pictures, but it's so different now."

"Do you have an imagination?"

"Yes."

"Use it."

Ouch. Mary screened out the stores and

the traffic, and finally could imagine the scene the way it had been. Acres upon acres of flat crops, row after row of leafy, dark greens. Amadeo had walked here. He dug beets from this ground, and it didn't matter that it had been paved over. It became real to Mary then. "So this is where they worked, in the beet fields?"

"Yeah. The war left the sugar companies short-handed, so they used Eye-talians from the camp." Mr. Milton squinted against the brightness, but he didn't flip down the green shades over his bifocals. "They worked in the sugar beet fields and in the town. In the forests, too, cutting down trees. They liked the work. The Japanese, they had a tougher time of it. Lots of folks didn't like when they went to work in town. You couldn't blame us, really. It was a crazy time."

"Sure." Mary didn't judge. "People get nuts in wartime. They get scared. That's only human."

"That's right." Mr. Milton looked over the car at her and smiled gently. "Not many people understand that."

"Hey, it's only with beets I'm a rookie."

Mr. Milton snapped his clubby fingers.

"See that? How you're always makin' jokes? That's 'cause you're Eye-talian. That's how they all were, the Eye-talians. That's why everybody loved 'em. Loads of fun."

Stereotypes can be good for something. "So this was a beet field. Tell me—"

"You keep sayin' beet field. It's a *sugar* beet field."

"I stand corrected." Mary was flunking Montana. "*Sugar* beet."

"Ever seen a sugar beet?"

"Not unless it takes the C bus."

Mr. Milton smiled, and they became friends again. "It looks like a big fat carrot, only white."

"Does it taste good?"

"You can't eat sugar beets, city girl."

"Why not? I eat beets. They come in cans, from Harvard. They're geniuses. Genius beets."

Mr. Milton didn't smile. "Now you're just bein' silly. Sugar beets make sugar. They plant 'em in early spring and harvest in September through October, depending on frost and freeze."

"How do they make sugar?" Mary asked, actually starting to care.

"They slice 'em, extract 'em, put 'em in a diffuser to get the juice out. Press 'em and you're good to go."

"They grind it fine enough to make sugar?"

"No, the sugar doesn't come from the pulp, it comes from the juice."

D'oh.

"Well, anyway. Back in those days, laborers did all the work with the sugar beets. Topped 'em and dug 'em out, put 'em in burlap bags until they ran short on burlap, during the war. That was when they switched to paper. The Eye-talians used to come out here and do it all." Mr. Milton scanned the parking lot, and Mary could tell he was using his imagination, too. Older people were better at imagining, and she could almost see the bright green rows reflected in his watery eyes. "A border guard would take 'em out in the morning in a deuce an' a half and bring 'em back at night."

"What's a deuce and a half?"

"Truck. A two-and-a-half-ton truck. That was Sam. Sam would do the driving mostly. He had a lead foot, Sam did. His truck was in the shop all the damn time. Sam Livingstone, he died five years ago. Heart."

Another ghost. On the drive up Reserve, Mr. Milton had told her all the people he knew who had died and what they had died of.

"There used to be trees over there, way far. Out there." Mr. Milton pointed past the Costco. "A group of trees there, shade trees. The Eye-talians used to eat under the tree, come lunchtime. There was one tree, an oak, bigger 'en the rest of 'em. That fella you're askin' about, what was his name?"

"Brandolini."

"He hung himself on it."

No. Mary hadn't known Amadeo had killed himself that way.

"Hung himself right here one day, when he was out in the field, working."

Mary looked past the Costco, shielding her eyes. From the sun. From her imagination.

"They say his wife died while he was in the camp."

He'd hung himself. Mary imagined a huge oak tree, with branches that stretched like a hand, reaching for the clear blue sky, ripping down that blue cloak and exposing heaven itself.

"Mary, ready to go?"

"But how did he hang himself, if the others were around?"

"There wasn't, that day. It was a small crew, only him and another 'un, his friend. The friend fell asleep during their lunch break, and when he woke up, your Mr. Brandolini had hung himself."

"Who was the friend?"

"I don't know."

Mary didn't get it. "But wait, Amadeo climbed a tree and hung himself, and the border guard didn't stop him? He wasn't asleep, too, was he?"

"What border guard? There was no border guard."

"Wasn't anyone here guarding them?"

"You mean like in the movies, standin' over 'em with a gun? Like that Paul Newman movie?" Mr. Milton chuckled. "Nothin' could be further from the truth. No need to have a border guard when the Eye-talians worked. Where was they gonna go? It was all sugar beet fields, and they lived here."

"But still, how could they not be guarded? They were enemy aliens, prisoners of war. If they were dangerous enough to arrest and put behind barbed wire, weren't they dangerous enough to guard?" Mary heard resentment edge her voice, so maybe she did judge after all.

"We didn't make the decision to arrest 'em or pen 'em up. We never treated 'em that way in Missoula." Mr. Milton shrugged bony shoulders. "The Eye-talians worked independent during the daytime. They were trusted, like friends. The ones that worked in town, they came back at night to the camp, like it was home from a job. Hell, some even dated gals in town. And the ones in the sugar beet field, we picked up at the end of the day. Sam did. Passed away five years ago. Cancer."

Heart. Mary didn't correct him. She was thinking about Amadeo.

"Okay, ready to go?" Mr. Milton patted the Toyota's roof, and though Mary could tell he was tiring, she couldn't leave just yet.

"I don't understand why Amadeo would come out here to kill himself. Why not do it in the camp?"

"I guess he'd a been stopped there. Too many people around. The internees slept a hundred to a room. They didn't have any privacy."

"Wonder how he did it, I mean logistically."

"Easy. Climb the tree with the rope, tie it around your neck, tie it to the tree, and jump off the branch. It would snap your neck pretty good. Okay, good to go?"

No.

Mary blinked. That voice. Did she really hear it, or was it her? Maybe it was the wind. Her hair was blowing in the gusts, whipping around her face and ears. She stared past the Costco. "Where did he get the rope?"

"Always some rope layin' around the truck. Tie the hoes together and such."

"So when did they discover that he had done this?"

"Not 'til Sam came to pick 'em up." Mr. Milton shook his head. "Didn't have no cell phones then."

"So Amadeo lay there all afternoon, dead?" Mary shuddered, trying to picture the tableau. The spotless blue sky, a flat expanse of green crops, a man hanging from a tree. And another, with him. "Who was the other guy?"

"I don't know."

"But he was an Italian internee?"

"Yes."

"A friend?"

"Yes."

No. That voice. Mary didn't know if it was the wind or not. Maybe she just had jet lag. She'd had to travel all day yesterday, with two takeoffs and landings. And she hadn't slept well last night because the Clark Fork River ran right outside her hotel room, making annoying nature sounds. In fact, she hadn't heard a single police siren all night and was considering filing a complaint.

"Are you okay, dear?" Mr. Milton's eyes narrowed.

"Sure."

"You're not related to Mr. Brandolini, are you?"

"No, just the estate's lawyer." Mary shook it off. "Who would know who the other internee was?"

Mr. Milton shook his head. "Nobody left would know that, I would guess. Bert, he's one a the internees, he might know, but he's back visitin' Italy. Maybe the director at the fort would know. He has those archives, upstairs."

"Archives?" Mary's ears pricked up. She should have guessed as much. Museums had archives. Even the Mario Lanza Museum.

"You gotta ask the director about it. He keeps it. Seen enough?" Mr. Milton asked again, and Mary took pity on him.

"Yes. May I treat you to a burger, to say thanks?"

"You sure can, if there's a vanilla milkshake with it, too."

"Done and done, sir!"

Mr. Milton ducked inside the car, but Mary waited a minute, looking at the place where the hanging tree had been, letting her hair blow. A voice was telling her that she had to know more about how Amadeo had committed suicide, and she didn't know if the voice was hers or his.

But she was going to find out.

SIXTEEN

The words ST. MARY'S were chiseled into the stone pillars that flanked the cemetery entrance, but Mary barely noticed the coincidence, having understood long ago that her first name was the most marketable brand in the Catholic Church. She took a right onto a driveway of soft black gravel that ran down the center of the cemetery and was lined on both sides by tall shade trees, so old that their heavy branches made a leafy canopy. The grass covering the graves had been newly mowed, releasing a fresh, green scent, and a few old-fashioned verdigris sprinklers sprayed leaky arcs of water into the sunlight, saturating the air with an uncommon humidity.

Mary drove slowly up the road and raised the Toyota window to avoid being drenched. She scanned the cemetery, which had a small and humble feel, no more than one city block square. Brownish, tasteful tombstones dotted the damp lawn, which told Mary that it wasn't an Italian Catholic cemetery. It lacked the requisite archangels with six-foot wingspans, chilly marble mausoleums, or fountain-ridden tombs. It's no accident that Hadrian was Italian.

She glanced around for a cemetery office but didn't see one, and there wasn't a soul in sight, at least not living. The office had to be along the road, so she cruised slowly ahead. The Toyota's soft tires rumbled as she drove, and when she had passed the sprinkler, she lowered her window, eyeing the tombstones for Amadeo's. She saw tombstones for SKAHAN, MURRAY, MERRICK, and one granite tombstone that was heart-breakingly smaller than the others, which read ELIZABETH, OUR BABY.

Mary felt a familiar pang, though she obviously hadn't known the child. She felt for the parents. Grief connected people, made them part of the same unhappy but thoroughly human club. Suddenly, mourning for Mike blindsided her like a fresh body blow, knocking the wind out of her. The Toyota rolled to an unplanned stop, and Mary sat stalled. Trying to breathe. Watching the drops of water from another sprinkler dot her windshield. She had been so single-minded in her search for Amadeo's grave, she hadn't stopped to think that she'd be visiting *graves*. The sprinkler began its turn her way, like her own personal rain cloud.

Get it together, girl. You have a purpose.

She gritted her teeth, pressed the gas, and drove forward, turning on the wind-shield wiper. She eyed the tombstones, but none was Amadeo's. She didn't know why she sensed he was here; he couldn't be, un-der church law, but still. Dappled sunshine shifted the shadows on the granite, and she drove around the perimeter of the cemetery, expecting to find an office. But after one cir-cuit and row after row of tombstones, all she could find was a battered white pickup down by an exit gate. She made a beeline for it, parked the Toyota, and climbed out. An older black groundskeeper in baggy jeans was loading a Scott lawn mower onto the bed of the truck, and he smiled in a friendly way when Mary approached.

"Excuse me," she said. "I'm trying to find out if someone is buried here, an Italian internee from Fort Missoula, but I don't see an office. Isn't there an office here?"

"Across the street," the groundskeeper answered, extending a long finger, which Mary followed. Outside the cemetery, directly opposite the main gate, sat a white clapboard house trimmed with green, which she hadn't noticed when she came in. She was about to thank the man when he said, "But you don't have to go ask the office about that. I know where those fellas are buried. I been here twenty-three years."

"Do you know if someone named Amadeo Brandolini is here?"

The man gestured, by way of response.

Mary stood alone, her hands linked in front of her, confronting the graves of the four internees. They had bronze memorial plaques, not tombstones like the other graves, different from the others even in death. The plaques, flush with the ground, were dusted with leftover blades of grass and sat in a solemn little row. They were identical, with an embossed depiction of the praying hands to the left of a name: Giuseppe Marchese, Born Catania Italy, 1913–1942. Aurelio Mariani, Born Genova Italy, 1914–1942. Giuseppe Marazzo, Born Torre Del Greco Italy, 1896–1943. And:

AMADEO BRANDOLINI
BORN ASCOLI-PICENO ITALY
1903–1942

Mary stood at the foot of his grave, in pain. Pain for the loss of Amadeo, pain for the loss of Mike; it was hopelessly bound up now. Maybe she hadn't been right to come here. Maybe it would make everything worse. Her chest tightened and she bit her lip. Amadeo's grave made his death real to her. He had died out west, far from his family, far from the city he had made his home, far even from the sea. It seemed so strange. And even though the cemetery was lovely by any measure, Mary couldn't help an uneasy sensation that crept over her, standing there. A sense that Amadeo didn't belong here at all. And it had nothing to do with the lack of Italian surnames or showy statuary.

She walked between the graves to his memorial plaque, knelt down, and ran her fingers along the embossed letters. BRANDOLINI. Odd. They felt warm to the touch. But they were shaded by the tree, weren't they?

Mary looked up. A tall, full tree sheltered the memorial, bathing it in cool shade. So why would the letters be warm? She felt them again to double-check. Warm. Maybe this type of plaque retained the day's heat? To test her theory, she turned around and touched the plaque of the grave next to Amadeo's, Giuseppe Marchese's. The letters were cold to the touch. Mary ran her fingers back and forth over the name. Cold, definitely cold, in the same shade. Then she touched Amadeo's name again. Warm.

Alive.

Mary edged away, rising. Then she heard a voice behind her, like a whisper.

"Yes?" Mary said, turning, thinking the groundskeeper had come back. But no one was there. Nothing stood behind her except the polished back of a granite tombstone, and beyond it, another monument, under the same massive shade tree.

Huh? What's going on? She listened again, cocking her head, but the only sound was the rhythmic spray of the sprinklers.

That must have been it. A spray sounds like a whisper, doesn't it? Mary listened again, harder, her heart beginning to thump.

No, she heard, with a softness of a Bitterroot breeze, its inflection clearly Italian. *No.*

She waited, trying to decide whether she was crazy, jet-lagged, or just Premenstrual Mary. Or whether she had simply heard a voice. Because her third secret was one she joked about, but had never truly admitted until now: *I believe in ghosts*. It was impossible not to, wasn't it, for a good Catholic? Growing up, she had blessed herself to the Holy Ghost, studied the miracles and the lives of the saints, and had swallowed whole the stigmata thing. So it wasn't completely inconceivable that a ghost was speaking to her now, was it? Amadeo's ghost.

No, he said again, and Mary waited, trembling. Listening. Watching the shadows flit across the letters on his memorial plaque. AMADEO, beloved of God.

And then it was gone.

Leaving Mary standing there. She didn't feel afraid. She didn't want to run or scream.

All she wanted was to know the truth.

SEVENTEEN

Mary went back to the Doubletree Inn and stopped at the brownish counter at the front desk, where the ponytailed clerk was on the phone. On the left sat a metal rack of fold-up Osprey schedules and Bitterroot Valley brochures, but Mary wasn't interested in the sights. She waited for the clerk, who hung up and looked over expectantly, her ponytail swinging in its white scrunchy. Mary asked, "Did a fax come for me? Room 217."

"You with the U?"

"The University? No, I'm just by myself." *If you don't count the ghost.*

"Be right back." The clerk disappeared behind a door and returned a minute later with a manila envelope, which she handed across the counter. "Here we go."

"My death certificate!" Mary said, excited, and didn't bother to explain when the clerk recoiled. She had applied at the recorder's office for Amadeo's death certificate this morning, on her way to the fort. She thanked the clerk and went upstairs but couldn't wait to get to her room to open the envelope. She slid it from the envelope and hit the hall.

At the top, the fax read DEATH CERTIFI-CATE, and it was divided into two parts. At the top half, each entry was neatly handwritten: Decedent's Name: Amadeo Brandolini. Alias: None. Age: 38. Date of Birth: August 30, 1903. Date of Death: July 17, 1942. Marital Status: Widowed. Occupation: Unknown. Armed Forces: Not Applicable. Residence: Fort Missoula Detention Facility. Race: Caucasian. Nationality: Italian.

At the bottom half of the certificate was a section filled out in almost illegible handwriting, evidently by a coroner whose exact name she couldn't decipher. Cause of Death: *accidental asphyxiation*. Time of Death: *7:18 P.M.* Place of Death: *Missoula City Hospital*.

Mary read it again and again, but she didn't get it. What was accidental asphyxiation? And the time and place of death didn't jive with what Mr. Milton had told her. Amadeo was supposed to have hung himself in the field at lunchtime and had been dead all afternoon. But that wasn't true, according to the death certificate.

Mary slid the certificate back in the envelope, hurried up the stairs and down the hall to her room, and perched on the edge of the bed to call Missoula information for Mr. Milton's number at home. When she heard his soft voice on the line, she said, "Mr. Milton, it's Mary, sorry to bother you."

"It's no bother, dear. I did enjoy our lunch together."

"Me, too. I'm calling because I got a copy of Amadeo's death certificate and it says that he died by accidental asphyxiation, which sounds impossible to me. And it also says that he died around seven o'clock at night. Does any of that make sense to you?" Mary paused, and the line went silent. "Mr. Milton?"

"Yes."

"I don't understand."

"I guess, well, I only told you part of the truth."

Mary felt a jolt of surprise. "Okay, what is it?"

"I didn't tell you because I didn't want to upset you, and it didn't matter. I told you what happened, pretty much."

"Please tell me everything. Like they say, the whole truth and nothing but."

"The accidental part, well, I don't know for sure. I guess it says accidental so they didn't make your client look bad. You know, a suicide and all. It was kinda embarrassing to him."

Not to mention to the camp. Or maybe the FBI wanted it covered up. In any event, that must have been how Amadeo was buried in the Catholic cemetery. He wasn't listed as a suicide. "But what about the time difference? You said he died around noon."

Mr. Milton paused. "Well, uh, this Brandolini, your client, he didn't die right away. As I recall it, he was unconscious when Sam picked 'em up, but he didn't die until later, in the hospital."

It jived with the certificate. "Why is that? Do you remember?"

"Oh, I remember. You know, my memory is very good."

Mary remembered he had told her that, even if *he* didn't. "So what happened?"

Mr. Milton paused again. "You really have to know? It's kinda upsetting, the gory details."

"Tell me."

"Well, the rope he hung himself with? It didn't hold."

"What do you mean, it didn't hold?"

"It broke. It wasn't strong enough to hold him."

Mary swallowed her distaste. "But he was only a hundred and fifty-five pounds." She remembered from Amadeo's alien registration card. "What kind of rope was it? Just string or something?"

"No, it was strong enough rope, that wasn't the problem. Problem was, he made the rope by tyin' two ropes together. They weren't long enough, either one of 'em. They musta been ropes they used to tie the tools together, like I said. The rope broke where he tied it."

No. Mary heard someone whisper. *Okay, officially, there are no sprinklers or wind in my hotel room.*

"Mary, you all right?"

"Sure, fine."

"Sorry I didn't tell you, but you can see how come I didn't want to mention it. And don't think on it, too much. Your client, he didn't suffer."

Yes, he did. "Is there anything else you remember?"

"No, dear. That's all. I'm sorry about your client."

"Thanks so much," Mary said and hung up.

She sat on the edge of the bed a minute. The hotel room had been cleaned, and housekeeping had opened the curtains on either side of her sliding glass doors. Outside her window, the sun was glimmering on the ripples of the Clark Fork, which was doing its gurgling and rushing thing. A little boy in a striped shirt and rubber overalls was fishing in the river, which came as high as his knees, and his father stood behind him, holding on to him by a strap of his overalls. The father wore a green vest with a wooden net hanging from his collar in the back. Mary watched them idly. She had never gone fishing, but she felt like she was fishing now. Casting a line into waters she didn't know, seeing what would bite. Amadeo had evidently joined her, as a guide. Thank God one of them could fish.

Mary tried to imagine the day of Amadeo's death. The rope tying him to the tree, coming undone. Amadeo falling to the ground. The horror of the friend when he woke up, unable to call anyone to help. Not that anyone could have helped anyway. Mary had worked on enough murder cases to know a little about strangulation. The rope would have ruptured the carotid and other vessels in Amadeo's neck, and he would have bled to death, internally, over a period of hours. He would have known that he was dying. Would that have made him happy? Finally given him peace, knowing that he would join Theresa? Mary couldn't help but shudder at the thought. Even in her grief over Mike, she had never considered suicide. Her parents would have killed her.

Part of her wished Mr. Milton hadn't told her the truth, because it hurt to think of Amadeo suffering. She tried to dismiss the thought but couldn't. She sighed, needing suddenly to lie down. She took off her blazer, folded it in half, and laid it flat on the other bed, near the glass sliders. Outside, the father was bending over the little boy, evidently instructing him as he tied something to the end of his fishing line. A lure, she guessed, or a fly of some kind. Last night there had been people fishing in the same spot, not fifty yards from the Doubletree. Mary knew that fly-fishing was big in Montana, from a movie she'd seen on Encore with Brad Pitt. *Broad Street Runs Through It*.

She kicked off her loafers, went back to bed, and sat down, bending over and pulling off one nylon knee-high, then the next. Nobody else at Rosato bothered with nylon knee-highs, but Mary had grown up watching the *mamarellas* on the C bus wear them with dresses and had nursed a secret fondness for their taupe ugliness. She was about to drop the *mamarella* socks on the floor and lie down, but she looked at them again. They were the cheap kind from the Acme and had shriveled to nothing without her calf to give them shape. In fact, they looked like two pieces of brown rope.

Just then Mary heard an excited yelp from outside her window and looked up. The little boy's fishing rod had bent almost to breaking, and he was reeling something in, braced against the strain and the moving water. His father held on to him with a sure hand under his arm. In the next instant, a fish shimmering with color and water burst from the river into the air, its long body torquing before it fell sideways into the river, with a splash.

Mary watched, transfixed; the fish was a strong, wild animal, fighting for its life, which is not the kind of thing you see at Tenth & Ritner. The boy cranked his reel, the father held on tight, and the trout jumped from the river again, thrashing more weakly. It happened one more time, the boy and the fish locked in a lethal battle that the boy eventually won, reeling in the fish close enough for his father to scoop it into the net. The boy jumped with glee, and the father gave him a hug. Then they bent together over the fish, and the father reached into the net. After a minute, they let the fish swim away.

Mary smiled at the happy ending. She had no idea that a fish could be so big or so powerful; they were so calm in the Chicken of the Sea can. Whatever the boy had tied on his fishing line had done the trick, and the line itself had to have been strong. She considered it. Fishermen had to know how to tie things onto other things. Knots were something that fishermen knew about. Even a city girl like Mary had heard the term fisherman's knot.

On impulse she went with the *mamarella* socks to the borrowed laptop she'd set up on the desk, then hit the enter key to wake it up. She logged onto Google, typed in "fisherman's knot," and the cheery blue-and-white screen yielded the results of her search. She eliminated the first few links, which looked irrelevant, then about the middle of the page came upon what she was looking for: **Get Knotted! Animated Knots for Scouts!** She clicked on the link, and the screen changed as the computer found the website, which was for a Boy Scout troop in East Sussex, in the United Kingdom. Underneath the title was a bright blue list of all sorts of knots: **bowline, clove hitch, figure-of-eight knot, fisherman's knot**.

Bingo! Mary stopped there and clicked. **Fisherman's Knot**, read the heading of the new page, next to a definition:

The fisherman's knot is used to tie two ropes of equal thickness together. It is a useful and common

knot used by fishermen to join fishing line, and is very effective with diameter strings and twines.

Instantly, at the top of the page, two animated pieces of rope, one bright red and one bright blue, started tying themselves into a very solid knot. She watched the rope tie and untie itself a few times, slowly enough so that even a Philadelphia lawyer could follow. She scanned the page and underneath were directions: **Tie a thumb knot in the running end of the first rope**—and Mary had to click on a link to learn about the thumb knot part—**then tie a thumb knot in the second rope, around the first rope. Note the thumb knots are tied such that they lie snugly against each other when standing ends are pulled.**

Mary double-checked the directions, picked up the *mamarella* socks from the desk, and followed the directions for the fisherman's knot to tie them together. Then she pulled the reinforced toe of each sock. Presto! She had joined her *mamarella* socks! She yanked hard. Nothing would make them come apart. She was screwed if she needed to wear them, but she had taught herself one thing. No rope joined by a fisherman's knot would ever come apart.

What had Mr. Milton said on the phone? *Problem was, he made the rope by tyin' two ropes together. . . . The rope broke where he tied it.*

Mary felt a bolt of excitement that was almost electric. The knot in the rope hadn't held. Amadeo, a fisherman by profession, would have known how to tie a fisherman's knot. So only one conclusion followed logically, and to confirm it, she didn't need a ghost. Amadeo hadn't tied that knot. Somebody else had, and there was only one other man with him in the beet field that day.

Mary reached for the phone.

EIGHTEEN

"It's almost closing time," said the cashier at the Fort Missoula museum. It was the same woman in the denim shift, who had helped earlier today and was undoubtedly regretting it now. Mary was on a new mission, to find a mystery man.

"I know, and I'm sorry." *Sorry, sorry, so very sorry.* They were upstairs at the museum, and on the way over, Mary had called Frank Cavuto and Jim MacIntire again and left more messages. Skinny Uncle Joey wasn't in either, and it gave her a pang of homesickness she was too old for. She considered calling home and asking her mother why she was so frigging thin, but stopped because she'd have to reveal she was on Pluto.

"I do have some paperwork to finish up, but then I'll have to get home." The cashier hustled down the hall on the museum's second floor, past the administrative offices, and halted at a door bearing a red sign that read: STOP! YOU ARE ENTERING A CURATORIAL ZONE! "Can you be done in an hour, Mary?"

"If I can't, I'll come back tomorrow, if that's okay with you."

"Certainly. The director said to help you in any way we can." The cashier nodded. "What you're looking for might be in here. If it isn't, the U has a lot of archival information in the Mansfield Library, as you know."

"Yes, thanks." Mary had read as much, and was a library fan from way back. She would never have learned to love books if not for the Free Library of Philadelphia. She'd grown up in a household where there was only one book other than the Bible. *TV Guide.*

"Our archive is more specialized, as you'll see. It pertains strictly to goings-on and internees at Fort Missoula, during the internment." The cashier opened the door with a jingling set of keys and flicked on the light in the small, windowless room, which was wall-to-wall history.

"Wow," Mary said, meaning it.

"Wonderful, isn't it?" The cashier went to the end of one of the gray accordions, pulled a sheaf of papers from the last one, and handed them to Mary. "This may help you. It's an index made by a volunteer named Dale."

"Thanks." Mary flipped through to a page in the middle, which read: P. 2001.048.223—Photograph, Internees, Italian—Woods camp; P. 2001.048.224— Photograph, Internees, Italians—Woods camp. Next to each catalog number was a description of the internees engaged in all sorts of activities: "doing forest work," "bathing at camp," "firing the furnace," "working in laundry," "raising chickens," "feeding cats," and "meeting with priest." The index would save Mary tons of time. "Thanks so much, and God bless the Dales of the world."

"I agree." The cashier headed for the door with a little wave. "Good luck," she said, and Mary got busy.

An hour later, the door reopened, and the

cashier stood in the threshold, bearing a light jacket and her handbag, but it was an excited Mary who greeted her.

"Look what I found!" she said, putting the last of the accordions away. In her hand were two photos.

"Let's see. I have a minute."

"Great." Mary set the two photos down on the top of the nearest box, and the cashier bent over them with her. They were two cracked group photos taken at different times; one was in the beet field on a sunny day, with eight Italian internees posed like a graduating class, four in front and four in back. Amadeo stood on the far right of the front row, recognizable from the alien registration photo. Mary pointed at him, delighted. "That's the man I've been looking for!"

"Mr. Brandolini." The cashier grinned. "Good for you! I guess these photos weren't displayed downstairs because of the cracking."

"I guess so." Mary set out the next photo proudly, as if it were a trump card. It was another group photo, but of only five internees including Amadeo standing in a loose ring, leaning on hoes in the beet field. "Look at

the first photo and the second. Notice anything similar about them, even though they
were taken at different places and times?"

"Yes." The cashier pointed. "Your man,
Brandolini, always stands in the front row,
far right. He was short."

"True. That's half of it." Mary moved her
fingernail past Amadeo's head and one up,
to the top row, where a tall man wearing a
cap stood. "Also, in both photos, the man in
the cap stands behind him."

"He's tall."

Ouch. "Okay, but he also has his hands on
Amadeo's shoulders in both photos."

"Interesting." The cashier looked over, intrigued behind her glasses. "And?"

"It suggests they were friends, doesn't it?"

"Yes."

"I'm wondering if this is the friend who
was with Amadeo in the beet field, the day
he died. Do you know how I can find out
who this man is? Are there any camp
records here? Any list of internees?"

"No records other than these." The
cashier gestured at the boxes, but Mary had
looked through everything and still had finished before menopause.

"Would Mr. Milton know?"

"Probably not. He worked in the motor pool."

Mary remembered. She'd double-check later. "Anyone else alive? Any of the other internees?"

"No. Some of the internees settled here, but they're gone now." The cashier shook her head, deep in thought. "There is the one internee, Bert, everyone knows him, but he's out of the country now."

Mary remembered that Mr. Milton had mentioned him. "What about any of the Japanese or German internees?"

"They didn't mix, from what I understand."

Mary had read as much. "What about anyone else from the camp staff? Mr. Milton can't be the only one alive. Is there a listing of the staff, a directory I can use to track them down?"

"Hold on." The cashier cocked her head, her steely hair catching the overhead light. "There was someone, the camp adjutant actually, who lives in Butte. He worked closely with the men, I understand. Maybe he would know."

"What's his name?"

"Aaron Nyquist."

"Is Butte far?"

"Just down the road," the cashier said, and Mary translated. In Montanaspeak, that meant two hours.

But the evening was young.

NINETEEN

The Montana sky deepened from cobalt blue to a rich, grapey purple, until blackness fell like a bolt of felt in a photographer's darkroom. Mary drove a very flat two hours into the pitch dark, leaving behind all the colors. A moonless nightfall obliterated the horizon and obscured even the peaks of Bitterroots. The only illumination on the empty highway was two jittery cones of light from her headlights, faint owing to the underpowered rental, and she flicked on the high beams for company. She thought she saw a herd of bighorn sheep running alongside the highway, but it could just as easily have been a group of Hell's Angels in weird helmets. She hit the accelerator.

The Nyquist home was a small farmhouse of white clapboard with sharply peaked gables, typical of the Victorian houses Mary had seen out here. She pulled up in front and cut the ignition, looking over. Adrenaline had powered her drive, but it was ebbing away at the sight of the dark house. All the windows on the front floor were black, and the only light shone through the curtains on a second-floor window. The FOR SALE sign on the lawn told her she was just in time, but the lights upstairs told her that it was past Mr. Nyquist's bedtime. She sat in the car, wrestling with her conscience. Was she really going to wake up the whole family, just to get the answers she wanted?

Go, girl. If it was Amadeo talking, he was cranky from the drive. And his English was better than everybody thought.

Mary got out of the car into the darkness, but the lamp from the second-floor window cast almost enough light to illuminate the front walk. She headed up the walk, her gaze on the window, and the crunching underfoot told her it was made of pebbles, an oddly suburban touch. The house was silent, and she slowed her step. Maybe she should come back in the morning. She was about to turn around when she spotted it. A light, around the back of the house, shining down the gravel driveway. She walked toward the light and saw the outline of a small barn behind the house, on the right. It had a three-peaked roof, like the cut-off top of a star, which was barely visible against the night sky. Its bay doors hung open, and light poured from within. There were no animals inside; it was a barn converted to a garage, and under a bright panel of fluorescent lights sat a vintage pickup truck.

Mary walked toward it and got a closer look. The bed of the truck had shiny sides of varnished wood, and its green back door read HARVESTER in gleaming yellow paint. A large blue machine sat next to the truck, which looked like a compressor or something equally foreign, and the walls of the tiny garage were blanketed with white Peg-Board, displaying tools hung in graduated order. Mary reached the doorway and stood there a minute, not seeing anyone around the truck.

"Hello? Mr. Nyquist?" she called out, but there was no answer. She stepped inside the garage, which smelled of grease but was cleaner than her apartment. Plywood workbenches built into both walls on either side of the garage looked like they'd been wiped down, and even the cloth rags hanging on the handles of the homemade base cabinets underneath were white and fluffy. "Mr. Nyquist?" she said, louder.

"Wha?" came a voice from underneath the truck, and Mary peered around the front. A pair of wrinkled jeans stuck out from under the chassis, ending in a scuffed pair of Nikes. The Nikes walked themselves out on their thick rubbery heels, and the bottom half of a man in jeans was lying on his back on a dolly. The face hadn't emerged, but a voice from underneath said, "Grandma?"

Mr. Nyquist's grandson. He'd be about the right age. "No, I'm Mary DiNunzio," she called back, leaning over.

"Who?" The man rolled himself out from under the truck, and from the bottom up appeared a gray T-shirt too faded to read, a handsome, if grease-streaked face, brown eyes that wore a puzzled expression, topped by a green baseball cap that read AGRO. The young man did a sit-up with ease, boosted himself off the dolly, and rose, wiping his hand on his jeans before he extended it. "I'm Will Nyquist. What did you say your name was?"

Mary reintroduced herself. "Nice to meet you, and sorry to bother you so late. I was looking for Aaron Nyquist. I was told he lives here."

"That would be my grandfather."

"Great! I was hoping it wasn't too late at night to see him."

"I'm sorry, he passed away about six months ago," the young man answered, without evident emotion, and Mary's heart sank. She *was* too late.

"I'm sorry."

"Thanks, but it was a blessing, for him. For my grandma, too. He'd been sick a long time. Why'd you want to see him?"

"I had some questions, about Fort Missoula. He was on the officers' staff there, wasn't he, during the war?"

"World War *II*?" Will flashed Mary a familiar ancient- history look. "I don't know, he worked for the government during the war, I think. He didn't like to talk about it a lot." Will glanced toward the house. "Grandma would know. I'll take you in, and you can ask her. She reads upstairs until late. Says she's more comfy, readin' in bed."

Mary felt a guilty twinge. "But I don't need to bother her. It was him, really, who would know."

"She'd enjoy the company. She's been so bummed since Gramps died." Will took off his baseball cap, revealing a thick mess of brown hair and a severe case of hat head. He slapped the cap against his jeans and dust flew out. "I'll take you in to meet her. It'll make her night to have a guest. And she's got some wicked pie, made fresh tonight."

"Pie?" Mary asked, hiding her interest.

Mary had barely introduced herself when she was shown to a cushioned seat at a kitchen table of knotty pine. Mrs. Nyquist was about five four, still trim, and she wore a gray sweatsuit outfit and bifocals in no-nonsense plastic frames. Her pale blonde hair had been clipped into a practical, short cut, gone gray at the temples, and deep wrinkles creased the corners of her blue eyes and her mouth. Her nose was tiny and her smile sweet. She was probably in her early eighties, and her manner was warm, friendly, and fragile with fresh grief. Mary wanted to grab and cuddle her, but Mrs.

Nyquist was fortunately oblivious to her secret love attack.

"You've *never* had huckleberry pie?" Mrs. Nyquist asked, incredulous. She set in front of Mary a large wedge of pie, its golden crust dusted with grainy sugar. Thick purple goop oozed from the side, encroaching on the plate like lava. If lava contained fructose.

"No, I've never even seen a huckleberry. What's a huckleberry? I thought it was a book by Mark Twain."

Mrs. Nyquist smiled, which made Mary happy. She was enjoying going around Montana, making old people happy. She was a roving ambassador of codependency.

Mrs. Nyquist said, "Huckleberry, especially wild huckleberry, tastes a lot like gooseberry."

"I never tasted a gooseberry, either. I've tasted gnocchi, and that's all that grows in Philadelphia."

"That where you're from? I was wondering with your accent, and you talk so fast."

Accent? "Yes." Mary tried to talk slower. *Ye-es.*

"Would you like some tea with your pie, dear?"

"Only if you're making it already."

"I am. We're not much for coffee in this house. My husband can't—couldn't—tolerate it. His stomach."

"Tea's great, thanks. May I help you?"

"No, thanks. It's good for me to move around. This is exercise, for me."

"Thanks, then." Mary couldn't remember the last time she'd drunk tea, but she wasn't about to put Mrs. Nyquist to further trouble. The older woman was placing a white teapot on a burner at the stove and she could have been Mary's mother, except for her perfect command of English and nonviolent nature in general.

"My goodness, I sit all day nowadays, except when I'm cleaning." Mrs. Nyquist bustled around the gleaming kitchen, an Early American type with red-and-white cushions tied to the backs of the wood chairs. The counters and appliances were a spotless white, and the air smelled vaguely of orange-scented Fantastik. On a side table next to some old photos stood a grouping of brownish figurines, which Mary thought might be Hummels, but wasn't sure. In South Philly, statuary was restricted to a dashboard St. Christopher or a bobblehead Donovan McNabb.

Mrs. Nyquist was shaking her head. "I even cleaned the garage last week, it gave me something to do. Aaron was so disabled by his stroke in those last years, and taking care of him was a full-time job. Now I have all this free time." She waved her hand in the air, as if shooing away a bumblebee. "Please, taste your pie."

"Wow, this is great!" Mary said, scooping a forkful. It tasted like blueberry pie, only sweeter. She took another bite and hadn't realized how hungry she was. "It's so nice of you, to feed me so late."

"It's my pleasure." Mrs. Nyquist bowed her head graciously. "Will's right about one thing, I do like the company. He's worried about me, thinks I'm getting blue. He even wants to set me up with a man from church, on a date!"

"You, too?" Mary laughed, and so did Mrs. Nyquist. "What is it with the blind dates? I'd rather watch TV."

"Me, too." Mrs. Nyquist returned to the table and set a steaming mug in front of

Mary, with a fragrant triangle of a Lipton tea bag inside. "How do you take your tea?"

"How should I take my tea?"

"I take it plain."

"Then so do I," Mary said, making Mrs. Nyquist smile again as she went back to the stove and poured herself a mug of tea, then came back to the table with it and sat down. An oversize men's Timex slipped down from her wrist, undoubtedly her husband's, and she still wore her wedding band. *I'm a widow, too,* Mary thought, but for some reason, couldn't say. She settled for, "You must miss your husband."

"Every minute." Mrs. Nyquist sighed. "You know, they say everything happens for a reason, but I'm not sure I believe that anymore." Behind her glasses, the older woman's blue-eyed gaze was direct and even, and it struck Mary that this was going to be a real conversation and not just small talk. It was hard to bullshit an old lady, which was only one of the things she liked about them.

"Honestly, I never thought that everything happened for a reason. I still don't. It's just something we say to each other to get us over it, whatever it is. The hard part."

"Maybe. I used to believe that God has a plan for us, each of us. The longer I live, the less sure I am of that, too. What do you think?"

"I believe in God, but I think he's a lousy planner."

Mrs. Nyquist smiled over her steaming tea. "So is there a plan, at all?"

"Not unless you have one."

"So what's left then, if there's no plan?" Mrs. Nyquist set down her mug. "What is it that your generation believes in?"

Mary smiled. "You're asking the wrong girl. I can't speak for my generation. I'm not even sure which generation I'm in, half the time."

"So, then, what do *you* believe in, Mary?" Mrs. Nyquist waited expectantly, and all of a sudden, Mary knew the answer. She had just realized it, sitting in a dark farmhouse, with a very kind stranger, in the middle of Montana.

"I believe in justice. And in love. And in *not* getting over it, because that's too much to ask of a human being." Mary collected her thoughts. "Getting over it is the wrong thing to want, anyway. You should never expect to get over it, the best you can hope is to

live past it. And you go on. Your past be-
comes a part of you, you just fold it into the
gnocchi dough and keep rolling." Mary was
surprised to hear her voice break, so she
scooped another forkful of pie, and Mrs.
Nyquist seemed to let it register, still listening, until her unlipsticked mouth curved
slowly into a smile.

"You know, you may be right, Mary."

"It's possible. I'm wrong so often, the
odds are on my side."

Mrs. Nyquist laughed. "No, I can't believe
that. You're a very thoughtful young girl."

"It's the huckleberries. They have superpowers."

Mrs. Nyquist laughed and sipped her tea
with the tea bag still inside, and so did Mary,
because she felt like they were friends now.
"But you came to see my husband, and I've
gone on and on. What was you wanted to
see him about?"

"I understand from Mr. Milton that your
husband was at Fort Missoula, during the
war."

"He was," Mrs. Nyquist answered, and her
voice suddenly echoed the clipped tones of
a military wife. "He couldn't serve because
of his heart, which bothered him so much.

He always felt he could have served, he felt quite fit and healthy, and took some pride in it. In fact, the doctor said a less fit man would never have survived his first stroke. It was the second that killed him."

"I'm sorry." Mary had said it before, but this apology was sui generis. The ultimate apology. "I am doing some research and trying to identify an internee I found in some old photos."

"Maybe I can help you. I worked at the camp for a time, as a secretary."

"You did?" Mary asked, surprised. "The cashier at the museum didn't mention that."

"I doubt they know, at the museum. I was unofficial, you see. They were so short-handed during the war, Aaron had them hire me. For free."

"You needed a lawyer."

Mrs. Nyquist laughed.

"Well, if you wouldn't mind looking at the photos, I brought them with me." Mary went digging in her bag and pulled out the two photos.

But she had barely set them on the red-and-white placemat when Mrs. Nyquist emitted a gasp.

TWENTY

"My goodness!" Mrs. Nyquist said.

"What? Do you know them?"

"This does take me back. I'm sorry, it's just so surprising to see these!" Mrs. Nyquist's aged hand fluttered to her throat. "I do know that man."

Yes! "Which one? It's win-win, to me. One is named Amadeo, and I don't know the other, the man in the cap." Mary pointed at the mystery man, and Mrs. Nyquist met her fingernail to fingernail.

"I know him, this man, the man in the cap. I recognize him. Everybody in our office knew him. He always wore that cap, just that way."

"You're kidding!" Mary edged forward on her slippery cushion. "Do you know his name? I think he may have been a friend of the other man, the shorter one, Amadeo Brandolini. Do you know the short one in front?"

"Let me see." Mrs. Nyquist picked up the photo and looked at it through her bifocals. "No, I don't know him."

"You sure? Amadeo was a fisherman from Philly." Mary was trying to jog Mrs. Nyquist's memory. "He committed suicide. He and the man in the cap worked in the beet fields together."

"Oh, wait, I had heard about that." Mrs. Nyquist set the photo down on the place-mat. "I didn't know him, but I heard about that. That one of the internees killed himself, sometime after his wife died." Mrs. Nyquist tapped on the photo. "But for sure I recognize the man in the cap, I *knew* the one in the cap. We all knew him, the girls in the office, that is. He was one of the youngest internees, very talkative. A *wolf*, we used to call his type."

"Really?"

"My, my, my," Mrs. Nyquist said, shaking her head at the photos. She almost seemed to forget about Mary's presence. "His English was very good. We used to use him as a translator around the office. He wasn't really an *Italian* Italian, like the others."

It jived with what Mary knew. Most of the internees at Fort Missoula spoke only Italian, and the inventory sheets she'd found in their files at the National Archives showed that almost all of them owned an English dictionary, apparently for teaching themselves the language. But she didn't get one thing. "Why would an internee be hanging out in the office? I mean, they were in prison camp, right?"

"It depended. The Japanese, when they came, were always under light guard, and my husband had border guards on them often. We kept an eye on the Germans, too. I have to admit, I'm not proud of that. Those groups were treated different, and they kept more to themselves." Mrs. Nyquist nodded. "But it was much looser for the Italians, and we all got to know each other. They helped us out in the office or delivered things. They were just a bunch of young sailors, most of 'em from the cruise ships, and they were all so happy-go-lucky."

Mary smiled. She had never been happy-go-lucky. She was the only unhappy-go-lucky Italian on the planet.

"They helped out a lot at the camp, in town, and with the logging and the sugar beet fields, and the way the camp was set up, the barracks were close to the administrative offices and the officers' homes. We were always running into them. My husband and I lived on a house at the camp, like the other officers. It was a white house, very pretty."

Mary flashed on the black-and-white aerial views of the camp, then she thought of something. "If the Italians weren't under guard, then how come guards monitored their visits?"

"They didn't."

"Yes, they did."

"Did they? That surprises me."

"I think so, at least sometimes. I found a memo that shows a guard monitored a visit Amadeo had with his lawyer, and they even sent a copy of that memo to the FBI."

Mrs. Nyquist blinked behind her bifocals, then shook her head. "I have no idea why that was, but I wouldn't know everything. And I was only there a while."

Mary made a mental note. "Okay, back to the man in the cap. Tell me about him."

"As I recall, he'd been educated, too, back where he was from. He could read and write. He'd had a year or two in an American high school."

"Where was he from?"

"I don't recall, offhand. Give me a minute." Mrs. Nyquist lowered her hand, still holding the photo, and squeezed her eyes shut.

"Maybe your husband had some photos around, or papers that could jar your memory?"

"No, no, no." Mrs. Nyquist shook her head, her eyes still closed. "Aaron wasn't the sentimental sort. He didn't save a thing from those days."

"Not even some pictures?"

"No, none." Mrs. Nyquist was rubbing her lined forehead, as if she were trying to scratch the answer from her brain. "The war wasn't the happiest time for Aaron. He did feel so terrible, being left behind with all us women, when the others were fighting. He didn't want to remember anything of those days. He never even talked about it."

Mary remembered that was what Will had said, back in the garage. She shut up and let Mrs. Nyquist think in peace.

"Let me see. The truth is, the other girls in the office liked him, but not me. I thought he was too smooth. You know, bedroom eyes and a slick smile. I don't like that type. He was my age, in his twenties, but he acted a lot older, and he had a lot of city ways." Suddenly Mrs. Nyquist snapped her fingers. "Oh, he was from the East Coast— Philadelphia. Like *you*!"

"He was from *Philly*?" Mary asked, amazed. No one was ever from Philly, except her. And she had been assuming that although Amadeo and the man in the cap had been friends, they had met in the internment camp. But what if they hadn't? What if they'd known each other before, from the city? She felt her heartbeat quicken, but it could have been the fructose lava.

"I remember now, his name was Saracone. Giovanni. Giovanni Saracone. The girls in the office called him Gio."

"Giovanni Saracone! Gio!" Mary jumped out of her chair, came around the table, and gave Mrs. Nyquist the hug she'd wanted to give her at the beginning. "Giovanni Saracone is his name?"

"Yes!" Mrs. Nyquist emerged from her clinch, smiling. "Why are you so happy? Do you know him?"

"No, I don't."

"Oh."

"I know the other man, Amadeo." Mary caught herself, as she returned to her seat. "Well, I don't *know* him, either. I'm trying to find out more about him. I wonder if this Saracone went back to Philly after he was released. Do you know?"

"No."

"Do you know anything else about Saracone?"

Mrs. Nyquist thought a minute. "No, just that. His name, and that he was a wolf."

Mary thought a minute, taking in Mrs. Nyquist's pretty blue eyes and sweet smile. She must have been lovely in her younger days. "A wolf, huh? Did he hit on you?"

"*Hit on?*" Mrs. Nyquist's eyes flared behind her bifocals. "Is that what they say nowadays, for making a pass? No, he didn't make a pass, not at me. I was a married woman, and I can shoot."

Mary laughed.

"Hold on, let me show you something." Mrs. Nyquist rose abruptly, walked over to the side table, and picked up a photo in a wooden frame and handed it to Mary. The photo was in black and white, of an attractive woman in fringed leather chaps and a cowboy hat, riding a bucking horse. Despite the death-defying arch to the horse's back, the woman rider hung on with a huge grin, and Mary looked at Mrs. Nyquist in amazement.

"Is this *you*?"

"Sure enough. I rode rodeo, roping and penning, I did it all."

"You were a cowgirl?" Mary handed her back the photo. "How did you learn it?"

"From my mother. I was a rancher's daughter, like my mother. She became a rancher after my father died. She kept the place herself, she even knew Calamity Jane. Jane was a real Montana cowgirl, born Martha Jane Cannary, she was."

"Calamity Jane!" Mary knew about her only from a Doris Day movie she'd seen on TMC. If it weren't for TV, she wouldn't know anything about Montana. "You were so brave to get on a horse like that! Weren't you afraid?"

"Surely! It's no fun if you're not afraid."

Mary laughed. The notion was as foreign to her as, well, Montana. "I wish I could be that way."

"You can. Anybody can." Mrs. Nyquist took the photo from Mary and replaced it on the side table, then came back to her seat. "You just climb up on the horse and stay on. Why can't you?"

"I don't know. I just can't imagine it."

"Haven't you ever been on a horse?"

"Are you kidding? I can barely drive. I'm not brave."

Mrs. Nyquist set her lips firmly. "I'm not brave, either, but I'm determined, and the horse can sense it. People can, too. Can you be determined, Mary?"

"I think so. It's like stubborn, and the DiNunzio women are good at stubborn."

"Well then, you come by it honestly." Mrs. Nyquist nodded. "If you can't be brave, be determined. And you'll end up in the same place."

Mary blinked. "Is that true?"

"Try it."

Determined. "I will." Mary looked down at the photos from the camp, which she had almost forgotten about. "Well, yes, where was I? Okay, do you know anyone else in the office, anyone you knew, who would know more about Giovanni Saracone?"

"No, I'm sorry." Mrs. Nyquist quieted, her mouth falling into the sad line she'd worn earlier. "They're all gone, now. The last one, Millie Berglund, she worked with me in the office. Millie passed right before my son and his wife did."

Mary felt her words like a weight. "Your son and his wife?"

"Yes, they were killed in a car accident, last year. A drunk driver, out on I-93. That's when Will came to live here. He was their only child. He's saving to get back to the U, but they didn't have insurance and the burial expenses alone . . ." Mrs. Nyquist's voice trailed off.

Mary hadn't realized. The older woman had seen so much pain, in only a year. But she had gone on. Determined. Mrs. Nyquist sat stoic in her sweat clothes, and Mary got up, went around the table, and gave her another hug. This time Mary didn't say she was sorry. The words, for once, couldn't come. After a minute, Mrs. Nyquist patted her arm, and Mary released her. "You okay?"

"I'm fine, dear." Mrs. Nyquist reached for

her napkin to wipe her eyes. "Why is it you want to find this Saracone fellow, Mary?"

"It's a legal matter."

Mrs. Nyquist frowned. "Are you a *lawyer*?"

"Hard to believe, huh?"

"But you're so nice!"

"I'm the nice one."

Mrs. Nyquist smiled, her eyes glistening. "What kind of legal matter is it?"

"I represent the estate of the other man, Amadeo Brandolini. And I actually think Saracone may have had something to do with the death of my client."

Mrs. Nyquist's lips parted in surprise. "But didn't you say it was suicide?"

"I'm not sure it was. I think it may have been murder."

Mrs. Nyquist's pale eyes widened. "My goodness, how awful!"

"I'll say. But I can't figure it all out. There are too many pieces to this puzzle."

"You think it was a *murder*? What do the police say?"

"I haven't asked. Yet." Mary got up to go, regretting that she'd even brought it up. "Well, thank you so much for your help. I've probably overstayed my welcome."

"Not in the least." Mrs. Nyquist suddenly

looked crestfallen, for a cowgirl. "You can stay and have another piece of pie, if you like. I'm a night owl. I read for an hour or so, then watch the television."

My routine, too. Mary thought a minute. She would love to get back to the motel, but Mrs. Nyquist looked so alone. "Who do you watch, pardner? Leno or Letterman?"

"Jay Leno."

"Right answer!" Mary smiled. "Now for the tough one. Conan or Craiggers?"

"Conan!"

"Yes!"

Mrs. Nyquist grinned. "I'll get more pie!"

Later Mary hit the road, rejuvenated by caffeine, Conan, and her first break on the case. When she had almost reached Missoula, her cell phone started ringing. She grabbed for her purse, fumbled for her phone, and flipped it open, all at top speed. "Yo," she said, and the voice on the line was Judy's.

"Mare, you have to come home. Now."

"You're damn right I do. Listen to this, I don't think Amadeo committed suicide. I think he was murdered, and I think the killer is from Philly!"

"Then that's *two* murders we have to solve."

"What?" Mary asked, stricken.

TWENTY-ONE

"Frank Cavuto is dead?" Mary asked, in pain. She slumped in the soft chair opposite Judy's desk. It was almost seven o'clock at night, and the offices of Rosato & Associates were quiet and still. Mary's briefcase, purse, and suitcase were beside the chair where she'd dropped them, damp from the downpour outside. It had taken a full eight hours to get home, including a layover, and in all that time, Mary still hadn't been able to process the news. "Frank is dead? I can't believe it. What happened? Any more details?"

"He was killed in his office during a break-in, at about ten o'clock last night. Taken by surprise as he was working late. Shot twice, robbed." Judy buckled her lower lip, atypically grave. "I'm sorry. I know you liked him."

"I did." Mary swallowed the tightness in her throat. She flashed on a younger Frank Cavuto, waving her into third base. Now, he was gone. Yet another ghost, this one too close to home. "I don't know why he wanted to fire me, but I still liked him. I'm sorry he's dead."

"Your parents okay?" Judy's blonde bangs had been brushed off her face, and she must have been in court today because she was wearing a blue linen dress with real leather shoes, even if they were the official slingbacks of Rosato & Associates, from the office closet.

"Are you kidding? They're freaked. The *circolo*'s freaked, too. I called Frank's house, but nobody's answering." Mary's temples began to throb and she didn't bother telling herself it was jet lag, trail mix, or the hassle at baggage carousel B. "I don't think it happened during a break-in. I don't care what they made it look like, I ain't buying."

"What do you think?"

"Frank never worked late. He wasn't a lawyer like us, writing briefs and reviewing documents at night. He was a hustler kind of lawyer. At night he went to softball games. Church bingo. Justinian Society cocktail parties. Sons of Italy receptions."

"You're sure?"

"Positive. So maybe he was meeting somebody at his office. And I can't stop thinking about that guy in the Escalade." Mary eyed the gifts she'd brought for everyone from the Missoula airport, lying forgotten on Judy's desk. A copper elk pin, huckleberry gummy bears, fuzzy bear claw slippers, and Moose Drool Soap. Mary had even bought herself a straw cowboy hat. Montana used to seem so far away. Now it wasn't. In fact, it had come home. "I think it's all connected, somehow, to Amadeo."

"I knew you would say that."

"Let's get real." Mary held up a certain hand. Something felt different in her, and she didn't know why. Whether it was Montana or Amadeo she didn't know, but something had gotten under her skin and stuck there. "I investigate Amadeo and Mr. Escalade starts following me around and a reporter shows up. I checked online and there is a reporter by that name at the *Philly*

News, but my Uncle Joey doesn't remember cutting his hair."

"That's strange, and there hasn't been an article in the paper about it. You don't know what the reporter did with the information, or who he gave it to, either."

"Right. So where were we? Frank tries to fire me, then somebody breaks into my office and takes Amadeo's file, and I go to Montana, where I find out that Amadeo may have been murdered by a man named Giovanni Saracone. Then Frank himself is murdered. Jeez, poor Frank."

"I looked Saracone up on the web. No one by that name or any reasonable variation in Philly or the subs." Judy's phone rang and she let voicemail pick up.

"Don't you have to get that?"

"It's a conference call in Alcor, which turns out to be the mother of all securities cases. Let them get the other three hundred lawyers on the line, then they can patch me in."

"Sorry."

"Forget it."

"I searched for Saracone online, too, until my laptop battery *and* my cell phone battery gave up." Mary fell silent a minute, watching rain slake the window. Nimbus clouds darkened the sky, and this high up, she could see lightning flash behind the storm clouds. It was better than seeing it from seat 17A. "It ain't rocket science, Jude. Even I can put this together."

"Meaning what?"

Uh. Gimme a minute. "Well, basically, there must be something about Amadeo, a reason he was killed, and it's behind everything." Mary was convincing herself as she went along, but she still felt like she was fishing.

"So why did whoever it is kill Cavuto?" Judy's phone finally stopped ringing.

"I don't know. Maybe to keep him quiet, to keep secret whatever he knew. Frank seemed worried to me that morning, and he wasn't that good a liar. He could have been getting nervous, as I was digging around, maybe getting closer to the truth. Do I flatter myself?"

"Somebody has to."

Mary laughed, which felt good, temporarily. "I knew Frank, and whatever his role in this mess, he couldn't have been a principal. He wasn't a real bad guy at heart, he was just a guy whose law firm had some involvement. Maybe that's why the house sale at bargain prices."

"This isn't my main concern." Judy's face darkened, matching the clouds. "I'm worried about you."

Me, too. "I'm worried about my job. Am I fired yet?"

"You caught a break. Bennie didn't ask where you went on vacation, so I didn't volunteer it. She sent her condolences for Cavuto, but she can't get an extension on her trial. We're free at last, free at last." Judy frowned. "But I'm still worried about you. I think we should go to the police." Her phone started ringing, and she ignored it again. "Tell them the story."

"I'm on it. I called the Homicide Squad on the way in and left a message for Reggie and his partner, Detective Kovich. Remember them?" Detectives Reginald Brinkley and Stan Kovich had become Mary's friends on an old murder case, and Reggie still stopped by her mother's house for meatball sandwiches, raising the African-American population on Mercer Street to one. "I know they'd help, but the detective answering the phone said they were out on jobs."

"Who's assigned to Cavuto?"

"He wouldn't tell me. I left a message. I even told the desk detective all about the Escalade, so they can issue an APB."

"Which they won't do."

"Not yet."

"So you gonna wait for him to call back?"

"What do you think?" Mary smiled.

"He leaves us with no alternative, does he?" Judy grinned back, but Mary's smile faded.

"Us?"

"Of course, us. It's always us."

"Not this time." Mary rose and picked up her purse and bag. She'd stow the bag in her office. It would only burden her, where she was going. "You have a conference call, you should take it."

"I'll say I got sick."

"No, I'm going on my own."

"But it's dangerous."

"Not really. I'm just going to look around a little."

"Alone? You?" Judy's eyes flared. "You get scared by yourself. Remember the Della Porta case? You got heebie-jeebies at the murder scene. You wouldn't even get out of the car."

Mary smiled. It was true. That was before Montana. Now she was *determined*. "I can do it alone. If you got shot, I couldn't take the guilt."

"You got shot on one of my cases, and I didn't give it a thought."

"Ha! You know you love me." Mary laughed, hoisting her heavy bag higher onto her shoulder. "See ya."

"No, wait!" Judy called out, but the phone started ringing again, and Mary was off and running.

Rain pelted Mary's shoulders in her go-to navy blazer, and she stood as close as possible to Frank Cavuto's building. Wet crime-scene tape crisscrossed the front door, collecting rain so that DO NOT CRO was all anybody could read. It made her sick at heart. She had seen way too much crime-scene tape even in her short career; now it was all over TV shows and party gags. For Mary, murder would never be remotely funny. As far as she was concerned, all crime-scene tape should read: SOMETHING UNSPEAKABLE HAPPENED HERE.

Soggy Acme carnations wrapped in crinkly plastic blanketed the front stoop, next to sprayed daises and wilted roses, their stems encased in green plastic straws. Hallmark cards had been Scotch-taped to the door but were now drenched, and one hung open, showing all the nouns under-lined in now-dripping marker; *Sympathy* and *Sorrow* and *Sadness*. A tiny Italian flag had been wedged in the mail slot, and it moved slightly in the rain. Frank had mat-tered so much to this community. He had been loved.

Frank, what did you do that got you killed?

She stood on tiptoe and peered through the small glass window in the door. It was dark inside; she couldn't see a thing. Then she heard a sound behind her and turned, startled. A homeless man was standing there, in a Phillies cap and a stained Dorney Park T-shirt. It was raining on his skinny shoulders, which were already saturated, but he didn't seem to notice.

"That guy got shot," the man said. "They shot him, they did."

"I know."

"Neighborhood's goin' to hell," he said, shuffling on, and Mary's blood pressure re-turned to normal. She glanced around, un-easy. She'd taken the bus to get here, making sure she wasn't followed, and hadn't seen the Escalade. She glanced again, double-checking, but it was nowhere in sight. Not that she felt safe. She wouldn't feel safe until Frank's killer had been caught and she learned the truth.

Mary glanced around one last time and saw nothing amiss, so she left the stoop to walk around the front of the building to the corner, where Frank's office was. The large window with dirty glass was covered by a drawn curtain. *Damn!* Mary reached into her handbag, rummaged around, and pulled out a brown spongy cowboy hat on a key ring, one of her presents to herself from the Missoula airport. At one end was a tiny pen-light, and she flashed it around the window, discovering nothing except that the curtain had a cheap cotton lining.

Thunder clapped in the night sky, and rain soaked her suit and hair. She was getting nowhere fast and was cold and wet to boot. She looked around, blinking water from her eyes. Only light traffic sped in the hard rain down a slick Broad Street. A mostly-empty SEPTA bus barreled along, churning gutter water in its huge corrugated tires, spraying watery grit. The bus zoomed past the empty kiosk in front of Frank's office. The sidewalks were completely vacant, owing to the thunderstorm, and evidently even the crazy man in the Phillies cap had sought shelter.

Mary glanced around one more time, to make sure the coast was clear. When it was, she made her move.

TWENTY-TWO

Mary edged away from the window, hustled along the Broad Street side of Frank's building, then took a right at the corner. Typically the cross streets were residential except for the mom-and-pop corner grocery/beauty parlor/florist, and well-kept rowhouses stretched in a line of unbroken brick down the street, their gray marble stoops light spots in the downpour. It was a nice, safe neighborhood, except when girl lawyers were on the prowl.

Mary stole down the street in the darkness, following a hunch that turned out to be correct. On her right, tucked behind Frank's building, she found what every resident of South Philly longed for—a parking space. Frank's space was in a paved lot that was the exact footprint of a rowhouse, which he had undoubtedly bought, torn down, and paved for this purpose. And unless she was wrong, there would be a back door to his office. She stepped onto the asphalt of the parking lot and froze.

A motion detector! Bright light flooded the tiny lot, suddenly illuminating the back door, a window next to it, and a paralyzed lawyer. Mary sprang backward out of the brightness, then flattened in the shadow against the building, its coarse brick clammy beneath her palms. She edged sideways while the light remained on, and she could tick off the seconds with the sound of her own nervous breaths.

Rain hurtled down and she spent a fleeting moment wondering if she was about to commit a venial or a mortal sin, then reconsidered. THOU SHALT NOT STEAL didn't necessarily encompass THOU SHALT NOT BREAK IN, and after all, someone had broken into her office, so turnabout was fair play. At least she was furthering the cause of justice, which should count for extra credit in the God Department.

Click! The security light went off in the

next instant, and she waited a minute more, getting thoroughly drenched. Then she hurried back to the parking lot and the window, and when thunder shattered the sky, hopefully deafening the neighbors, she shoved her fist in her purse and put the entire assembly through the glass window, which broke easily. Then she climbed inside.

The window dumped her into darkness and she landed on her butt in what felt like a hallway, because her head was against one wall and her wet shoes against another, less than three feet away. She didn't dare turn on a light, but she reached for her bag on the floor next to her, got out her trusty Montana penlight, and flicked it on. A pool of light roughly the size of a dime roamed uselessly over the walls of the hallway, and Mary got up. Shards of glass tinkled to the floor. She grabbed her bag and shook herself off, hearing more tinkling sounds, and aimed the penlight down the hallway, then hurried into the dark corridor. Frank's office would be on the right, closest to the corner, and she turned.

Into a wall.

Clunk! She rubbed her nose and reminded herself not to go faster than she could see, then waved the penlight around until she found an open doorway and walked through, casting the flashlight around. It was the reception area, so she must have been near the front of the office building. *Damn!* She walked again to the right, looking for Frank's office and after she'd tripped only twice, she found it. Partly because of the odor.

Mary wrinkled her nose. That smell, she knew from other crime scenes. It was blood, decomposing blood. The old Mary would have run screaming or maybe cried, but the new Mary scorned such lame-ass, estrogen-fueled responses, so she gritted her teeth and moved forward through the threshold she knew led to Frank's office.

She cast the penlight around, watching it wander like a laser pointer over certificates and law degrees and finally, her own photo in the group shot of the old softball team. She experienced a pang of times lost, then of Frank. He was dead, someone had murdered him, and now she wanted to know who. She took a step toward the desk, and the scent of his blood intensified here, becoming part of the office forever. She became vaguely aware that she was avoiding whatever Frank's desk looked like, since he had been shot there.

Lame, lame, lame. Grow up, cowgirl. Look.

The penlight found a splotch of brownish blood on the desk, where papers had been undisturbed, and Mary felt her stomach turn over. Or maybe it was somebody else's stomach, since she was tougher now, and she walked around the desk, the primal smell filling her nostrils. She gasped when the penlight inadvertently found blood spatter against the wall behind the desk, blanketing the photos that hung there.

The penlight fell on Frank's desk, which had been ransacked, every drawer pulled out and left on the floor. Bills, receipts, pencils, and pens spilled everywhere, just as they had in Mary's office. She squatted on her haunches and aimed the penlight at the first drawer in the middle. The penlight seared a white circle into the drawer, and the lock had been broken, wedged completely out of the drawer, leaving even the walnut splintered like balsa.

Mary crouched closer and turned a sharp piece of wood over with the penlight, like a kid examining driftwood on the beach. The killer had taken whatever papers, if any, Frank had in the desk. The cops would think they were looking for money or petty cash, but she wasn't buying that either. What could have been in there? She took one last look around at the debris scattered behind the desk but saw nothing that mattered. All the time, she was wondering, if Frank had papers relating to Saracone, where else would they be? Then it hit her.

A safe. Mary rose and started looking behind the certificates and photos. No safe. She remembered that Frank had mentioned a will vault. Was it literal? She searched his bookshelves, behind his books, and through the drawers in a credenza against the wall. No safe or vault. Then she realized she'd been going about it the wrong way. She should just troll the office and see what the killer had destroyed; if he'd found a safe, she'd found a safe. She took a slow once-over of the office again, trying not to breathe the horrible odor or see anything too upsetting, which was a neat trick at a murder scene. But there was nothing. No safe. No vault. Strike one.

She left the office and cast a light around the secretary's area, then reconsidered.

Frank had to have a file room, didn't he? All lawyers had file rooms, and he had even mentioned one at their meeting. She hurried past the reception area, toward the hallway leading to the parking lot, but right before she got to the hallway was an open door. She flashed the light and walked in, where it smelled oddly rosy. She cast the light around.

A toilet, seat up, and on the back rested a can of pink Glade air freshener. Strike two. She went out again and cast the penlight around the hallway. There it was; another door, halfway open. She went inside and found herself in a room that even smelled tiny and cramped, the air stale with old coffee. She flicked the penlight around her, full circle. A wooden table held a Mr. Coffee coffeemaker and the usual array of cups, sugars, plastic stirrers, and powdered creamers. Mary scanned the file room, pivoting quickly on her heel, and noticed that the room had no windows. Good. She went back to the door, closed it securely, and found a light switch, which she flicked on. Fluorescent panels went on overhead, filling the room with harsh light, which was when she saw it.

A recessed frame in the wall near the baseboard had been completely demolished. White and gray plaster had been cut away, wire mesh wrenched out of shape, and wooden studs in the wall had been cut, as if with a crude saw. Mary knelt before it, examining it. Even an idiot could tell that a safe had been extracted from this spot, like a diseased tooth. Was it the will vault that Frank had mentioned? How had they carried it out? Put it on a dolly and wheeled it? Mary considered it. It would have made more sense than trying to bust it open here, and taking it away would clinch the police theory of a break-in.

Damn. She rose slowly, looking at the file cabinets next to the hole. Banks and banks of them; beige, standard-issue Hons in four-drawer stacks. She set upon the filing cabinet, pulling each drawer out and closing it again. Each drawer contained only case files in legal-size manila folders, suspended on Pendaflex hangers and filed by plaintiff's name, and she went through the first few. There was nothing remotely suspicious about the files, then Mary had another thought.

She eyed the carefully hand-printed labels

in the front of each drawer, starting with
Ab–Ar. She took a quick look at the *B*
drawer for *Brandolini*, but there was no
Brandolini file for Amadeo or Theresa. But it
was at least possible that there was a
Saracone file. Mary scanned the drawers
until she reached the *S*s, then yanked on
the third drawer, fourth row: *Sa–Su*. Inside
were more case files, starting with *Sabella v.
Oregon Avenue Painting and Plastering*,
and she thumbed through the case files until she reached where Saracone's would be.
There was no manila folder.

She stopped, momentarily stumped.
Either there was no case file for Saracone or
the killer had taken it, leaving no sign that
the file cabinets had been disturbed. Smart.
Had he left a sign, the cops would have suspected it was more than a robbery for cash.
Mary tried to think what to do next. No safe,
no nothing, no sign of anything linking
Saracone to Frank.

She felt her shoulders slump. Maybe her
Saracone search was a dry hole. Maybe it
really had been a robbery and murder.
Maybe huckleberries didn't have superpowers. She sighed audibly and lowered her
head, resting it on her arm as it lay on the

open file drawer, which was when her gaze fell on the two bottom drawers, after the Zs. BILLING, read the label, with last year's date, then this year. Of course! Why hadn't she thought of that? Every lawyer kept a copy of his bills in a separate file, in addition to the copy that would be in the case file, for tax and accounting purposes.

Mary closed the drawer, squatted on the carpet, and pulled out the drawer for last year's bills. The first manila folder read JANUARY, and the others were the months of the year, in chronological order. She flipped through January, reading bills sent to a variety of South Philly residents and small businesses, most of them for a few thousand dollars. Nothing. Mary paged through February, which was more of the same, then continued through March, April, and May. By June, she was beginning to lose hope, but then she hit the middle of June and stopped cold.

There it was. Right in the middle of the stack. A bill, and under the client name, at the top, it read: Giovanni Saracone. Mary read the bill, which merely stated: Payment on semiannual retainer. The amount— $250,000.

What? A retainer of two hundred and fifty thousand dollars? Mary almost laughed out loud. That was insane! Not only was it way out of line with Frank's other bills, even her old white-shoe firm, Grun & Chase, didn't have more than a handful of clients with retainers of that magnitude. A case demanding those fees would be in the news every day! What type of case could Frank be handling for Saracone that would justify those fees? And twice a year?

Mary skipped back to the year before that, and thumbed through the bill copies. Again, midway in the pack, on the fifteenth, was a file copy of a bill to Giovanni Saracone. The amount was $250,000. Again, unlike the other bills, not even a brief description of the services rendered. What kind of client accepted that for a retainer accounting? None. Mary could barely contain herself.

What gives? Five hundred grand a year billed to Saracone? For what? For how long? And did it have anything to do with Amadeo? It must have. Here was a link between Saracone and Frank. Mary just didn't know what it meant. Her gaze shifted to the drawer with even older bills, and it took her only five minutes to find the June and

December bills to Saracone, again totaling $500,000. She checked the year before that and the two before that, going back a total of five years. Each year had the same bill copies, coming to half a million dollars for five years. *Two and a half million dollars.* It bought a lot of softball jerseys. How long had it been going on, and why?

If there had been a Saracone case file, it had been taken, but Mary didn't think there had been a case involving Saracone at all. Ever. The timing didn't make sense; most small litigation matters didn't last that long. And the killers hadn't thought to look here in the billing files because they didn't know about them—for once, the bad guys *weren't* lawyers. Mary's thoughts raced ahead. These had to have been some sort of payments from Saracone to Frank, disguised as legal bills. Did Frank know something— maybe about Amadeo's murder—that Saracone wanted silenced? If so, why not kill him a long time ago? And who *invoiced* for blackmail?

Mary's hands trembled as she held the folder. She didn't want to risk Exhibits A through F disappearing when the bad guys figured out what they'd left behind. She'd lost enough documents for one case, in the drawings. She took the Saracone bill from the file folder, then went back to the other folders and took out all the Saracone bills going back all five years. She stacked the bills, folded them over, and stuck them in her purse; then she replaced the file folders, closed the drawers, and left the file room, turning off the light. Good girls conserved electricity *and* avoided detection.

She hurried down the hallway, climbed back out of the shattered window, and headed down the street in the rain. She had broken at least one commandment, THOU SHALT NOT STEAL LEGAL BILLS, but she was too jiggered up to question her conduct or even to feel guilty. She clutched her purse protectively to her chest, out of the rain. Because inside were the bills, with a very valuable address.

So she knew exactly where to go next.

TWENTY-THREE

The thunderstorm showed no signs of letting up, and rain pelted the roof of Mary's ancient BMW and struck her windows, clouding what her breath didn't fog. She'd gone home for her car and never once thought about turning back or even stopping for coffee, she was so excited. She drove pedal-to-the-metal past acres of dark hills, shadows of cornfields, and winding country roads, to a place called Birchrunville, then looked around for the house. It wasn't hard to find in such a small, apparently exclusive place. The town boasted one intersection, a quaint post office, and an elegant restaurant called the Birchrunville Cafe, and was moneyed in a completely tasteful way. Mary never would have guessed that an Italian from Philly would end up in such ritzy country. But then again, she didn't know enough about Giovanni Saracone.

His house was at the end of a long, narrow road, and she pulled up across the street from an apparently indestructible green mailbox, cutting the ignition. She'd broken a sweat that she knew wasn't from the humidity. Mary couldn't believe she was actually here, at Saracone's house. A man who had been with Amadeo when he died. Was Saracone even still alive? The bills indicated he was, and Mrs. Nyquist had said he was one of the youngest in the internment camp. What had really happened the day Amadeo died? Had Saracone actually killed him? Part of Mary believed it already, but that was the part of her that jumped to conclusions. She told herself to calm down, then rubbed the steam from her car window with a fist and looked outside.

Colonial glass lanterns mounted atop stone pillars cast the only light on a seven-foot-high cedar gate that blocked the driveway and the entrance. It had to be an electric gate, because a gold-toned keypad on a gooseneck stem sat beside the cobblestone driveway. Mary tried to see over the gate, but rain and dense trees obscured her view. She rolled down her window, blinking against the rain, when suddenly the front gate started to open.

Mary slumped in the driver's seat just as a black sedan glided from the gate and took a left turn down the road. She followed its red lights with a nervous gaze, and when it had driven out of view, she slid up in the seat. The cedar gates were closing. She only had a minute to make a decision. She wanted to see inside. She flung open the car door, grabbed her purse, and bolted into the rain. The gate was closing, narrowing her entrance to three feet, then two. Mary darted through the opening as the gate closed noiselessly behind her and she ran for the shelter of a huge, leafy oak tree and looked around.

A winding driveway slick with wet cobblestones and lined with low lamps curled to a huge stone mansion, four stories high and constructed entirely of fieldstones, their natural earth tones vivid with rainwater and illuminated by bright lights aimed at the house. How did Saracone come to afford such a place? What did he do for a living? How had he come so far? And the mansion was only part of the compound. Beyond the house along the driveway sat a large stone carriage house, and next to it, a barn converted to the most swanky four-car garage in history. In front of it were parked two black Mercedes sedans, the model favored by Eastern Bloc diplomats. Mary looked over the cars to a stone cottage, also of fieldstone, and to the cedar fence beyond that apparently enclosed a built-in pool.

Her gaze returned to the stone mansion and its massive front door, of dense mahogany with an ornately cut glass. Giovanni Saracone lived behind that door. If he were still alive, he'd be in his early eighties and was evidently wealthy. He would have survived a world war and maybe killed a man with his bare hands, alone in a Montana beet field.

If you can't be brave, be determined. And you'll end up in the same place.

She left the shadows of the oak tree and walked directly down the middle of the driveway toward the front door, with far more bravado than she felt. She reached the front step of a slate flagstone, too high-rent to be called a stoop. Tall white pillars on either side of the front door soared two stories high, supporting a white-painted porch that sheltered the entrance from the storm. Mary braced herself, pressed the lighted doorbell, and tried to remember that she was a cowgirl.

The door was opened by a young African-American woman wearing a fresh white nurse's uniform embroidered with the slogan *HomeCare, WeCare.* Above the stitching glinted a fake-gold pin that read KEISHA. Keisha was a pretty twenty-something, with her dark hair close-cut and her lightly lipsticked mouth forming a puzzled frown. "Did somebody ring you in through the gate?" she asked.

"No, I was about to push the button for the intercom, but a car went out, so I just walked in."

"You shouldn'ta done that." Keisha took in Mary's wet blazer and khakis with disapproval. "Are you selling somethin'?"

"No. I'm a friend of Mr. Saracone's and I'm here to see him."

"A friend?" Keisha repeated uncertainly, blinking against the rain spraying under the porch.

"Maybe if I could come in for a second, we wouldn't both get wet."

"If you're Mr. Saracone's friend, you know he's very ill." Keisha was still squinting against the rain, or maybe in suspicion. "He's not taking visitors except for family, and certainly not tonight."

"To tell the truth, I'm not really *his* friend." Mary scrambled to cover, digging a business card from her purse and handing it to the nurse. "I'm really a lawyer, and I represent a man who's a very old friend of Mr. Saracone's. A man named Amadeo Brandolini. I really do need to see Mr. Saracone, about him."

"I don't know." The nurse edged away from the door, but on impulse, Mary thrust her hand inside.

"I swear, Mr. Saracone would be angry with you if you sent me away. He might even fire you." Mary was winging it, but the nurse stopped closing the door.

"You serious? I need this job."

"I'm very serious."

"*What's* your client's name?"

Mary repeated it. "Please, just show Mr. Saracone my card, and tell him I'm here. I promise, if you tell him that name, he'll want to see me."

"Well, wait here for a minute," Keisha said, her voice softening. Her gaze lifted to the rainstorm. "Sorry I have to make you wait outside in this weather. I can't let you in until I ask Mr. Saracone."

"I'm fine, thanks." Mary waited while the front door closed and was locked. Not only was Saracone alive, she would be meeting him any minute. Mary had no sooner had the thought than her determination evaporated, replaced by good old- fashioned fear.

Still she managed not to run back to the car and made herself stay until the front door opened again.

TWENTY-FOUR

Five minutes later, it wasn't the nurse who opened the front door, but instead a beautiful woman about Mary's age. She had glossy black hair that grazed her shoulders in a chic cut, dark almond-shaped eyes with no crow's feet, and a body that strippers would kill for. She looked way too young to be Saracone's wife, which had to mean she was Saracone's wife.

"Hello, I'm Melania Saracone, Giovanni's wife." She pursed thin lips and extended her manicured hand in a confident, if not friendly, way. "Please come in."

"Thanks." Mary felt her hand gripped a little harder than necessary as Mrs. Saracone fairly pulled her inside the house and shut the door behind her.

Okay, I'm intimidated. It had been a stupid idea to come here without telling anyone, putting herself inside this house, alone and vulnerable. Her determination had vanished, evidently figuring she would get them both killed. She could only hope it was calling 911.

"Would you like a drink? Diet Coke, or water?" Mrs. Saracone asked, leading her over a thick Oriental carpet through a dimly lit entrance hall, with one of those pretentious staircases that curved around in a costly curl. Her hair bounced like a shampoo commercial and her head was cocked stiffly to the side, as if awaiting the answer.

"No, thanks." Mary followed her into an immense living room lined with books that reached all the way to a vaulted ceiling, topped by a dramatically arched skylight. Plush couches and matching wing chairs clustered in three different areas—one near a stone fireplace, one on the right, and one on the left—but the furniture looked more stage-set than living room. Mrs. Saracone sat down in a navy velvet chair next to a mahogany end table and motioned Mary into the identical chair opposite her. "Thanks," Mary said, sinking into the down cushion. "This is a lovely house, Mrs. Saracone."

"You can call me Melania. So you're the lawyer for a man named Amadeo Brando-lini." Melania crossed one long leg over the other and brushed down charcoal slacks that broke above pointy black velvet mules. She wore a pressed white shirt with darts that emphasized the curve of an amplified C cup, and her waist didn't bulge at her belt when she sat down. It was easy to see she worked out, and Mary tried not to imagine how many lawyers she could bench-press.

"Yes, actually, I represent his estate."

"Then your client died?"

"Yes, a long time ago. In 1942, by sui-cide." Mary didn't want to show her hand, at least not until her determination got off the cell phone and came back. All was forgiven. "It's my understanding that your husband was with him when he died."

"That's odd, he never mentioned it." Melania cocked her head again, either by habit or affectation, and Mary wondered what she really knew. It was doubtful that Giovanni would have told his trophy about Amadeo's death, especially if he was involved, and there was nothing in Melania's manner that suggested she was uneasy. If anything, she seemed interested, if only politely. "You say your client committed suicide?"

"Yes. He and Giovanni were very good friends, and ended up in an internment camp together in Montana. During the war." *That would be World War II.*

"I so didn't know that. Are you sure?"

"Yes, positive." Mary reached in her purse, carefully avoided the Saracone legal bills, and pulled out a scanned copy of the photos she'd found at the camp. She had made three copies of the photos and left them at work, hiding the original in the coffee room; this time she was taking no chances. She showed the paper to Melania, both photos on the same page. "Isn't that Giovanni, in the hat?"

"Whoa!" Melania's liquid-lined eyes flared. "God, he looks hot! He must have been twenty or so!"

Read it and weep. "Yes, he was younger then. The short man with him is my client, Amadeo Brandolini. Giovanni never mentioned him? They were good friends."

"No, not at all." Melania handed the picture to Mary, who tucked it back in her purse. "How did your client commit suicide?"

"He hung himself."

"Eeew." Melania wrinkled her nose like a varsity cheerleader, and Mary stopped missing her determination. If the bad guys were going to kill her, they would have already. They had probably assumed that she'd told people she was coming here, thus making the classic bad-guy mistake of overestimating her.

"Melania, I know it's late, but do you think it would be possible for me to meet your husband?"

"No, sorry, but you can't. He's really ill."

Mary wondered if she were telling the truth, but she seemed to be, and the nurse had said the same thing. "I'm sorry. What is he ill with?"

"He has cancer, pancreatic cancer."

"How terrible," Mary said, with an inward moan. She thought reflexively of her mother. "Can I come back another time? Tomorrow, maybe? I promise I'll be brief, and I—"

"To be honest with you, he's terminal. I'm not sure how much longer he has left."

Melania blinked away tears that barely challenged waterproof mascara. "The doctor can't say, so we take it day to day."

"I'm so sorry," Mary said, with regret, not grief. She had come so far, from the National Archives to Montana and back, tracing Saracone to this very house. If he was alive, it wasn't too late. "So there's no way, just for a minute, I could see him?"

"No, I don't think so." Melania swallowed in premature grief, but Mary wasn't buying it for a minute. Anytime a sophomore marries a rich eighty-year-old, she's not only prepared for the death part, she's counting on it. Melania added, "I only let you in because Keisha said you were so nice. It's really only family at the house at this point."

"Family, of course. Do you have children?" Mary switched tacks for the moment, taking discovery.

"Giovanni does, from his previous marriage. A son, Justin. He should be here any minute." Melania checked her watch, a gold Rolex. "He must be running late, with this weather."

Mary could meet him if she stalled. "Oh yeah, I think I met Justin once. In town."

"You might have. He did graduate from

law school, but he doesn't practice anymore."

Melania smiled with new interest. "Where
did you meet him?"

"If memory serves, it was at a bar function
of some kind," Mary answered vaguely. "So
many lawyers quit practice, nowadays. I think
of quitting all the time. Why did he quit?"

"Justin didn't really quit, he works for the
business."

"What business?"

"Giovanni's. You know, his investments."

How had Saracone made all this dough?
"What type of investments?"

Melania's smile faded. "Why do you ask?"

"I'm just making conversation, to distract
you from your grief. Is it working?"

"No." Melania laughed, and Mary leaned
over.

"Look, I know this sounds weird and awful, but can I please see Giovanni? I swear,
I'll stay three minutes and that's it. I could
show him the photo of—"

"No, of course not." Melania recoiled. "My
husband is on his *deathbed*."

"Is he awake now? Did he get my message about Amadeo?"

"Yes, Keisha told him."

"You're sure?"

Melania bristled. "I was there. What's wrong with you? Why do you ask?"

"It's just that it matters so much, to my client's estate. My client had a special affinity for your husband. What did he say when Keisha told him?"

"Now stop right there." Melania's fair skin flared in anger. "That's none of your business!"

"I know it seems rude, but it *is* my business." Mary struggled for an explanation. "It would mean so much to my boss if I could tell him what your husband said. Could you just let me know, girl to girl, so I don't get fired? I need this job." It was Keisha's line, but it had hit home with Mary, and it seemed to hit home with Melania, too.

"All he said was, 'Amadeo.' Okay?"

Amadeo. "He didn't say anything else?"

"No. He put his head back on the pillow and fell asleep."

"You sure he didn't say anything else? Something that didn't mean anything to you could mean a lot to my boss."

"No, nothing else. He's been saying things all the time, things that make no sense, because of the morphine and the other drugs."

"Things that make no sense? What do you mean? What things?"

"The man is dying! The man is dying, and he knows it. Have some decency, why don't you!" Melania stood up suddenly and brushed her wool slacks down over her taut thighs. "I tried to be nice, but I'm over this. I'm going upstairs, and you're leaving. Right now. I'll walk you to the door."

Mary couldn't walk out, could she? She'd come so far and if she waited another day, Saracone could be dead. She rose to go, hoisting her purse to her shoulder. She couldn't just give up and go home, but she didn't know what else to do.

"You have some nerve, you know that?" Melania was saying, over her shoulder, but Mary was thinking.

Should I take a chance? No. Yes. No. "Sorry," Mary said. She followed Melania to the front door, but her determination re-turned in the nick of time. As Melania opened the door, Mary spun about-face and bolted for the carpeted stairwell that led up-stairs. She didn't stop to question or won-der or even double-check.

She just *ran*.

TWENTY-FIVE

"What! No! Hey! Don't you dare!" Melania shouted from the door, but for once Mary didn't apologize.

Go! She darted up the stairs as fast as she could. She could get there. She could see Saracone. She wasn't too late, not if he was alive. She reached the landing at the top with Melania on her heels. Where was Saracone's bedroom?

"Stop!" Melania shouted. "No!"

Mary looked wildly right and left, panting hard. Two rooms were at either end of the long carpeted hall. Which was Saracone's? An open door, with lamplight behind it! *Left! Go!* She bolted for the lighted bedroom just ahead of Melania, fueled by thoughts of

Amadeo, the hanging tree, and the noose, which trumped a StairMaster any day.

"No! Chico, help! Chico, hurry!" Melania screamed, the sound reverberating in Mary's ears.

Go, go, go! Mary tore down the hallway. There! She could barely stop in time as she reached the bedroom door and grabbed the doorknob. She scooted inside the bedroom, slammed the door closed behind her with a *bang*, and twisted a brass thumbscrew above the doorknob to lock herself inside. *Thank you, God!*

Almost instantly, Melania started pounding on the other side of the bedroom door, which shook with the force of each blow. "Get out of there! Chico! CHICO!"

Mary didn't want to meet anybody named Chico. She whirled around on her heels and came face-to-face with Giovanni Saracone himself.

The old man sat bolt upright in his huge, fancy bed, his wobbly head egg-shaped and bald. His dark, sunken eyes had gone wide with alarm in their withered sockets, and his parched lips formed a wasted circle of alarm. A transparent greenish oxygen tube snaked from under his nose to a portable tank beside the bed, and he was hooked up to an IV and a small home monitor for his vital signs.

The sight took Mary aback, or maybe it was just the shock of what she had just done, breaking into his bedroom. But what she saw in Giovanni Saracone was stark, cold fright. Saracone was *afraid* of her, terrified *of her*, and in that one instant, eye to eye, she knew exactly why. Because he had killed Amadeo. He had been told she was here and he knew why she had come. He must have been dreading this day, and now it had finally come, on his deathbed. The knowledge flooded Mary with unholy power.

"You killed Amadeo Brandolini!" she shouted at Saracone, against the pounding on the bedroom door.

"Stop!" Melania screamed from outside the door. "Chico, here! Break it down!" In the next minute a huge *thud* pounded against the door, almost tearing it from its hinges.

"Please! Please!" Saracone rasped, and his head tottered. He put his hands up feebly, the IV tubes slack. "Please don't hurt me! Please! God!"

"God won't help you!" Mary shook with a rage she didn't know she had. "God doesn't help *murderers*! You strangled Amadeo with your *bare hands*! You tied a rope on his neck and you tried to make it look like he killed himself! You got away with *murder*!"

Suddenly, the door began to splinter. Melania's shouts were joined by a man's. "Let me in, you bitch! Let me in!"

"No. Please. No!" Saracone's head kept shaking, and Mary saw wetness spring to his eyes, but his tears didn't soften her heart. He hadn't denied what she said. He was afraid only for himself. He had done it. He had killed Amadeo and now he was crying for himself. Only she stood for Amadeo, traveling across space and time to face his killer, at death's door. Saracone might never be called to court to pay for what he had done, but after all this time, he would account to her.

"You killed him! You murdered him, and I want to know why." Mary stepped toward the bed, and Saracone didn't recoil from her but instead inclined toward her, seemingly transfixed. He raised his arms as if to embrace her, and Mary wondered fleetingly if he was so drugged that he thought she was an avenging angel. In a way, she was. "Why did you kill your friend Amadeo? A man who trusted you? An innocent man? *Why?*" Then Mary heard herself speaking to him in Italian, which she hadn't spoken in years. "*Perché, Gio? Dicami! Dicami perché!*"

"Miss DiNunzio, please don't hurt him," said a woman's voice, almost drowned out by the clamor at the breaking door. It was Keisha, who had risen from a chair in the back of the room. Mary hadn't noticed her in her frenzy, but the nurse's expression remained calm. "Please. Don't hurt him."

The bedroom door was about to break from the pounding. "No! Stop! Come out of there!" Melania screamed.

Saracone wept fully now, tears trickling down his slack cheeks, and Mary knew she wouldn't hurt him. It wasn't for her to hurt him. The bedroom door was about to burst open, and she felt nothing but pity for the terrified man. Not even anger anymore, but merely sympathy. She leaned over the bed and whispered to him in Italian:

"*Dica al vostro Dio perché. Dica al Dio.*" Tell your God why, Giovanni. Tell God.

Mary went weak in the knees, and in the next instant, the bedroom door burst open and a huge man rushed through like a charging bull. He was followed by another man, short but brawny, and Melania, who hurried to the bed to check on Saracone.

In the next instant, a force with the impact of a freight train rammed Mary, grabbed her by the shoulders, and hurled her backward into the entertainment center. The back of her head exploded in pain. Her neck snapped backward, then forward. It happened so fast she caught only a glimpse of her attacker. Pitted skin. The Escalade driver. He came after her, picked her up by her shoulders, and was about to hit her again when she thought she heard the other man shouting, the man who must be Saracone's son.

"No, Chico! Stop!" the son shouted, clearly an order.

Thank God. Mary's heart eased and she slumped in the Escalade driver's powerful arms. Her eyelids fluttered open long enough to see the son standing before her, his face contorted with rage.

"Mind your own business!" the son shouted, spitting in her face, and the last thing Mary saw was the awful blur of his balled fist.

And the sneer on the face of Justin Saracone.

TWENTY-SIX

Mary regained consciousness in the dark, slumped in the driver's seat of her car. Her keys and her purse rested in her lap. The car's clock read 3:18. Rain pelted the roof, and the sound made her head throb. Her thoughts were muddled. She closed her eyes a minute and waited for her head to clear, but it didn't. Her right cheek stung, and she touched it gingerly. *Ouch.* She flipped down the car's visor, checked the mirror, and even in the dim light, almost yelped in surprise. Blood covered her right cheek, the skin broken, and her right eye was red and swollen.

She turned her head, and pain arced

through her neck. Saracone's front gate stood closed, as if she had never been inside. Her brain struggled to function. So Saracone had killed Amadeo. And the Escalade worked for Saracone. Saracone must have had him follow her after she'd started investigating Amadeo. But now that she'd seen Saracone, she didn't understand. The old man had terminal cancer. There was no statute of limitations on murder, but could he seriously be worried about being prosecuted at this point? What about Frank's murder? Had Saracone, or his wife or son, been involved in it? And what were those legal bills for?

The bills. Mary reached for her purse. Her wallet, cell phone, and date book were inside, but the legal bills and the scanned photo were gone. Her mouth went dry. They had taken the bills, and they were originals. There were no copies that Mary knew of. With the legal bills missing, there was no physical evidence linking Frank to Saracone. What was she gonna do now?

She didn't have time to puzzle it out. She wanted to get out of here before Chico and Justin came back for her. She jammed her keys in the ignition, started the car, and headed back to Philadelphia.

It had to be safer than Birchrunville.

The next day dawned bright and clear, and Detective Daniel Gomez turned out to be young for a full detective, at about thirty-odd years old. He had a warm, friendly smile and looked compact and powerful in sleek gray pants and a white European-cut shirt. He had sounded so professional on the phone, but his eyes softened to a sympathetic frown when he met Mary and saw the angry red bruise on her puffy cheek.

"You told me it was bad, but that's a beauty." Detective Gomez peered at her like a family doctor. "Who'd you say hit you?"

"An SUV named Chico, then his boss, Justin Saracone."

"You want to charge them with assault?"

"No, I want to charge them with murder." Mary sat down, looking briefly around. She hadn't spent as much time at the Roundhouse as the boss and she needed to get oriented. Interview Room C was small and windowless, painted a dingy green, and scuffed by heel marks halfway up the wall to a largish two-way mirror. The only furniture in the room was a rickety old-fashioned typing table and a mismatched metal chair, on which rested a white legal pad and a sheaf of blank forms. Mary cleared her throat. "It really started as a lawsuit, a document case. Ancient history. Should I begin at the beginning?"

"Please do, I'm listening," Gomez answered, pulling over the metal chair, and Mary began telling him about Amadeo while he started to take notes on a pad that rested on his crossed legs. She went on to tell him about Montana and how she figured out that Amadeo's suicide was really murder, but then she slowed the story when she got to the part about her breaking into Frank's office. *Oops.* Detective Gomez looked up sharply, his Bic poised above the legal pad. "Did you say you *broke into* Cavuto's office last night? The office on South Broad?"

Gulp. "Well, yes."

Detective Gomez frowned, a tiny pitchfork appearing on his otherwise smooth forehead. "That office is a crime scene, Ms. DiNunzio."

"Please, call me Mary."

"*Mary*, it's a crime scene. *My* crime

scene." The detective set the Bic down and leaned back in his chair, and Mary could see they were about to have their first fight.

"I didn't compromise any evidence, and I don't think of it as a crime scene, since I knew Frank so well."

"Are you trying to tell me, if it's not a crime scene to you, it's not a crime scene?" Detective Gomez's dark eyebrows flew upward, so Mary shifted gears.

"There's no way he was killed during a robbery, Detective. Frank Cavuto wasn't the type to work at his desk late at night. I think he had arranged to meet the bad guys, Chico and Saracone Junior, or maybe the wife, at the office. And there's also that reporter I told you about, we can't forget about him. I showed him the circle drawings and told him about Frank."

Gomez made another note.

"It's possible that Frank let them in, that's why there was no sign of a break-in, and they killed him to silence him."

"Silence him about what?"

"About whatever he knew about Amadeo's death, and Saracone."

That pitchfork again. "The evidence points to a robbery gone wrong. The vault was taken, and the secretary said it had almost ten thousand dollars in it. The whole office was ransacked, all the petty cash stolen, as was everything else of value. Computers, adding machines, a portable TV, even gold earrings the secretary kept in her top drawer."

"They took that stuff after the fact, to make it look like a robbery. And in the files, I found—"

"You looked in the files?"

"—a series of legal bills from Frank to Saracone, who owns the thug who hit me in the face. The bills totaled five hundred thousand dollars a year for five years. That's over two million dollars in payments, for no apparent pending case, which I still can't explain, but at least I got Saracone's address from the bills and that's what led me to—"

"You found bills where? In that file room, where the vault was?"

"Yes." Mary noted that Detective Gomez was getting bogged down in the details. "I had the bills with me last night when I went to Saracone's, but they took them after they beat me up."

"Mary." Detective Gomez folded his arms,

testy. "Are you telling me you took evidence from a crime scene, in an uncleared case? I can't imagine you would take evidence from a crime scene and carry it around with you."

Uh. "Yes." *Sorry.* Mary felt her face flush with embarrassment.

"And now, thanks to you, this evidence is gone?"

"But I can testify that I saw them, because I did. And we can subpoena the files and maybe find copies of them."

Gomez had stopped listening. They were beyond pitchfork now. "That's hindering, obstruction of justice. Tampering with evidence. Destroying the chain of custody."

"You could still bring Saracone and Chico in, ask them about the bills, and investigate their connection to Frank. Saracone has some kind of investment business and maybe Frank had dealings with that."

"You want me to pick up a dying old man who you think is guilty of a sixty-year-old murder?" Detective Gomez looked at her like she was nuts. She was rapidly losing any credibility she'd earned by her busted cheek. "Whose only connection to Cavuto's murder you carried around in your *purse* and then *lost*?"

"They took it, I didn't lose it," Mary said, but it sounded lame, even to her. "Don't you think it's strange that the Saracones didn't call the Birchrunville cops? That I'm the one who had to come to you?"

"No, I don't." Detective Gomez was shaking his head. "Not everybody would call the cops on a prying lawyer, and who knows what they got out in that burg? The force can't be that big."

"Why don't we go over to the Saracone house and investigate? I swear, if I confront that old man in front of you, he just might admit that he killed Amadeo." Mary had thought about it all night. As pathetic as Saracone had been, he was still a murderer and he should still be brought to justice. For Amadeo. "He was *this close* to telling me last night. He *wants* to confess. He knows he's on his deathbed and he's getting religion. I can see it, it's an Italian thing."

"No, no, no. I can't take you over to Saracone's. I can't get involved with this, or you. I have to talk to my sergeant." Gomez shook his head. "Obtaining evidence by burglary! You should know better, as a lawyer."

"Okay, so don't take me over, then." Mary

switched tacks. "Just go to the Saracones yourself. Talk to them. Don't tell them I was here and told you what happened last night. Tell them it came in through an anonymous tip."

Detective Gomez thought a minute. "Were there other witnesses to this conversation you had with Saracone?"

"Sure. A nurse was right there. Saracone's nurse." Mary flashed on the gold lapel pin. "Keisha, from HomeCare. I'm telling you, I think Saracone, or at least this Chico guy, killed Frank Cavuto. I'll testify that I saw the bills from Frank to Saracone. They exist, and I bet they exist in back files, too. If we ask Frank's secretary and—"

"Quiet now, I've heard enough." Detective Gomez stood up and hoisted his pants by his thin black leather belt. "I need to end this interview, Ms.—Mary."

"Why? We're just getting started."

"For your own good. I do have to talk to my sergeant. What a mess." Detective Gomez kept shaking his neat head, solid as a cinder block. "We're sitting here, you tell me you have information on the Cavuto case, and you end up confessing to bur-

glary, obstruction, and evidence tampering."

"I didn't tamper with evidence, I lost it."
Eeek. "I mean, somebody stole it from me."

"After *you* stole it!" Detective Gomez
rested his hands on his hips and eyed Mary
unhappily. "You need to get yourself a
lawyer."

"You're going to charge me? I'd have a
criminal record?" It was almost beyond belief for Mary DiNunzio, valedictorian at St.
Maria Goretti High School. She didn't even
curse. Out loud.

"If I have to, I assume. I'm new, and I can't
say I have a lot of experience with this type
of thing. Evidence stuffed in a *purse*."
Detective Gomez snorted. "I heard your law
office was like this. My partner warned me
about the Rosato firm, but I didn't listen.
Dumb, dumb, dumb. Now, I don't think I
have to arrest you—"

"*Arrest* me?" Mary jumped to her feet and
felt instantly dizzy, either because she got
up too fast or her career was over.

"I don't think that's necessary, yet. But
don't you dare make a fool of me."
Detective Gomez pointed a thick finger in
Mary's face. "I'm releasing you on your own

recognizance. Don't leave the jurisdiction, you hear me?"

"I won't, I promise. I love this jurisdiction. It's my favorite jurisdiction."

"Well, then, this is ass-backward, since you've already incriminated yourself, but I'll play it safe and inform you of your rights under Miranda. You have the right to remain silent, you have the right . . ." Detective Gomez recited the Miranda warnings, facing Mary squarely in an on-the-spot ceremony that reminded her oddly of being sworn in to the Pennsylvania bar. He cleared his throat when he finished. "Do you have any questions?"

"Yes. When are you going to follow up with Saracone?"

"As soon as I can."

"You can't waste a minute, Detective. Saracone is dying and you need to get over there right away. If Saracone isn't behind Frank's murder, he'll know who is. And he'll know why. Will you call me as soon as you've seen him?"

"Yes." Detective Gomez walked to the gray door of the interview room, opened it, and gestured to Mary to leave. She didn't.

"You have my office number, right?"

"Yes."

"Did I give you my cell number?"

"When we spoke on the phone."

"Try there, too. And please make the appointment this morning."

"I'll do it right away, dear." Detective Gomez made another gesture for her to go, but Mary had a second thought.

"Wait! Why didn't I think of this before? How about I stay right here while you call—"

"No."

"Or I can wait in the squad room, to give you some privacy?"

"No. Absolutely not. Now, if you please." Detective Gomez gestured again out the door, and beyond it lay the squad room, which, unlike on TV, was always quiet and still in the daytime. Two of the detectives looked up from their desks, obviously eavesdropping. A woman in a suit walked by, and Gomez eyed her. "I'll follow up as soon as I get back to my desk, get it? The sooner you leave, the sooner I call."

"Okay, then I'm leaving." Mary went to the door. Detective Gomez rested a heavy hand on her shoulder, then all of a sudden he poked her in her swollen cheek.

"That hurt?"

"Of course!"

"Good. Bullets hurt way more than that, and you only feel the pain if you live."

Mary knew as much, but she wasn't about to skip down memory lane with him.

"Leave the police business to the police from now on. Stay away from the Saracones. No more investigating, breaking and entering, or any of that funky stuff. Next time I lock you up! You hear me?"

"Yes, Detective." Mary hurried out, feeling as if she'd just dodged a bullet. In fact, she was starting to feel positively bulletproof.

Which even she knew was a bad sign.

TWENTY-SEVEN

"My God in heaven! What happened to *you*?" Marshall asked. She glanced up from the reception desk and did a double-take when she saw Mary's bruised cheek, then stood and examined the wound with the laserlike absorption of a new mother. "Mary, what *happened*? You need to get that looked at!"

"I'm fine." Mary was about to explain but noticed the reception area was full of clients ensconced on rental furniture. One of them was that reporter, Mac, who was already making a beeline for Mary. His eyes weren't espresso anymore but were closer to shit brown. Mary said under her breath, "I have a deposition, right?"

"Great minds," Marshall muttered back, and Mac joined them at the desk, his handsomeness arranged into a mask of concern.

"Mary, what happened to your cheek? It looks like you took a really nasty punch!"

Marshall interjected, "Mary, you remember Mr. MacIntire. I told him you have deposition this morning, but he insisted on speaking with you."

"I have a deposition," Mary repeated matter-of-factly. "Sorry, I can't talk now. Though I checked with my Uncle Joey and he said he doesn't know any reporter named Mac from the *Philly News*."

"He calls me Jim, and I never told him I was from the *News*. I doubt he knows what I do."

Mary filed it away. Skinny Uncle Joey wasn't the sharpest tool in the shed. Still she didn't trust this guy. "Also I called you twice. Did you get my messages?"

"No, so what happened to your face? Did somebody punch you?" Mac leaned over and squinted. "It's so fresh, like you just got slugged."

"It's not. I didn't." Mary prayed for a good lie. "It happened when I was out west."

"Someone hit you in Montana?"

"No, it was a horse." *Yikes.* "A horse kicked me."

"A horse kicked you *in the face*?" Mac's eyes flared. "I had a friend who got kicked in the face by a horse, and it broke her cheek. She needed a whole series of operations to even talk again."

"No, that's not what happened." *Please God help me. I said a good lie.* "The horse didn't kick me in the face. It kicked me on the *leg*, and I fell down and hit my face."

"Now, I understand," Marshall said helpfully, and Mary faked a smile, which stung.

"Sorry, Mac, I have to go get ready for my dep."

"But we said we'd meet again, so I could write the second installment of our Brandolini story, remember?"

"You never did the first installment, and I have to go." Mary started to leave, but Mac fell into step with her.

"I was waiting until both installments were done, to show them to my editor. And we should talk, since Frank Cavuto has been murdered. Shame, isn't it? You two went way back, didn't you? I heard you played softball on his team. Word is, you had a mean right arm."

Mary picked up the pace. "How did you know that?"

"I called Frank after we met. He liked you very much. He said you were a great lawyer, doing your best for Brandolini."

Hmm. "My comment is that it's awful and sad that Frank Cavuto was murdered. Now I have to go." Mary turned on her heel in the tight hallway. "Listen, you can't follow me to my office. I have to get ready for a dep."

"I can wait until after your deposition is over. I need to catch up, and you could tell me what you learned about Brandolini at Fort Missoula. After all, I was the one who suggested you go there."

Mary gritted her teeth. "I have another dep in the afternoon. It's wall to wall today, and I didn't learn anything in Montana anyway."

"Is that for the record? Because that's not what the director said, at Fort Missoula. He and the staff were very impressed with you. He said you'd tracked down an old mechanic, a Mr. Milton, at the camp." Mac frowned. "He said you found some old pictures, and even identified a friend who was with Brandolini when he committed suicide."

The reporter had learned everything. I hate the First Amendment.

"Then he put me in touch with a widow you met, who said the friend was named Giovanni Saracone. I spoke to her yesterday, and she really liked you. She seemed to think you'd head right for this Saracone."

Die, asshole! "Nah, I have to get back to work. Please, I gotta go."

"Call me ASAP!" Mac called out as Mary hurried away.

She escaped into Judy's office, where she closed the door with herself on the inside. When she turned around, she let out a little yelp of surprise. Judy was sitting behind her cluttered desk, and leaning against the wooden credenza opposite her was Bennie Rosato herself, her blonde hair up in its tangly twist and her arms folded in her trademark khaki suit.

Help! "Bennie, you're back!" Mary tried to sound delighted, but her cheek wound and true emotions combined to thwart her. "Did you win, boss?"

"DiNunzio?" The boss's eyes widened when she saw the bruise, and Judy's jaw dropped open.

"Mare, are you all right?" the associate

asked, rising alarmed from her desk chair. "What happened?"

Mary quickly considered her options, and there were none. One woman was her boss and the other her best friend. She was fresh out of lies, even lousy ones. *Busted*. So she wasn't bulletproof after all. She dropped her bag, set down her messages and mail, and sank into the chair opposite Judy's desk to give her second confession of the day. When Mary was finished telling them everything, both Bennie and Judy looked terribly grave, their lips set in almost identical hyphens, so that side by side their mouths formed a dotted line. At times like this, Rosato & Associates would morph into the Supremes; Bennie would became Diana Ross, so she'd yell in the lead, and Judy, or any another associate, would yell backup, like Cindy Birdsong.

"DiNunzio!" Bennie began, her hands on her strong hips. "How could you possibly, ever, ever, get yourself in this much trouble? What were you thinking? *Were* you thinking?"

"I was thinking. I had to follow up on Amadeo, and when I found out that—"

"Don't backtalk me! You lied to me!

Running around Montana, breaking into murder scenes, stealing evidence, losing evidence! How'd you act so nuts?"

"I'm sorry. I'm sorry, I'm really sorry." Mary reverted instantly to her old forte. It was a serviceable forte, applying to so many different situations, and she should never have abandoned it. Also, not everyone was good at apologizing, and Mary had heard of people who couldn't part with a single I'm sorry, even when they were totally in the wrong.

"You almost got yourself killed! Do you realize that? Instead of dumping you in your car last night, they could have dumped you in a shallow grave! You could be dead today!"

"You could be dead!" Judy yelled backup. *Doo-wap, do-wa.*

"I know, and I'm sorry," Mary said, meaning it. She did feel bad. She could be dead, and she had lied to Bennie, which was even worse. The phone on Judy's desk started ringing but everybody ignored it, and Bennie began to pace the office like a Bengal tiger. In a bread box.

"I have no idea what to do about this! I'm too furious with you to even think straight! I came down this weekend, thought I'd give you a little support at the funeral, and this is what's going on?" The phone's ring turned to buzzing, which meant Marshall was trying to signal Judy to pick up. "Get that call, Carrier!" Bennie yelled, not even breaking stride, then she focused again on Mary. "DiNunzio, this time you've gone too far! This is over, you get it? Over! No more Brandolini! No more Saracone! It's done! You hear me? DONE!"

"Yes, Bennie," Mary said, and Judy turned her head to listen to her phone, clamping a free hand over her other ear.

"Starting right now, DiNunzio, you will get back to work, unless I decide to fire you! You will write briefs, bill time, and go on blind dates! Above all, you will start acting like yourself again!" Bennie stopped pacing long enough to glare down at Mary, her skin color shading to Harvard beet. But Mary tried not to think about beets right now. Or Fort Missoula. Or knots.

"Excuse me, Bennie?" Judy said, turning with the phone in her hand. "The phone—"

"Tell whoever it is I'll call back!"

"No." Judy looked at Mary. "It's for you, Mare. Marshall transferred the call to my line."

"Who is it?" Mary and Bennie asked in unison.

"Detective Gomez from Homicide."

My God. Mary jumped to her pumps, but Bennie reached for the phone first.

"Gimme that!" she shouted, then cleared her throat before she spoke into the receiver. "Detective Gomez, this is Bennie Rosato speaking. We haven't met, but I expect we will soon."

Mary went weak in the knees. What was Bennie going to do? Had Gomez talked to Saracone? Was he on his way to Birchrunville right now?

"Detective," Bennie continued, "I want you to understand that I'm representing Mary DiNunzio in the event that she's charged with burglary or any other crimes. I've talked with her, and our position is that she acted appropriately in every respect and that any such charges would be frivolous!"

Mary couldn't believe her ears. Two minutes ago, Bennie had been screaming at her. Now, she was screaming *for* her.

"Before you file, Detective Gomez, I want you and the department to understand that I'll fight any such charges with every resource my firm can muster. Charges like that could destroy the career of one of the finest young attorneys in this city!"

Huh? Me? Mary swallowed hard at the praise. It felt good and bad at the same time.

"I won't permit you or the D.A.'s office to ruin this lawyer's good name. You'll have to get *through* me to get to her, do I make myself clear? My next call is to the sergeant, and I'm sure that he and I can come to terms before this goes any further. Thank you so much." Bennie seemed to catch her breath, and the redness ebbed from her face. "I'll permit you to talk with Ms. DiNunzio, provided that I'm a party to the conversation. May I put you on speakerphone? Thank you." Bennie pressed hold and turned quickly to Mary. "Okay if I'm on with you? You're represented now, by me."

"Yes, thanks," Mary answered, overwhelmed, and Bennie winked, then hit another button on the phone. The red light went on and they were on speaker.

"Detective Gomez," Bennie said. "My associates, Judy Carrier and Mary DiNunzio, are here. What is it you want to discuss?"

"Mary, can you hear me?" It was the detective's voice, and it didn't sound good.

"Yes, Detective Gomez. I'm listening."

"I see you got yourself a good lawyer."

"Damn right. Did you call Saracone?"

"I have some bad news," Gomez began.

TWENTY-EIGHT

Mary spent the afternoon in her office behind a closed door, feeling sorry for herself. She had decided long ago that everybody was entitled to feel sorry for themselves, and its bad reputation was completely undeserved. She therefore ignored the phone when it rang, didn't bother to recall clients she couldn't reach the first time, and didn't do productive work on any of her cases, least of all Amadeo's. She'd tried online, only briefly, to find out some background information about Justin Saracone, Melania, or Chico Escalade, but she gave up when she got nowhere.

She let her coffee get cold and sat slumped in her chair, propping her face up by a fist to her one good cheek. Sunlight poured through her window, but she wouldn't let it cheer her up. On the contrary, she made a point of noticing that it reflected harshly on the internee files scattered across her desk, none of which mattered anymore. All her work had been for nothing, almost a year's worth. She had figured out that Amadeo had been murdered by Giovanni Saracone, only to have the killer himself pass away this morning.

Mary felt like crying but her eyes remained dry. Her heart was hollow, her chest oddly empty. She hadn't gotten to Saracone in time. If only she'd gone to Montana when she'd first gotten the case. If only she weren't such a chicken. Montana wasn't scary, it was just another state. The people there weren't aliens, they were normal. Airplanes weren't all that amazing, they were just three billion tons of sheet metal, bolts, outdated copies of *Forbes,* and little tiny soaps which managed not only to stay aloft but also to fly through thin air.

Okay, maybe airplanes were amazing.

Mary sighed. At some level, even she had to admit it was time to lay Amadeo to rest. She had to let him go. Stop thinking of him as some sort of a ghost, George Clooney, or even Mike. She had discovered the unspeakable, but both Amadeo and Saracone had passed from this earth; murdered and murderer, good and evil. They would reconcile with their God; one embraced and the other reviled. She would have to be content with that justice.

And, after what Gomez had told them, there was no chance now of proving that Frank's murder was connected to Saracone. Gomez liked his lead in Frank's murder, and the police were about to arrest a man who had committed another office burglary farther down Broad Street, also in which a small safe had been wheeled away. Gomez hadn't gone out to Saracone's house, and the Cavuto case was officially cleared. Saracone was dead. Amadeo was gone.

It was over, all of it.

It was history.

The parish church brimmed with neighbors, nuns, priests from the Archdiocese, beat cops, bowling buddies, and the latest softball team Frank had sponsored, girls and boys squirming next to an array of small businessmen. Mary flashed on the bills she'd seen in the file drawers: dry cleaners, carpet cleaners, window blind cleaners; car repairs, shoe repairs, roof repairs; plumbers, electricians, carpenters. All of them mourned the passing of Frank Cavuto. And she knew that miles outside the city, far from the auto body shops and the check cashing agencies, in an elegant country mansion in a lovely town called Birchrunville, people were gathering to mourn the passing of Giovanni Saracone—his very young wife, his son, that felon in the Escalade, and undoubtedly an array of businessmen in custom suits and silk ties, who trafficked in stocks, bonds, and mysterious investments.

Mary sat with Bennie and Judy behind Frank's grieving wife and sons, in one of the glistening wooden pews toward the front of the parish church. Mary's parents clutched soggy Kleenexes, and the rest of the weepy *circolo* filled her pew and the three pews behind her. The church was dark because the sun wasn't bright enough to penetrate the stained glass depictions of the Stations of the Cross, in jewel tones of merlot and rich midnight blue. Refrigerated flowers and everybody's best perfume sweetened the air.

Mary raised her eyes to the altar, where the white-robed priest was holding the host over his head, reciting the familiar prayer. She responded with the rest of the congregation, as she had her entire life, but her thoughts kept straying to work. She had ten active cases piled on her desk and clients shaking their fists at her. She had briefs to file and motions to write. She had depositions to take and defend; cases to settle or try, the day-to-day business of being a trial lawyer. Part of her missed it, which came as a surprise, even to her. Amadeo had taught her that, brought her that; she had never felt happy with her choice of profession before this case. She sent him a silent prayer of thanks.

She bowed her head to the sound of sobs and sniffling, the cadence of praying and chanting, and next an unwelcome sound. The intrusion of a cell phone, set on generic ring. *Briing. Briinnnggg.* It rang startlingly close to Mary, and she glanced over at Bennie, who remained impassive. *Briiinnngg.* Everyone began looking around the pews; the cell phone Nazis on alert. Her mother heard the ring, swiveling her puffy pink-gray hair, but her father remained oblivious, since he never wore his hearing aid in church. *Brriinngg*. Then Mary realized the ring was coming from her own purse.

She opened her bag, grabbed her cell, flipped it open, and pressed Power, instantly turning it off. Her mother frowned. Her father smiled. Bennie eyed her coolly, then looked away. Mary felt redness warm her aching cheek. She hadn't recognized the caller's number on the glowing blue display, but the call had been from a 215 area code, local to Philly. Probably one of the clients she'd been avoiding. She wished her cell number wasn't on her damn business cards.

Mourners were rising to receive Holy Communion, and with a crowd this size it would take twenty minutes at least, so Mary got up on autopilot, helped her mother to her orthopedic shoes, and the DiNunzios excused their way out of the pew to join the line, hands folded and heads bowed. She tried to focus again on her work, but all she could think about was Amadeo, Saracone, and Frank, and the emotion she felt most fully was grief. Grief for all three of them, oddly. Sorrow that they had all gone. Her heart weighed in her chest as she walked to the altar, hearing people sniffling, the occasional smoker's cough, and the regular *clack clack clack* of her pumps on the hard marble floor. And when she reached the altar and it was her turn to kneel, the Communion wafer tasted bitter and her eyes were wet. Mary was in mourning. For everything.

After the funeral mass, crowds thronged outside on the granite steps of the church, covering the pavement and spilling off the curb and onto a busy Sixteenth Street. Cars couldn't afford to be heedless of the crowd letting out and gave the foot traffic wide berth. Men talked in groups at the curb, lighting up cigarettes and puffing cigars, blowing cones of gray smoke into the gray clouds, where it was carried off and disappeared. Women chattered in small groups, hugging, kissing, and dabbing their tears from the side, so as not to smear their mascara. The *circolo* formed a large group of its own, swarming around Mary, thanking her, kissing her, and even pinching her. With love.

"Mary, you're such a good lawyer! So

good to us! So hard, you worked!" they all said, and Mary's mother nodded, her father beamed, and Mary accepted the congratulations, feeling like a complete fraud. She hadn't recovered even a dime of Amadeo's estate and she hadn't vindicated his murder. She hadn't even told any of them that he had been murdered, though in truth, they seemed to have forgotten altogether about Amadeo. It was as if Frank Cavuto had been Mary's mentor, and with his death, she had succeeded him in being the *circolo*'s favorite lawyer. A prominent woman in the community, Bernadette Gibboni, grabbed her hand with glistening eyes, and said, "Poor Frank, he loved you so! He thought the world of you! He told us, if anybody can get justice, it's Mary DiNunzio!"

"Mary! Mary! Itsa sin, that Frank's gone!" yelled Joe Grassi, from the back. "He woulda been so proud, to see what you accomplished. He tol' me last week, you been workin' for no pay!"

"No, wait, everybody!" Mary put up a hand. Enough was enough. "It was my boss who paid, Bennie Rosato. Give her the credit!" She pointed to the edge of the throng, where Bennie had been collared by a *circolo* member who wanted to franchise his chain of nail parlors. "Pop, take Joe over, to thank Bennie!" Her father and the *circolo* changed direction as quickly as a school of guppies, leaving Mary and her mother standing face-to-face with Jim MacIntire, the reporter. He'd evidently been at the funeral, because he'd slapped a tie on his workshirt. It was a look Mary used to love.

"My God, you have lots of fans, Mare!" Mac said. "The *circolo*, is it called, they all want you to take over Frank Cavuto's practice, now that he's gone."

"It doesn't work that way," Mary said, recoiling. *He's not even buried yet, you jerk.*

"This must be your mother!" Mac boomed, and Mary was figuring out a way she could turn his doggedness to her advantage.

"Ma, meet Jim MacIntire. He's a reporter, so don't answer any of his questions."

"Ah-ha!" Her mother sniffed, making no disguise of her instant dislike, which only confirmed Mary's doubts. Her mother's instincts about people were positively canine. She could take one whiff, and you were either sunk or made. German Shepherds came to her for advice.

"You must be so proud of your daughter!" Mac boomed again, sounding more the proud parent than Mary's own proud parent, who gave her daughter's arm a familiar squeeze, turned on her thick rubber heel, and without another word, walked off into the crowd. Mary tried not to laugh.

"Tough room," Mac said. "Listen, I want to talk with you about Brandolini. I guess you heard that Giovanni Saracone died yesterday. If you're going to ask me how I know, we have an obit section, and I saw the notice."

Mary kept her middle finger to herself. She was so near church and all.

"Let's talk, Mare. Like we did, that first time, in your office." Mac's tone softened, and she gathered it was his Love Voice. The one that made her check if he had a wedding ring on. *Fool me once, fool me twice.* Mac took a step closer. "I felt for you when I heard. Just as you started to find the only man who knew Brandolini, he died. Did you ever get to see Saracone?"

"Did *you*?"

Mac blinked. "What do you mean?"

"I mean exactly what I said. You had the same information I did, you copied my research. You gonna tell me you didn't go to the Saracones? Track him down like you did the director at the museum?"

"I didn't say that I didn't."

"You didn't say that you did, either." Mary thought it was fun, turning the tables. "When did you go? Who did you see?"

"I went there yesterday afternoon and met Melania. Giovanni was too sick to see me."

"Then you didn't really learn he was dead from the obit." *Liar.* "You knew he was on his deathbed way before any obit got called in."

"I didn't know for sure."

"Bullshit. I don't think Uncle Joey told you anything about me and Amadeo. I think somebody at Saracone's did." Mary wasn't even sure she was right on the facts, which made accusing him even more fun. "I think you're on Saracone's payroll, and you're using the fact you're a reporter to find out what I know."

"What?" Mac's mouth dropped open, but Mary didn't intend to elaborate. This was a hit-and-run. She wanted to shake him up.

"Who are you working for now that he's

dead, Mac? The son, the wife, Chico? Or somebody else? When you want to talk, I'll want to talk, got it?" Mary looked past his head, and her father was pumping his hand wildly, waving her over. She was finished anyway. "Excuse me, I gotta go." She left Mac before he could react.

Wait a minute. Mary had almost forgotten. The cell phone call that had interrupted the funeral Mass. She should check the message, if she expected not to get fired. She dug into her purse, pulled out the cell phone, and powered it on to check for a message.

On the display screen was a text message that made her heart stop:

call me, it's important. keisha

TWENTY-NINE

Mary hit *86 to double-check if there was a message.

"MARY, MARY! HERE YOU ARE!" Her father came over, shouting because he couldn't hear himself without his hearing aid. He looped a meaty arm around a smiling, dark-haired man about Mary's age, dressed in a white shirt, jeans, and no wedding band. "MARE! I WANT YOU TO MEET A REAL NICE FELLA! THIS IS PETE CIROCCI! PETE OWNS THE FRUIT TRUCK WE GET THE LETTUCE FROM! THE GOOD LETTUCE, NOT THE CRAPPY LETTUCE!"

"Great. Please, hold on, Pop."

"MARE, YOU KNOW THAT LETTUCE

YOUR MOTHER LIKES SO MUCH? IT NEVER HAS THE BROWN LEAVES ON THE OUTSIDE? SHE GOES TO PETE SPECIAL TO GET IT, THEY DON'T HAVE IT AT THE AC-A-ME!" Her father turned to shout at Pete, who stood an inch away from him. "MY WIFE HATES THE BROWN LEAVES! YOU GOTTA THROW HALF OF IT IN THE SLOP! THAT'S FIFTY CENTS, RIGHT THERE! SO WHO'S STUPID, AC-A-ME OR ME?"

"Pop, please, gimme one second," Mary said, gently. She didn't want to disrespect him in public, even though he couldn't hear her disrespecting him in public.

"MARE, PETE OWNS THREE TRUCKS! HIS BUSINESS IS GOIN' GREAT! HE GETS ALL HIS PRODUCE LOCAL FROM JERSEY! HE BUILT THE BUSINESS UP FROM SCRATCH! IT USED TO BE CALLED PETE'S PRO-DUCE, THEN HE GOT A DEAL ON SOME BROOMS AND HE STARTED SELLIN' THE BROOMS, AND GUESS WHAT? THE BROOMS TOOK OFF!"

Mary struggled to hear the voicemail re-sponse, which came in maddeningly, me-chanically slow. "You have three new messages," she thought it said, but it could just as easily have been, "Boo boo boob boo sages." She hit the number 1 anyway, to retrieve them. The number of messages didn't matter, only what Keisha had called about.

"SO HE CHANGED THE NAME TO 'PETE'S PRODUCE *PLUS*'! AIN'T THAT GREAT? NO FLIES ON THIS ONE, EH? HE'S GOT A GREAT SENSE A HUMOR!" Her father turned to Pete. "MARY'S GOT A GREAT SENSE A HUMOR, TOO! AN' SHE DOESN'T ALWAYS HAVE THAT THING ON HER CHEEK! SHE GOT IT WHEN SHE FELL DOWN AT WORK!"

Argh! Mary couldn't hear the phone message over her father's shouting and was about to tell him so when Bennie appeared at her elbow with Jeff Eisen, one of the clients Mary hadn't been able to reach. What was Jeff doing here? Both he and Bennie were frowning.

"Excuse me, DiNunzio," Bennie said, her blue eyes hard as ice. Jeff Eisen stiffened beside her. "You might hang up and take that call later."

"MARE! WHO WOULDA FIGURED

OUT THAT BROOMS WOULD SELL AS
GOOD AS LETTUCE! PETE CIROCCI,
THAT'S WHO!"

"Boo sageges," said the voicemail, and
between her father, Pete's Produce Plus,
Bennie, and Jeff Eisen, Mary finally surren-
dered and closed the phone. She smiled
and extended a hand to Eisen.

"Jeff, I didn't expect to see you here. How
have you been?"

"Not so good." Eisen puckered his mouth
unhappily, his back rigid in his expensive
suit, fancy striped tie, and shirt with a cutaway collar. "It's a shame about Frank, murdered like that. We knew each other from
the Chamber of Commerce. Frank's the one
that recommended I hire you, when my
partner sued me. Last year, remember?"

"Of course." Mary had forgotten for a moment. She felt off balance, preoccupied by
the cell call. She was never that good at
multi-tasking, and her father and Pete were
waiting to be introduced, so she made intro-
ductions all around. There followed a flurry of
handshaking, but it was a schizophrenic
foursome, half of them loving Mary and half
of them looking daggers.

"I was hoping to see you here, Mary,"

Eisen continued. "Maybe we can talk about my lawsuit. It's keeping my wife up at nights. I had my girl call you all last week, but you didn't call back. They're taking my deposition on Monday."

I'm sorry, I'm sorry. "I'm so sorry, I was out of town." *And I forgot. Oh Jeez.*

"Didn't you call in for your messages? I would think you'd call in for your messages. I've had my deposition taken before, but we only talked about it the one time."

"WHA?" Her father scowled, and his forehead wrinkled unhappily all the way up, like ripples in a cranky pond. "WHA'D YOU SAY, PAL? SHE'S WORKIN' AS HARD AS SHE CAN! SHE EVEN HURT HER FACE AT WORK, FOR CHRIST'S SAKE! THAT'S WHAT YOU CALL DEDICA-TION!"

"I didn't mean anything by it, Mr. DiNunzio." Eisen backed off in surprise.

"SURE YOU DID! SHE SAID SHE WAS BUSY, PAL! WHAT ARE YOU, *DEAF*!?"

Oh, no. "It's okay, Pop." Mary touched her father's arm, but she couldn't help feeling touched. He would defend her even when she was totally in the wrong. Especially when she was totally in the wrong.

"YOU DON'T DESERVE THAT, MARE! YOU WORK TOO HARD FOR THESE INGRATES!"

Bennie turned to Mary, only apparently calm. "DiNunzio, I'd like us to take Jeff to lunch *right now* and discuss his deposition. Then you two won't have to play phone tag anymore and you can mend some fences. Jeff would like that very much. Wouldn't you, Jeff?"

"I'm free." Eisen nodded. "No time like the present. I paid my respects here, and it's only immediate family going to the luncheon after."

"Okay, sure. Great idea." Mary gave her father a soft kiss on the cheek, flashed Pete's Produce Plus a thumbs-up, then found her mother on the way out and said good-bye, introducing her to Jeff Eisen. Her mother took one sniff and hated him. Vita was in the zone today. But walking to the curb and hailing a cab with Bennie and Jeff, Mary couldn't think of anything but that phone call. How did Keisha get her cell? Then she remembered. She had given the nurse her business card, at Saracone's door.

Mary would find out why she was calling

as soon as she could find some privacy. The restaurant had to have a bathroom.

"How can you *not* have a bathroom?" Mary asked in disbelief, and the tuxedoed maître d' took cover behind a carved lectern more appropriate at Harvard Law.

"I'm sorry, there was a . . . malfunction and it's closed until it's in working order."

"When will that be?"

"When the plumber arrives. He's on his way."

Go to Plan B. "I could use the men's room, I don't mind. Where's that?" Mary craned her neck, and the maître d' sniffed with disdain.

"I'm sorry, mademoiselle. There was only the one water closet."

Bennie leaned over. "DiNunzio, get over it," she whispered. "How old are you? Three?"

Nothing but the truth. "That was Saracone's nurse on my cell," she whispered back. "I need to hear her message."

"Don't you *dare*. This client is about to fire us. *Focus,* child."

"Ladies, we can go to another restaurant," Eisen offered, since he was a gentleman and Mary was evidently having Female Trouble.

"No, this restaurant is fine," Bennie countered firmly. "This is your favorite place, and she'll be fine. Won't you be fine, DiNunzio?"

"I'll be fine," Mary echoed, and the maître d' plucked three impossibly padded menus from their provincial cradle and ushered her, Bennie, and Eisen to a round table in the corner.

The small dining room was softly lit, a converted colonial house in Society Hill, filled with well-dressed diners conversing in low, polite tones. Burgundy paisley drapes blanketed the windows, covered the tables to the ground, and made elegant skirts on the chairs, so the furniture was dressed better than Mary was. She had to find a way to take Keisha's call. She left her cell phone powered on, and they sat down and opened menus softer than a Sealy's.

"I love the foie here," Eisen said, and Bennie nodded.

"I'll join you, Jeff. In fact, why don't you order for all of us? We've never been here."

"Terrific." Eisen smoothed down his shiny tie, and the waitress arrived in the next instant with not one but two bottles of French water, one in each hand, asking if they wanted their water with gas or not. Mary hoped the answer was not. Who *wants* gas? Then Eisen ordered them an appetizer of foie gras, the double-cut lamb entrée with wild rice, and a bottle of red Château Whatever.

"So, Jeff," Bennie began, sipping some water. "Why don't we get straight to business, and you tell us what's keeping your wife up at night? I know that having your deposition taken can be stressful, for everybody, and—" Suddenly she was interrupted by the sound of a ringing cell phone.

Brriinngg! Briinnnggg! Like Pavlov's experiment, the entire restaurant responded by reaching instantly inside suit pockets, purses, and belt holsters, but Mary this time recognized her cell.

It has to be Keisha, calling back! "Excuse me, I'm really sorry, I have to get this," she said, and before Bennie could stop her, she'd reached for her purse, grabbed her cell, and flipped it open. "Yes?"

"MARE! ARE YOU STILL WITH THAT INGRATE?! PUT HIM ON! YOUR MOTHER WANTS TO TALK TO HIM!" It was her father, shouting so loud he could be heard by the eastern United States, not to mention Jeff Eisen.

Eeek. "Pop, I have to go. Call you later. Love you both." Mary flipped the cell closed just as the waitress materialized at her elbow and leaned over.

"Mademoiselle, cell phones are not permitted in the dining room."

And gas is? "I'm sorry," Mary said, and when she looked up, Bennie was glaring at her and so was Eisen. "Sorry," she added, like punctuation, but she felt like she was going to explode if she didn't hear that message.

"So, Jeff," Bennie began again, forcing a smile. "Why don't we go over the facts of the case? It's a good idea for you to review them, and then we'll take it from there and tell you what the other side is likely to ask you in your deposition."

"Sure. Well, as you know, Marc and I used to be in business together. Partners. We had the furniture stores, three locations, for the past oh, say, eight or nine years, and then all of a sudden last year, we start fighting. Disagreeing. Everything's a problem." Eisen threw up his hands, with a heavy gold ring. "First, it's the inventory. He wants to keep too much inventory, and he develops this *thing* for recliners . . ."

Mary sipped her water and tried to listen, but she couldn't.

". . . he likes the Broughley recliners the best, they got the suede, all kinds a suede, and I admit, it's a nice design and it's recliners for cool people. But in half a year, Marc's got the showrooms in all three locations wall-to-wall with Broughley, and then I find out that the new Broughley rep named Ricky is really a *girl* named Rikki . . ."

Mary couldn't sit still. If she could just get that message, she could listen to Eisen's problems with a clear head and everything would be okay. She needed one lousy moment of privacy with her phone. Then she got an idea.

". . . and next thing I know, my partner, who's got a wife and three kids in private school, one with ADHD and can't eat wheat products, my partner who never in ten years took a vacation, is now seeing more of Tortola than Mick Jagger, and I got enough Broughley to . . ."

"Excuse me a second," Mary said, rising nervously. "I know this is rude, but I can't concentrate on the story, as much as I want to, because I need a cigarette."

"You *smoke*?" Bennie demanded, and her incredulous eyes telegraphed, *DiNunzio, you know you don't smoke. You never smoked a day in your life. You don't even know which end to light.*

"I do smoke. I smoke. I do everything bad." *I even fly on airplanes. I smoke on airplanes, in fact. While I swim.* "You knew that I smoked, didn't you?"

"No, I thought you quit," Bennie countered, and her eyes glinted evilly in the soft lights. "You told me you quit."

God, she's good. That's why she's the boss. She lies better. "I fibbed a little, and now I'm jonesing for a cigarette. I need to go outside and smoke. I'll be right back, I'll only take a puff and be right back."

Eisen interjected, "I knew you were jumpy. I could tell, right off." But at this point, neither woman was listening. This was litigation in which the client had become irrelevant. The battle was between boss and associate.

"I'll be right back, I swear." Mary eased out of the corner seat and reached for her purse, but Bennie caught it by the shoulder strap.

"No, sit down." Bennie held fast to the leather strap. "I won't let you go. How can you quit smoking if you keep backsliding?"

"Everybody backslides a little." Mary tugged her purse, but Bennie was too strong and held on. All that stupid rowing.

"Not everybody backslides, when their heart is as bad as yours. You know what your cardiologist said. You could—"

"Cardiologist?" Mary blurted out, then caught herself. "He changed his mind. He said it's okay to smoke while I'm weaning myself off."

But while the women were playing tug-of-war, Eisen was standing up at the table. Suddenly Bennie stopped talking, and Mary looked over in dismay. *Oh, no.* He was going to fire her. He had had it. She had pushed him too far. But in the next minute, Eisen burst into a smile and threw a friendly arm around Mary.

"I'm with you, Mare," he said, and there was a new warmth in his voice. "I quit, too, so I know what you're goin' through. Let's go outside and fall off the wagon together, and I'll tell you the dirty parts of the Broughley story. Ha!"

No! "Sure," Mary said, tugging her purse free in defeat. She let Eisen lead her away from the table, and when she looked back, the boss was laughing her ass off.

As soon as she was alone in the cab, Mary finally listened to the cell message:

"I called you at work and left a message but it's Saturday and I guess you're not there." Keisha's voice sounded vaguely panicky. "I need to see you, but I don't want to say more on the cell. Call me as soon as you can." She left a number with a 215 area, and Mary called it immediately. When the ringing stopped, an answering machine picked up.

"This is Keisha Grace. Please leave a message at the sound of the beep," it went, and Mary left a message telling her to call back anytime, day or night.

She snapped the phone closed in the backseat of the cab as it whisked her home through the city. Her stomach felt shaky, but it wasn't from her first—and last—cigarette.

Mary couldn't let go of Amadeo, just yet.

THIRTY

LAWYER IN MURDER MYSTERY, screamed the headline on the thick Sunday morning newspaper, and Mary went white when she saw her own photo plastered underneath, the one she had posed for in her office. The byline of the article belonged to Jim MacIntire, and she skimmed the first two paragraphs:

Lawyer Mary DiNunzio is a fighter. She fought her way to the top of her hotshot Philly law firm, Rosato & Associates, and she is fighting to discover what happened to a man who has been dead for over sixty years. She traced that trail all the way to Montana and back, and though she was once cooperating fully with this reporter, she now has no comment about the story—and denies tracing the death to one Giovanni Saracone, now deceased.

However, a well-placed source assures this reporter that DiNunzio believes that Saracone himself may have been responsible for Brandolini's death, only apparently by suicide. And the same source reveals that Saracone is responsible for the mysterious injury that DiNunzio has been sporting about town. Only with Mr. Saracone's death yesterday, of cancer, can the full story be told.

"He's got it all," Judy said, flopping into the chair opposite Mary's desk. They'd both come into the office on yet another rainy day to get some work done, but this threw a major wrench into their plans. Judy had brought the paper in, having just picked it up on a Starbucks run.

"My God." Mary skimmed the rest of the story, which detailed her initial interview with MacIntire and all the stuff he'd learned by calling everyone from Missoula, piggybacking on her work. The article went on to raise the same questions she'd had about Frank's murder, though Mary hadn't breathed a word to him. She felt sympathy for Frank's family and betrayed for herself. And she couldn't help but wonder about the identity of the well-placed source. "Think his source is someone at Saracone's or a leak at the Roundhouse?"

"Would Detective Gomez have talked to a reporter?"

"I doubt it, not him. He seemed like a decent guy." Mary flashed on her conversation with the detective, the end of which had taken place at the open door to the interview room. She remembered the eavesdropping detectives and the woman in the skirt. "But people in the squad room definitely heard us. One of them may have leaked it."

"Lucky for you that Bennie went back to New York. She probably picked up the newspaper, but even she can't turn a Metroliner around."

"Don't bet on it." Mary shoved the paper out of her sight. She was thinking about Keisha. She'd already told Judy about the nurse's call to her cell phone. "I called Keisha again this morning, but she didn't call back. This could explain why."

"How so?" Judy pried the white lid off her coffee, releasing hazelnut steam, and took a sip.

"Our cover is blown. This whole thing is no longer our little secret." Mary was thinking aloud, trying to wrap her mind around it. "If Keisha wanted to talk to me before, she'd be wary of me now. She may not trust me anymore at all."

"Right, or she might not want the media attention." Judy looked fresh in a plain white T-shirt, denim shorts, and bright red flip-flops. She'd pulled her hair back in a stubby ponytail, stiff as a blonde paint-brush. The indirect light from the window brought out the alert blue of her eyes.

"What are you going to do?"

"Have a cigarette."

Judy laughed. "Have some breakfast, do your work, and get yourself ready for this dep."

"But this screws me up! People will read it,

or hear about it. Saracone's son will see it, and his wife, and Chico The Escalade." Mary considered the timing of the article, then realized something. "That must be why Mac ran the story right now. He lucked out when Saracone died, because he and the paper can't be sued for defamation now. You can't libel a dead man, isn't that the law in Pennsylvania?"

"Yep. Good for you." Judy sipped her coffee. "When the other papers pick up on the story, I'm sure the calls will start. It's just you and me in the office, and we probably shouldn't answer the phones. We can avoid Premenstrual Tom and Premenstrual Bennie."

"He still calling?" Mary had almost forgotten.

"Don't worry about it. I have them all recorded, and the TRO hearing will be scheduled as soon as I can serve his ass. So don't get the phone."

"But what if Keisha calls here, instead of on the cell?"

"Why would she, and anyway, you don't sound like you're putting Brandolini behind you." Judy's eyes darkened. "Your cheek is barely healed, Mare. You want a repeat of the other day?"

"I'll give it up after I talk to Keisha." Mary reached for the phone. "I better call my parents about that article. I'll call Eisen, too, so he doesn't freak when he sees the papers. Then I'll get us both ready for his dep, so by the time Bennie hears about the newspaper story, she'll love me again."

"Don't bet on it," Judy said, peering across the desk. "You gonna eat that croissant?"

"No, you are."

By midafternoon, Mary had finished preparing for the Eisen deposition and had made all her calls. Keisha still hadn't called. Mary hadn't answered the phone but just kept checking the messages: a slew of reporters, her father, assorted clients who had forgiven their celebrity lawyer, and a prisoner who wanted a date with her legs. When she couldn't take waiting for Keisha anymore, she got proactive. She picked up the receiver, dialed information, and waited until it found the number and connected her.

"HomeCare, WeCare," answered a pleasant voice, a woman's. "Leslie Eadeh speaking."

"Yes, Leslie, maybe you could help me." Mary put on a cigarette voice, inspired by last night. "I have a problem. I'm looking for one of your nurses, Keisha Grace."

"It's Sunday, dear. The business office is closed."

"I know, but this nurse, Keisha, is due at my house today, and she can't get here. She called and said her car broke down."

"What's your name?"

Mary's gaze shifted to the papers scattered across her desk, order forms from E & S Furnishings. The top name belonged to Rikki Summers, offending Broughley sales rep, the body that launched a thousand recliners. "Broughley. Rikki Broughley."

"Like the recliners?"

Uh. "Exactly. But we're no relation."

"Too bad. I love the suede."

"Everybody does."

"Please wait a minute, Ms. Broughley," the woman said, and Mary could hear the *click, click, click* of computer keys over the line. "We don't have a record of Keisha coming to see you today, Ms. Broughley. We show she hasn't worked since Friday."

Since Saracone's death. "There must be some mistake with your records."

"I doubt that highly, Ms. Broughley."

"Everybody makes mistakes. Keisha was here at my house just yesterday, Saturday."

"Keisha was?" Leslie asked, in a way that sounded like she knew her. "You sure you got the right girl? Sometimes our patients get confused."

"Certain of it. She's African-American, pretty, young, about five three, same as me, with very large eyes and a pretty smile. Her name tag reads Keisha, I remember seeing it."

"That's her. Hmmm." Leslie sounded stumped.

"She left me her phone number." Mary gave her the number. "I called but there's no answer. See, she called and said her car broke down and could my son pick her up."

"Her car broke down? I thought it was new."

Oops. "I know, it's an outrage. Anyway, my son left an hour ago but he lost the address and I don't remember it. So now I need her address."

"Ms. Broughley, we don't give out that information. I can call her for you."

"You won't get her. I just called her at home and got no answer. There's no answer on her cell, either."

"Keisha gave you her cell?"

"Sure enough." Mary read her the number. "We got along very well. I thought the world of her, that's why I sent my son out to fetch her. I hate to think of Keisha standing in the rain. She wouldn't do that to one of us patients, not for a minute."

"You're right about that, and this weather is so awful. Sometimes I think we'll never see the sun again."

Mary knew the feeling. "And it's so cold for this time of year. Even the rain is so cold. If I could just have her address. I think my son's only a block or so away."

"Well, I guess it's okay, just this once. Tell Keisha I said hello."

"Will do." Mary jotted the number down, thanked her, and hung up. She grabbed her purse and hurried to Judy's office to make her escape, taking personal inventory. She was wearing jeans, Jack Purcell's, and her old Penn sweatshirt, and her hair was loose under a Paddington Bear slicker and rain hat. It was a good outfit for a stuffed animal, not an amateur sleuth, but she had no choice. With one last hurdle, she was good to go. She stuck her head in the door of Judy's office. "This is me, leaving," she said.

"Is it that time already?" Judy squinted at her Swatch watch, which Mary knew was a tumbling circle of smiling baby heads.

"You can't tell time with that thing, admit it."

"Yes I can. It's half past baby nose." Five seconds later, Judy was still squinting.

Mary faked a yawn. "Listen, I'm beat. I couldn't sleep last night. I'm going home to take it easy, to be fresh for tomorrow."

Judy scoffed. "Please don't bullshit me. You've got something up your sleeve."

"No, I don't."

"What is it? Give." Judy leaned over her messy desk.

"I would tell you. Gimme a break."

"Did Keisha call?"

"No."

Judy's eyes narrowed. The alert blue had been replaced by eyestrain pink. "Did you call her?"

"No."

"Truth?"

"Yeth."

Judy seemed placated. "Okay, I believe you. Go home and chill. You're the best."

Ouch. "You, too," Mary said. That much was true.

Then she hurried out in her sneaks.

THIRTY-ONE

Mary had got off the D bus in West Philly, in a residential neighborhood that was truly integrated. At the moment, however, Mary's was the lone white face on the street, and her Paddington Hat screamed Dumb Things Only White People Will Wear. The rain slowed to a drizzle, so she took off the hat and rolled it like a hoagie into her slicker pocket. Then she turned left on Gingko Street. The sky was permanently cloudy and prematurely dark, but residents were still out, enjoying the last night of the weekend. A young couple walked by with a golf umbrella held over a baby bouncing in a Snugli, and kids played Wiffle ball in the street, hitting foul balls with a wet *thwick*.

Gingko trees lined the street, and Mary eyed them, loving their primitive branch system, if not the stinky berries they dropped all over the sidewalk. Gingkos were as Philadelphia as snapper soup, and they scented even the best of her pumps.

She traveled down the street, walking past 5207 and 5209, four-story Victorians with Cape May paint jobs, and she inhaled a great-smelling back porch barbecue, which she'd take over foie gras any day. But she wasn't thinking about food now. She was thinking about Keisha Grace. At the end of the street lay a newer limestone apartment building, and Mary raised her eyes to the second floor. One of those windows belonged to the nurse.

She went to the building's front door, painted a forest green, and was about to knock when she noticed it was slightly ajar. She opened the door and went inside an entrance hall that bore a large homemade sign, PLEASE CLOSE THE FRONT DOOR BEHIND YOU! She read the stainless steel mailbox covers until she found 2F, Grace/Whitman. *All right!* She pressed the black button, and the walls were so thin she could hear a loud buzz overhead. A man answered almost immediately.

"Yes?" On the cheap intercom, his voice sounded like it was underwater.

"This is Mary DiNunzio, and I'm looking for Keisha Grace."

"She's not here."

"Well, may I come up and see you? She's been calling me, and I'd like to talk with you, if I may."

A pause. "Okay. Come on up."

The buzzer sounded and Mary crossed the hallway to open a thick front door, which swung onto a red carpeted hallway and ended in a set of narrow stairs. The hallway smelled vaguely of gingkoes and Glade, and she went upstairs to the second-floor landing, which contained a long hallway with several doors, but no sign. She took a flyer and went right. 2D, 2E, 2F. The door had been painted navy blue, and as soon as Mary knocked on it, any worries she'd had about going alone to a stranger's apartment vanished at the sight.

The man at the door was a tall but slight African-American in black nylon gym shorts, a red Temple T-shirt, and round rimless glasses. His dark eyes were bright and intelligent behind the glasses, and he had short close-cropped hair and a slight over-bite. He extended a hand with long fingers. "Bill Whitman," he said, shaking Mary's hand. "You're the one in the papers, aren't you? The lawyer."

Mary cringed. "Yes, that's me."

"I knew I knew that name." He smiled, and the tips of his front teeth popped into view. "Nice picture."

"Thanks." Mary stepped inside the apartment, which was large and had high ceilings. It was neat for a guy's apartment and simply furnished, with a black cloth couch she'd seen in the IKEA catalog, a teak coffee table, and a wool rug in earth tones. Abstract paintings hung in a trio on an exposed brick wall, and the overall effect made her jealous. "This is a really nice apartment. Mine's so small."

"Where do you live?"

"Center City."

"Got more space up here." Bill gestured at the couch the way boys do when they're playing host, halfheartedly swinging his hand from the shoulder. "You want a water or somethin'?"

"No, thanks." Mary looked to her left,

where three desktop computers with three oversize monitors, two CPUs with the motherboards exposed, and two laptop carcasses covered the dining room table. Even she could sleuth this one out. "You're a computer guy."

"Yeah. I do consulting and repair from here. It's my own business, I started it two years ago. You know anybody who needs IT help, call me." Bill sat down on the end of the coffee table, feet flat-footed on the floor. "So, you must be here because Keisha worked for Saracone."

Smart. "Yes. I met Keisha at Saracone's, the night before he died." Mary edited out the rest of the story, now that she was learning to shut up on occasion. "I got a call from her yesterday, asking me to call her back. I did, but that's the last thing I heard."

"Sounds like Keisha. She comes and goes."

"When is she coming back?"

"Dunno."

"Where is she?"

"Dunno that, either."

Huh? "Doesn't she live here?"

"Yes."

"Doesn't she tell you where she's going when she goes out?"

"Used to, all the time. But things have sorta changed." Bill looked down, examining his Adidas slip-ons. "Lately, we're, she and me, we're kinda shady. She met somebody else. Been seeing him off and on, tryin' to decide between me and him. Sometimes she goes with him for the weekend, then she comes back. I'm hopin' this week she'll come back."

Are you a saint? "That must be difficult."

Bill shrugged. "I love the girl."

You are a saint. Do we have a black saint, yet? "How long have you two been together?"

"A year. We met at school. I graduated Temple, in IT. She was taking nursing courses, but she quit and got the job as a day nurse. Started at Bayada, went on to HomeCare. She doesn't like to stay with one thing too long. She's restless. The job suits her, I don't." Bill laughed softly. "She says I'm the only black geek in the world."

Mary winced. "Who's the other guy, if I can ask?"

"Dunno, but he's got money. He bought her a new car."

"A new car!" *It's over, dude.* "You can't let him buy her a car!"

"What am I gonna do about it?" Bill spread his large hands, palms up.

"Fight for the girl! Tell her you love her! Find out who he is, snoop around her top drawer, follow her, spy on her, look through her stuff." It was so obvious to Mary, since she'd gone to Montana. Maybe Bill needed to go to Montana, too. "There's lots you could do, if you wanted to."

"Not my style."

Mary decided to change the subject. "How long did Keisha work for Saracone, do you know?"

"Two months, off and on. She didn't like him. He used to order her around."

Mary recalled how Keisha had protected him, that night. "But she was good to him, right?"

"I dunno. She was a good nurse. She did her job, I'm sure."

"Did she ever talk about Saracone?"

"Not much."

"What did she say about him?"

"Not much."

"Did Keisha ever mention a Chico? He's the guy who hit me."

"No."

"Chico drives a black Escalade. Have you ever seen a black Escalade out front?"

"In this neighborhood?" Bill smiled and his teeth tips peeked out. "I got three neighbors have a black Escalade. Everybody wants a black Escalade, even me."

Okay, forget that. "Did she know what kind of business Saracone was in, or the son?"

Bill thought a minute. "Don't remember her saying."

"I think it was investments. Sound familiar?"

"News to me." Bill shrugged, and Mary switched tacks.

"When was the last time you saw her?"

"Wednesday morning, when she went to work. She was here all last week. Then she didn't come home Thursday night, or any night since."

Mary felt a twinge of concern. "Aren't you worried?"

"No, happens all the time. She's with him."

"Did you try her cell? I did, and she doesn't answer. I think I left three hundred messages so far."

"She never answers when she's with him."

Mary wasn't taking no for an answer.

"Could she be with her family, or would they know where she is, for sure?"

"Nah. She's only got a mom, and she lives in Birmingham. They don't talk much."

"Doesn't she have any girlfriends who would know where she is?"

"She's not big on friends, and I *know* where the girl is." Bill shook his head with a sad smile. "I don't *like* where the girl is, but I sure as shit know where she is. She's with him, and I don't know where he lives."

"Do you think she'd go to Saracone's funeral?" Mary had seen the notice in the paper. The funeral was tomorrow, but it was private.

"I dunno."

"So you have no idea when you'll see her again?"

"None."

Mary tensed. "You're assuming so much, Bill. Something bad could have happened to her. It's at least possible, even if she's seeing someone else. She's an attractive girl and she's missing."

"She's not *missing*." Bill laughed ruefully. "She's with *him*."

"But you don't know that for sure! *I'm* worried about her, and I don't even know her."

Mary couldn't help but freak. Some people never got emotional, and she woke up emotional. "Bill, I didn't tell you this before, but when I went to Saracone's the other night, I accused him of killing a client of mine, and they did this to my cheek." She pointed at her badge of honor, and Bill's eyes flared, but only briefly. "Keisha was there for the whole thing. She heard what I said, saw me get hit. Her being missing, it may be related to that, and not just her being with another guy. You read the article in the paper today, so you know that this Saracone guy is a killer."

"Saracone is dead."

Uh, right. Still. "But something else may be going on. Ask yourself, why would she call me, anyway? Her call to me sounded worried. I saved the message, you wanna hear it?" Bill nodded, so Mary opened her purse, got her cell phone, and played him the message on repeat, then saved it again. His eyelid twitched just the slightest behind his glasses when he heard Keisha's voice. Mary watched him and softened her tone. "Doesn't she sound worried to you?"

"A little."

"I think we should call the police."

"Call the cops? No way! I'm not going to." Bill waved her off. "I don't want any part of that. I'd embarrass myself."

"You said you love the girl. Why take a chance? You think you can't lose someone you love?" Mary heard the words escape her lips, then realized why.

"Let me think about it." Bill bit into his soft lower lip, but Mary couldn't take it any more. She reached into her purse, pulled out her cell phone, and plugged in the number.

"Detective Gomez, please. I'm a friend of his, and it's personal."

"Gomez," he said, when he picked up.

"Detective, it's Mary DiNunzio. That nurse I told you about is missing. Keisha Grace, the one who witnessed my discussion with Saracone. She called me on my—"

"DiNunzio, you told the desk it was personal."

"It is. To me. My face hurts. And that's not a straight line."

"I'm not laughin.' Not after that stunt you pulled."

"What stunt?"

"With the paper, with that reporter. Got my name in ink, and yours, too. You fed him that story while the case was under investigation."

Mary's mouth fell open. "No, I didn't. I talked to him last week and he ran with it on his own."

"Sure he did. He had details only you could give him. He talked to your *uncle,* for Christ's sake! You think you're a smart-ass, breaking into a crime scene, stealing evidence. You don't respect the process, and I don't appreciate it."

"I do respect the process. I didn't leak anything, I swear."

"Try livin' in Mexico, honey, like my brother. The cops there don't bother to do any investigating, they just beat a confession out of you." Gomez's tone had an unhappy finality to it. "I'm working this case, I'm all over this case, and I don't need you or any other lawyer—including Ms. Rosato—talkin' to the papers and makin' me, my sergeant, and the department look bad."

"Wait, hear me out. I thought *you* leaked it."

"Bullshit!"

"Listen, set our stuff aside for a minute, I'm calling because of this nurse, Keisha

Grace." Mary tried to modulate her voice. "She's missing. She hasn't been home since Wednesday. She saw my fight with Saracone. She heard me accuse him. Yesterday, she called me on my cell, trying to reach me. It's too coincidental that she disappears right now."

"So tell her family to file a missing person report. This is Homicide, not baby-sitting."

"Her family doesn't live here."

"So how do you know she's missing?"

"Her boyfriend told me, I'm here with him now."

"Then put him on. I'm done talking to you."

Mary handed the phone over, but not before she covered the receiver with her hand. "Back me up, please."

Bill nodded and put the phone to his ear. "That's right, Wednesday morning. She worked for the Saracone family for two months."

Mary started nodding encouragement.

"It isn't that unusual for her. I mean, she does disappear from time to time."

Mary stopped nodding encouragement.

"Last week, for two days. Week before

that, one day, and the week before that, too."

Mary kicked his big foot in the flip-flops.

"No, she never said anything like that to me. She didn't tell me much about the Saracones or about any of her jobs."

Mary gave Bill a shove, and he almost fell over.

"Nothing," he answered. "No, I don't think she ever felt threatened or anything."

No! Mary grabbed the phone. "Detective Gomez," she said into the receiver, but his only response was a very pissed-off *click* as he hung up.

It was dark and pouring when Mary left the apartment building, so she pulled the White People Hat out of her pocket and put it back on. She hurried back down the street in the downpour, over the gingko berries and through dirty puddles formed by the cracked sidewalks. Water drenched her sneakers, and hard rain pelted parked cars, sidewalks, and her hat so hard it was like a dull roar, obliterating all other sounds.

Mary broke into a light run, keeping her head down against the slant of the drops. The front of her pants got soaked, and her sneakers were waterlogged by the time she turned the corner onto the cross street.

Which was when she became aware of a dark sedan, turning left onto the cross street, a few lengths behind her.

THIRTY-TWO

It was a black Town Car, behind her. Mary wouldn't have noticed it but for one thing. The windshield wipers weren't on, despite the downpour. She picked up the pace, using the absurd brim of the hat to sneak a look backward. Was the car following her? Was she being paranoid? Still. It was pouring rain. Who would drive with no wipers? It was a late-model car, the wipers had to be working.

Then she realized. The only reason to drive without windshield wipers in a rainstorm was if you wanted to hide your face. And Chico would have known Keisha's address. Or maybe he had followed her there, and she just hadn't seen him from the bus window. Was it *him*?

Mary broke into a light run, but she wasn't afraid. Not completely. Not her. That would have been the old Mary. This was Cowgirl Mary. She ran to the corner where the bus stop was, but she had to see if the Town Car was following her. She took a right on Chestnut and kept running. She ran past a closed dry cleaner but kept her eye on the left side of the street.

The Town Car turned onto Chestnut, taking a right at a distance. Its wipers still weren't on. She couldn't see the driver at all. It could have been Chico. He would have ditched the Escalade. She wondered fleetingly if he had a gun and burst forward, panicky. She kept her pace, panting from fatigue and nerves. Only a few other cars were on the street, a green Jetta and a red Saturn. She jogged to the end of the block, and when she reached the corner, turned right, keeping up the pace. Her hat brim flopped with each step and doused her face with cold water. She held her breath until she reached the middle of the block.

The cross street was darker than Chestnut, and she felt suddenly panicky.

Maybe this wasn't such a hot idea. In the next second the Town Car turned onto the cross street. Its panel of bright headlights switched to the high beams. Light flooded the narrow street, illuminating parked cars, trash cans at the curb, and wet trees and sidewalk. It couldn't have been a normal driver. If a normal driver wanted to see better in this weather, he'd turn on the wipers. Unless he didn't want to be seen. It had to be Chico.

Oh, no. No one was on the sidewalk. There was no traffic on the cross street. He would have a good shot if he shot her here. There was no shop to duck into or anyone to witness what happened. Except.

Mary reached into her pocket for her cell phone and tried to open it on the run, but a sudden rush of cold rainwater from her sleeve made her drop it. She barely heard it clatter to the sidewalk in the downpour and she couldn't see it in the dark. She didn't have time to stop and look for it. She left the phone and kept running. Her lungs felt like they were going to burst. Her thighs ached in the soggy jeans. She ran until she couldn't anymore. She was sick of running. She had to end this. Now.

She turned around suddenly and ran straight for the car. The car kept coming. She intercepted it in three strides, grabbed the passenger's side door, and flung it open. She was about to start screaming when somebody else did.

"Help, police!" Mary screamed back, before the scene registered. The driver wasn't Chico Escalade, but a very old woman with curly gray hair and eyeglasses as thick as her mother's.

"Don't hurt me, please! Please, please God!" The old woman grabbed her purse from the seat and thrust it at Mary in terror. "Please, take it! Just don't hurt me!"

"I'm sorry. I'm so sorry." Mary flipped up the brim of her hat, dumping rainwater onto her shoulders and the car's black leather upholstery. Her chest was heaving, she was out of breath. "I'm really, really sorry. Your wipers aren't on, do you know that?"

"My wipers aren't on?" The old woman looked at the windshield wet with rain, then looked back at Mary. "Goodness! I thought they were! No wonder I couldn't see anything! Please don't give me a ticket!"

"Okay, I won't give you a ticket, if you make me a promise."

"I will! What is it?"

"Promise me that the next time you drive in the rain, you'll double-check and make sure your wipers are on."

"I promise, Officer!"

Mary saluted her from the wet brim of her rain hat. "Atta girl!" she said, and went off to find her cell phone.

It was going to be a long night, and even so, she knew it would be nothing compared to tomorrow.

THIRTY-THREE

By Monday morning, the sun was struggling to burn off the Philadelphia humidity, a task even a fiery planet couldn't accomplish. The weather hardly mattered to Mary, who was back at work. Not at the office, but outside the Saracone mansion in bucolic Birchrunville. The newspaper had said that his funeral was this morning, so Mary knew that the Saracones and even Chico The SUV would be out of the house. Burglars read funeral notices to see when a house would be empty, so why couldn't lawyers?

Mary scoped out the scene. The street was even more splendid in the daytime, with a dappled sun peeking through lushly overgrown oaks, their leaves dripping residual rainwater onto the grayed asphalt. The country-road quiet was disrupted only by a series of trucks making their way through the Saracones' front gate. In the short time Mary had been sitting here, two white gourmet-catering trucks had passed, three florists' trucks in elegant pastel shades, and a big blue Taylor Rental truck, its open back revealing stacks of extra chairs, of fancy white wood. Mary could have guessed as much. Even bad Italian-Catholics had guests to the house after a funeral.

She opened the car door, climbed out, and walked toward the house with purpose. If the Saracones were hiding something, even after the old man's death, then she wanted to know what it was, and she couldn't think of a better place to start than at his house. The electric gates were held wide open, which made sense. There were so many deliveries that they couldn't be bothered to keep buzzing everyone in, and they weren't worried about security with so many people in the house. She walked down the street, her pumps clacking on the asphalt, which reminded her that her navy blue suit limited whatever role she'd play this morning. She was dressed for work, not

the white-shirt-and-black-pants that caterers wore or the jeans-and-T-shirt of a florist.
She looked like a lawyer. *Uh-oh.*

Mary shrugged it off as she strode with
authority through the open gates, down the
Belgian-block driveway, and toward the
front door. A young gardener hurriedly
mulching a bed of hosta near the doorway
looked up as she passed, but her manner
telegraphed *I-belong-here, minion* and he
looked away. This could work. She hit the
front step and rang the doorbell, her
thoughts racing.

An older woman wearing an old-fashioned
black-and-white maid outfit, a flat, steely
bun, and a polite if puzzled expression answered the door. "Hello, who are?" she
asked, with a Hispanic accent. Behind her
rushed a young girl with a huge spray of
calla lilies, and going the opposite direction
hurried a caterer with a crystal bowl of egg-
glazed rolls. Florists. Catered food. Fancy
white chairs. It was like those weddings on
the Discovery Channel.

Eureka! "Pleased to meet you." Mary
shook the maid's hand. "I'm the funeral
planner."

"Funeral planner?" The maid frowned. "What is funeral planner? I never heard."

"You know, just like a wedding planner, I'm a funeral planner! I coordinate the flowers, the food, the linens!" Mary stepped inside the entrance hall, edging the door aside and gesturing grandly at the activity. "This is all happening because of me. One doesn't leave funeral planning to amateurs! I planned it with Melania."

"Melania? She no say."

"Yes, don't you recall? I'm here to see that everything is in order, for the memorial luncheon! Giovanni would be so proud!" Mary snapped her fingers at another florist, passing with a huge bouquet of pink gladiola. "Stop right there! Those go in the living room, behind you!" She referred to the layout of the house to bolster her feeble credibility in a job no one had heard of, because it didn't exist. "And put them right by the fireplace, with the stone mantel. On that mahogany end table, like Melania wants!"

"Oh, sorry!" the young florist said, then turned around, but the maid was following Mary like a hound dog. It wasn't going to be that easy.

"What you say your name is?"

"Rikki Broughley." *Well, it had worked before*. "Didn't Melania mention me? No?" Mary didn't wait for the answer. "We've been working together, I guess she wanted to keep it to herself. Some people feel that it's unseemly, planning for the death of a loved one, but we must be realistic, mustn't we? Poor Giovanni, she loved him so. She must have cried her pretty blue eyes out. I was with her the night before he died, you know. She was a wreck, even in that great white blouse! And she still found time to work out!"

The maid listened, her head cocked.

"And Justin, he will be so upset, too. All those investments to look out for, all on his own now. Buy, sell! Sell, buy!" Mary was running out of inside information. "How's Justin holding up?"

"He fine."

"And Chico? He'll be strong for everyone. He's a rock, isn't he?"

"Fine, too." Finally, the maid seemed to relax a little. "I no like Chico," she whispered, leaning over. "He mean."

You're telling me. "Now, dear, everyone has their good points!" Mary said lightly. The key to good funeral planning was saying everything lightly. She was getting the hang of it.

"Not Chico. No good point." The maid shook her head. "He plain mean."

"Okay, well, gotta go! Gotta get everything in place before they return!" Mary grabbed the sleeve of a caterer's helper bearing a mounded tray of crudités with dill dressing, then plucked a bright carrot from the bowl and bit it with a loud crunch. "Perfect!" she announced and shooed the caterer into the dining room before she turned back to the maid. "Will you make sure they don't start the coffee yet, in the kitchen? I don't want it to burn! And come to me if they give you an ounce of trouble!"

"Okay, sure," the maid said, turning back toward the kitchen.

Mary hustled into the living room, where florists were setting tasteful flower arrangements on the various side tables that had seemed so vacant before. She made only the corrections that would be obvious to anyone with a law degree. She moved a vase of calla lilies to the right, and her gaze fell on a closed door, off to the right. If the bedrooms were upstairs, what could that be? Maybe a den or a home office? That could be helpful. She edged toward the paneled door, and after a florist had plunked down the last gladiola and left the living room, she opened the door, slipped inside, and closed it behind her.

Mary found herself in a large den, lined with light-pine magazine racks, displaying rack after rack of fashion magazines. *Cosmo, People, W, Vogue, Vanity Fair,* even an array of British magazines like *Hello!* and *Tattler.* A flowery print sofa and two soft chairs in one corner clustered around a decidedly non-funereal display of white daisies. An array of silver-framed photographs adorned a large, whitewashed desk of ersatz antique pine. It was clearly a girl home office and of someone who didn't work. Melania. Not helpful. But it suggested there was a boy office, too. Giovanni's.

Mary cracked the door, peeked out to make sure the coast was clear, and slipped back into the living room. Just then another deliveryman entered the room with a huge vase of red roses, and she put up a hand. "Stop! Take that arrangement right back to the dining room!" she began to say, then caught herself. "No, wait! Come with me!" She stalled a moment, eyeing the living room for another paneled door. On the other side. *There!*

"This way!" Mary strode to the paneled door and opened it, ushering the florist inside, as she looked quickly around. Dark blue walls, navy leather couches and chairs, and the faint odor of cigars clinging to navy-striped curtains. It was a home office, apparently Saracone's. Mahogany bookshelves held a few books, various photos, and a black custom entertainment center and television, directly across from a matching mahogany desk. She itched to get at that desk. Why would Saracone have paid so much to Frank in legal fees? There had to be legal files somewhere, or an explanation.

Mary pointed at the desk. "Please set those roses by the phone, to soften the effect, no?"

"Whatever," said the man, obviously unentranced by her horticultural wizardry. He tramped in untied Timberlands to the desk, plunked down the vase, and walked out of the room, leaving Mary inside. She closed the door and locked it with the thumbscrew, just to be sure. She hurried across the thick carpet, almost tripping over an AstroTurf putting green, then went around the desk, and opened the top drawer.

It was full of pens, almost all of them black Montblancs, and next to the Montblanc log-jam was dirty loose change and paper clips. Not probative. Mary opened the top right drawer and found it full of papers, which she rifled though. Stray Amex bills, from two years ago, Mobil gas receipts, an anniversary card from Melania, and cash machine tapes. Saracone obviously hadn't used the desk in a long time, which Mary guessed was to be expected, but why keep this crap? She had the feeling of a businessman carrying an empty briefcase, for show.

She opened the Amex bill and scanned the charges. Morton's Steakhouse, Ruth Chris, the Palm; an array of carnivorous restaurants. How did Saracone pay for these meals, this house, and this wife? She opened the next drawer. More of same, with photos besides, of a young Justin in front of a Christmas tree, then in a Boy Scout uniform, and finally in a graduation gown. She switched sides to the next set of drawers and it looked more promising. Financial statements, from a PNC brokerage account in his name only. Mary's eyes widened at

the first balance—a whopping $19,347,943.
Jeez!

She went to the next balance sheet, which
read $18,384,494. The other balance sheets
went back three years, all in a neat, chronological stack with a three-hole punch on the
left side. Twenty mil and change, ten mil,
eighteen mil; the balances fluctuated with
the market, but the account always hovered
in the extremely healthy twenty- to twenty-
five-million-dollar range. *Wow!* Where did
Saracone get all that money? The deposits
didn't tell the source, just the amounts, and
a quick glance suggested they occurred
twice a year. Mary went to the next drawer.

More of the same. Bank checkbooks, at
least five of them, with a stack of canceled
checks stacked behind like bricks. She
grabbed the first check register and opened
it. The entries read PECO, Verizon, PGW,
Time magazine, the *Inquirer*; the amounts
were higher than hers, but otherwise it
looked like her own checkbook. No checks
to Giorno & Cavuto. Was there a business
checkbook? There were only a few deposits; again, no source, just a modest
amount. Hmm. She continued ransacking.

Behind the registers was an array of mutual fund accounts with amazingly high balances. In the $30 million range, with deposits twice a year, but there was no indication of where all this money came from. Just then Mary heard a noise outside the door and froze. The door remained untried. She had to hurry. She closed the drawer and opened the next. More mutual fund accounts from an array of houses; Merrill Lynch, Smith Barney, and other institutions. But the dates on these reports were older—1982, 1983, 1984—so the money had been made a long time ago. How much could Saracone be worth now? Where would the recent records be? She double-checked the top; the address on the sheets wasn't the home address like the more recent accounts, but an address downtown under the account name: Saracone Investments, Inc.

Mary thought a minute, rereading the office address. Why hadn't she been able to retrieve that address from the computer, when she'd searched earlier? Maybe because the phone number was unlisted. But what kind of investment company had an unlisted number? No time for answers now. She grabbed the sheet, folded it up, and stuck it in her purse. The records of an incredibly wealthy man, with no evident source of income. What gives? Drugs? Money laundering? The mob? And what, if anything, did it have to do with Amadeo?

She closed the drawer and was about to leave when her gaze fell on the photos on the desk. All of them were of a Giovanni Saracone, flashing that smile Mrs. Nyquist had mentioned, standing tan and tall on the decks in a series of white sailing caps. The boats got bigger and bigger as Saracone got older. The end of the biggest boat— Mary didn't know if it was called the prow, the bow, or the stern—read *Bella Melania.* There were photos of Saracone and Melania on the boat, and Saracone, Justin, and even a sunburned Chico holding fishing rods. Mary looked over the desk, and on the opposite wall hung a huge fish with a pointy bill. Or beak, whatever. A marlin, a tuna. It was a fish.

Saracone fished, too? Why hadn't she thought of it? She had learned from Mrs. Nyquist that Saracone was from Philly. What if he and Amadeo were both fishermen? It wasn't impossible, and in fact, these photos suggested it was likely. But then why didn't Saracone know about the fisherman's knot? Mary didn't have time to figure it out now.

She hurried to the drawer just as she heard another noise from beyond the door, in the living room. She'd have to make sure the coast was clear, then start talking lightly all the way out the front door. Soon the Saracones and their guests would return, and she had to get out. Or did she? Mary paused with her hand on the doorknob. The guests at the luncheon would have to be the people who knew Saracone the best; maybe even his fishing buddies or other people he boated with. Maybe they would even have known Amadeo. Could she take the chance of being recognized? There was talking on the other side of the door. She couldn't stay any longer. She opened it. Waiting for her were three florists, two caterers, and a heavyset guy holding a laundered stack of white linen tablecloths.

Eeek! "Yes?"

The heavyset man spoke first: "My boss told me you were the funeral planner and to ask you where to set up the tables." The young caterer next to him added, "Also we're out of Sterno. Do you know where the nearest market is?" "Are there enough lilies in the dining room?" asked another florist's helper, holding the umpteenth vaseful.

Mary waited a beat, then started directing, answering their questions in character and improvising when she got to the Sterno. But all the time in the back of her mind, she was wondering. Should she stay? Could she take the chance? Then she solved her problem, the answer coming to her in a flash. She followed the smells of baking ziti and chicken cacciatore and hurried into the kitchen, where caterers were running around and the maid was struggling to keep the place clean, wiping black-and-tan granite counters until they glistened.

Mary made a beeline for her, looped an arm around her shoulders, and said *sotto voce,* "We have problem."

"What?" The maid looked up, setting her little wipecloth aside.

"I forgot my guest list."

"Guess list?" The maid looked confused again, and Mary kept her tone light, light, light.

"Melania gave me a guest list, of course, to make sure that only Giovanni's best friends would be admitted."

"Giovanni no have friends. He worse as Chico."

Okay. "That's not what Melania thinks, and after this article in the newspaper, I'm sure you saw it, people may try to get in today that shouldn't. Reporters even." Mary leaned closer as a white-jacketed chef dashed past with a mountain of shrimp cocktail on crushed ice. "Do I have to tell you how private the Saracone family is? I wouldn't want to be responsible for letting a reporter in, would you?"

"No, no." The maid's short forehead creased under her little white hat. "So we do what?"

"You get me a copy of your guest list, and I'll check it as the guests come in."

"I no have lis'. She no give me!"

"Okay, then, let's make a new list." Mary grabbed a pink Melania's Memos pad from the counter and slid it in front of the maid. "Write down all of Giovanni's friends, especially the ones from fishing or from his boat. But don't forget the ones from his business, too. All his friends. Anybody you think will be here to pay their respects."

"Okay, okay, good." The maid opened a

drawer and reached for a pencil, and Mary watched her write down the first few names.

"Now, are these the ones from fishing?"

"Yes, yes, these. And more, I know."

Wahoo! "Oh, and one more thing," Mary added as the maid wrote. "Let's let this be our little secret. I don't want anyone to know that we lost our lists. Chico was supposed to make sure I had it, and he wouldn't like that I lost it."

"Okay, okay."

"In fact, don't tell anybody I was even here. I told Chico I'd have all of this done on the phone. We don't want Chico mad at us, do we?"

"No, no, no," the maid said, shaking her head as she wrote.

Mary sent up a silent prayer to the Patron Saint of Escalades.

THIRTY-FOUR

Mary eyed the shiny skyline of her hometown from inside the conference room at the law offices of Shane & Baker. That afternoon she had to return to her day job, having left the Saracone house before family or guests arrived, including Chico. The pink list of Saracone's friends was burning a hole in her purse, but she couldn't do anything about it yet, though she couldn't resist leaving another message on Keisha's cell phone. The nurse hadn't called back, so Mary had no idea if she'd gone to the funeral. The Saracones' maid hadn't included Keisha on the guest list. Mary pushed it from her mind and concentrated on defending Jeff Eisen's deposition.

The plaintiff in *Schimmel v. Eisen*, Marc Schimmel, was represented by Joe Baker himself, who sat across the glistening conference table; a forty-year-old lawyer in a slick gray suit, bright yellow Hermès tie, and brownish handlebar mustache waxed at both ends. Mary liked mustaches, but wax was for tables, and any man affecting an eighteenth-century look in the second millennium had Something Seriously Wrong. She liked better his down-to-earth court stenographer, a compact man named Jim who wore a flowered cotton tie and an earnest expression. The stenographer had positioned himself, as was typical, at the head of the table, with his gray steno machine off to the side.

Mary snuggled shoulder-to-padded-shoulder with Jeff Eisen, who wore an open-collar white shirt with a tan wool suit that reeked of cigarettes. He was smoking again thanks to Mary, having puffed two Winstons outside the building before the deposition. She had guiltily declined to join him, telling him she was back on the patch, but his relapse made her feel like Mary Magdalene on Nicotrol. Eisen had eventually settled down and the proceedings had been a day-long question-and-answer session—until this minute, when the plaintiff, Marc Schimmel, suddenly opened the door and entered the conference room.

Eisen's moussed head swiveled to Mary. "You told me he wasn't gonna be here. He's not allowed in here!"

Mary quieted Eisen with a touch and addressed Baker. "Joe, I thought you said your client wouldn't be attending Mr. Eisen's deposition today."

Baker went palms up, nonplussed. "I didn't know he—"

"I decided to come in the end," Schimmel interrupted, rounding the polished conference table and taking a seat beside his lawyer. He was a solidly built man of medium height, with layered brown hair. He blinked too frequently from blue-tinted contacts and sported a leathery tan from expensed jaunts to the Caribbean. He glared at Eisen from across the table, his fake-blue eyes bright against his dark skin. "I have a right to be here. I'm the plaintiff."

"It's *my* deposition," Eisen said.

"It's my *lawsuit*," Schimmel shot back, and Mary half rose.

"That's enough of that, Mr. Schimmel,"

she said, from the squat that trial lawyers learned early. It was the I'm-almost-outta-here squat used for profanity breakouts, fisticuffs, or when the coffeepot was empty. The only reason Mary's thighs were reasonably toned was because of this specialized maneuver, which required a law degree to perform. "You're a party, so you have the right to be present, but you don't have the right to abuse my client. Once more and I end this deposition."

"Yeah, kiss my ass, Marc," Eisen added.

"Wait just one minute!" Baker shouted, squatting to I'm-almost-outta-here.

"Your client started it," Mary said, and it took the ensuing five minutes to send everybody to their figurative corners and settle down.

Baker continued his questioning: "Now, Mr. Eisen, beginning in January of this year, how many recliners did plaintiff, Mr. Schimmel, order for E & S Furnishings?"

"I don't remember," Eisen answered, simmering. The court reporter tapped silently away on the black keys of the steno machine, and Mary thanked God transcripts didn't record the bubbling of testosterone.

"You may consult Exhibit 62 to refresh

your reflection," Baker said. On cue, Mary flipped through the stack in front of her and showed Eisen Exhibit 62, which was an order sheet. Baker cleared his throat. "Now, how many recliners did plaintiff order in January?"

"Depends on what kinda recliners you're talking about." Eisen pushed the sheet away like cold leftovers. "You're question isn't specific enough."

Good boy. Mary had instructed him not to answer general questions, though she had no illusion that Eisen was following her instructions. He was just making trouble, and she liked that in a client.

"What kind of recliners do you sell at E & S Furnishings?" Baker asked.

"We sell Broughley Lady Executive recliners, Power Glide recliners, Merrie Olde England recliners, Long-Leg recliners, Massage Me recliners, Big Boy recliners, and the top of the line, the Comfort Regent Recliner." Eisen rattled them off without the exhibit.

"So, why don't you break it down by recliner and tell me how many of each were ordered in January of last year? Again, you may consult the exhibit."

"I don't need the exhibit, I know our inventory." Eisen folded his arms. "In January, last year, Marc ordered three each of the Lady Executive, the Power Glide, the Merrie Olde England, the Long-Leg, the Big Boy, and the Comfort Regent. And he ordered eighteen of the Massage Me because his girlfriend loved to screw him on it."

"Jeff, please," Mary said, but her client was too angry to hear.

"Screw you!" Schimmel yelled back, going bright red under his tan. "I ordered eighteen because they *flew* out of the store for Christmas. They dissolve tension, reduce pain, and revitalize the entire body! You don't know the product line, Jeff! You never did!"

"Marc, please!" Baker said, but his client was too angry to hear, too.

"Who do you think you're kiddin,' Schim?" Eisen leaned over the table, with Mary hanging on to his arm like a baby monkey. "This is me, your old partner, your old *room-mate*! Remember freshman year? Speakman sucks, remember? You gonna lie to my face?"

"The Massage Me has the Lovin' Touch System!" Schimmel leaned over, too, and the former partners were screaming nose to nose. At the head of the table, the court reporter tapped his keys, recording everything but the noses. Schimmel had launched into recliner frenzy. "The Lovin' Touch is a genuine innovation in recliner comfort! It has remote-controlled accuracy! It gives a lifelike, professional massage, right at home!"

"Gimme a break!" Eisen roared. "You charged our company for your girlfriend's *vibrator*!"

"Jeff, please stop!" Mary shouted, and just then the melee was interrupted by the ringing of a cell phone. Silence dropped like a bomb, and they all froze in place, then the men's hands flew instantly to their belt holsters. But Mary recognized it. It was *her phone.* She dove under the table for her purse, as fighting resumed.

"Then how come they sold, Jeff?" Schimmel screamed. "Every single one of the Massage Mes sold! All of 'em! The proof's in the pudding!"

"That was January! But what about February? Ten sold! And March? *Seven!*"

Mary found her phone and flipped it open. Shouts flew overhead.

"It's not my fault the economy went in the toilet!"

"Gentlemen, please!" It was Baker. "Stop this right now! This isn't serving anybody!"

"In April, Marc, we're down to one lousy sale! One lousy unit!"

Oh my God. Underneath the table, Mary had a text message. The blue display on her cell read:

**meet me at 5. 18th & Walnut.
keisha.**

"I told you, it's the economy, stupid! Everybody took a hit in April! There was a war on! Don't ya read the papers?"

"Then why'd you keep ordering the Massage Mes? They weren't goin' anywhere, we couldn't *give* 'em away! But you got two times, three times, the normal order! Don't lie to me, Marc, I *know* why! So your girlfriend could double her quota and win the trip to Tortola!"

"Where do you get your information? She *hates* Tortola!"

Under the table, Mary had to read the message again to believe she was really seeing it. Keisha wanted to meet with her.

Why? It had to be about the Saracones. She checked the display for a little electric envelope but there wasn't one. No voicemail message. She couldn't hear over the yelling anyway.

"You should be ashamed of yourself! Your wife and kids never even *saw* Tortola! You send 'em to *Ventnor,* if they're *lucky*! You don't even go down with 'em, like Jake! Not even on the *weekends*!"

"*You* spend the weekend with my mother-in-law! I *wish* that on you, just once! See how *you* like it, Mr. Perfect Marriage! And what about that secretary, at the auto tag place?"

"Gentlemen! Marc, please! Sit down! I want this on the record! Mary? Where's Mary?"

Under here. Mary wasn't ready to come out yet. They weren't hitting each other, and she needed a minute alone to think. She crouched under the table with her phone. Keisha wanted to meet her at five o'clock? How would she ever make that? She checked her watch. 4:35. The dep would go to until six, easy, and at this rate even later. And on top of it, Eighteenth & Walnut was ten blocks away.

"I never said I had a perfect marriage! And Courtney didn't mean anything to me! At least I didn't leave my wife and kids for her! I have some *self-control,* unlike you!"

"Oh, please! You just don't have the *balls* to leave! You've been miserable for years, but it's easy to stay! It's simple! You're just settling! You don't know what real love is!"

"Don't lecture me about love, Marc! Love is stickin' by somebody, no matter what! Good times, bad times! You bailed on Linda when it got tough! Just like you bailed on *me*!"

"Mary? Mary!" Baker said, and the next minute his mustachioed face popped underneath the table, where she was on all fours with her cell phone. His eyes narrowed in professional anger. "Mary! Get off the phone and talk to your client! He's out of control!"

"Shhh!" Mary said, hushing him with an index finger to her lips, and both lawyers fell silent for a minute.

"*I* didn't bail on you, Jeff! You bailed on *me*! *You're* the one who wants to dissolve the partnership! *You* sent *me* the termination letter!"

"Only because you're never around! You

showed no interest! I was *carrying* you! It was always *her* and the trips to Tortola! What, can't the broad stay home for one second?"

"It's Tortuga!"

"Same difference. Anyway I thought it was Tobago. You said Tobago."

"Oh right." A pause. The decibel level lowered above the table. "You're right. It *is* Tobago." An uncomfortable laugh emanated from the plaintiff's side, followed by one from the defendant's side.

"If it ain't Jersey, I'm lost."

"Me, too." They both laughed again.

Awww. Mary came out from under the table, slipped her cell back into her purse, and straightened up on her side at the same time that Baker straightened up on his side. "Joe," she said, "are you thinking what I'm thinking?"

"Yes," he answered, and his handlebar twitched in a way that suggested he was smiling. "Off the record," he said to the court stenographer, who lifted his hands from the keys.

Mary put a gentle hand on Eisen's shoulder. "Jeff, I think this marriage can be saved. Why don't we end this deposition, and Joe and I drop out for a while? I think you and Marc should go to dinner and see if you can settle this thing. Go to that French restaurant you took me to. Smoke yourself silly."

"Maybe," Eisen said uncertainly, and across the table, Joe was nodding at his client.

"I agree. It's a good idea, Marc. You two can resolve this thing without us. If you don't, we can always continue the dep. You're the plaintiff, it's your call."

Schimmel frowned so deeply that fissures appeared in his tan forehead like cracks in dry clay. Mary read his eyes. It wasn't going to be that easy. He wasn't sure, but she was. She had to get to Eighteenth & Walnut. Ten blocks in ten minutes. Keisha could be in trouble.

"Marc," she said, talking across the table, "you're the one who came to the deposition, when you weren't going to. I think you did that because you were mad. So go out and yell at each other. Get it out of your system. Even a lawyer knows that peace is better than war, if you don't make a habit of it."

Marc looked at Eisen. Joe looked at Mary.

Mary looked at her watch. 4:49. She had to *go*. Ten blocks in ten minutes, at rush hour.

In the next minute, Schimmel smiled and said, "So. You *smokin'* again, Jeff?"

Mary grabbed her exhibits and ran.

THIRTY-FIVE

Mary hit the humid air outside with her purse swinging from her shoulder. Her briefcase weighed down her arm; she'd packed it for a deposition, not a sprint. She launched herself into the rush-hour crowds of businesspeople, salesclerks, and students heading for the trains at Suburban Station, SEPTA buses, and the subway line. She'd been going with the flow in the down elevator, now she was swimming upstream. And she still couldn't swim.

"Excuse me! Excuse me, please!" she said, wedging sideways through a sea of loosened ties, damp oxford shirts, sweaty silk dresses, briefcases, laptops, backpacks, bulging shopping bags, and a rolling

Samsonite overnighter that she tripped over. She checked her watch on the fly. 5:10. "Excuse me, please!" she said, pressing forward to Chestnut Street.

She reached the corner of Fifteenth & Chestnut just as the traffic light turned red and stepped off the curb anyway. A bus headed straight for her, and she jumped back on, almost sideswiped by a poster of J. Lo in the shower. 5:16. Fifteen minutes late. Would Keisha wait? *Could* she wait? The light stayed red for so long it seemed intentional. So many buses roared down the street Mary couldn't slip across. She waited on the corner, sweated though her navy jacket, breathed in acrid diesel exhaust, cigarette smoke, and fading Shalimar. It took a long business day to kill Shalimar. *Go!* She took off at the very next break in traffic, sprinting into the street against the light and hitting a wall of people at the other side.

"Excuse me! May I get through!" she kept saying, plowing through the crowd. 5:23. Hurry!

Mary hustled her way to the curb and barreled ahead, still going against the grain, bonking her briefcase on a cab driving the other way on an always-congested

Fifteenth. She grabbed it back, ran across Sansom, then headed through the crowds for Walnut. Only one block more to go, then a few more uptown. You could walk the entire business district in Philly in half an hour. Mary was trying to fly it. 5:34. The crowd was noisy, laughing and talking, many yapping on cell phones as they hurried along. The air was thick with noise, heat, and smoke, and somewhere Mary heard her cell phone ringing. She reached for her purse, grabbed the phone, and opened it:

help me! keisha

Mary felt her heart leap into her throat. Keisha was in danger. Go, go, go! She bolted full-tilt through the crowd, shoving people aside with her shoulder. Her thoughts raced her footsteps, outstripping them. Why didn't Keisha call the cops? Mary couldn't think of a reason, but she wouldn't take a chance. She raced to the corner of Walnut Street, flipped open the phone on the run, and pressed speed dial for emergency. The dispatcher answered, and Mary shouted, "Please help! There's a woman being attacked at Eighteenth & Walnut!"

"Eighteenth & Walnut?" The woman's voice was calm and even. "Does the attacker have a gun?"

"I don't know! I'm not an eyewitness!" Mary huffed, almost out of breath. "She just messaged me on my cell! She may not be able to talk!"

"How do you know she's being attacked?"

"She said she needs help, on the cell. Send a squad car! I'm on my way there now!"

"You're in a car?"

"No, I'm running. Please!"

"Eighteenth & Walnut, that's Rittenhouse Square. How do you know where she is?" The dispatcher asked, but her question got lost when Mary banged into a businessman.

"Watch it!" he yelled. "Hang up and walk!"

"I was supposed to meet her there, on the corner at five! I think somebody got to her first because I was late! Ask Detective Gomez from Homicide! He knows all about it!" Mary was only using his name to bolster her credibility. She knew the two departments couldn't be more separate, and there wasn't time for a referral.

"Okay, stay on with me. Can you stay on with me?"

"Sure, yes. Thank you! Please hurry! Send a car!" Mary sprinted past Burberrys, rounded an overflowing wire trash can in front of McDonald's, and jumped over a smashed Big Mac wrapper, scattering a trio of pigeons. She was only two blocks away. *Go, go, go!* "Are you sending a car?"

"I'm seeing if I can locate one close to the Square. There usually is one. It's a busy time of day. Where are you now?"

"I'm *there*!" Mary tore down Walnut and finally hit Eighteenth, cell phone in hand. She stopped when she reached the intersection, thronging with businesspeople. Buses, cars, and cabs clogged the street. Keisha was nowhere in sight. It was the busiest time of day in the busiest corner in town. That must have been why Keisha had wanted to meet her here. It was where she felt safe, with so many people around. Mary looked wildly around, panting. "I'm at the Square, but I don't see her!"

"I have a car on the way. I've located one three blocks south."

"Please, hurry! Hurry! God, where *is* she?" Mary saw everyone but Keisha. Secretaries, businessmen, students, moms, kids, even poodles crammed the Square. "I don't see her!"

"Stay calm and keep looking."

"Okay, okay," Mary said, her voice jittery from panic and exertion; Keisha wasn't on this corner, if she ever had been. She took off when the light turned green, loping around the Square, lapping a real jogger in running shorts. She searched the crowd for Keisha but didn't see her. Anybody who wanted to hurt Keisha would have to take her away from witnesses. Stick a gun in her ribs, threaten her so she wouldn't scream. Where would he take her? To a car? No way. He couldn't get a parking space around the Square. And if he double-parked, a cop car would be on his ass sooner than if he committed murder. So most likely, he was walking Keisha some-where away from the crowd or to a waiting car. *Right now*.

Mary picked up the pace, her breath coming in ragged bursts. Her arm hurt from carrying the briefcase and purse. She looked frantically around for Keisha. Passers-by looked at her like she was nuts. In the next instant she heard the distant blare of a police siren. The cavalry! "Is that siren the squad car?" she asked into the phone.

"Should be. The car's on Spruce, heading toward you. Did your friend message you again?"

"No." Mary ran harder.

"You're sure you're for real? I'm comin' after you myself, if you aren't."

"I swear it!" Mary turned left onto the west side of the Square, thinking again. West or south were the residential sections, with less traffic than the business district. And they had parking. A bad guy's dream.

The thought gave Mary her second wind and she veered around the corner at a streak. The Square was lined with the swanky restaurants, the busiest branch of the Free Library, therapists' and plastic surgeons' offices, and a ritzy art gallery.

Think! Then the answer popped into Mary's head. Where else in a city did nobody ever go? *A church!* The Church of the Holy Trinity was right on the Square! She whirled around and doubled back. The police siren blared closer now. Help was on its way! She bolted across the street between cabs and sprinted toward the church, a huge brown sandstone edifice with a castle-like Norman tower, on the northwest corner of the Square. She shot toward its red doors.

"Keisha! Keisha!" Mary shouted as she ran up the church steps toward the door and yanked on the iron handles. It was locked! The church was closed! Police sirens screamed closer. They were almost here. Mary looked around, frantic. The Rittenhouse hotel sat beside the church, and cars drove in and out of the hotel's circular entrance. Then she noticed a narrow concrete driveway tucked between The Rittenhouse and the church. An iron gate covered the entrance but the doors hung open, half-painted brown.

"Keisha!" Mary yelled. She ran for the driveway and grabbed the iron gate to stop her momentum, leaving rust- colored paint on her hand. A padlock and chain hung uselessly from the gate, which had been left open. A white painting truck was parked in the narrow driveway and beside it was darkness, where The Rittenhouse completely blocked the sun. Midway down the driveway was Tiffany's stained-glass depiction of St. Paul, his palms open in appeal. Mary looked directly underneath it, in the shadow between the truck and the wall.

"No!" she screamed. Keisha, in a dark T-shirt and jeans, had collapsed in a sitting position. Beyond her was the silhouette of a man, running for the end of the driveway and the side door to the church. The man was large and thick. Chico.

"STOP!" Mary yelled, but Chico escaped through the door. She wanted to chase him, but she had to see about Keisha. She dropped her briefcase and purse and flew toward the fallen woman, throwing herself down on the concrete. Keisha slumped against the stone wall, her head tilted forward like a broken doll and her legs splayed out next to a few paint cans. Her eyes were closed and her mouth slack, but her lips moved as if she were trying to speak. Then Mary looked again, in horror. Keisha's T-shirt wasn't dark, it was drenched with blood. Blood bathed her neck and bubbled like a gruesome freshet from under her chin. Her throat had just been slit.

"HELP!" Mary screamed at the top of her lungs. She fought panic long enough to raise the cell phone and start talking.

THIRTY-SIX

Access Hollywood played on a TV mounted in the corner, and fluorescent lights glared harshly overhead, behind pebbled panels recessed in a white tile ceiling. Outdated copies of *Cosmo, Time,* and *Car & Driver* lay in a glossy fan on a low wooden table, and in the corner stood a Formica cabinet holding a Bunn coffeemaker. An orange-handled pot of coffee burned in its hot plate, filling the room with the odor of stale decaf. The small waiting room, reserved for families of patients in the intensive care OR, had been painted an allegedly calming blue and adorned with gauzy landscapes in forgettable hues. Its blue padded chairs sat empty except for Mary, who was in a sort of shock.

Hail Mary, full of grace, the Lord is with thee. Blessed art thou among women and blessed is the fruit of thy womb, Jesus.

Drying blood stained Mary's white silk shirt and navy suit, stiffening its light wool in patches. She had managed to wash most of it from her hands, but fine dark lines etched the network of wrinkles on her palm. She should wash again, but Keisha had been taken to the OR half an hour ago, and Mary didn't want to be in the bathroom when everybody got here, especially Bill.

Holy Mary, Mother of God, pray for us sinners now and at the hour of our death. Amen.

The words struck home. Mary prayed it wasn't the hour of Keisha's death. It couldn't be. Not because of Saracone or Amadeo or even Frank, or anything logical or tangible. Just because it *could not be*. There had been too much death and it had to be over. Keisha had to live. Mary willed it to be so, the only way she knew how. She started the rosary over again.

Bill arrived a half an hour later and sat slumped in the chair as Mary recounted a

sanitized version of how she had found
Keisha. He sank deeper and deeper into his
clothes, flipping up the collar of his jean
jacket as if to ward off a winter wind. Judy,
her face a mask of well-scrubbed worry, arrived right after, and she couldn't take her
stricken gaze from the blood drying on
Mary's suit. "You okay, girl?" she asked, her
tone hushed.

"I'm fine. Keisha's in the OR still. She lost
a lot of blood." For Bill's benefit, Mary didn't
add the details about the slicing of the
carotid. Evidently, Chico had known what
he was doing. "The doctors said we'll know
more later."

"They're great doctors here," Judy said to
Bill, and he nodded.

When Detective Gomez and his partner
arrived, Bill listened only idly, all over again,
as Mary filled them in. Gomez's partner,
Matt Wahlberg, was a grayish blond detective of about forty-five years who was as tall
as Gomez was thick. His blue eyes seemed
sunken in a gaunt face that Mary understood when she spotted his triathlete's
watch. Insanely fit, he wore a light tan jacket
and khaki slacks, and sat back in the

padded chair, legs crossed and arms folded, while Mary leaned toward Gomez.

"I'm telling you, it was Chico," Mary said as she finished. "He left her for dead in the driveway. He must have gotten out through the church."

"Did you see his face?" Gomez looked at her directly, and her mouth went dry.

"If I said I had, would you arrest him?" Mary was so tempted to lie.

"We'd question him."

"Would you question him anyway? I mean, how many people does he have to kill? He killed Frank and now he tried to kill Keisha!"

"In other words, you didn't see his face." Even Gomez sounded regretful. His soft mouth had formed a deep frown and his thick eyebrows sloped unhappily.

"No, not really. But I saw him. His back, his shoulders, his *outline*. I know it was him. At least go out and question him."

Wahlberg snorted. "An outline isn't probable cause."

"Who are you kidding?" Judy interjected. "What do you call a racial profile?"

Mary wanted to get back on track. "Didn't anyone in Rittenhouse Square see Keisha with Chico? There had to be a hundred witnesses. She may have walked with him from Eighteenth & Walnut to the church."

"We got uniforms canvassing right now. If they find anybody who can ID this Chico, we'll haul him in for a lineup."

"Detective Gomez, I know it was him. It makes sense it was him. Chico is a violent man, Saracone's muscle, and he was there the night I accused his boss of Amadeo's murder." Mary felt a deep pang of guilt. If she hadn't burst into Saracone's bedroom that night, Keisha wouldn't be in the OR right now. "I'll swear out an affidavit, I'll do whatever it takes. I'm making a formal complaint. He assaulted me. Please, please, please, at least go out there and question Chico."

Gomez frowned. "Where does he live, do you know?'

"I don't know, but I think on the Saracone property."

"But didn't Saracone just die? The funeral should be when?"

"Today, this morning." Mary didn't add that she was moonlighting as a funeral planner. Gomez was already frowning deeply.

"I'm not going out there tonight. They buried the man today." Next to Gomez,

Wahlberg nodded in agreement. "And anyway, your theory that it was Chico, or connected to Saracone, doesn't make sense. What would be the motive for an attempt on Keisha? Saracone is dead, so what's the reason for it?"

"Honestly, I'm not sure." Mary wracked her brain. "I accused Saracone of killing Amadeo and maybe Saracone confessed to Keisha. Or said something that admitted it. Something that the Saracones don't want to come out."

"So what if Saracone confessed to Brandolini's murder? Both men are dead. What can they be hiding?"

"I don't know, they have lots of money and I have no idea how they got it. Maybe illegally. Drugs, money laundering, whatever." Mary thought of the investments in the drawers in Saracone's office, but she couldn't tell Gomez that. "Maybe stocks and bonds, something corporate, with IPOs. It could be anything. What if Saracone was going to call the cops and confess? What if the wife or the son had to kill him to stop him?"

"*Killed* him? Why would they kill him? He was already on his deathbed." Gomez frowned. "Why would they care, anyway? So he gets prosecuted for the murder, so what?"

Judy, who had been listening, looked over at Gomez. "They didn't do an autopsy on Saracone and he was buried today. Can we exhume—"

"No way, I can't order one unless there's credible evidence of a homicide. This is getting way out of hand." Gomez shifted his weight in the hard plastic chair. "Look, we have enough questions that we'll consider taking a drive and talking to Chico. But not tonight."

Wahlberg looked at his partner in disapproval. "Dan. Cavuto is cleared. We start running out there, moving too fast, without the facts, we'd lose the evidence in motions—"

"Then consider this as independent of Frank," Mary interrupted. "Somebody tried to kill Keisha and you have to catch that guy." She didn't bring up that Homicide had no jurisdiction unless Keisha died. "You can at least question him. What's it going to cost you?"

Gomez glanced at his partner. "We can

check it out, can't we, Wally? Aside from Cavuto? You got a problem with that?"

Mary sensed she should shut up but couldn't. "Just see what Chico's alibi is. I bet he won't have one, and if you want me to look at some mug books, I will. He probably has a record, being a thug ain't exactly a white-collar line of work. Did you recover the knife in the driveway or the church?"

"No. There are crime scene guys looking for it."

"So he didn't drop it." Mary knew from Bennie that this was significant. Also from *Forensic Files* on the Discovery Channel. "He saw me coming and didn't drop it. He risked getting caught with it, so that means he didn't want you to look up his prints. Somebody who had no record would have dropped it." Mary was impressed with her own powers of deduction, but Gomez waved her off.

"Quit while you're ahead. Wally and me will go out to the house and check it out."

"When, if not tonight?"

"Soon as possible. We'll follow standard procedure."

"Thank you, thank you!" Mary leapt impulsively out of her seat and into his arms.

Gomez felt solid and smelled wonderfully of roast beef hoagie.

Suddenly, Bill, who had been sitting quietly off to the side, rose stiffly on his long legs. "You're all assuming Keisha's not gonna make it through this operation. I think she is, and it would be nice if you thought so, too."

Mary felt a twinge she knew the others shared, except possibly Wahlberg. "We're not assuming that. We're just talking. Trying to figure it out."

Bill's expression said, *Well, don't*. His dark gaze shifted away.

Later, the detectives left, and Mary and Judy tried to distract Bill by asking him computer questions, which he answered ad nauseam. The three of them were in the middle of his lecture on Microsoft XP when the surgeon entered the waiting room on soft paper booties.

And slid off his mask to give them the news.

THIRTY-SEVEN

When Mary got home, she dropped her briefcase and bag at the front door of her apartment, ignored her bills and other mail, and went almost mechanically upstairs, kicked off her pumps, stripped off her bloody suit, climbed into the shower, and cranked up the temperature. Hot water coursed over her body, and she closed her eyes and stood under the spray, letting it soak into her skin and loosen her muscles.

Thank you, God.

She felt tears of relief well up under her eyelids. Keisha had survived the operation and was in intensive care, but she hadn't yet regained consciousness. The loss of blood had left her in a coma, and the surgeon wasn't sure when, or even if, she would recover. They couldn't determine the damage the oxygen loss had caused to her brain. A somber Bill had stayed at the hospital, saying he'd sleep in the waiting room, but he'd wanted Mary and Judy to leave, and they did, reluctantly.

Mary worried that Keisha wasn't safe in the hospital. That when Chico found out he hadn't killed her, he'd come back to finish the job. But Bill had promised to stay by her side, and Mary knew he would. He loved the girl. And he said he'd call Keisha's mother, so she'd be flying in today. She'd be safe with all those people around her. Now all she had to do was live.

A wave of exhaustion washed over Mary, with the hot water. She shampooed her hair, feeling the sudsy foam slick on her shoulders, but she was too bummed to shave her legs. At least it was a good excuse. She got out of the shower, toweled off, and slipped into her McNabb jersey, then tucked herself into bed. She couldn't stop thinking about Keisha and wishing that she'd remembered her before she rushed into Saracone's bedroom that night. She lay sleepless in the dark and didn't even consider reaching for the remote.

Mary took a right turn, then a left, and ended up in the same place she had started, having gone around in a circle for the third time. On a bright Tuesday morning, after a lousy night's sleep, she'd hit the road early to find Saracone's office in the suburbs, right off the Schuylkill Expressway.

LEHIGH VALLEY INDUSTRIAL PARK read the red-and-yellow letters on the sign, but once she was in the industrial park, everything looked the same. Clusters of four-story brick buildings were laid out like a corporate honeycomb, and lush lawn curved around the buildings, bordered by overmulched beds of tulips planted in bands of red and yellow, evidently the team colors. Some evil genius had embedded the red-and-yellow signs for the various companies among the tulips, destroying forever any chance a South Philly girl had of finding Saracone Investments. But if Mary had crashed a funeral, an industrial park should be a piece of cake.

She gripped the steering wheel and took another turn. Only a few cars were parked in the pocket lots at this hour, and she didn't see anyone she could ask for directions. She turned left, found another tulip bed, and searched for the sign. Dearborn Computers. Mary was losing her sense of humor. The attempt on Keisha's life had raised the stakes, and she had fought all last night to suppress the horrific image of the woman slumped bleeding against the alley wall. She had called the hospital from the car, and the intensive care nurse had told her that Keisha hadn't awakened and Bill was asleep in the waiting room. She cruised to the next cluster and the next tulip bed. Household Plastics, Inc.

A white Cadillac drove past, and Mary followed him to the next chamber of the hive, where they both parked, side by side. The man, in casual dress, got out of the car carrying a bronze Halliburton, his cell phone bud plugged into his ear. Mary frowned. This ear-bud thing had all started with the Sony Walkman, and she didn't like it one bit. She flagged him down, raising her voice to be heard. "Excuse me, do you know where Saracone Investments is?"

"No idea," the man answered without breaking stride or further conversation, and

Mary growled under her breath and backed out of the space. She drove around reading tulips and with only three missed turns, asked five more people where Saracone Investments was. None of them had any idea. It was getting weird. After another wrong turn, she found a gardener in a yellow jumpsuit with a red Lehigh Valley patch and she jumped out of the car and accosted him.

"On the end," he said, pointing, and she went back to the car and drove to where he pointed. Then she understood why she hadn't seen it before. The last brown building had a tiny tulip bed in front and the smallest sign of all, with an array of company names in smaller fonts: Rate Foods, Inc, The Steingard Foundation, Francanucci Insurance, Ltd., Juditha Corporation, Simmons Partners, and Saracone Investments. The pocket lot was empty even though the others had been filling up. Why? She'd see for herself; she had found Saracone's office. Mary felt a tingle of fear but chased it away.

She got out of the car, her jacket suddenly sticking to her back. She had dressed in her favorite nondescript beige suit, had her hair pulled back, and was wearing her glasses, so Justin wouldn't recognize her from the newspaper photo. It was an abundance of caution, because she doubted that he'd be back at work so soon after his father's death, but maybe she could sweet-talk the receptionist and get into his office. She walked up the elegant flagstone walk, past the evil tulips, and reached a brown door, hoping it wasn't locked. She pulled on the door, and it opened into a hallway with a panel of mailboxes. Each one was labeled: Rate Foods, Inc, The Steingard Foundation, Francanucci Insurance, Ltd., Juditha Corporation, Simmons Partners, and Saracone Investments.

No! A mail drop? She had driven all the way out here to find a mail drop! She went to the Saracone Investments box, which was stainless steel like the others, and locked, with a little clear window in the top. No mail showed in the window, so it must have been empty, saving both the decision of whether to break in and Mary's immortal soul. But she couldn't be stopped now. A dry hole!

She hit the mailbox in frustration. She couldn't believe an empty mailbox was all there was to Saracone Investments. Where did Justin go to work, and Giovanni before him? Did they work at all? She had seen something like this only once before in her life. At Grun & Chase, her old law firm, she had met a client whose father had made money in the stock market in the early 1950s. The children and grandchildren spent their lives investing and reinvesting the money he'd earned in the fund but were never employed in real jobs. Was that what she was seeing with the Saracones, and Justin? Where had they earned all that money? She couldn't just give up and go back to the office. She had forgotten how to be a lawyer. And just when she started to like it, too.

Ten minutes later, Mary had successfully located the management office of the industrial park and was standing before a reception desk with a cardboard box she'd had in her trunk. She placed it on the reception desk next to a nameplate that read TONI BRUNETTI and waited for the receptionist to get off the phone. It didn't look like it was going to happen anytime soon. Toni, a young woman with spiky black hair and a fake-diamond stud pierced through her left nostril, had flashed Mary the one-minute sign five minutes ago.

"And then I find out, just this morning when I get his email, that he was seeing her *and* her friend and *all* the chicks from the chat room. *All* of them. Even *hillbillygirl*!"

Mary averted her eyes but there was nothing to see. A plain office with white walls, furnished with a tweedy sofa and chairs, a whitish laminated coffee table, topped off with a dreaded vase of company tulips.

"How could he *do* that? *Hillbillygirl?* Who *knows* what you could catch from a *hillbillygirl*?" Toni tore a Kleenex from a gaily patterned cube on her desk and dabbed at her nose with it. Mary wondered what the deal was with that nose pierce. Did it get in the way of heartbreak?

"I *knew* he was fooling around. He started working out and he got his eyes lasered and his teeth whitened. Since when did he ever care about his eyes or his teeth? Until February, the only thing he cared about was basketball!"

Mary tried not to eavesdrop but she couldn't help it. The woman's voice bore the unmistakable inflections of South Philly— adorably warped *o*'s and deliciously nasal *a*'s, and with a name like Brunetti, she was clearly a *paesana*. And unwittingly, Toni was giving Mary a better idea than the one she'd had.

"Oh, yeah, and he bought an Ab-Doer, can you believe that? An Ab-Doer? How could I have been so stupid?" Toni gritted her teeth without smearing her lip liner. "Listen, I gotta go. I'll call you back, I have to help someone here. Thanks. Bye." She hug up, sniffed hard, and looked wetly at Mary, who felt a tug for her.

"You want to go freshen up?"

"No, I'm fine." Toni blinked back tears. "I *so* wouldn't give him the satisfaction."

"I *so* understand," Mary said, ramping up her accent, which had barely survived an Ivy League law school. "You're from South Philly, aren't you?"

"You got it. Sixteenth & Wolf."

"Get out!" Mary grinned. "St. Monica's? I graduated Goretti, too. What year were you?"

"We moved to Delco for high school. I went to Interboro."

"It's all good." Mary smiled. Having traded both high schools and parishes, the two girls had just transferred billions of information-bytes faster than any Pentium chip. They had learned that they had everything in common, and in fact, might be the same person. "So what are you doin' out here?" Out here could be west of Fifteenth Street, or Montana.

"My loser boyfriend was from out here."

"He'll get his," Mary said, with a twinge. She felt bad, but she had a mission to accomplish, and she was hoping another white lie wouldn't hurt. It was a venial sin, at worst. She summoned the frustration of her morning, her newfound hatred of tulips and a pathetic frown. "I can't believe this, you and I have so much in common. More than you think. I'm in the exact same situation as you, with your boyfriend."

"You are?" Toni's damp eyes widened.

"Yes. That's why I'm here. I've been seeing Justin Saracone, from Saracone Investments. The rich family with the mail drop here, at the end?"

"My God!" Toni's manicured hand flew to her mouth. "I know that turd! He hits on me every time he comes in—and he's married! He thinks that smile will get him anywhere."

"I'm not surprised. He told me he wasn't married when I met him, so now I'm dump-

ing him." Mary moved her empty box forward on the counter. "This is his stuff."

"What is it with men?" Toni asked, bewildered.

"Don't ask me." *If I knew any, I'd tell you.*
"He's a pig."

"A tool."

"A *dog*." All this name-calling was making
Mary feel unaccountably better. But back to
the point. "I came to leave his stuff in his
mailbox, but I had a second thought. I want
to take it to his *house*. And deliver it to his
wife!"

"What a great idea!" Toni clapped in delight, as Mary had hoped she would.

"Why should these guys get off scot-
free?"

"They shouldn't!"

"We're not gonna let them treat us this
way, are we?"

"Hell, no!"

"We don't have to take their crap!"

"No way!"

"We can fight back!" Mary raised her
palm, and Toni slapped her five.

"We *will* fight back! Do it! Do it! Do it!"

"I don't have his home address!"

"I do, it's in the file!"

"Let me have it!"

Suddenly Toni's triumphant smile faded and she lowered her hand. "I can't. Saracone signed up for the lockbox and he pays the bill, but I can't give you his address. I'm not allowed."

Damn! Another casualty of a parochial education. A girl who followed the rules. Mary used to be that. Before Montana.

"Don't you have his address?"

"No, he never gave it to me. He didn't want me to know he was married."

Toni bit her lip. "I really want to give it to you, but I can't."

"You sure? We're homegirls."

"I'm so sorry."

"It's okay, I understand. You've been through hell this morning." Mary picked up the empty box. "I don't want to get you in trouble."

"You're not mad?"

"Not at all. I'll find another way to get his address." Mary reached across the counter and gave Toni a warm hug. "And throw that guy out. He doesn't deserve you."

"Thanks."

"Take care now." Mary turned to go to the door, but Toni called out:

"Yo, wait a minute!"

Mary turned on her heel, with the box.

"Where you going after this?"

"To the office."

"Where's your office?"

"Center City."

"Let me give you directions. I bet you don't know the shortcut." Toni beckoned her back to the desk with a polished finger-nail, and Mary returned to the counter.

"Shortcut?"

"Yeah. I know a great shortcut back to the expressway." Toni grabbed a pen and a piece of paper from her desk, then bent her spiky head over the paper and began draw-ing a wobbly line. "Go this way. It'll save you half an hour, easy. And if you keep your eyes open on the way—God knows what you'll find."

Mary finally came up to speed, with a smile. She watched Toni finish the map, which was a long wiggly line, with no *X* to mark the spot. It was like a treasure hunt for Mensa members. How would she know which house was Saracone's? "You think I can do this?"

"No worries. You're from South Philly, so

you'll recognize it right away." Toni slid the map across the counter, with a sly smile.

Not five minutes later, Mary was in her car, following a convoluted series of switch-backs that could qualify as a shortcut only if your destination were Mars. She drove through gorgeous countryside and passed her umpteenth rolling hill, still ponds with cattails not attached to cats, and immense new mansions, where the only neighbors were Canada geese. She eyed each house on the shortcut, but after six winding miles began to worry that she would never find Justin's house, or that she had already driven past it by accident. Then she took a right turn as the road wound around a bend, glanced out the window at the house on the curve, and hit the brake.

Mary laughed out loud at the sight. Toni had been right. There would be no mistak-ing this house, not for a girl from Mercer Street. A huge wrought-iron gate spanned the driveway, and its black bars formed a mile-high, scrollwork S. The same as the screen doors on Mercer Street and every other street in South Philly, only about three billion dollars more expensive.

Mary pulled the car up a little out of the

line of sight, found a sheltering oak tree, and cut the engine, eyeballing the house, which was situated near the street. Thank God that Saracone the Younger didn't share his father's obsession with privacy. He lived in a huge mansion, hewn of gray-and-black stone, with a sloping Tudor roof, genuine slate, with little iron stoppers so the cable guy didn't slide off. A circular gravel driveway curved gracefully in front of a grand, gabled facade, and cars lined the driveway bumper to bumper, too many for one family. There must have been some kind of get-together going on, maybe associated with the father's funeral.

Mary scanned the lineup of cars for an Escalade, but there wasn't one. *Whew*. Then she reconsidered, wishing the Escalade were there. It would be better to know where Chico was at all times, rather than not. She suspected he had been sent out of the country, or at least the jurisdiction, after his attack on Keisha. And Mary hoped that he or Melania hadn't talked to the maid about the funeral planner, because she didn't want anyone in the Saracone camp to know what she was up to. It was only a matter of time before they did.

There was no traffic on the street, so she sat outside the house a minute, wondering what to do. Crash the party? Sneak around the back? And she wasn't sure what she'd learn by going in. *No, not yet.* And she had better leads to follow anyway, when she launched the next stage of her investigation.

Starting as soon as she got back to the city.

THIRTY-EIGHT

Only fifty-six more to go. The late-morning sun peeked through Mary's office window as she typed at her laptop. She was researching the Saracones' funeral guests and finding their home addresses. She hit the enter key and checked the monitor.

Richard Matern, Business address: 1837 Chestnut Street
Phone: 215 546-2982
Home address: 314 Delancey Street, Philadelphia, PA 19103 215 454-9848

She copied the information to a new document and penciled a checkmark on the pink sheet, underneath Melania's Memo. Then she plugged in the next guest's name, hit enter again, and in a second, the next address and phone number popped onto the screen. Ten addresses and phone numbers, so far. The Internet made all sorts of information public, and home addresses were a warm-up to bra sizes and HDL levels.

"Missed you this morning," Judy said, appearing in the doorway. She looked remarkably corporate in her blue sleeveless dress, but she still had bedhead, her blonde hair going every which way. Mary thought it might be intentional, because nobody but her actually *parted* their hair anymore, especially everybody in whatever generation she was supposed to be in.

"Sorry, I was out." Mary kept typing.

"Where were you?"

Uh. "Out."

"What're you doin'?" Judy asked, her tone suspicious.

"Stuff."

"Translation, you're back on Brandolini. Me, I've been in a deposition all morning. *Your* deposition in Alcor."

"Thanks. How's it going?"

"It's all finished, it went great, and you don't have to feel guilty about it."

"Then why'd you give me guilt?"

"For fun."

Mary smiled.

"I also successfully served Premenstrual Tom, and the TRO hearing is next week. It's yet another deposit in the karma bank for me. I'm beating you, even though you surged ahead with all this pro bono work." Judy entered the office and came around the desk to snoop. "Guess you know that Keisha's still unconscious."

"I called, too." Mary ignored the sinking feeling in the pit of her stomach. The way she could help Keisha best was by doing exactly what she was doing. She cut-and-pasted another address into her document. *Fifty-five more to go.* "Bill's with her, so at least she's safe."

"I know."

"Tell me what the papers say. I didn't take the time to grab one this morning, and they barely mentioned it on the radio." Mary had listened on the way in, after the shortcut. The attempt on Keisha's life rated three whole seconds of airtime, and only because the knifing took place in Rittenhouse Square. "They don't get excited unless you die."

"Or you're white." Judy shook her head. "The newspaper has the attack as only a small piece. That reporter evidently didn't make the connection between Keisha and Saracone, so it's just street crime."

"For the moment." Mary kept working. *Fifty-four to go.*

"Hear from Gomez?"

"No." Mary had left two messages.

"Bet he didn't go to Saracone's yet."

"No takers here." *Fifty-three.* Only one phone unlisted, so far. Mary tried to ignore Judy, who was reading her computer screen, and she braced for the inevitable lecture. "Isn't this where you tell me this case is too dangerous?"

"No. This is where I make you give me half that list, so that it gets done in this century."

"Really?" Mary looked up, feeling a rush of gratitude.

"Gimme." Judy held out her hand, and Mary complied.

"Thanks. You're going straight to heaven, girl."

"Since what happened to Keisha, I'm all about you getting those animals."

"Even the Dalai Lama would approve."

"Bennie wouldn't."

"So we'll keep it a secret," Mary said, but she was worried. She couldn't keep a lid on everything forever. Sooner or later, Bennie or Chico was going to blow, and Mary wasn't sure which was worse. Okay, she was. "How much longer can I keep ducking her phone calls?"

"You can't. Beat her to the punch."

"What do you mean?"

"You disappoint me, Mare. Call her cell right now and say hi. Act like everything's fine. Don't give her any reason to worry." Judy made a little skating motion with her hand. "Smooth as glass."

"Call her now?" Mary checked her watch. 10:30. "She's on trial. Her cell will be turned off."

The two girls locked eyes. "Perfect!" they shouted, in happy unison.

And Mary reached for the phone.

By midafternoon, she was sitting in front of the glistening mahogany desk of Richard Matern, a V.P. at Philadelphia National Bank. He looked to be about fifty years old, much younger than Saracone. It probably would have saved time to call the guests on the maid's list instead of meeting them, but Mary could learn more if she saw them face-to-face. Also they couldn't hang up on her. She'd gotten in to see Matern only by harrumphing her way past his secretary and dropping Saracone's name. And right now he was looking at her expectantly, his smile coolly professional.

Showtime. "Thank you for seeing me, Mr. Matern," Mary began. "I'm Rikki Broughley, an investigator here on behalf of Melania Saracone. She would have called you to introduce me, but she's resting today, understandably."

"Of course she is. It's awful about Giovanni."

"Yes, it is. Melania mentioned that you were at the house for the luncheon and also sent her some very nice calla lilies." Mary had remembered one card, and shot her wad.

"Thank you. It's the least we could do."

"Mr. Matern, for my records, could you give me some background about yourself?" Mary pulled a small legal pad from her purse, as a prop. And a security blanket. "How long have you known Mr. Saracone?"

"Ten years or so. He was a client of mine."

Mary would have to get back to that. "Now, Melania tells me that you often fished with Mr. Saracone, on the *Bella Melania*."

"Yes, my wife and I have gone out on the boat, as his guests." Mr. Matern cocked his head in a critical way. "What did you say this was about?"

"Well, confidentially," Mary said, lowering her voice, "it's come to Melania's attention that certain guests on the boat have had some of their valuables go missing after their fishing trips, and she suspects the culprit may be one of the crew. She's asked me to look into it, to substantiate terminating him."

"Oh, I see." Mr. Matern's shoulders relaxed, and Mary guessed he bought the story. She had made it up with Judy, who said it was more fun than working.

"As you were saying, you used to go fishing with Mr. Saracone."

"You're half right. I didn't fish, I'm a golfer. All I did was sit on deck and drink margaritas." Matern chuckled, leaning back in his chair.

"You don't fish?"

"Nah. Giovanni didn't fish either, truth be known."

Huh? "He didn't?"

"Nah, he loved his boat and he made great margaritas, but he didn't fish. He thought it was boring. Face it, it is boring."

"I see." Mary made a note on her pad, only to hide her surprise. How could that be? It didn't square with all the fishing pictures in Saracone's office. "Did you or your wife ever miss any valuables after a trip on the *Bella Melania*?"

"No."

"Does the name Amadeo Brandolini mean anything to you?"

"No. He on the crew?"

"Not that I know." Mary let it drop. It was risky to even go there, but she had to ask it. Her disguise was good enough, and it was a safe bet that Matern didn't remember the details of the newspaper story from days ago. "Now, also for the record, I understand that Mr. Saracone made certain investments with you. Substantial investments, in the neighborhood of twenty million dollars." Mary was remembering the financial statement in Saracone's home office. "Twenty million with you, and slightly more with Merrill Lynch. I probably shouldn't specify how much, exactly."

"More with Merrill?"

"I can't confirm."

Mr. Matern arched a graying eyebrow. "I'm surprised you know all that."

I am, too. "Don't be. Melania trusts me completely, Mr. Matern."

"She never mentioned you."

"I'm *that* confidential, and of course, Melania requests that you keep this visit strictly between us. To do otherwise would not only jeopardize the investigation, but it could also make you vulnerable to a defamation suit, should the culprit decide to sue her."

"Of course." Mr. Matern sat suddenly upright. The word *lawsuit* could do that to anyone, even executive vice presidents. Especially executive vice presidents.

"Now, you were discussing the source of the investment funds."

"The source?"

"Of course, we were discussing Saracone's investments, and you were saying how it was amassed."

"No." Mr. Matern shook his head, puzzled. "I wasn't saying how it was amassed."

"Of course not, and you keep getting me off the point." Mary tried shooting him a stern glance and may have succeeded. If so, it would be the first time in her life. She rose to go, slipping her legal pad back into her purse. "Well, thank you for your time. I do appreciate it, and your discretion."

"Of course. Please give my best to Melania."

Ten minutes later, Mary was sitting in front of another mahogany desk in another ritzy office in Center City. Thomas Richter sold home and car insurance, and was a younger version of Mr. Matern, only with blue eyes. Mary went through her spiel and ended with: "And so, how often did you and your wife Lynnie go fishing with the Saracones on the *Bella Melania*?"

"At least ten times, I guess."

"You must be an avid fisherman."

"No, not at all." Richter laughed. "I only went along because Giovanni invited us. But we never fished, we just sat around in those little chairs on deck and drank Bloody Marys."

"Giovanni didn't fish?"

"Not that I saw."

Weird. "Thanks for your time," Mary said, closing her pad to go.

Ten offices later, in a double-checking

frenzy, she had met most if not all of Saracone's guests, all young or middle-aged professionals who had sold him his car, home entertainment system, or stocks; fixed his bridgework, his sundeck, or Porsche Carrera; prepared his taxes, his will, or his pension fund. All of them had been on the *Bella Melania* with Saracone and had guzzled vodka gimlets, Tanqueray-and-tonics, whisky sours, Manhattans, daiquiris, or Heineken. None of them fished, and all of them confirmed that Saracone didn't, either. None of them knew him that well. None of them knew the name Brandolini, except for one who swore it was a delicious entrée, with clams and white sauce. None of them went back to the old days. Mary didn't get it. Somehow, some-where, *somebody* had to know Amadeo, or at least fish, or there was no connection to Amadeo at all. And she would be, as they say, dead in the water.

By five-thirty, Mary was standing in front of her last reception desk of the day, facing the final secretary she'd have to barrel through, beg, or sweet-talk.

"Hello, I'm Rikki Broughley," she began, glancing around the insurance office. "I'm here to see Mr. Jackmann." It was a one-man law office in an unfashionable part of the city, and the secretary chain-smoked brown Capri cigarettes.

"Mr. Jackmann's gone for the day."

"Will he be back? It's an important matter, on behalf of his friend Melania Saracone."

"No." The receptionist belched smoke. "Melania? She the wife?"

"Yes. Giovanni's wife."

"Oh, Gio, we know."

Gio. Giovanni's nickname. The last time she'd heard it was from Mrs. Nyquist. Melania never used it, Mary realized now. "So Mr. Jackmann goes back, with Gio?"

"Way back."

"How old a man is he?"

"Almost seventy-five. He's semi-retired, hardly comes in anymore."

"If he's not coming back, can you tell me where he lives?" Mary asked, intrigued. Jackmann would be the oldest on the list. "It's urgent. Or at least would you mind calling him and asking him to call me?"

"Sorry. He has a cell phone, but he won't answer it. He can't be reached today unless you're the Coast Guard."

Mary couldn't believe her ears. "What did you say?"

"He's fishing."

Wahoo! "What time does he finish? When is he coming in? Docking, whatever? Better yet, where does he fish from?"

"You want to go to the marina?"

"I have to, it's my job. It's that important to him. Money is involved. Major money."

The secretary's eyes lit up. "Oh, I see. A *will*. Did Gio leave him money?"

Yeah, right. "I'm not at liberty to say. Just tell me, where does he come in from fishing? From." *Huh?*

The secretary rattled off a marina address, and Mary thanked her and scooted out the door.

THIRTY-NINE

The sun was setting on the other side of town, and Penn's Landing was losing its light. The marina was located on the Delaware River at the eastern border of the city, just off the newly renamed Christopher Columbus Boulevard, tucked behind Dave & Busters. Mary wouldn't have guessed that a marina could be a twenty-minute cab ride from Center City, much less next to a sports bar.

The marina was smallish, with only a few skinny wooden walkways between lots of gleaming white boats, bobbing gently in the murky river. People on the boats were laughing, sporting fresh sunburns, and they looked relaxed even as they busied themselves unpacking things, untying things, and undoing things after a day's fishing. Mary looked around, not wanting to miss Jackmann coming in, and scanned the names of the moored boats. *Donna. Julie. Tiffany*; must be first, second, and third wife's names. There were bad puns, too: *Full of Ship. Sea More. Ocean's Eleven Grand*. And then the one she was looking for, already in: *Outta Here*. It was a white boat, about twenty feet long, with a matte finish and navy stripes along the side and it flew the American flag. An older man was unloading a spool of white rope off the boat and onto the dock. Jackmann.

Mary hurried down the walkway, pretending she wasn't a landlubber, and burst through a cyclone fence gate in defiance of the MEMBERS ONLY sign. She waved her hand to get Jackmann's attention. "Ahoy! Mr. Jackmann!" she called, caught up in the nautical spirit, but he didn't look up and the effort made her cheek wound throb. *Loser*. She tried again when she reached the back of his boat. "Mr. Jackmann!" Mary was almost breathless, and he finally raised his head.

Jackmann had a weathered tan that brought out the sea blue of his eyes, and he was tall and still fit, in a white polo shirt, raggedy shorts, and untied sneakers. He sported a bushy beard, a headful of thick, grayish hair, and forearms like Popeye. *Hot, for an old salt*, Mary thought, then stopped cruising a septuagenarian. "Excuse me, are you Floyd Jackmann?"

"Every day." Jackmann squinted at her, not unfriendly, merely puzzled. "Do I know you?"

"No. Your secretary told me you'd be here." Mary sized him up. He looked like a no-nonsense kind of guy and she was sick of lying. "My name's Mary, and it's important that I talk to you. I wanted to get some information about Giovanni Saracone."

"Take this can, would you?" Jackmann handed her a rusty blue Maxwell House coffee can sitting on the deck, next to a pile of other fishing gear and supplies. Mary accepted it, but it emitted such a stench, she had to look inside.

"Argh!" She jumped back in horror, almost dropping the can. Long alien-worms with zillions of legs slithered all over one another. One looked up at her with three little black eyes. "Gross! What are they?"

"Bloodworms. Don't put your hand in

there, hon. They attach right to ya."
Jackmann laughed with a smoker's throati-
ness. "Now, whaddaya want to know?"

"I understand you were at Mr. Saracone's
funeral lunch, and your secretary said you
two go way back. I was wondering if you
could tell me—"

"You want information, you can work for
it." Jackmann handed her a red Playmate
cooler, mercifully sealed. "Take this and set
it over there."

"Okay." Mary set the cooler down as instructed. "So how long did you know
Saracone?"

"Long time." Jackmann locked a white
plastic box fixed to the deck of the boat. In
front of the box was a blue padded driver's
seat, a blue steering wheel, and over it, a
panel of black control switches that read,
NAV AFT BILGE WASHDOWN ACC.

"Since the war?"

Jackmann's eyes flashed a minute, a surprised shot of blue. "Yeah."

"How did you know him? How did you
meet?"

"Everybody knew Gio. I was in college,
working part-time with my dad, outta the
shipyard. Gio was around all the time, with

the lunch truck." Jackmann handed her a rusty green box with a rusty handle, then pointed to the dock. "Tackle box goes over there."

Mary set it down with the other stuff, and it rattled. "Did you say lunch truck?" *Saracone had a lunch truck? Can you get to Birchrunville on a lunch truck?*

"You know, a lunch truck. Sold soda, egg sandwiches, and hoagies to the guys fishing off the docks. That's how hoagies got its name, you know." Jackmann went to the front of the boat and pulled a fishing rod from a chrome holder, one of four rods and holders affixed to the roof of a shelter over the driver's seat. The rods soared so high in the air it looked like they combed the clouds. "Guys sold them to the longshore-men and sailors down the old Navy Yard, off Hog Island. So they called 'em hoagies."

"Really?" The one thing about Philly that Mary hadn't known. It was a whole new world down here. She kept looking at the fishing rods. "Why do you have so many rods? You switch 'em around when you fish?"

"No, there's rod holders. The rods go in there when we drop anchor." Jackmann pointed to the chrome cups ringing the boat as he brought Mary the fishing rod, which was heavy as hell, with a cork handle and a very wiggly top. She took it, feeling vaguely like those guys who spin plates. Jackmann said, "Gio used to sell sandwiches, drinks, cigarettes, sodas. He charged too much for the smokes, which he boosted anyway."

Gio. "Did you know anyone named Amadeo Brandolini, from when you worked on the docks? He was older than you or Gio, by about twenty years."

Jackmann thought a minute, going back and sliding out the next rod. "No. Italian?"

"Yes, an immigrant. He didn't speak much English. He had a wife and son."

"Don't know him." Jackmann handed Mary the second rod, and she took it, discouraged.

Damn! It was a dry hole. Jackmann didn't know Amadeo. She set the rod down on the dock with the other one. "You sure? Did you fish in those days? In the late thirties, early forties?"

"Yep. Always did. Born on the water."

"Amadeo Brandolini was a fisherman, too."

"You're a lawyer, right?"

"I didn't know it showed."

Jackmann laughed thickly as he handed her the third rod, and Mary set it down, distracted. She couldn't just give up. It was her last lead.

"But Amadeo started a small fishing business. I don't know where exactly he fished, since it's all built up now, but I think it was right off the port."

"There were plenty of places to fish, then. Still are."

"Right on the Delaware?"

"Then, sure. Myself, I always fished in the bay, downriver." Jackmann retrieved the fourth rod, brought it to the back of the boat, and handed it to Mary. "The river takes you to the C & D canal, then down to the Chesapeake. But in the bay, you can get weakies, tons a weakies, now that they're back."

"Weakies?"

"Weakfish, like a sea trout. No pin bones, my wife grills them." Jackmann nodded. "I used to know a contractor, his father bought a house on the weakies he sold. There's stripers in the rips, too. It's the current from the ocean, and plenty of guys fish in the rocks, for tog."

Stripers? Rips? Tog? Okay, whatever. Mary set the rod down. "But what about the port? Could you fish off the port? Did people do that, before the war?"

"Sure. Then, you could fish right off the port. Lots of Italians from South Philly did that right off of Washington Avenue. I didn't know any of those guys. I was a college boy."

"But Saracone knew Amadeo. I'm thinking they knew each other from fishing together, or the lunch truck."

Jackmann snorted. "Had to be the truck. Gio didn't fish."

Mary blinked. "I saw a stuffed fish on the wall, in his den. It was big."

"Then he bought it."

Mary felt sure, now. Jackmann had the ring of authority. "Gio owned boats, though. Fishing boats."

"Sure. Boats weren't about fishing, for a guy like him. Boats were about showing off. The kinda boats he had anyway. Gio loved boats. He collected boats. Sold 'em used, kept buyin' more, until the end when he got sick." Jackmann closed the lid of the box, with a heavy *slam*. "His last boat was a Bertram 60. A sixty-footer. Staterooms, master bedroom, unbelievable. Beautiful yacht. The *Bella Melania.*"

"You went out with him on the boat?"

"Sure."

"You fished, he watched?"

"I fished, he drank my Bud."

Mary was trying to piece it together. "You think Saracone and Amadeo could have met because of the lunch truck?"

"Who's Amadeo?"

"Brandolini."

"Possible." Jackmann paused on the deck, resting a hand on his back and stretching it back and forth. "Gio went all along the river with the truck, and he spoke English and Italian. He was the friendly type, always with a big smile. So it's possible he got to know your friend, Brandolini, that way."

Mary considered it. It would explain a lot. How they knew each other even though Saracone didn't fish. She was trying not to be completely discouraged, but she didn't know much more than when she came. Jackmann stepped down, knelt on the deck, and opened a small hatch in the middle of the boat as Mary watched him, hating life. Then she blinked. The hatch was round and thick, about eight inches in diameter. Where had she seen that before? All of a sudden, she realized.

Amadeo's drawings. The circles on the papers in his wallet! Mary couldn't believe her eyes. She had forgotten about them. She pointed at the hatch. "What is that?"

"What's what?"

"That hatch!" *It was Amadeo's drawing, come to life! Or at least, to plastic!* Mary jumped into the boat, which rocked in response, and scrambled to kneel down on the deck over the hatch. Just like on the drawings, there was even a small steel catch on the side. Mary pressed it in and out. "Is this a hatch? What does it do?"

"It's a type of hatch. It's an inspection port. The fuel gauge is underneath."

"And the spring?" Mary pushed the catch in and out, and it sprang back each time. "This is a lock. It's automatic, this mechanism."

"Yeah. Keeps it watertight. Now I gotta go, hon."

"One minute." Mary closed the lid of the hatch and read the outside. Embossed on the top in plastic were two letters: GO. GO? *Go?*

"That's Gio's hatch."

"*What?*" Mary raised her eyes slowly, as it dawned on her. "*Gio's* hatch?"

"He named it after himself. Get it? GO."

"What do you mean by 'Gio's hatch'?"

"Gio invented it, the lucky bastard. Got a patent on it." Jackmann bent over and closed the hatch. "There's no patent anymore, it's just the brand name, GO. But it's the top of the line in that type of hatch."

"Saracone *invented* it?" Mary repeated in disbelief.

"Yeh. It's used on fishing boats, then got picked up for commercial boats of all kinds. It was the first to have the automatic closer. It was such an innovation, Gio was able to sell licenses on the patent and get a grant back on each one, giving him the royalties and the credit on the ap. Helluva business-man, Gio was." Jackmann clucked. "I don't think he worked a day in his life after that thing got patented, way back in—"

"1942?"

"Right."

"He *patented* it." Mary came fully up to speed, flashing on the laundry line in Amadeo's backyard. It was practical, useful, ingenious. An *invention*. Amadeo was the mechanical one and he was the fisherman, too. He had three fishing boats when Saracone was driving a lunch truck. In one blinding moment, it all fell into place. Amadeo had invented this hatch, and Saracone had strangled him for it, under a lonely tree in Montana, in the midst of a world war.

"Yeah." Jackmann shook his head. "I never woulda thought Gio was the mechanical type, but there you have it. Probably made fifty mil off that thing."

"*Fifty million dollars?*"

"Easy, and Justin told me at the funeral that now that his father's gone, he's gonna sell the whole shebang to Reinhardt."

"What do you mean?"

"Reinhardt's the second biggest hatch maker. The competition. Justin told me he's selling the trademark, the rights, and all. Next week. They'll put the GO hatch out under the Reinhardt trademark, for a boatload of dough. It's one big payday for the kid."

Not if I can help it. Finally, Mary had figured out why Saracone had committed murder.

Now all she had to figure out was what to do about it.

And go do it.

Right now.

FORTY

Mary was back in her semi-repaired war room at Rosato & Associates, where it had all started, typing furiously online. She had practically run here from the marina and hit the office on fire. She still couldn't believe it. She had figured it out. She had Saracone. She would bring him to justice. She would set it right. For Amadeo. It was after hours, and the office was empty. The glass window behind her was black and opaque, and the conference room reeked of stale coffee. Mary had already called in reinforcements, but for now the only sound was the clacking of her keyboard.

The website of the United States Patent and Trademark Office came onto her laptop screen, and she clicked to Search Patents, where she was stumped. The search for issued patents by keyword went back only to 1976. The GO hatch would have been patented in 1942 or thereabouts. *Damn*. Mary had learned enough about patents in law school to know that they were frequently altered and improved, in some cases to extend their life past the permissible term of seventeen years. She moved the mouse and in the box, typed: "Saracone" in "all fields" AND "hatch" in "all fields." Onto the screen popped:

Results of Search in 1976 to present db for:
Saracone AND hatch: 24 patents.
Hits 1 through 24 out of 24

Bingo! The screen showed twenty-four listings, which set forth the patent number, the title, and a short description of the patent. She skimmed the first four, but none of them seemed to have anything to do with hatches. Still it looked like Saracone had been busy, if it was the same Saracone. Mary clicked the first listing and started reading. It was a patent issued to Giovanni

Saracone just last year, for a larger hatch than the one on the boat deck, and one that had the same configuration as the one on the boat deck. And according to the site, the GO hatch was used on bunkers in disaster areas.

She clicked the next patent, also issued to Giovanni Saracone, the year before. It was a patent for the same hatch, now issued to keep light out of certain industrial applications, such as commercial darkrooms. She read on, clicking each one, and in time discovered the myriad applications of the original patent: pressure relief hatches, vehicle sunroofs, telescopic winch drives, whatever that was, and underground shelters. She thought a minute. Saracone didn't manufacture any of these things—or indeed anything at all—which meant that he had to have sold licenses for all of these doohickeys to others to manufacture.

Mary could barely wrap her mind around it. There had to be hundreds of licenses, each requiring the license holder to pay money to the Saracones for the use of the invention. It was the key she had been looking for. No wonder they were rich as sin. Licenses for these applications—in addition to the marine applications from the earlier patent—would bring in millions and millions of dollars. First to Giovanni Saracone, then to Justin.

For doing absolutely nothing.

Then she made another connection. Saracone hadn't filed the original patent application on his own; he couldn't have. Mary was willing to bet that it had been prepared and filed by Joe Giorno. They had been in it together, from the beginning. That was why Giorno made Amadeo the gift of the house on Nutt Street and later went to Missoula to tell him about his wife's death. Giorno and Saracone were pretending to be his friends, cultivating him for the invention. They were smiling, all the while they buried a knife in his back. Then Amadeo's son Tony had died, both ordering and funding the lawsuit by his will. Frank Cavuto must have taken over for Giorno, and when Mary started to expand her investigation into Amadeo's death and close in on the truth, Frank must have panicked, and they'd killed him.

The scope of the scheme took Mary's breath away. No wonder that Giovanni, stricken with guilt, had sat up on his very deathbed at seeing her, an avenging angel.

He had carried that terrible secret his whole life—murdered his friend for his inventiveness, for his creativity, and stolen it to further his own ends. And Justin had to know that his father hadn't invented a deck hatch, or anything else over the years. What had Justin said, before he hit her?

Mind your own business.

Mary clicked to the oldest patent on the screen, in 1976. At the end, it contained a reference to the original patent and its patent number. She clicked the blue link and held her breath. A patent, with a series number in the two millions, appeared on the screen:

UNITED STATES PATENT OFFICE, it read in the center, and underneath, the title of the patent was **Hatch Frame and Hatch Cover,** next to the name of the inventor: **Giovanni Saracone.**

Mary felt her breath catch. She had been right. Saracone had killed Amadeo for his invention, then patented it. She had it in front of her and she still couldn't believe it. She felt tears come, with anger and with relief. She had been right, which was amazing, because she was never right about anything.

Her gaze fell on the first line under the title:

Application: July 27, 1942.

Mary blinked. Why did that sound familiar? Then she knew. She searched through the file on the conference table and found the accordion of the documents and notes she'd brought from Missoula. She pulled out the death certificate and double-checked the line:

Date of Death: July 17, 1942.

My God. Saracone had killed Amadeo and only ten days later had told Giorno to file the application for the patent in his name. A patent application was so technical, it would take months to draft, and they probably had to engage a patent lawyer, at least as a consultant. Saracone and Giorno had to have been planning this for a long time, maybe years. Then World War II and the internment intervened, which Saracone exploited to his advantage. He used the camp as the perfect opportunity to get away with murder.

Mary's eyes blurred with bitterness, then she refocused on the first lines of the patent description: **"My invention, which in gen-**

eral, relates to the closures has been devised as a deck hatch. . . .”

His invention? She read the rest with a growing fury. Saracone had stolen the invention, every word, and claimed it for himself. She read to the end and clicked onto the exhibits, which were two technical drawings. They were Amadeo's circles, with the funny closing on the side. Now she knew it was a special type of closing, so original and practical that it was patentable. And Saracone had exploited the patent and its many applications, from shelters to telescopes. It was ingenious, and evil. And at the bottom right of the second page of the drawings, Mary's supposition about the lawyering was confirmed by the signature:

Inventor, Giovanni Saracone. By Joseph Giorno, Attorney.

She leaned forward, clicked back to home, and searched under Patent. In a few clicks, the words of the patent statute came onto the screen:

Whoever invents or discovers any new and useful process, machine, manufacture, or composition of matter, or any new and useful im-

provement thereof, may obtain a patent therefor. . . .

Mary read it again and again, inspired. The law had a force of its own, even a beauty. Its letter was clear, as was its intent. She was finally glad she had become a lawyer, because she knew just what to do next.

Less than an hour later, she was writing like a girl in a fever, surrounded by open law books, photocopied cases, and a stack of tentative exhibits. She had written two pages and only had fifty-six more to go. It would take all night, but she would get it done. Most lawyers would have balked at the task, but not Mary.

"You need a break, Mare," said a cheery voice from the threshold. It was Judy, grinning in her hot pink sweatshirt, clashing cobalt sweatpants, and red clogs with black fake- ostrich dots, all topped by a Stanford backward-baseball cap. Her ensemble was Cirque du Soleil meets Best-Friend-Forever, and Mary didn't say a thing, because Judy had dropped everything to come and help her. Also she was carrying a brown bag that smelled like take-out lo mein, chicken curry, cold sesame noodles, and spring rolls.

Mary smiled. She couldn't remember the last time she'd eaten. "I love you, you know that?"

"About time you realized it, girl," Judy said, with a crooked grin, and set the bag on the table. "Let's eat."

In time, Mary filled Judy in on all the details of her plan, the lawyers got down to work, and the night sky outside the conference room window lightened to streaky gray. The take-out containers littering the table were joined by Styrofoam coffee cups, empty Diet Coke cans, discarded cellophane from two packs of chocolate Tastykakes, a tiny plastic tub of Light 'n Fit strawberry yogurt, and an organic apple, which came prebruised, so Mary refused to eat it. By dawn, Judy was getting tired and looked up, red-eyed from the law books.

"You know what we need, Mare?" she asked.

"Fruit with pesticides."

"No."

Mary thought of the case. "A miracle?"

"No. Tunes! We need TUUUUUUNES!" Judy yelled, throwing up her arms, because she was beyond punchy. She leapt out of her swivel chair, leaving it spinning, flew out of the conference room, and before Mary could protest, returned with a white Bose CD player from her office and a stack of slippery CDs, which she set on the credenza. "Tunes have arrived!"

Mary peered over her laptop with suspicion. "Got any Sinatra?"

"No way. I have Steven Tyler and Aerosmith! Yeeeesss!" Judy giggled, slipping a black CD into the tray, hitting some buttons, and cranking up the volume. An earsplitting guitar riff blasted the conference room, ten thousand drums thundered, and Judy started dancing around, shaking her tight butt in her loose sweatpants, and clicking off her clogs so she could jump around better. Aerosmith started singing at full volume.

"This doesn't sound like 'Night and Day'!" Mary shouted, covering her ears, but Judy segued into dancing like an Egyptian, boogying around the room.

"It's 'Dude Looks Like a Lady!' Come on, get up and shake your booty!"

Mary scoffed, then reconsidered. She needed the exercise and she couldn't work with all that noise anyway. She pushed back the laptop, got on her feet, kicked off her pumps, and shook her butt as hard as she could in a skirt from Brooks Brothers. And the rock music wasn't bad at all. He was no Francis Albert, but Steven Tyler rocked!

Later, Mary became aware that Judy had fallen silent and she looked across the table. Judy was buckling her lower lip, eyeing what she'd written on her screen. Under the Stanford cap, her brow knit unhappily. Mary knew it wasn't just fatigue. "What's the matter, Jude?" she asked, setting down a warm Diet Coke.

Judy looked up. "I'm worried."

"About what?"

"About you, about this." Judy slid off her baseball cap, revealing a flat ring around her shorn blonde hair. She spiked it up with her hand, and Mary knew she was stalling, because she never cared about hat head. Judy cleared her throat. "Listen, let me say right out that I think it's great that you put all this together, and figured out what that snake and his son did."

"Thanks."

"You went all the way to Montana, and I'm not denigrating that. I told you how cool that was."

"Hold the positive reinforcement. Just give."

Judy sighed. "But I'm not sure about this new idea of yours. I'm not sure it holds up to a standard cost-benefit analysis. Can I be your sounding board?"

"Of course."

"Let's review." Judy straightened up. "Cost. Bennie will hate this idea."

"True."

"Cost. You probably need her permission to do it and you're not asking."

"Right."

"Cost. She could fire you for it."

"And the bad news?"

Judy smiled, but it faded quickly. "Cost, and worst cost of all, it could be really dangerous. Justin Saracone has a fortune to protect, and the power and means to come at you. Even if Chico's out of the picture, Justin has the dough to hire somebody else. He's a killer, Mare. Look at Keisha, she's still in a coma."

"I know." Mary felt her stomach tense. She had called the hospital during the dinner break, and Bill had said Keisha's prognosis wasn't good. The longer she stayed under, the worse it got. It made Mary feel guilty, and angry, all over again. "All the more reason to do this."

"Maybe, but it means it's definitely dangerous."

"Okay, it's a little dangerous."

"Or a lot."

"Okay, a lot," Mary admitted. Even though she felt a tremor of fear, she was determined, but she didn't tell Judy about Mrs. Nyquist. It would be Mary's replacement secret, because now she could fly with abandon.

"So, you would agree, there are costs to this idea of yours. Great big downside?"

"Me, dead. That can't be good."

Judy couldn't manage a smile, which showed what a good friend she was. "Now we come to the benefits. I don't mean to hurt your feelings, Mare, but I think you're gonna lose."

Ouch. "You do?"

"Yes. Honestly, it's a high standard of proof at this stage of the game, and you don't have much. I'll buy that you have irreparable harm. The sale of rights to Reinhardt and the change in trademark would render Brandolini's patent worthless, over time. But you can't show you'll win on the merits."

"Yes, I can."

"Try it on me, try it right here." Judy leaned back in the chair and put her Stanford cap back on. "I'll be the judge. Judge Judy, get it?"

"Calm yourself."

"And suck up a lot. We judges like that."

"Please." Mary stood up and gathered her exhibits. "I'll keep it short. Basically, I'm asking the court for a temporary restraining order. I want the court to restrain, or stop, Justin Saracone and Saracone Enterprises from selling the rights to the patent and trademark to Reinhardt and ultimately, from getting any more royalties from licenses of the hatch patent or its improvements, because they obtained the original patent by fraud."

Judy nodded. "So to get a TRO, or a temporary restraining order, you have to show that when this case goes to trial, you have a reasonable chance of success on the merits. In other words, you have to prove that Giovanni Saracone stole the invention."

Mary tilted her head. "You talkin' down to me, Your Honor?"

"I'm the judge. It's my job."

"Okay. First, I prove that Amadeo Brandolini registered as an enemy alien. Exhibit A." Mary set down a stamped copy of his alien registration card. "Second, I prove that he was arrested and sent to Fort Missoula. I can't prove it through me, because I'm not a fact witness, but you can. You saw the FBI memo, too." Mary set out an affidavit she'd drafted about the FBI memo from the National Archives as Exhibit B. "Third, I prove that Saracone was sent to the same camp, and that they knew each other in the camp." Mary set out Exhibits C and D, which were copies of the photos she'd gotten from Fort Missoula's archives. "I'll authenticate them by affidavit of the museum director. Are you dazzled yet?"

Judy smiled. "Keep going, counsel."

"Fourth, I prove that Amadeo died by asphyxiation in the camp, on July 17, 1942." Mary set down the death certificate as Exhibit E. "Fifth, I prove that Giovanni Saracone was the only other person with him when he was asphyxiated." Mary set down a piece of paper for Exhibit F. "Pretend this is an affidavit from Mr. Milton, which will be faxed to me tomorrow morning."

"Better be. Blank paper carries no weight with me."

"Remember, for these purposes, I don't have to prove that Saracone murdered Amadeo, which he did. It's not a murder trial, it's a civil case of fraud. *Capisce?*"

"Then why are we in federal court? Fraud is a state court cause of action, counsel."

"Under the Patent Act, the provision is 'correction of a named inventor.' And we're squarely in dicta in *Stark v. Advanced Magnetics*. Also there's ancillary jurisdiction because of the amount in controversy. You want me to get technical, Judge?"

"I'm already bored. Proceed, counsel. You got bigger problems than jurisdiction."

"Now. Sixth, I prove that Giovanni Saracone, who was with Amadeo in the camp, filed for a patent application roughly ten days after Amadeo was killed." Mary set down a copy of the patent application for the hatch as Exhibit G. "Seventh, I prove that Amadeo made a number of drawings of a marine hatch, which were given to me by his previous lawyer, Frank Cavuto." Mary set down another blank piece of paper as

Exhibit H. "This will be another affidavit from you, detailing what the drawings look like and that they were stolen from our offices during a break-in."

Judy cocked an eyebrow. "You gonna question me on the witness stand, counsel?"

"Yes, and you'd better behave. I can't sign it because lawyers make bad witnesses and they get disbarred besides." Mary cleared her throat. "Eight, I refer to your affidavit and prove that Amadeo Brandolini's drawings were identical to those submitted with the patent filed by Giovanni Saracone." Mary set down a copy of the patent application, as Exhibit I. "Finally, I prove, by a copy of the police report, which we'll get in the morning, that my office was broken into, which is why I can't produce those drawings in court." Mary sat down a piece of paper as Exhibit J. "Finally, I prove that Saracone had a lunch truck and was not a fisherman. Supported by a one-paragraph affidavit to that effect, faxed to me by my new best friend. Mr. Jackmann. That's all he will say on the subject, and I'm only getting that much because Justin has made more enemies than Satan. The acorn doesn't fall far." She looked across the messy table expectantly. "Well?"

Judy had on one of those let-her-down-easy faces. "You still have no proof that Saracone stole the invention from Brandolini, and that is the critical fact. I mean, you can assert all you want, but without the drawings, you don't even have a prayer."

No. "The drawings weren't proof anyway. Amadeo hadn't signed or dated them, and I couldn't authenticate them even if he had. I have no other sample of his writing, except the *X* on his alien registration card. But I *can* prove the fact that they were stolen, and that fits perfectly."

"That's not enough, Mare," Judy said softly.

"It has to be. I have to make this work. I know I'm right, Jude. I know I can win."

"You can't."

Mary flinched. "I can. At least I have to try."

"No, you don't. Not with the stakes this high. You're too wrapped up in this case, you have been from the beginning. Be logical." Judy spread her palms. "Why take such a big risk, if you're only gonna lose?"

"Do you fight only the fights you're gonna

win, Jude?" Mary shot back, then she heard herself, and to her surprise, she sounded like she was actually making sense. It came as a revelation, suddenly lifting her spirits. "I mean, if you know you're gonna win, it's not really a fight."

Judy sat back and broke into a slowly growing smile. "You know, you just said something that was either incredibly dumb or incredibly smart."

Mary laughed and slipped on her cowboy hat. "We'll see, lil' pretty. We'll see."

FORTY-ONE

At noon, Mary stuck her head out of the conference room door and looked right and left. No one in the hall. No one in the waiting room. Everyone was at lunch. Most important of all, the reception desk was empty and Marshall was nowhere in sight. She was the one who'd tell Bennie on them and she must have gone to lunch, too. The coast was clear.

"*Andiamo,*" Mary said, gesturing. According to plan, she had one stack of finished papers under her arm, and Judy had the other, and they hustled through the empty reception area to the elevator and hit the Down button.

"We did it!" Judy cheered, but it caught in

her throat when the elevator doors opened and Marshall was standing inside.

Busted! Mary stayed calm. Judy stayed hyper.

"Hello, ladies," Marshall said, her eyes narrowing to secretarial slits. She stepped out of the elevator cab and intentionally blocked the doors, which slid closed behind her. She looked unusually stern this morning, in a severe braid and a black shirtdress with a white collar that reminded Mary of every nun she'd ever had. Marshall folded her arms. "Where were you going?"

"Out," Mary answered, and Judy added:

"Fine, thanks."

Marshall cocked her head. "What are you up to?"

"Nothing," Mary answered, and Judy added:

"Not today, thanks."

Marshall looked from one to the other. "Why are you wearing stupid hats?"

The cowboy hat! Mary had forgotten she had it on. Judy wore her Stanford cap. "For attitude?" she answered, and Judy added:

"I always wear stupid hats."

Marshall put her hands on her hips. "This can't be good. Both of you locked in the

conference room all morning, with chocolate and Joe Perry. This can't be good. I'm
responsible for you guys when Bennie's not
here, you know, and she's going to be calling in again. You going to tell me what's going on, or do I have to beat it out of you?"

"It's better if you don't know just yet,"
Mary answered, and Judy added:

"Better for us, that is."

Marshall frowned at Judy. "Hey, Miss, I
held your calls all morning, and you have a
ton of mail on my desk, some of it on those
cases of Bennie's that you're supposed to
be watching. Mr. Reitman called twice."
Marshall turned to Mary and began counting off on her fingers. "And as for you,
you've got phone messages from MacIntire,
that reporter, two from a Gail Lasko at the
Daily News, one from Steve Levy on
Channel Ten, one from the *Legal Intelli-
gencer,* one from COURT-TV, one from your
Uncle Joey, and a bunch of other personal
ones. Some have been on my desk for
days, with your mail."

"Sorry, gotta go." Mary hit the elevator
button and the doors slid open immediately,
proving that her cause was just, if a little
wacky and dangerous. She bolted into the

elevator and hit the button to close the door. "Don't worry, Marshall. We'll explain later!"

"Don't wait up!" Judy added before she slipped inside, the doors closed, and the elevator spirited them away.

By the time they had gotten downstairs and left the building through the back alley to avoid the press, Mary had lost her sense of humor and remembered her original purpose. She had made a plan and was executing it, and they had to part company among the rusty blue Dumpsters that lined the cruddy brick alley, which smelled coincidentally of chicken curry.

Mary gave Judy a big hug. "Thanks for all your help. I really owe you."

Judy hugged her back, then released her, her brow dark with doubt. "You really have to go alone, Mare? I could go with you. It's safer if we go together."

"Nah. It's a two-pronged attack. We have to hit at the same time." Mary peeked out of the alley for any stray reporters. There weren't any; just the typical crowded sidewalk at noontime on a workday, with businessmen and women walking in groups, smoking, laughing, and talking on cell phones. She could blend right in and go. "I'll be fine."

"But I have the easy job. You have the dangerous job."

"That's as it should be. It's my case, and my score to settle." Mary managed a smile. "On your cases, you get to keep the dangerous jobs."

Judy eyed her unhappily. "Just be careful, okay? Do what you have to do and get out of there."

"I will." Mary shooed her out of the alley. "Now, skedaddle! You go left, I'll go right."

"You're sure you'll be okay?" Judy said, but Mary only gave her a gentle push in response, and she hit the sidewalk running and flowed into the foot traffic, manila envelope in hand.

Good girl. Mary tucked her papers under her arm and hurried out of the alley.

It was late afternoon by the time Mary arrived at the house, and she felt grim, professional, and purposeful, her anger simmering in her chest. There was no one on the exclusive tree-lined street, and she pulled into the driveway in front of the scrollwork S. She set her jaw and took off her cowboy hat, since she already had enough attitude. She eyed Justin Saracone's property through the wrought-iron bars.

Saracone, you bastard.

The fieldstone mansion looked still in the sun, and the property was quieter than the other day, though not deserted. The front door was closed, but a sprinkler system was running on the vast lawn, watering the already lush bushes on the perimeter. On the circular driveway sat a shiny red Hummer and a black Mercedes sedan, either of which qualified as pretentious enough to be Justin Saracone's. Mary hoped he was home. She cruised up to a squawk box on a gooseneck stem and hit the black intercom button.

"Yes?" A man answered.

It was him. Mary would never forget that voice. Her mouth would have gone dry, if it hadn't gone dry three exits ago. Not with fear this time, but with fury. "This is Mary DiNunzio and I'm here to see you, Justin."

The box went silent, and she worried fleetingly that he wouldn't let her in. She had figured that anybody who wanted to hit you himself was spoiling for a fight, and now, so was she. But in the next instant, there was a *clunk* as the iron gates parted slowly, dividing the S in perfect halves. Mary drove through, parked behind the Hummer, and cut the ignition. She grabbed her envelope and slipped a tiny green spray can of mace into her jacket pocket, just in case. No cowgirl went anywhere without her mace.

She strode up the brick pavers and knocked on a tall front door of dark wood, with a frosted glass window she couldn't see through. In a minute the door was opened and she felt the chill of central air-conditioning. On the rose marble threshold stood Justin Saracone.

"Hello, Mary," Justin said coolly, his dark eyes glittering and his mouth a mirthless smile. He wore an open shirt of a silky fabric with European vents and a black belt with gray trousers and expensive tasseled loafers. He extended a hand, and Mary put the manila envelope in it.

"Consider yourself served." Mary found herself shaking with controlled anger. "This complaint is being filed in court as we speak, on behalf of the estate of Amadeo Brandolini. I'm suing you and Saracone Investments for fifty million dollars, the profits you and your father got by stealing Amadeo's patent in 1942 and licensing it illegally since then."

"You can't be serious." Justin's smile stayed plastered on his face, as if he were humoring her, which only made her madder.

"I'm also seeking a TRO to stop you from selling the rights under the patent and licenses to Reinhardt and from destroying the GO trademark. All of that would render Amadeo's patent unmarketable and valueless, and that's not happening as long as I draw breath. By the time this is over, I'll make sure you don't collect another penny in royalties for the illegal licensing of the original patent, or any of its applications."

"You don't learn, do you?" Justin's smile faded to the sneer she had seen right before he hit her, and Mary felt a new power surge through her body.

"Actually, I do, and I also fly on planes, but that's neither here nor there. I'm turning off the faucet on you. No more money, as of tomorrow. The hearing's at ten. See you in court, pal. And by the way, if I lose tomorrow, I'll take it to trial, and if I lose there, I'll appeal it. I'll never let you go, Justin.

Cowboy up, pal. You're in for a long, *long* ride."

"Are you done with your little speech?" Justin clapped.

His arrogance sent Mary's blood boiling over. She flashed on him punching her, and before she knew what she was doing, she balled her hand, hauled off, and hit him square in the face, smashing her hand into his obnoxious sneer.

"Agh!" Justin cried out, in surprise and pain. He staggered backward, losing his balance, pinwheeling his arms in his fancy shirt, and in the next minute, he slipped on his slick marble entrance hall and fell flat on his designer ass.

"Next time you hit a girl, remember that we hit back," Mary said with a smile, and she closed the door on him.

Then she ran like hell.

Okay, it really really hurts to hit someone with your hand.

Mary drove with her left hand on the steering wheel while she opened and closed her right hand, trying unsuccessfully to make a fist. Her fingers had swollen quickly, turning pink, and her middle knuckle killed her. She didn't know if she had broken it, but it al-most didn't matter. She felt high, adrenal-ized, exhilarated. Filing lawsuits only went so far. You should get to hit somebody back. You might even have a First Amend-ment right to hit somebody back.

Mary considered it, keeping an eye on the road, and luckily the traffic was light, since nobody was driving into the city at the end of the business day. She had so much more to do. She got off 202 North and negotiated the King of Prussia construction that fun-neled her onto the expressway, going east to Philly. She whizzed past an orange blur of Home Depot, Chili's, and an Outback Steak-house, and accelerated.

Time for stage two of the plan. Mary had a zillion cell phone calls to make, starting with her new best friend. She fumbled with her Filofax, managed to find the number, then pressed it into her phone with a combina-tion of teeth, nose, and little finger.

"Mac?" she said, when he picked up. "Jim MacIntire, from the *News*? This is Mary DiNunzio, returning your call."

"Mary!" the reporter exclaimed. "I need to talk to you. I can't get over what you said to me, what you think of me! What's going on?"

"Here's the scoop, Jim," she began, then launched into the details of the suit papers Judy had just filed for her, including everything she had learned about the original patent that Giovanni Saracone had stolen and how Justin Saracone continued to profit. She answered every question as fully as possible, defaming both the living and the dead, because it only suited her purposes if Justin countersued her for defamation. She ended by telling Mac to be at the hearing for the restraining order.

"You're going for a TRO?" he repeated, salivating audibly.

"Be there or be square," Mary answered, then hung up with her teeth. She consulted her Filofax for the next reporter's number, decreased her speed in a concession to auto safety, and plugged in the next number.

"Shannon," she said when he picked up, then she told him the whole story, too, beginning at the beginning and ending with the TRO hearing at ten tomorrow.

"I'll be there," the reporter promised, and after that she took her life in her hands and called five other reporters, then she hung up, satisfied that the word would spread. Telling a reporter was almost as good as telling Skinny Uncle Joey, and Mary wanted to make as much noise as possible. She wanted the whole scheme brought to light and the Saracones dragged along, kicking and screaming. The Reinhardt deal would collapse, and as soon as the licensees found out that the validity of the original patent was being questioned, as well as subsequent patents relying on it, they could stop doing business with Justin. The licenses would fall like dominoes. Justin's world—and his income—would collapse and end. One way or the other, she was taking him down.

Mary switched into the fast lane and was about to check on Keisha when her cell phone started ringing. She picked it up, recognized the number on the lighted display, and felt her heart plummet to her pumps. How could she be so happy and so unhappy in the same moment? "Hi, Bennie," she said into the phone.

"DiNunzio, what's up? You okay, or still upset over Cavuto?"

"No, I'm not." *Frank seems like years ago, and I have so much more to be upset about.*

"And Brandolini's doing what?"

"It's quiet right now." *Or being filed in federal court.*

"You're letting it go?"

"Absolutely. It's gone." *What had Judy said? Smooth as glass.*

"Then you're all ready."

"Ready for what?"

"Don't tell me you forgot!"

"Forgot what?" Mary asked miserably.

FORTY-TWO

The restaurant in Fairmount turned out to be dark, smoky, and crowded, putting Mary in an even worse mood. Another blind date was the last thing she wanted right now, with her hand killing her, a TRO hearing to prepare for, and a night's sleep to catch up on, but she had no choice. Bennie had set it up a few weeks ago with a good friend of hers named Gary Haddon, and Mary had forgotten about it completely. She couldn't have cancelled this late without arousing the boss's suspicion. Or her fury.

She glanced around the packed bar, looking for Gary. He should be here already, since she was almost twenty minutes late. She had wasted so much time at home, trying on different outfits, finally deciding on a little black dress and black heels. She'd even changed her purse to match her outfit, which was one of those things that women thought essential and men never noticed. Mary wanted a good report card from this guy, even if she wasn't looking for Mr. Right. Him, she had already met and married. Nobody gets two Mr. Rights in her life, even if she's a good Catholic.

Mary didn't see Gary at the bar. Bennie had said he was hot, hot, hot; a tall, thirty-five-year-old lawyer with black hair and an incredibly hunky body, because he was the Vesper crew's stroke. Bennie had said that meant he was the best rower in the boat, as if Mary cared. He was supposed to be wearing a dark polo shirt and biceps. She peered though the carcinogens for dark hair and a dark shirt, but she didn't see him. Maybe he was waiting for her at a table. The dining section of the restaurant looked like it was toward the back.

She waded into the crowd, ignoring the degrading sensation that men were looking her over, and the equally degrading sensation that they weren't.

"Can I get you a drink?" asked a man to

her left, and Mary looked over. He was tall, but skinny and bald. Not Gary Haddon.

"Uh, no, thanks. I'm meeting someone."

"Maybe next time?"

"Mrphm," she answered, just to be nice. Then a man turned to look at her from the far side of the bar, catching her eye. He was about thirty-five years old, tall, with thick, dark hair. He wore a dark polo shirt and had the requisite musculature. Gary Haddon. *Wow!* This guy *was* seriously hot, if you happened to have a sex drive, which Mary didn't. She gave him a little wave with her good hand, and he waved back, then got up from the bar. She squeezed her way over, extending her good hand when she reached him. "Gary Haddon?"

"Mary? I'm Gary." Gary smiled almost shyly, which she found instantly cute. He was a great height, maybe six two, and when he shook her hand, his grip felt warm and strong. "Nice to meet you."

"You, too. Sorry I'm late."

"No sweat."

"Did you make a reservation or was I supposed to?"

"I think you were supposed to."

Argh. "Sorry. Please don't tell Bennie."

"No sweat."

Mary decided he was big on *no sweat*. Gary had a jock-y way about him for a lawyer, like Bennie. She could see why they'd be friends, even if Bennie's biceps were bigger.

"Maybe they'll have a table anyway," Gary said, and they both looked at the dining section. There were about thirty tables and all of them were taken, to a one. Mary hid her dismay. This date would never begin, so it couldn't end. Still, Gary seemed nice and he was really good-looking. For a stroke.

"Sorry, I should have called."

"Forget it. I'll check the wait." Gary left her and wedged his way to a gorgeous hostess, who held the menus under her ample breasts, like push-up menus. Mary watched Gary speak to her, and he didn't seem to notice the cleavage display. Nevertheless, she countered with a matching-purse display as he returned, his expression unhappy. "Bad news. The wait is an hour, maybe more."

Blind date hell. "Oh no."

"I'm too hungry to wait."

Good. Let's call it a night.

"I say we find another restaurant."

Oh. "Uh, okay, it's too smoky here any-way."

"I hate smoke, too. I quit smoking."

Me, too. Wonder how he feels about Sinatra. Or Aerosmith. "Where else can we go? I don't know this neighborhood that well. This is Bennie's turf."

"I don't know it either, but we can go any-where. I have a car. Come with me." Gary turned around and plunged into the crowd, reaching back to clasp Mary by her good hand.

Hand holding? Mary let herself be tugged along, even though hand holding was a boyfriend thing, not a blind date thing. Still, it wasn't an altogether unpleasant feeling. For once, she didn't have to be in charge, and Gary took over very naturally. Maybe it was a stroke thing. Gary had them outside in no time, and Mary breathed in a gulp of fresh air. It was a lovely evening, the sky over the city darkening. Rush-hour traffic had died down, and there were only a few cars on the street. Just the same, Mary looked around, tense. There was no Escalade in sight, or anybody who looked like Chico or Justin driving any of the other cars.

"My car's down the street," Gary said. He released her hand, which she appreciated. A gentleman.

"Great." Mary fell into step beside him. He was wearing tan slacks and loafers, and she took two little strides to his one long one, feeling like a windup doll.

"So, tell me about yourself, Mary."

"Oh, there's nothing to tell. I work for Bennie, I live in town." *And I hate talking about myself.* "How about you?"

"Ha!" Gary walked with his head cocked, at listening angle. "You think you're getting off that easy?"

Mary laughed. "I know I am. Now, let's talk about you."

Gary smiled. "So, you're stubborn."

"And you're perceptive. Unfortunately." Mary laughed again, vaguely aware that she might be flirting. But for once, she didn't tense up. Maybe because she was outside? Maybe it was okay to flirt outside, where the flirting went into the air and didn't land anywhere? At least it was dark. She tried not to think about it. "What kind of law do you practice, Gary? Bennie didn't say."

"You know, regular."

Mary smiled. "You mean general practice?"

"No, I mean regular practice. Yes, I'm a regular lawyer. A regular guy." Gary grinned again. They had reached his car, an older bronze Lexus, parked at the head of the line. He opened the car door for her grandly. "I drive a regular car. I even have a regular dog at home. Didn't Bennie tell you?"

"Not a golden retriever, I hope. Our firm is lousy with 'em."

"No, a mutt. A regular mutt."

"What's his name?"

"Joe. What else?"

Mary laughed as she climbed into the car and Gary closed the door gently. The Lexus interior was tan and smelled faintly of aftershave. A Norah Jones CD had been tossed onto the console and the cloth upholstery remained remarkably unfurry for a dog owner. "Either you're a very neat guy or you don't let your dog in the car," she said when he climbed in the driver's side.

"All of the above." Gary turned on the ignition, gave the car some gas, and pulled out of the space. "So, you're from South Philly, right?"

"Right." *You gotta problem with that?*

"I love South Philly. We can eat down there if you want to. The Saloon, if you're feeling classy, or Marra's. South Philly Bar & Grill. Even Triangle Tavern."

Mary smiled. "Any one of those is fine." *And not a website among them.*

"How about Marra's?"

"I love Marra's."

"Me, too. It's a *regular* place." Gary smiled, turning left onto the Ben Franklin Boulevard, where the traffic got heavier, funneling out of the city. They rounded Eakins Oval in front of the Art Museum, and Mary watched a herd of joggers running back from the river. A few couples walked together, carrying shopping bags, and businesspeople who worked late walked home, bearing briefcases or talking on the cell. It was a warm Spring night, and Mary pushed the button to open the window.

"I just put on the air conditioning." Gary looked over. "Unless you want the windows open."

"No, that's okay."

Gary turned the wheel, and the muscles in his forearm actually rippled. "You know, Bennie didn't tell me you were so *hot*."

Yeowch! Mary felt herself flushing. She

was suddenly uncomfortable, being so close to him in the car, with him rippling and flirting. Plus they weren't outside anymore, so there was no place for the flirting to go. Especially with the window closed. She felt nervous again as the Lexus picked up speed and curved onto the ramp for the expressway.

"I'll take the expressway. It's faster to hop on here and get off on Oregon." Gary rested his large hand on the steering wheel and refocused on his driving for an awkwardly silent stretch. The car accelerated. Everybody always sped on this stretch of the expressway, near the old Vare Street exit, because they were leaving the city's congestion for the open road. Mary's gaze fell on the rearview mirror on her side of the car. In the darkness, she could see part of the chrome grille of a dark sedan, coming up behind them, fast. She couldn't see the whole car in her parallax view, but she felt a tiny tremor run up her spine.

"Gary." Mary edged up in her seat. "You see that car behind us?"

"The black?" His attention shifted to the rearview mirror. "Yeah."

"It's going kind of fast, isn't it?"

"No, not really. You gotta keep up with the speed of traffic. My dad always says that."

"But I think he's going way too fast. He's tailgating you."

"Not really. Relax."

"I can't." Mary couldn't see the driver in her mirror, so she turned around in her seat, straining against the shoulder harness. On top of the grille glinted the slivery emblem of a Mercedes-Benz. *Justin has a black Mercedes.* "It's a Mercedes!"

"Right. An SL. What a ride. If it's the 500, it has a five-liter engine. One of the most powerful cars on the road."

Oh, great. Mary was trying not to panic. The Mercedes was speeding up to them, but she couldn't see the driver's face in the darkness. "Is it a man or a woman driving? Can you tell?"

"No." Gary looked in the rearview again. "Does it matter?"

"How long has that car been back there?"

"I don't know. What are you worrying about?" Gary looked at her like she was nuts. "So he's tailgating, so what?"

"Why would he? It doesn't make sense." Mary sized up the traffic, which was light as the road stretched out toward Jersey. "All the other lanes are totally open. Why doesn't he just go around us?"

"I don't know!" Gary laughed, softly. "Sit back down and relax, will you? I can't drive with you popping around like—"

"How fast can this car go?" Mary blurted out, panicky.

"Fast. Not as fast as the SL, but fast."

"Then lose this guy. If you can lose him, I'll calm down. If you can't, I'm calling 911." Mary twisted back onto her seat, reached for her purse, and took out her cell phone, so it was ready.

"You gonna call the cops for *tailgating*?" Gary's mouth dropped open, but Mary was beyond explaining.

"Just *go*!"

"Okay, sit back and hold on!" Gary hit the gas, and the Lexus surged forward with surprising power.

Mary fell back in her seat. They barreled forward as if the highway were greased for them, whizzing past the Oregon Avenue exit. Dinner could wait. She tried to figure out what was going on. Chico had evidently changed cars. He had followed her to the restaurant. He was going to run them off the road or ram them. Poor Gary, mixed up in this. In the wrong place at the wrong time.

"Gary, go faster. Go!" She turned around and looked over her shoulder. The Mercedes was falling behind. She felt a leap of hope in her chest. *"Go!"*

"Sit down!" Gary shouted back, and as soon as Mary sat back down, he floored the gas pedal. The Lexus burst forward, shot like a rocket.

Mary looked back. The Mercedes was way back, evidently making no attempt to catch up to them. They had lost it! Thank God!

"They're gone! Ha!" Mary heard herself laugh with nervous relief. She turned and double-checked, but the purplish head-lights of the Mercedes were pinpoints. She exhaled, finally. The car could have been nothing, but she wasn't taking chances. It could have happened the way she thought, but it hadn't. Not this time, at least. She was safe again. The Lexus slowed, bringing its speed nearer the limit.

"What was *that* all about?" Gary asked her, almost laughing. "Are you crazy or what?"

"It's a long story." Mary looked over, and

his dark eyes shone with that excitement men get from high speeds and St. Pauli Girl. Another disastrous blind date, but he might call her back. *Guys love crazy chicks.*

"Tell it, for Christ's sake! This I'd love to hear."

Mary sank into her seat, her adrenaline buzzing in her ears. Her heartbeat returned to normal, her mouth felt less dry. She tried to process what had just happened. How could she explain it? Should she explain it? And could she swear Gary to secrecy, or would he run back to Bennie and get her fired? He hadn't come down yet, from his excitement.

"Hell, Bennie didn't tell me you were nuts! He told me you were a nice, quiet girl!"

He? Mary must not have heard him right. "What did you say?"

"I said, Bennie never told me you were so wild! Wait'll I get my hands on him!"

Her, Mary was about to correct him, then froze. *He? Him?* It was a natural mistake, but it would never have been made by a friend of Bennie's. It would never have been made by anyone who had even met her. Mary's thoughts jumped back in time. A *regular* lawyer? No dog hair in the car?

Suddenly it all fit together. This man wasn't Gary Haddon. This man worked for the Saracones. He must have followed her to the restaurant, then stationed himself at the bar. And she was in a speeding car with him, alone. She had to stay calm, and play along.

"He didn't tell you that, did he?" Mary asked, but even she heard a new fear in her voice. It made the man look over, and his smile faded. They locked eyes and in one glance, he knew. She couldn't pull it off. *Oh my God, no.* "Help!" Mary screamed and lunged for the door lock, but her injured hand couldn't hold her grip.

"NO!" the man yelled.

"HELP! PLEASE!" Suddenly all hell broke loose in the car. Mary was yanked backward by her hair. Her neck almost broke. Her scalp exploded in pain.

"HELP!" Mary kept screaming, trying to pull him off. Her cell phone fell from her hand. The Lexus careened into the next lane. There was no other traffic. No one to see the struggle. It was too dark.

"HELP!" She struggled to free herself. Reach the door. The window. Anything. "HELP!"

The next thing Mary knew, her face was pushed into the car window with the impact of a head-on collision.

One that happened again and again and again.

FORTY-THREE

Mary woke up in darkness, lying down on her side. Something heavy covered her completely, like the biggest blanket in the world. It made it hard to breathe. Hot. Sticky. Her head was killing her. Her thoughts were cloudy. Confused. Pain seared into her brain from her forehead and her right eye.

god my head my head hurts so much

She reached up to touch the spot, but she couldn't move her hand. She tried to move it again, but it wouldn't budge. It was behind her back. She pulled harder, hurting her shoulder, but it still didn't move. Something was binding her wrists. Both wrists. She could feel the pulling. The same

thing with her legs. They were stuck together, one on top of the other. She couldn't
separate them. They were bound at the
ankle.

Mary couldn't see anything. It was the
blanket, on top of her. Wetness poured from
somewhere into her eyes, warm. She
blinked and blinked but she couldn't clear
her eyes. They stung, drowning in the liquid.
Her forehead burned. It felt like her hair was
on fire. She tried to speak, she couldn't
open her mouth. She couldn't move her
lips. Something tight was covering them. It
cut into her nostrils. It was so hard to
breathe. She could feel moisture under her
nose, she was leaking, warm and wet. Then
she remembered.

The Lexus. The man. The car window. Her
gut twisted at the memory. And the realization: her hands were tied behind her back.
Her mouth was taped. Her head was probably bleeding. It was dark. Justin. In the
next second, whatever she was in lurched
forward, jostling her. She heard a powerful
car engine. She smelled exhaust. Moving
now.

She was in the trunk of a car. The Lexus?
The Mercedes? Were both drivers in it to-

gether? Did it matter? Mary felt herself surrender to panic. Her heart thundered. She screamed, emitting only a muffled *mmmm,* a cry that began and ended in her throat. Terror rose in her chest. She couldn't breathe.

MMMMMMM! MMMMMM! MMM-MMM!

Mary told herself not to panic. Think. Plan. Figure it out. Be brave. No, be determined. She was determined to live. The Lexus picked up speed. The jostling was almost constant now. She could hear road noise. Other cars. She was lying on her right side. Judging from the pull, she was facing the front of the car. Her hands were tied at the back. She forced herself to think. Assess the situation.

Okay, okay, in a car trunk, going somewhere fast. Legs, mouth, and hands taped. Cell phone? Lost in the fight in the car. No one knew where she was, not even Bennie. Bennie thought she was with her friend Gary Haddon.

Mary tried to move her hands. Feel for a latch. Find the trunk lock. She wrenched her hands apart but they wouldn't come undone. Duct tape, there, too. She could feel it up her arms, wrenching her shoulders almost out of their sockets. She ignored the stabbing in her forehead. Blinked blood from her eyes. She pulled and pulled, yanking her wrists apart with all her might. Nothing.

She raised her hands bound together, trying to feel for the latch. The lock. A wire. Anything. The blanket kept getting in the way, wrapping her up. Stiff and scratchy, a tarp. It smelled of garbage and motor oil. Wet splotches around her face. Her blood. Mary tried throwing off the tarp but couldn't. There were yards and yards of it. Every time she moved, weight shifted on top. *Clink. Clink.* It made a clinking sound when it moved. He had weighted the tarp down with things. Tools. A shovel?

She kept moving her hands, scratching frantically around for a latch. All she could feel was the tarp. The car roared forward, with no turns in the road. The expressway. He had it planned all along. Out toward the airport, away from the city. There were warehouses. Industry. Distribution centers. The shipyard. The piers. Long stretches of roads, desolate after business hours. Then Chester, Delaware. Farther south. Or north.

No! She wriggled, trying to roll herself over, twisting this way and that, feeling frantically for any kind of latch. Her eyes filled with tears but she squeezed them shut. She thought of Mrs. Nyquist, riding bucking broncos. Bennie, rowing hard on the river. Judy, climbing huge rocks. Mary could never do stuff like that. She could never do it their way. She had to do it herself. Her way.

What can I do? Make funny noises or wiggle. What can't I do? Move, scream, or save my own life. Guess what? My way sucks.

Mary had to do something. This man was taking her somewhere to kill her. The secondary location. *Huh?* Where had she heard that term? Not in law school. How did she know that term? Where else? She didn't do anything anymore. Or go anywhere. Since Mike, all she did was work and watch TV.

TV! That was it! The Lifetime Channel! That was where she had heard it, on some show on Lifetime. Television for Women. The secondary location was where the bad guy took you when he wanted to kill you. The secondary location was the place you were never supposed to go.

MMMMMM! MMMMMM!

Mary found her train of thought before it derailed. Now what else had she seen on that show? One of those survival shows for girls, with reenactments and lipliner. What else was on that show? It came on Saturday morning, when she should have been at work, and again on Sunday mornings, when she should have been at church.

It showed how to survive carjacking, attempted rape, avalanche, if your car went in water, or quicksand, or if you were locked in a basement, a refrigerator, or a CAR TRUNK!

The Lexus curved steeply to the left, accelerating. An on ramp? An off ramp? Hurry! Then she remembered something else, another save-your-lifetime tip, and one that she was in an excellent position to do. And she even had the weapon of choice.

She started kicking backward, ramming her high heel against the blanket. Kick, kick, kick. She had to kick with both feet, since they were tied. Her stomach muscles protested, then screamed, then begged for mercy. She kept kicking, aiming for the taillight with the spike of her high heel. The Lexus was slowing. No! Were they there?

Was he coming to get her? She kicked like crazy, fighting terror.

Yes! Mary succeeded in the first step. Kicking upward enough times to shimmy the tarp off one foot, leaving her high heel free, and lethal! She kicked hard! **That one's for Keisha!** She kicked again. *This one's for Frank!* She kicked harder. *This one's for Amadeo!* She kicked hardest of all. Then she kept on and in the next minute heard a cracking sound at her heel. She was doing it! The taillight was cracking!

She kicked in a frenzy, heedless of the pain in her head, stomach, legs, or wrists. She could do it. She could save herself. She was going to live! She couldn't see if light was coming through the tarp, she didn't see the progress she was making. But she could hear it. One crack, then another. And another, the plastic cracking and giving way. If she didn't electrocute herself, she could live! It was night. Couldn't someone see a light being kicked out?

The Lexus was slowing, and she heard the sound of engine noise. *HONK! HONK! HONK!* Honking, right near her bumper! Someone had seen it! Someone was trying to tell the driver! *He knows, stupid.* Call the

cops! Call 911! She kept kicking, determined. *For Keisha! For Frank! For Amadeo!*
Kick! Kick ! Kick! She kicked like her life depended on it, because it did. The taillight
had to be demolished. She pictured it,
cracked, its bulb smashed to smithereens.
She could feel cool air on her foot. She had
broken through! She could have fit her foot
through the hole if it had been free! Still she
kept kicking.

HONK! HONK! HONK! Suddenly, the
Lexus took off. She lurched violently to
the back of the trunk and stayed there. The
honking sound got farther away. *No!* He
was going to get away! *Get the license
plate! Call the cops!* Kick, kick, kick! Her
foot was wedging in the place where the
taillight was. She squeezed her toes to keep
her high heel on. She'd kick through the
metal! She was determined!

MMM! MMMM! MMMM!

And in the next minute, she heard it.
Sirens! Far away. Getting closer? Yes! They
were coming! Cops! The Lexus shot away in
response. They were going to have to chase
him. He wasn't going down without a fight,
not with her in here. Mary kept kicking. Still
kicking. Trying to yell. Trying to stop crying.

don't kill me don't shoot the trunk please I'm in here I'm in here

The sirens blared louder and the Lexus hit top speed, barreling down the expressway. She rammed her heel into the back of the trunk and got stuck. The Lexus careened left and right. HONK! HONK! It was the Lexus, honking. She couldn't hear anything but road noise and sirens. Fresh air swept into the trunk through the hole. Mary kept trying to wedge her foot out of the taillight well so she could keep kicking.

I'm alive in here don't shoot the trunk don't shoot the

There were more sirens, louder now. They were chasing the Lexus, full court press. She could imagine it like it was on TV. *Cops, NYPD Blue*, every cable channel had its high-speed police chase. And now, she was in one. Mary was finally *in* the television. She almost laughed.

If I live, I promise I'll get a life.

Sirens were all around them now. Left. Right. Directly in back. They were racing ahead together, careening this way and that. The cops had to be surrounding him, at warp speed. Would they shoot her? Would they *crash*? This was worse than before! Mary kept kicking so they would know she was still alive. Suddenly the Lexus took a sharp right turn, almost ninety degrees.

Everything went crazy. The Lexus pin-wheeled around and round. Wheels squealed. Sirens blared. Mary screamed. Cried. The Lexus spun out of control, then it spun slower and slower. Mary hiccupped. Vomited. It filled up her throat. She couldn't breathe. Help! Help! God!

The Lexus was slowing its spinning.

I can't breathe I can't breathe I can't

CRAK! CRAK! CRAK! Gunfire! Right near the car! The cops weren't going to shoot her, but *he* would! He wanted her *dead*! *CRAK! CRAK! CRAK! CRAK!* A fusillade of gunfire thundered in her ears. There was no oxygen. She hiccupped and hiccupped. And finally, shuddered.

CRAK! CRAK! CRAK!

FORTY-FOUR

The examining room was white, ringed with institutional cabinets in regulation beige, and barely large enough to accommodate The Flying DiNunzios, two uniformed cops, Detective Gomez, his partner, a nurse, and the doctor.

Dr. Steven Weaver was an incredibly handsome, blond plastic surgeon, and the little rainbow pin under his red-embroidered name was the only indication he was gay. It took him an hour to carefully tweeze the glass from Mary's forehead and seventeen stitches to close the wound, and he was just finishing up. Mary hardly felt his touch, much less any pain, owing to the miracle of Percocet and her sheer happiness at being alive, tempered only by the fact that the Lexus driver had been shot to death during the police shootout, when he'd returned fire.

So he'd had a gun. He was going to kill her. Now he was dead.

Mary wasn't sure how she felt about that. Shaken. Upset. Surprisingly, not that good. Any death was awful, and the man had died taking valuable information with him. How would the cops link him to Justin Saracone now? They'd have had a chance if he'd been taken alive. On the other hand, part of her wasn't completely unhappy. He was evidently a hired killer, and he'd have gone on to kill other people. Not to mention that he *had* tried to kill her.

And would have succeeded if it weren't for cable—and a good pair of heels.

"Okay, let me take one last look." Dr. Weaver stepped back, eyeing his handiwork with a smile. "The stitches are at the hairline. When they heal, you won't even be able to see the scar."

"Thanks a lot," Mary said, though she could hardly hear over the background noise of her mother praying. A novena was in progress. The hospital had called her parents because she'd been stupid enough to list them in her wallet In Case of Emergency. They stuck together at the edge of her bed like conjoined twins, fused at their brown car coats. They wept, prayed, and felt faint in a continuous loop. They needed comfort, help, and medical attention. As touched as Mary was by their love, they were honestly the worst people to have around in an emergency. Thank God Judy was on the way.

"HE'S ALL DONE, MARE!" her father shouted. Of course, he'd rushed to the hospital without his hearing aid. Daughter-in-emergency-room was his best excuse yet. "YOU DID GREAT, KID! JUST GREAT!"

"Your father's right. You're a trouper, Mary." Dr. Weaver gathered his leftover sutures, flesh-toned curlicues, and shiny little scissors with the flat edge. "The nurse will be in with release papers for you to sign and directions for care of the wound."

"How was the X-ray on my right hand?" Mary asked. No need to tell the world she had slugged Justin Saracone. She had grandfathered the injury into the car trunk thing, like some insurance scam.

"Fine, it's not broken, just a soft tissue injury. I'll see you back in my office in two weeks. My address is on the form."

"SHE GONNA BE OKAY, DOC?" her father asked, and her mother paused in prayer, keeping God himself waiting.

"She'll be fine," Dr. Weaver answered, turning. "Her MRIs were fine. She needs to rest tonight and follow the directions for wound care, and she'll be good as new."

"NO PROBLEM! SHE'S COMIN' HOME WITH HER MOTHER AND ME! WE'LL TAKE GOOD CARE OF HER!"

The very thought evaporated Mary's cloud of Percocet, setting her thinking. She had to get to work, but if she went home, her parents wouldn't let her out of their sight. The whole block of Mercer Street would spy backup. Not to mention the reporters outside the hospital, many of whom she'd called on the way back from Justin's. The rest had picked up the sensational car chase down the expressway on their police scanners.

"Okay, champ," Dr. Weaver said, with a sympathetic smile, now that she was an Official Crime Victim. Even the detectives seemed to have found a new respect for her, standing stolid and waiting their turn to interrogate her. The doctor patted her arm. "It's all over now. Take care of yourself. Nurse'll be back in a minute, then you can go."

"Thanks again, doctor," Mary said, just as her mother sniffled loudly. "By the way, you got any Percocet for my parents?"

The doctor laughed and turned to shake her father's hand. "Mr. DiNunzio, it was a pleasure—"

"SEVENTY-FIVE!" her father yelled, inexplicably, throwing his burly arms open, and in the next second the startled doctor was group-hugged by her weepy parents. Mary should have warned him. She had never seen her father shake anyone's hand. Even with complete strangers, he had two speeds—hug and bear-hug. "THANK YOU SO MUCH, DOC! LIKE I SAID, YOU'RE WELCOME IN OUR HOUSE ANYTIME! COME FOR DINNER! YOU AND YOUR WIFE!"

"Thanks, Mr. DiNunzio, but I'm not married."

"YOU HEAR THAT, MARE? HE'S NOT MARRIED!" Her father poked his head around Dr. Weaver, who laughed.

"Gotcha, Pop!" Mary fought a smile.

She'd explain to him about the rainbow flag when he was ready, in about twenty years. And right after that, she'd tell him how she'd really met up with Mr. Lexus. When she was first brought into the emergency room, she'd been in no state to tell her parents or anyone else the full story, and Detectives Gomez and Wahlberg were waiting for her medical treatment to end so they could interview her.

"See you all later," Dr. Weaver said, with a wave, and on the way out almost bumped into Judy, who was barging through the curtain in gray sweats.

"Mary!" she shouted, her voice a crack of pain. She rushed to the bed and threw her arms around Mary, smelling of linseed oil. "Are you okay? They wouldn't let me through out front, I had to tell them I was your sister."

"Mrymph," Mary said, feeling an unexpected warmth in her friend's arms, realizing what had happened to her on more than an intellectual level. *I almost died. I almost lost my life. And Judy is closer than a sister. Closer than mine, anyway.* "I'm fine, really, I am."

"My God, I can't believe this!" Judy released her, her face a mask of concern. "This is unreal! There's like three hundred reporters out front! I didn't see the TV, I was working. What *happened*?"

Detective Gomez stepped forward and introduced himself. "Judy, you remember me from the other night, after Keisha was attacked? My partner and I would like to question Mary as part of our investigation. Your questions will have to wait."

"Go straight to hell!" Judy turned on him, fierce as a girl who climbs mountains for fun. "*Your* investigation? Mary's the one doing all the work! She's the one putting her life on the line! She had to file a lawsuit to bring that guy to justice! Did you ever even go to the Saracones, like she begged you to?"

"Not yet—"

"What were you waiting for? *This*? They tried to kill her! If you'd gone over, she wouldn't be in a hospital tonight! She wouldn't almost have been *killed*!"

"THE SARACONES? WAS IT THAT SARACONE GUY, MARE? WE THOUGHT IT WAS A GUY OFFA THE STREET!" Her father stepped toward the bed, even angrier than Judy, and her mother prayed harder.

"YO, DETECTIVE! IS IT TRUE WHAT JUDY'S SAYIN'?"

Mary put up a hand. "I have an idea. Judy, you stay here while I talk to Detective Gomez. Mom, Pop, I love you both, but you need to go outside, have a cup of coffee, and wait for me. This is going to take some time, and I have to talk to the police."

"MARE, *WAS* IT THAT SARACONE? I'LL KILL HIM WITH MY BARE HANDS!"

"It's okay, Pop," she answered, touched. "Please, you can help me the most by waiting for me in the waiting room. You don't want to put Mom through this, do you?" Mary shot her eyes toward her praying mother, caught in the middle of the third round of Hail Marys, and her father understood. Good thing he spoke Meaningful Eye Contact.

"AWRIGHT, AWRIGHT! I'LL TAKE YOUR MOTHER IN THE WAITING ROOM." He looped a heavy arm around her mother, who blew Mary a weepy kiss behind her Kleenexes as she was led toward the door. "LET'S GO SIT, VEET! WE CAN WAIT FOR MARY OUTSIDE. MAYBE WE CAN HAVE A NICE CUPPA COFFEE AND SOME CAKE!"

"Thanks, Pop." Mary watched with a little tug as they left the room. She had no choice but to deceive them. She'd have to make them understand later. She turned to Gomez. "Now Detective, let me tell you what happened. But first off, have you heard anything about Keisha?"

"No, she's still out." Gomez was already flipping open his notebook. Mary began the story about the blind date, then the lawsuit, then how she hit Justin, but she didn't expect anything from Gomez anymore. The cops had dropped the ball and it had almost cost her her life. There was nothing more they could do anyway. She knew that Justin had sent the Lexus driver, maybe even before she went over and slugged him, but he was too smart to leave an evidentiary link. It was up to her now.

Mary finished with, "So I think what happened was that Justin Saracone hired Mr. Lexus, who followed me into the restaurant and took a seat at the bar. He may have been following me for a while, for all I know. I got stalled looking around for my blind date, by this bald guy who asked me out, and then I spotted Mr. Lexus and made a mistake. It was a mix-up."

"I see." Gomez closed his book when she finished and slipped it into his back pocket. "Well, that was quite an ordeal. You must be exhausted."

"I'm okay," Mary said. Judy was the one who look like she needed a rest. Her pale skin had gone even paler and her blue eyes glistened. Mary had never seen Judy cry and looked away, at the detective. "What do you know about this guy?"

"We ran his prints and plate through VI-CAP. His name's Al Denser, with a couple of aliases, from outta Baltimore. He's wanted for murder in two states. We've been lookin' for him for a while."

Mary shuddered. "He seemed so charming. Smart. Good-looking. I can't believe I was fooled."

"He's a Ted Bundy type, but a hired gun."

"Definitely. Chico's replacement. Do you have any idea where that bad boy is? I didn't see him or his car, when I served Saracone with the papers."

"No." Gomez shook his head, buckling his lower lip. "Haven't been able to find him. We have called the father's house, and Mrs. Saracone said he's gone and she doesn't know where he is."

"Yeah, right."

"We're over there first thing in the morning, and we'll stop by Justin Saracone's, too."

"He'll be in court in the morning."

"You going forward with that lawsuit, after this?" Gomez asked, surprised.

"Of course," Mary said, without batting an eye. It hurt to bat her eye anyway.

"Just the same, we'll go to Justin's house and look around. Talk to his wife." Gomez shot a look at Judy, who managed not to flip him the bird. He shifted his pants up by the belt. "I'd like to show you a photo array for ID purposes. Can we arrange that?"

"For the Lexus driver? Why do you need me to ID him? You have his body, right?" *Yuck*.

"We batten down all the details." Gomez rose to go. "When's a good time to call? Noon?"

"Try my cell," Mary answered.

"Shall we go? I can give you and your family a lift home. You'll need us to get through the press, and of course, we would appreciate it if you wouldn't make any statements tonight."

"Of course." *But tomorrow, all bets are off.*

"I'll even take Judy along, if she'll let me." Gomez glanced over at Judy, whose blue eyes frosted over. The girl had learned something about vendettas over the years, but Mary decided on the spot to use their feud as an excuse.

"No, thanks," Mary answered quickly. "Judy and I will go together, she can give me a lift. But maybe you could give my parents a ride now, and I'll meet them at home, after I sign the form for the nurse. I would really appreciate it, if you could get them home right away and tell them I'll be right there."

"Sure. What about the press?"

"We can handle them."

"Okay. See you later. Rest easy, now." Gomez smiled and touched Mary's shoulder like Dr. Weaver had.

"Thanks, doc," she said, managing to return the smile. She was beginning to hate being a Crime Victim. Everybody was looking at her funny since she had Survived a Brush With Death.

Judy closed in, eyes narrowed, as soon as Gomez had left. "That jerk."

"He's doing his best."

"It's not good enough."

"It doesn't have to be. I have a secret plan."

Judy burst into a grin. "I knew it! What are we up to?"

"We're escaping from my parents. You have to take me to a hotel tonight so I can work. They'll know if I go to your house or to the office, and so will the press. Where are you parked?"

"Outside, illegally. But the press is out there."

"Okay." Mary thought fast. "Maybe we can get you some scrubs and you can go and get your car, then meet me out front. I'll go through the hospital."

"Sounds like us!" Judy's eyes lit up. "We're back in business! I bet I can find a nurse to lend me some scrubs. And maybe one of those puffy hats! I need a puffy hat!"

I've created a monster. "Whatever. Go. I'll meet you out at the main entrance. Don't let my parents see you."

"Okay, got it." Judy hustled out of the room, and Mary eased off the bed, her head spinning a little. She held on to the bed for a moment, hoping the dull pain throbbing in her temple would stop, but it didn't. She tiptoed out of the room anyway, making sure the coast was clear. To her left was the nurses' station, bright but still and empty. Beyond the station was a large plastic window, and she could see her parents being led out by Detective Gomez and his partner.

Excellent. Down the hall to her right was a single white exit door, beside a sign that read RADIOLOGY. Presumably it was another way out of the emergency department and would get Mary back to the hospital, where she could find her way to the main entrance by the time Judy scored a new wardrobe.

She snuck out of the room and made a beeline for the door. She almost had her hand on the doorknob when she heard a noise behind her.

And she turned.

FORTY-FIVE

"MARE!" It was her father, hailing her with a smile. "YOU'RE GOIN' THE WRONG WAY! WE'RE OUT FRONT!"

Busted again. "Dad, Jeez. Oh. Right."

"HOLD ON A MINUTE, I FORGOT MY LUCKY CAP. SEE, IT WORKED GOOD TONIGHT, DIDN'T IT?" He gestured at the door to the examining room, where his grimy tan cabbie hat hung on the doorknob. His lucky cap, easily older than she was, was the only dirty article of clothing in the house, because her father refused to let her mother wash the luck out. Mary had long ago forgotten why it was lucky, but she realized that he had worn it tonight for her. Her father plucked the cap from the doorknob and flopped his cap on his head, where it landed a little off center. "MARE, IT'S THIS WAY, THE EXIT!"

"Pop, I know, I just—"

"HOLD ON TO ME SO YOU DON'T FALL OVER." He shuffled to her and offered her his arm, bunchy at the elbow, where his brown car coat wrinkled in its worsted way.

Mary stopped, struck. It was just the way he always offered his arm, down the shore, when they were about to walk the boardwalk to get soft ice cream. Or when they were about to walk down the aisle, on her wedding day. Or at Mike's funeral. Now, he offered it to steady her. Pick her up. Retrieve her. Help her. He had always been there, offering his arm. When she was little, it was practice, and later, it was support. That arm was the greatest gift a father can give a daughter, and he gave it to her, without question, and always. Suddenly his arm sank slowly, his expression bewildered.

"WHAT? WHAT'SA MATTER? LET'S GO! YOUR MOTHER'S IN THE COP CAR, WAITIN'!"

"Pop, there's something I have to do tomorrow, on the Saracone case." Mary collected herself. "I was gonna meet Judy out front and have her drop me off at a hotel or something. If I come home tonight, you and Mom will never let me do it."

"WHA'?" Her father blinked, then understood. She saw the realization creep over him, and his gaze traveled from her to the exit door and back again. "You were sneakin' away *from us*?" he asked, his voice incredulous, his tone a fresh wound.

"I had to. I have to."

"I'm surprised at you, Mare." His brown eyes went round. "I can't believe you would do that."

"I'm sorry, Pop." *Sorrysorrysorry*. "But I have no choice."

"Yes, you do." His forehead wrinkled with the only disapproval she had ever seen on his face. "Lemme ask you somethin.' Were you doin' somethin' wrong?"

"No. I'm doing something I have to do."

"Then why you hidin' it?"

Mary didn't have an immediate answer.

"You don't sneak. You never sneak." Her father pointed a thick finger at her, and his eyes flashed. "You have to do somethin' tomorrow? Then, when the time comes, you stand up straight and you talk to us."

"But, Pop, Mom'll never go for it."

"You show your mother the respect she deserves. You talk to her. Tomorrow. But tonight, you come home and sleep." He sighed, his heavy shoulders letting down. "You're sick and you shouldn't be runnin' around, Mare. I signed the paper for you, they gave me the pills for your head. You gotta rest. Tonight you stay *home*."

Mary felt a tsunami of guilt wash over her. She would rather be locked in a trunk than this. And what were the odds she'd get out of her parents' house tomorrow morning? She'd have to defy not only her father, but also her mother, who still looked so thin. Mary seized the moment. "Pop, what's the matter with Mom?"

"That's not for now. That's for later. For her and you." His face softened, falling into familiar sad lines. "Come on, Mare. You don't want it to be this way. You were such a good girl, never snuck around. I heard the stories about the other girls at school, but not my Mary. Never you." He offered his arm again. "Come on, let's go home."

How much longer will I have that arm to hold on to? And what about Mom? Mary took his arm, appreciating its gift anew. "You win, Pop."

"Of course." Her father smiled. "Judy in the getaway car?"

"She's my wheelman."

They both laughed, and shuffled out together.

It wasn't until later, when she was putting fresh sheets on her childhood bed, that Mary got her mother alone. At least, alone except for the press outside, crowding tiny Mercer Street with their videocameras, klieglights, and microphones, waiting for Mary to come out. Earlier, Mrs. DiTonio had shooed them from the block with her trusty BackSaver snow shovel, but they'd come back in force, knowing Mary would have to come out sometime. But not tonight. Tonight was for family.

She and her mother were in the stop-time bedroom Mary had shared with her sister. Two single beds sat against the side wall, and between the front windows, a small white-painted bookshelf crammed with the artifacts of an American girlhood; stuffed Easter bunnies with legs that had inexplicably hardened like concrete; a chubby Latin-English dictionary, soft, blue hatch-marked copies of Nancy Drew, and random Archie comics; brown teddy bears with dilated pupils, eyelashes that stuck together and black noses that never wore off, and a mass grave of half-nude Barbies stacked on a shelf, so that only their stiff plastic feet showed. There was only a single desk that nobody used anyway, now cleaner than it ever had been, and above it hung a cork bulletin board cluttered with wrinkled track ribbons, photo-booth strips of girlfriends with matching braces, sewn felt letters in school colors for honors in English and religion, pointless sayings cut out of advertisements ("Slicker All Over. Yardley of London."), and a curling *Time* magazine cover of the Prince of Wales by Peter Max.

Between the beds stood a single wooden night table, and on it rested a plastic Flintstones lamp that nobody had the heart to discard, even when it went well beyond outgrown into campy and back again. Its yellowed paper shade had pictures of Pebbles and Bam-Bam, and its base was outdated enough to permit only a forty-watt bulb, which barely illuminated the room but emitted a soft, friendly, old-feeling glow. It bathed Vita DiNunzio's newly pale face with warmth, magically filling the hollows that had appeared in her cheeks.

"You got?" her mother asked, in her short-hand. She had both hands on her side of the sheet, wanting to know if Mary was ready with her side, and she didn't need to say more. Mary had made so many beds with her that she could do both sides of most of their conversations. But not the one they were about to have.

"I got it, Ma," Mary said, and they flipped the white flat sheet into the air, releasing a stored-up scent of mothballs, hard soap, and city air. The sheet would have been line-dried outside, on a clothesline less imaginative than Amadeo's, but equally useful. The sheet caught the air, making a momentary cloud between them, before it billowed soft to the bed. "So, Ma, tell me what's the matter with you."

"Nothing." *Nut-ting-eh*, it came out.

"Something's wrong, Ma. You're thin, I can see that. Tell me."

"I'm fine."

"Ma, you're making my head hurt more." Mary sat on the bed, refusing to make her hospital corner. "Tell me. I'm ready. I can handle it, whatever it is. We can handle it together." Her words rang with an authority unusual for Mary, and she realized she couldn't even have faked that tone before.

Her mother remained silent as she folded her corner, her lips forming a tight line. She smoothed out the sheet with the flat of each hand in brisk, practiced strokes, and in no time, her side of the bed was completely made and Mary's was a complete mess. Her mother pretended that she didn't notice as she picked up the white thermal blanket, bleached to the soft hue of city snow, and held it bunched in her hands, ready to put on the bed. Her mother tilted her head in appeal. "Maria."

"I'm not moving until you tell me."

"*Per favore.*"

"No." Mary folded her arms. It was stubborn meets stubborn, in a face-off over the hospital corners. Her mother couldn't stand an unmade bed. It was like a ringing telephone for some people, or a form of torture by electrocution for others. After a minute, her mother gave a small, final sigh and eased onto the bed, hugging the blanket to her chest. Mary swallowed hard. She was getting ready to say something.

"I'm a little sick." *Leetle seek.*

Mary felt her heart stop. "How sick? What do you have?"

"Little sick, inna, inna—" Her mother frowned in a squeamish way and made a swirling gesture near her pelvis. "*Ovaie*, itsa sick. Little bit, sick."

No. This isn't happening. What? Mary struggled to translate from the hand motion, "Like your ovaries? What does 'sick' mean?"

"Little bit sick."

It had to be. What else could it be? She didn't want to say the word. "Ma, did he say it was cancer, in your ovaries? That you have ovarian cancer?"

"*Sì, sì, è cancro*"—her mother made the swirling gesture again, yes, it's cancer, and Mary felt as if somebody had thrown a switch on all the circuits in her brain.

Her mother said quickly, "No worry, Maria, *dottore,* he say I 'ave operation." *Operaysh*.

"Operation? What kind of operation?"

"*Isterectomia,*" her mother answered in Italian, a word Mary had never heard, but she could guess.

"A hysterectomy?"

"*Sì.*" Her mother flushed, mortified.

She needed a hysterectomy. Maybe they

had caught it early. Maybe she'd be okay. Mary was terrified and relieved, simultaneously. She tried to collect herself. "Ma? You scared? It's a normal thing, a common thing, to be scared."

"No scared. I pray, I no scared. God, he take care of me." Her eyes remained unflinching, richly brown and clear, gazing back at her daughter, as always, with honesty, love, and something new. Bravery. Vita DiNunzio had never ridden a bucking bronco, climbed anything taller than a footstool, or kicked her way out of a Lexus. But she was braver than all of them, and Mary felt a sudden shame that she had never realized it before. She got up on weak knees, went around to the neat side of the bed, and put her arms around her mother, who felt so terribly frail in her arms.

"Don't worry, Ma. I'll take care of you, Pop will take care of you. You'll be fine." Mary searched for the words, never having comforted her mother in her life. "Ma, I'll make sure everything's okay for you, you'll see."

"*Sì, sì,*" her mother said, holding tight to the white blanket, and for a single moment, she permitted herself to be cradled like a child.

By the very child she'd brought into the world.

Mary had a sleepless night, between trying to work and trying not to worry about her mother, and was up at seven, showering in the bathroom down the hall, then changing into one of her sister's old brown suits, which almost matched a beat-up pair of Aerosoles she kept at her parents' for emergency Mass. Her black clutch bag and her cell phone had been confiscated for evidence, but she wouldn't need them where she was going today. She took a second to peek out the bedroom window, and there were only a few reporters out front, leftover from last night. MacIntire was among them, looking up at her lighted window, and she drew away. Mary was glad he had survived the snow shovel. He would come in handy today.

She headed out of the room but stopped at her bureau, taking the time to dab some cakey flesh-colored Clearasil over the purplish bruises on her forehead, which would fool no one and stung besides. She took no pain meds, despite the dull ache from the wound, because she had to think clearly today. She made her bed hastily, turned out the bedroom light, and padded down the hall, checking in on her parents' bedroom, almost hoping they'd be asleep.

But they weren't. Their bedroom was empty, dark, and looked the way it always did; their double bed flush against the flowered wallpaper, a wooden crucifix over the dark headboard, a blue plastic denture case on her father's night table. They were already awake and downstairs, waiting for her. *Good! Right?*

Mary had told her mother last night that she had to leave the next morning. They'd tacitly agreed that they'd had enough drama for one night and could postpone the fistfight until morning. Now. She left the room, steeled her nerve, and tramped downstairs to do battle over fresh coffee. *The DiNunzios may be crazy, but at least we're civilized.*

Five minutes later, Mary was sitting behind a scorching cup, opposite her father, saying nothing as they waited for her mother to sit down. Both her parents were fully dressed, her father in maroon Bermuda shorts, undershirt, white socks and black slippers, with his hearing aid curled in his ear like an electronic snail. *Uh-oh.* He had undoubtedly gotten an earful last night, and it was a bad sign that he wanted to hear this morning. Her mother wore her flowered housedress, her scuffy slippers, but no pink hairnet, which meant only one thing: she was going to early Mass this morning. A *definite* bad sign.

Mary sipped her coffee for strength while her mother put the pot down so hard on the stove it made a *clank,* unseating the cast-iron burner. Then she came over to the kitchen table and sat down behind her cup without a word. Her eyes weren't too tired to be stern behind the bifocal half of her glasses, which magnified her pupils in a black-and-brown window. Her lips were as tight as last night. "So, where you go, Maria?"

"To court, for Amadeo."

"You should stay home. You're sick. Your head."

"I can't. I have to go."

"The newspapers, out front again."

"I know. They should leave when I do, but if they don't, don't talk to them. Don't talk to them no matter what." Mary turned to her father. "Don't let her hit them with the spoon, either. That's assault."

He smiled, but her mother frowned. "Today, Judy goes?"

"No, I go alone."

"*E Benedetta*?"

"No, not Bennie either." Mary didn't even want to think where Bennie was or what she'd say about what had happened. She'd unplugged her parents' phone for a reason. They'd realize it sometime next year.

"These man, Saracone, he sent the one last night?"

"Yes, the son," Mary said, without hesitation. Justin Saracone was protecting his secret. No use sugarcoating it. Her mother wasn't stupid.

"And the police, why the police don' stop these man?"

"They can't prove he did it, and they have to prove it." *Like me.* "I can't wait for them anyway. Now, I have to go." Mary didn't know how to put it any differently. She was going to court no matter what her mother said. She couldn't ask permission to do her job, but this was beyond that. She couldn't ask permission to be herself. Not after Montana, or last night. They had two different paths to follow, mother and daughter. They were separate now. Changed, now and forever. Mary reached across the table and touched her mother's hand. "I can handle it, Ma. I saved my own life last night. You're going to save yours, too, right?"

Her mother didn't reply. Her father looked down.

"We can do it, Ma. You and me. But I have to go now. I'm gonna be late. You have to let me go, Ma." *You have to let me go.*

Suddenly her mother stood up, pushing back her chair, which made a familiarly unhappy squeak on the tile floor. Mary knew what would happen next because it happened all the time. Her mother would walk out of the kitchen. If Mary were going to leave today, it wouldn't be with anybody's blessing. But in the next minute, instead of storming out of the room, her mother opened her arms.

"Maria, good-bye, Maria," she said, in a shaky voice.

Mary's mouth dropped open. She rose reflexively and went around the table. But this time, she did cry.

And when she was finished, she wiped her eyes and went to work.

FORTY-SIX

The rain didn't faze the throng of reporters and photographers who mobbed Mary as soon as she got out of the Yellow cab in front of the United States Courthouse. They overflowed the wide sidewalk almost to the glamorous new Constitution Center, spilling off the curb, snarling cab, car, bus, and tourist traffic on an insanely busy Market Street. There were at least a hundred reporters, and Mary spotted ABC, COURT-TV, and CNN logos, as well as locals KYW and WCAU. And to think, all she had to do was almost get killed.

"Mary, Mary, Mary!" Everyone in the crowd was shouting, a reportorial cacophony. Mary had never heard her name so many times, except for Our Lady of Angels. "Mary, did you know the guy who kidnapped you?" "Mary, over here!" "Mary, smile!" "Mary, this way!" "Mary, did the Roundhouse identify the driver yet, Mary?" "Mary, how'd you get outta the trunk?" "Mary, is it true he was related to Justin Saracone?"

"After court! No comment until then!" Mary waved them all off as she made her way through the bubble microphones, boom mikes, and steno pads. They aimed videocameras, still cameras, and handheld klieglights at her Clearasil, and round flexible reflective screens bounced artificial light into her tired eyes. It was even better than she had hoped. "No comment until after the hearing! Thank you!"

Mary pushed her way inside the tall red-brick building, threading her way through its packed lobby of jurors, lawyers, spectators, and reporters who dogged her every step. She ignored everybody, barreling head down through security to the elevators, and she didn't look up until she reached the courtroom.

The courtroom was immense, with long dark wood pews and a matching wood dais under the huge golden seal of the United

States Courts, and even as large as it was, the courtroom was bursting at its federal seams. Spectators crammed the pews cheek by jowl, knee to knee, filling every inch of bench. They stood along the back wall of the courtroom, concealing its heavy acoustical wood panels, and along the sides, under the heavy oil portraits hanging there, framed in gilt. Beyond the bar of court, the courtroom deputies were at full staff, and every law clerk's high-backed chair was taken. The body heat challenged the air-conditioning, and the air was thick with aftershaves, perfumes, and pencil leads.

Mary stepped onto the blue carpet of the center aisle, and murmuring rippled through the crowd. Every single head turned toward her. She felt her face flush red as tomato sauce and kept her head down as she barreled down the aisle, with everyone craning their necks, or boosting themselves up to catch a glimpse of the lawyer who got locked in the trunk. Sketch artists held their gray pads sideways, and reporters scribbled on steno pads, including Mac, whose eye she avoided. The *circolo*, occupying two aisles on her right, waved frantically at her, and Mary acknowledged them with a nod, then practically ran up the aisle to the polished counsel table, where Judy was sitting, dressed up in a black suit, real eyeliner, and hair moussed into submission.

"Don't you look pretty," Mary whispered as she took her seat, and Judy smiled.

"How's first chair feel, big girl?"

"Terrifying."

"Go get 'em." They both looked over at the same time to defendant's table, where an older corporate-type lawyer sat next to Justin Saracone. Both lawyer and client were dressed in expensive dark suits with a sleek Italian cut, shiny black wingtips, white shirts with cutaway collars, and puffy silk ties. The only difference between them was that Justin had a swollen upper lip.

Mary smiled. "I do good work."

"You the *man*. BTW, you see the boss? She's here. Third row, in the middle."

Mary took a peek. *There*. Bennie in her trademark suit. Trademark hair. Trademark glare. Mary faced front, fast. "Am I fired?"

"Not this time. She feels guilty she almost got you killed on that last blind date."

Suddenly a paneled pocket door opened to the left of the dais, and the courtroom deputy appeared and took a position in front of the American flag, his chest puffed out. "All rise for the Honorable Lisa Gemmill," he called out, his ringing voice hushing the crowd instantly, and Mary, Judy, and everyone else rose as Judge Gemmill entered the courtroom. Mary had never been before her, but the number of judges Mary had never been before was legion.

Judge Gemmill nodded to the courtroom as she swept in and took her seat on the dais. She had long, dark hair, bright intelligent eyes, and wore a chic string of pearls with her robes. "Good morning, Ms. DiNunzio, Mr. Rovitch." Then her gaze took in the entire courtroom, her displeasure undisguised. "Ladies and gentlemen, I will have order in my courtroom today. I intend to keep these proceedings on a tight rein." She focused on Mary. "Ms. DiNunzio, you're the movant today. Please begin."

"Thank you, Your Honor." Mary gathered her papers and exhibits and went to the podium, trying to forget that five million eyes were staring at her. "Your Honor, if it please the Court, my name is Mary DiNunzio, and I'm here on behalf of the estate of Amadeo Brandolini—"

"Brava!" "Bravissima!" "Yeah, Mary!" The *circolo* burst into spontaneous whoops and applause, and the gallery laughed.

Crak! Crak! Judge Gemmill pounded the gavel with a frown. "Order, people! Order!" She waited until they had settled, then looked down at Mary. "Ms. DiNunzio. Given the crowd today, perhaps we can shorten this proceeding. I have read your papers carefully, and I do have a few questions."

Stay calm. Lots of judges do it this way.

"As you are well aware, you are before me today seeking extraordinary relief. Injunctive relief is granted in advance of a full trial, and enforceable by my contempt powers. Accordingly, the standard for such relief is quite high, whether it's a patent case or no." Judge Gemmill peered over the top of her glasses. "You are familiar with the standard courts must use for grant of a temporary restraining order, are you not?"

"I am, Your Honor." Mary wet her lips. "A trial court must consider whether the movant can show a reasonable probability of success on the merits, that he or she will be irreparably harmed by denial of the relief, whether granting preliminary relief will result in even greater harm to the nonmoving party, and whether the order will be in the public interest."

"Exactly." Judge Gemmill thumbed through Mary's brief. "Your brief is really quite well done, and I understand your irreparable harm argument with the sale of rights to Reinhardt. However, the glaring problem with your case is your likelihood of success on the merits. I am not sure that you can satisfy this essential requirement for the relief you seek."

Okay, this happens, too. The judge tells you what's worrying her, and you deal.

"In this regard, while I understand your proof problems—that the alleged fraud on the patent office occurred decades ago, and that both the patent holder, Giovanni Saracone, and your client, Amadeo Brandolini, are now deceased—I simply do not see that you have proven that Mr. Saracone misappropriated an invention of Mr. Brandolini's." Judge Gemmill peered over the top of her glasses. "Would you address that, Ms. DiNunzio?"

"Your Honor, I agree that my evidence is circumstantial, but it establishes the fact that Mr. Brandolini created a set of drawings for a marine deck hatch which were identical to those that ended up in Mr. Saracone's patent application. I have also proven that the application was filed the week after Mr. Saracone and Mr. Brandolini were working together alone and Mr. Brandolini was killed by strangulation, allegedly from a suicide by hanging."

"Objection, Your Honor!" Rovitch barked, but Judge Gemmill waved him off.

"Duly noted," she said. She turned to Mary. "Now, what is your proof that the drawings with the patent application were Mr. Brandolini's and not Mr. Saracone's?"

Mary swallowed. "Your Honor, those drawings were in Mr. Brandolini's wallet, part of his personal effects. As my affidavit shows, my associate Judy Carrier saw them. They were given to me by Mr. Brandolini's former lawyer, Frank Cavuto, who was murdered last week."

The courtroom burst into muffled comment, which Judge Gemmill silenced with a raised eyebrow. "Did Mr. Brandolini sign the drawings that you saw?"

"No, Your Honor. He couldn't read or write."

"Did he identify them in any way, on the drawings?"

"Aside from keeping them where he kept his most precious papers, no, Your Honor."

Judge Gemmill took off her glasses. "Isn't it equally possible, then, that the drawings in Mr. Brandolini's wallet were Mr. Saracone's?"

"No. The drawings were of a marine deck hatch used on fishing boats. At the time of the invention, Mr. Saracone owned a lunch truck. He was never a fisherman—"

"Objection!" Rovitch said, and Judge Gemmill nodded to Mary to continue, not that she needed encouragement.

"In contrast, at the time of the invention, Mr. Brandolini had been a fisherman all his life. He was an adult, almost aged forty, when he went to the camp. He owned three fishing boats."

"How would the Court know that, counsel?"

"Everybody knows that," Mary blurted out in frustration, and the *circolo* burst into righteous applause.

Crak Crak Crak! Judge Gemmill pounded the gavel. "Order! I will not have this! I will not!"

"Your Honor," Mary said, "if Frank Cavuto hadn't been murdered, I would have proof that Amadeo Brandolini was a fisherman. If those drawings hadn't been stolen, I could show you that they existed. If Keisha Williams hadn't had her throat slit, I could prove that on his deathbed, Giovanni Saracone's practically admitted that he murdered Amadeo!"

"Objection! Objection! That's an outrage!" Rovitch was shouting. Justin Saracone leapt to his feet, and the courtroom erupted in noise and chatter.

Crak Crak Crak! "Order! Order! Order!" Judge Gemmill slammed the gavel down again and again.

"Mary! Mary! Mary!" cheered the *circolo*, and others were shouting, too.

Crak Crak Crak! "Order! Order!"

"Mary! Mary!" someone called out, over the din.

"Order, order, I said!" Judge Gemmill was shouting. "Who is that, standing up in the gallery? Sit down, you! Sit down this very minute!" The judge gestured swiftly to the courtroom deputy, who rushed past the bar of court. Mary turned around to see what was going on. The gallery was talking, and every member was seated.

Except one.

FORTY-SEVEN

It was Mrs. Nyquist, standing up from the middle of the gallery and raising her hand. Her blue eyes shone, her crow's-feet deepened, and her mouth curved into that sweet smile. She stood barely unbended in the courtroom. Mary couldn't believe what she was seeing.

"Mary!" Mrs. Nyquist called out, loudly enough to be heard. "May I speak to you for a minute, please?"

"*Pardon* me?" Judge Gemmill said, astounded. "What is going *on* here?" The courtroom burst into new chatter, everybody craning their necks to see the action, and Mary went out the bar of court and hurried down the aisle toward Mrs. Nyquist.

"What are you doing here?" Mary asked, mystified, and Mrs. Nyquist made her way out of the packed pew as if she were at a Saturday matinee. When she got to the end of the aisle, she handed Mary some papers.

"Take a look at this, dear," she said, and Mary did.

"Ms. DiNunzio! Order! Deputy!" Judge Gemmill shouted, but Mary was armed with the papers and grabbed the deputy before he laid a hand on Mrs. Nyquist.

"Your Honor, I call Mrs. Helen Nyquist to the stand!"

"Objection! Objection!" Rovitch said, and the reporters scribbled away while the gallery kept talking.

Mary took the lectern. "Your Honor, Mrs. Nyquist has evidently come all the way from Butte, Montana to give testimony in this matter."

"This witness wasn't on the witness list," Rovitch argued. "She shouldn't be heard. Defendant wasn't given proper notice."

Mary appealed to the judge. "Your Honor, I had no idea Mrs. Nyquist would be appearing today. I listed all my known witnesses in my papers and even served defendant with a copy of the papers personally."

"Served me?" Justin Saracone jumped to his feet again. "You *hit* me!"

"Mr. Rovitch, silence your client!" Judge Gemmill banged the gavel. "I will *not* have further outbursts in my courtroom! Order! Order!" *Crak!* "I will *not* have this disruption! Order! Everybody! Now!"

In the meantime, Mrs. Nyquist strode toward the witness box, and by the time the gallery had calmed down, she had seated herself quite comfortably, crossing her legs in her long denim skirt, which she wore with a light blue cotton sweater. Her short gray hair was shaped in the same cut Mary had seen that night in the farmhouse kitchen, with no concession to vanity.

Mary looked up at Judge Gemmill. "Your Honor, may I proceed? It's well-established that Mrs. Nyquist didn't have to be announced on my witness list, in this sort of expedited proceeding. It isn't a trial, Your Honor, where those rules apply."

Judge Gemmill looked from Mary to Mrs. Nyquist, then leaned toward the witness box. "You say Butte?"

"Yes, Your Honor."

"I have a home in Bigfork."

"Flathead Lake's mighty pretty."

"I'll say." Judge Gemmill banged the gavel and smiled. "Swear her in. Proceed, Ms. DiNunzio."

"Thank you, Your Honor. Your Honor, may I get some copies of these documents for defendant and the Court?" Mary handed a law clerk the documents as Judge Gemmill nodded, and he disappeared out the pocket door while Mrs. Nyquist was sworn in. "Now Mrs. Nyquist, please tell the court where you were, from 1941 to 1943."

"I was living in Missoula, Montana, with my late husband, who was camp adjutant at Fort Missoula during the war." Mrs. Nyquist's face softened, and Mary knew she had to tread carefully.

"Mrs. Nyquist—"

"Please, call me Helen."

Mary smiled. "Thank you, Helen. Now, from 1941 to 1943, did you and your husband live on the internment camp grounds?"

"We did."

"Helen, I would like to show you Movant's Exhibit A, which is a photo taken at Fort Missoula during that time." Mary leaned over to counsel table, retrieved her exhibit, and took it to the witness stand, where she gave it to Mrs. Nyquist. "May I ask you to identify the men in this photo?"

"I know only the two. The tall man in the cap, that's Giovanni Saracone, and the shorter man in front, that's Amadeo Brandolini."

Mary felt her throat catch. Had Mrs. Nyquist lied before? "Helen, how did you come to know these men?"

"I used to work at the camp office during the week, filling in. My husband asked me to, so I did it for free, and I met them both." Mrs. Nyquist blushed slightly, and Mary tried to read her. She had called Saracone a wolf. Had he gotten to her?

"Helen, please tell the Court why, if Mr. Saracone and Mr. Brandolini were internees of the camp, would they be in the camp office and not under guard?"

Mrs. Nyquist turned to the judge. "It wasn't like that, they used to come and go freely, the Italians did. Giovanni—his nickname was Gio—was in our office all the time, flirting." Mrs. Nyquist didn't smile, but there was muffled laughter in the gallery, which she ignored. "Gio spoke very good English, so he was always dropping in, talking with the other girls, flashing his smile. Girls loved Gio."

There was laughter again, and Justin was grinning as if he'd won something. But Mary was putting it together. It wasn't Gio who had gotten to Mrs. Nyquist. If it had been, she wouldn't be here today. "Helen, did Amadeo Brandolini come into the office, too?"

"Objection, relevance!" Rovitch barked, and Judge Gemmill didn't bother to rule, but dismissed him with a wave.

"You were saying," she said, and Mrs. Nyquist swallowed visibly.

"Amadeo came in sometimes."

Amadeo.

"Gio would bring him in, and he would sort of tag along. He was very quiet, isolated from us, because his English wasn't good. Still, he was a very smart man. He could fix most anything." Mrs. Nyquist paused. "We tried to talk to him. He was the quiet type, and he got quieter after his wife died."

"Back in Philadelphia, right?" Mary was starting to suspect that Theresa's death wasn't accidental either, but she couldn't deal with that now. The law clerk returned with copies of the documents and handed them to Mary.

"Yes, we heard that." Mrs. Nyquist looked down, her gray hair glinting in the overhead lights, and Mary sensed she didn't need to go any further along this line.

"Helen, I show you the first of three documents you brought here today, which I am marking as Exhibit N-1, and I ask you to look it over while we all do." Mary took Mrs. Nyquist the top page, then distributed one to Judge Gemmill, one to defense counsel, and an extra one to Justin himself. "Here, as a courtesy, Mr. Saracone." Then Mary took the lectern without looking back.

Mrs. Nyquist finished reading the document, and looked up.

"Helen, what is the date on this document, Exhibit N-1?"

"It is dated July 1, 1942."

"Thank you. Could you please read Exhibit N-1 to the court?"

"Certainly." Mrs. Nyquist cleared her throat, and Mary looked down at the document. The paper felt soft under her fingerpads, yellowed and crinkly, and the typeface was the Smith Corona Courier she'd grown to love at the National Archives. The History Channel indeed; this case had a beating heart. As Mrs. Nyquist read the document into the record, Mary read it to herself.

CONTRACT

Giovanni Saracone and Amadeo Brandolini agree that Gio will make a translation into English for an invention of Amadeo's, which Amadeo says is a kind of cover that goes on the deck of his fishing boats and keeps the water out of the hull and closes by itself without him having to close it all the time, and Gio also agrees to help get for him the application for the Patent and to send to the United States Government. These are Amadeo's drawings that he made to show his invention for a cover. The drawings show the cover and the way it closes by itself. Amadeo already gave Gio fifty dollars ($50) to do this work and Amadeo promises to give Gio fifty more dollars ($50) when Gio finishes the translation for the Patent and we send it to the Government. This contract makes it legal and binding.

Mrs. Nyquist finished reading, and the courtroom fell completely silent. Then she testified: "The contract is signed with an X by Amadeo on the left, and by Gio here, on the right. And by me underneath, as witness. I typed it up and watched them sign it."

"Objection!" Rovitch was on his feet. "This document is hearsay! It's inadmissible! It's a compete fake!"

Mary faced the judge. "Your Honor, the document isn't hearsay. Mrs. Nyquist produced the document, she's a witness with knowledge, and she's here to authenticate it, if Mr. Rovitch would permit."

"Objection overruled. Go ahead," Judge Gemmill said, inclining her sleek head toward Mrs. Nyquist.

"Helen," Mary said, composing herself. "Where did you type this up?"

"In the office at the camp. At my desk."

"Why? Did Amadeo Brandolini ask you to?"

"Goodness, no."

Ouch. "Did Giovanni Saracone ask you to?"

"No. That shifty devil didn't want anything in writing."

"Objection!" Rovitch said, and Judge Gemmill slammed down the gavel.

"Counsel, will you give it a *rest*!" she said, and Rovitch slunk in his seat.

Mary hid her smile, and her confusion,

when she faced Mrs. Nyquist again. "Helen, who asked you to prepare this?"

"Nobody. It was my idea."

Mary blinked. "Why?"

"I never sold a horse without a contract. Never leased a horse without a contract. Never even hauled a horse without a contract," Mrs. Nyquist answered, matter-of-factly. "You gotta have a contract. Don't need a law degree to know that."

Mary broke into a smile, and the gallery and Judge Gemmill laughed with her.

"So," Mrs. Nyquist continued, "when I saw these two making this deal, I said, one a you is gonna need this thing on down the line." She eyed Justin coldly. "I knew just which one, and I'm sorry to say I was right."

Mary felt like clapping, but she'd be disbarred. The gallery was murmuring and Judge Gemmill was smiling. Mary returned to her exhibits.

"Let's turn now to Exhibit N-2 and N-3, Helen. What are these documents?" Mary looked down at hers, which felt like precious paper in her hands. They were drawings of the hatches, considerably more detailed than the ones she had found in

Amadeo's wallet, which must have been preliminary. Mary looked up at Mrs. Nyquist.

"These are drawings that Amadeo made, of his hatch," Mrs. Nyquist testified.

"How do you know Amadeo made them, and not Giovanni Saracone?"

"Because he drew them in front of me, right then."

Mary blinked. "While you waited?"

"It took an hour and a half, and he did it from memory, all of it. He was a smart man. Not an educated man, but a smart man."

"Helen, did you make copies of this contract?"

"I did. I made carbon copies when I typed it."

"How many?"

"Two. One for Amadeo, and one for Gio. I kept this one, the original, for safekeeping."

Mary thought a minute. "At whose request?"

"I did it on my own. I downplayed it, I guess you'd say. I don't think either man noticed I kept the original, they were so excited." At the recollection, Mrs. Nyquist had a faraway look. "Gio practically skipped out of the office."

And Amadeo had signed his own death warrant. Mary put together what must have happened. Saracone had undoubtedly gotten rid of Amadeo's copy of the contract, but he'd forgotten about the original. Mrs. Nyquist hadn't. Mary heaved a sigh. Her job was done.

"Your Honor," Mary said, "Exhibits N-1 through N-3 having being authenticated, I move for their admission into evidence."

"Admitted," Judge Gemmill ruled, nodding.

Thank you, God. "And thank you, Mrs. Nyquist. Your Honor, I have no further questions," Mary said, after a minute. She turned and sat down, catching Bennie flash her a thumbs-up. She sat down and stared straight ahead, because she knew if she looked over at Judy, she'd start laughing or crying or both. In the next minute, Judy passed her a note on a yellow legal pad that read: MARRY ME.

But Mary tensed as Rovitch approached the lectern.

Because it wasn't over until it was over.

FORTY-EIGHT

Rovitch drew himself up to his full height at the lectern. "Well, Mrs. Nyquist, that was quite a story."

Mary bit her tongue. She wouldn't object unless Mrs. Nyquist was in real trouble. The woman broke broncos for fun.

"It was the truth, sir," Mrs. Nyquist answered, folding her hands on the stand, and Mary thought she saw a slight tremble. Even cowgirls aren't bulletproof.

"Mrs. Nyquist, I find it strange that you appear with these documents that make Ms. DiNunzio's day, and just in the nick of time."

"Is that a question, Your Honor?" Mrs. Nyquist asked Judge Gemmill, and the judge shook her head.

"Not in my book."

"Mrs. Nyquist, my question is when is the last time you met with counsel for the estate, Mary DiNunzio?"

"A week ago, last Wednesday."

"And where did that meeting take place?"

"At my home in Butte."

"Was Ms. Carrier or Bennie Rosato present at the meeting?"

Mrs. Nyquist blinked. "Who are they?"

Judy laughed softly and passed Mary a note: NOBODY.

"Who else was present at your meeting?"

"Just us, and it wasn't a meeting."

"What was it then?"

"She came by for coffee and pie, she was trying to find out about Gio and Amadeo."

"Mrs. Nyquist, at this meeting, did you discuss with Ms. DiNunzio the testimony you would be giving today?"

"No."

"Did you discuss your testimony with her at all before you gave it today?"

"No."

"Did you discuss your testimony with anyone from her office before you gave it today?"

"No."

Rovitch blinked. "You mean to tell this Court that you simply appeared, here in this courtroom, with this document?"

"Yes."

At counsel table, Mary almost laughed out loud. *I know, I can't believe it either.*

Rovitch paused. "Has Ms. DiNunzio contacted you since your meeting in Butte?"

"No, she hasn't returned my call. I've left two messages but she hasn't called back."

Back at counsel table, Mary felt a pang of guilt. *Her messages.* She flashed on Marshall, lecturing her when she was on the way out of the office, with Judy.

Rovitch leaned over the lectern. "Then how, pray tell, did you even know to come here this morning, to this courtroom?"

"I didn't." Mrs. Nyquist shook her head. "I went to Mary's office but there were so many damn reporters there I couldn't even get in. Then one of 'em told me everybody was here, so I took a cab and came down here to see her. Then I saw her getting out of a cab, and I tried to call her, but there were still so many damn reporters louder 'en me, I couldn't holler over 'em."

The poor woman. Mary smiled, and the gallery chuckled, too.

Rovitch jingled some change in his pocket and rocked back and forth on his loafers for a minute. "Mrs. Nyquist, why is it, then, that you came all the way out to Philadelphia?"

"To bring Mary the contract."

"How did you know she needed it?"

"Because when she came to visit me, she told me she thought Gio murdered Amadeo, and I figured this might be the reason why."

Wow. Mary's eyes flared open at the revelation. The gallery startled, and even Judge Gemmill was surprised. Saracone looked like he could kill, and Rovitch stood at the lectern, wanting to object to his own question. Mary shuddered. *I'd go with no further questions, pal.*

Mrs. Nyquist added, "And it's been botherin' me, gnawin' at me, and my grandson showed me how on the Internet it was the big news story here in Philadelphia. I thought she might need my help." She nodded at Mary. "She's a hardworkin' gal and she's tryin' to do right by Amadeo."

Mary felt a rush of warmth for Mrs. Nyquist and couldn't help but nod in acknowledgment of her kindness.

Rovitch sighed. "No further questions, Your Honor."

Judge Gemmill turned to Mrs. Nyquist. "You may step down. Thank you for your testimony, and have a safe trip back home."

Mary was already on her feet. "Your Honor, we move now for a temporary restraining order against Justin Saracone and Saracone Industries."

"Granted, Ms. DiNunzio," Judge Gemmill ruled, banging the gavel, and the courtroom erupted into chatter and applause.

We won! Mary threw her arms around Judy, and when Mrs. Nyquist came over, Mary hugged her, too. In fact, she hugged the deputy, two of the law clerks, and the stenographer. The gallery exploded, the *circolo* started a conga line, and the judge pounded her gavel again.

Crak! Crak! "It is hereby ordered that plaintiff's requested relief is granted, the particulars of the order to be issued by chambers later today and released to the press. Dates for the preliminary hearing and subsequent trial to be scheduled later, counsel."

Crak! Judge Gemmill banged the gavel, with a final sound. "Lastly," she continued, "pursuant to Federal Rule of Civil Procedure 65, a security bond must be posted by the estate. I order that such bond be in the amount of one hundred thousand dollars. Ms. DiNunzio?"

"Yes, Your Honor?"

"I said, one hundred thousand dollars is your bond."

"My . . . bond?"

"Your bond. You've read the rule, correct?" Judge Gemmill frowned and picked up a piece of paper from the dais. "Rule 65(c) provides that 'no restraining order or preliminary injunctions shall issue except upon the giving of security by the applicant, in such sum as the court deems proper.'" Judge Gemmill peered over the top of her glasses at Mary, who froze in place.

A hundred thousand dollars? Where am I gonna get that kind of money? The estate is broke. I have $375 in savings. I mean, I didn't plan on actually winning.

"Counsel, as you know, I cannot issue a TRO unless the bond is posted. The reason, as you well know, is that in the event that you lose on the merits, the defendant is compensated for his loss. As I see it, his immediate loss would be the postponing of the sale of rights to Reinhardt, perhaps for one week, which delay would only be for a nominal amount."

A hundred thousand dollars is nominal? Plus, if I lose at trial, I lose the hundred thousand, too? Which I don't have? Is that even possible?

"DiNunzio!" called a voice, and Mary turned to the gallery.

Bennie Rosato was standing up. Trademark suit. Trademark hair. And trademark smile. "Your Honor, Rosato & Associates will post the bond. I'll accompany Ms. DiNunzio down to the Clerk's Office directly."

Really? Mary looked at Bennie, dumbfounded.

"I'd bet on you any day." Bennie beamed. "You're a winner, kid."

"Thank you," Mary said, and resisted hugging her, but just barely.

In the next moment, a defeated Justin Saracone stormed past her and out the bar of court, with his unhappy lawyer hurrying behind.

FORTY-NINE

The Four Seasons Hotel was where Philadelphia lawyers went to celebrate, and Mary, Judy, and Bennie had a little party there with Mrs. Nyquist and her grandson. They toasted one another at a marble table with peach-colored orchids in the center and a Steinway for background noise. Mrs. Nyquist got the most toasts of all, and Mary learned that after the first two glasses, Dom Pérignon tastes exactly like Crystal Light.

An hour or so later, Bennie and Judy excused themselves to go back to the office, and Mrs. Nyquist's grandson excused himself to go to the men's room, leaving Mary alone with her favorite cowgirl. She raised a glass to Mrs. Nyquist. "Helen, from the bottom of my heart, thank you very, very much."

"You're very welcome, my dear." Mrs. Nyquist smiled graciously.

"You saved the case, the day, my career, and most of the city."

"Not hardly."

"In fact, I think I love you."

"I like you just fine, too, Mary. We did have fun, watching Conan."

"We did. You're the best date I've had in a long time."

"That isn't saying much," Mrs. Nyquist offered, and they both laughed.

Mary raised a glass. "One more toast. To no more blind dates!"

"Here, here!" Mrs. Nyquist cheered, toasting.

They laughed again, and Mary couldn't remember if she'd thanked Mrs. Nyquist, and even if she did, it was worth repeating. "Helen, thank you so much for testifying today." Then she remembered how tight money was for Mrs. Nyquist. "And please, let me pay for your airfare and travel. That's standard for witnesses, and the least I can do."

"No, thank you. I won't hear of it. I never charge anything, but I charged this."

"Please, please, please let me pay."

"No." Mrs. Nyquist paused. "As much as I like you, Mary, I didn't do it for you. I did it for Amadeo."

"All the more reason."

"Although I admit, I'd thought you'd use that contract in a murder trial, not some patent doodah."

"I wish I could have. But Gio died after I got back from Missoula, I guess you heard."

"Yes."

They both fell silent a minute, and Mary took a swig of Diet Coke, as an antidote to champagne. There were so many questions she was dying to ask Mrs. Nyquist, but she couldn't go there. She sipped her Coke and listened to the lovely piano music. The pianist had segued into "I'll Be Seeing You," which Mary knew she wasn't supposed to like anymore, but still did. She felt suffused with the wonderful feeling of having won. For Amadeo. And the bittersweet feeling of having it all end, and having to let him go.

Mary raised her glass. "To Amadeo."

"To Amadeo." Mrs. Nyquist smiled, raised her glass, and they clinked and sipped. "I guess you know, he and I were in love," she confessed, softly.

Mary let the hushed words linger.

"Gio used to bring Amadeo around the office, and Amadeo and I became friends. He was shy, but I tried to teach him a few words in English. *Pencil. Pen.* Then one day, he fixed my typewriter. The *p* key stuck, and the *r*. Always those two." Mrs. Nyquist smiled. "I guess I kind of got a crush on him, from that day on. His wife was still alive at the time. He fixed the radio on my desk, and it wasn't even broken that bad. He took it apart, cleaned it, and put it back together again, and it got better reception after that." She shrugged, remembering. "Some girls like roses, and others like things fixed, I guess."

"I'd like both." Mary smiled.

"Then after his wife passed away, Amadeo was so blue all the time. My heart just went out to him, and our friendship, well, it turned into love." Mrs. Nyquist sighed heavily, and her hooded gaze met Mary's, on the level. "I'm not proud of it. I was a married woman. Aaron was so busy with the camp and his career, but that's no excuse."

Mary didn't say anything, but she didn't judge, either.

"Aaron knew about my feelings for

Amadeo, or at least he suspected. Even from early on, when I had my crush, he could tell. Later I found out he was having one of his men keep an eye on Amadeo, in the camp, from even before our affair began."

Mary remembered the FBI memo, from the National Archives, monitoring Amadeo's meeting with Giorno about Theresa's death. She had assumed Amadeo was being monitored by the government, but he wasn't. He was being watched on orders of Aaron Nyquist, who wasn't worried about betrayal of his country, but the betrayal of his *wife*.

"So I broke it off, in July. Right before the Fourth, because we were having a party at the house. I couldn't do it any longer, betray Aaron like that. I had made a vow to him, and I wanted to keep my word. Set things right between us." Mrs. Nyquist swallowed again, as she had in court. "Then I heard that Amadeo killed himself, and foolishly, I thought I had something to do with it. That he was upset over our breakup. I never gave a thought that it was murder. I forgot all about the contract until you came to Butte."

"It was lucky that I did, then."

"Or it was meant to be. Do you still think things don't happen for a reason, Mary?"

"Maybe they do," Mary conceded. "I'm in such a good mood, I can't disagree with anybody today. Least of all you, Helen." She noticed Mrs. Nyquist's grandson had come back into the lounge and stopped at the marble bar to talk with the bartender, a pretty redhead.

Mrs. Nyquist smiled sweetly. "I'm telling you all this, about Amadeo and me, because I think you understand him. You have a feel for him. He was a wonderful man." She leaned over. "I honestly think he was my one true love, and I think he loved me back that way, too. He couldn't do enough for me, he paid me so much attention. He even carried around a lock of my hair. Imagine!"

Mary would have said something but her throat felt kind of tight. She leaned over, unlatched her trial bag, extracted an envelope, and handed it across the table.

"What?" Mrs. Nyquist asked, puzzled. She opened the envelope and gasped. She took out the lock of hair, cupping it in her palm, and looked up, her eyes shining. "This is it! This is mine! How did you get this?"

"It was in Amadeo's wallet. I had it in my desk drawer with my personal stuff, because I showed it to Judy and didn't put it back in the case file. He kept it with him all the time, Helen."

"Oh, my." Mrs. Nyquist blinked the tears from her eyes and placed the lock back into the envelope with care, and Mary felt the love she felt for Amadeo. Because it was the love she had for Mike.

"To real, honest-to-goodness, no-joke love." Mary raised her glass. Someday she'd have that love again, she just knew it. She might even serve a subpoena on a certain engineering professor.

"To love." Mrs. Nyquist raised her glass, composing herself. "And to you, too, Mary. You're quite a little lawyer."

"Thank you." Mary sipped her Diet Coke, watching Mrs. Nyquist's grandson and the bartender, with their heads bent together over the bar. The plastic casing to the cash register was hinged open, and they were both looking inside.

Mary blinked. Her gaze traveled from the cash register to the grandson. Will Nyquist. His hair was dark, his eyes darker. She knew those eyes. She had seen them on

George Clooney. *Oh my God.* Mary turned to Mrs. Nyquist, whose gray head turned to her, and the two women regarded each other over the table for a minute.

"Yes, it's true," Mrs. Nyquist said, answering a question she hadn't been asked.

"Will is *Amadeo's grandson*?" Mary felt like shouting, but Mrs. Nyquist silenced her quickly with a wave.

"Aaron knew, I couldn't deceive him, not more than I already had. Still, he raised Amadeo's son as his own. He was a generous man, of heart and spirit." Mrs. Nyquist sniffed. "But I never told Will's father. And Will doesn't know either. That's why I didn't bring him to court today, in case it came out. I was afraid you would ask about me and Amadeo, but you didn't. Thank you for that."

"There was no need to, because you told the story so well." Mary's attention returned to Will, watching him. He did look so much like the way she had imagined Amadeo, now that she could see him uncovered by grease. And he fixed things—old trucks and evidently, cash registers. Will must have inherited his grandfather's mechanical ability and his movie-star looks. Mary turned to Mrs. Nyquist. "Are you going to tell him?"

"I guess so. I guess I will."

"I think that's a good idea," Mary said gently, then she thought of something. "Helen, you know what? If Amadeo has a living heir, which he does in Will, then that heir is entitled to inherit Amadeo's estate. I'm talking about the money that flowed from the original patent for the hatch." Mary leaned forward on the cushy shell-pink chair. "You understand? The money that's been going to Justin Saracone all these years will now go to Will."

"Excuse me?" Mrs. Nyquist asked, uncomprehending, and Mary felt a rush of excitement.

"Helen, before today, Amadeo's estate was worthless. You thought you were coming back here for a murder trial, but the hearing was about who gets the royalties for the hatch Amadeo invented." Mary touched her arm. She couldn't help it, she had to make contact with something. "The answer, thanks to you, is Will."

"My goodness!" Mrs. Nyquist blinked. "Is it enough to pay for the U?"

"It's enough to *buy* the U!" Mary burst into laughter, and Mrs. Nyquist's hand fluttered to her mouth in shock.

"Oh, my Lord!"

Mary beamed, feeling good all the way to her very soul. And then, though she couldn't tell if it was the champagne, the piano music, or the truth, she could have sworn that she heard a soft voice whispering.

Sì.

FIFTY

"Ma, what goes in next?" Mary asked, from over the big, dented pot of brewing tomato sauce. Beads of sweat popped on her forehead. Steam melted her contact lenses. The Panasonic radio on the counter played *Sunday with Sinatra,* Mass cards curled behind the switch plate, and Penny scampered between everyone's feet, chasing a tennis ball that nobody had time to throw. Mary stirred the tomato sauce, and a chicken wing, a bumpy meatball, and a piece of driftwood floated past. "Is it the garlic or the basil?"

"Garlic, Maria!" Her mother called from her seat at the kitchen table, where she was nestled like a baby bird in the pink folds of her chenille bathrobe. Mary's father sat next to her, in his Sunday undershirt and Bermuda shorts. They didn't try to help, because Mary had threatened litigation and now had the juice to deliver. Not only had she gotten her preliminary injunction, but Justin Saracone had been charged with conspiracy in Frank Cavuto's murder when Chico turned state's evidence. And in the process, Mary had become a major business getter at Rosato & Associates, with new cases coming in every day from three different parishes. *Today South Philly, tomorrow the world.*

"The basil gets too bitter if you put it in early," her father said, and next to Mary, Judy stirred spaghetti in another big, dented pot.

"Didn't they teach you anything in law school, girl? You embarrass the profession!" "You know you want me," Mary said, smiling. She grabbed a chipped china coffee cup, dumped in the chopped garlic, then stirred it up. She couldn't remember when she'd been so happy. Her mother's operation had been a complete success and she was cancer-free. Keisha had recovered, too, and was engaged to marry Bill. And

Premenstrual Tom had turned out to be harmless, but still completely annoying, so Mary had given him the cell phone number of a certain brown-eyed reporter at the *Philly News*.

"Ready, here!" Judy yelled. "We have spaghetti ignition!"

"Now basil ignition!" Mary sprinkled in the cheery green strips.

"Only a minute, Mare, with the basil," her father said, and her mother nodded in agreement, blessing the entire operation.

"Okay, lift off!" Mary and Judy sprung into motion as a team. Judy poured the boiling spaghetti into the colander, and Mary ladled the gravy onto the bare plates, mysteriously priming them for maximum spaghetti reception. It was a rookie kitchen dance, but in no time the table was complete with four plates of fresh spaghetti and homemade gravy, set in front of three hungry people, Mary's parents and Judy.

Mary was the last one to sit down because, for the first time, she was the one wielding the wooden spoon. She waited a minute, savoring the sight of the three people she loved so much, happy, whole, and about to be well-fed. And she sent up a silent prayer of thanks, for when it counted the most, all of the saints had come through for her.

Even St. Valentine.

AUTHOR'S NOTE AND ACKNOWLEDGMENTS

"Where do you get your ideas?" It's the most common question people ask authors, and my answer for *Killer Smile* is simple: The idea for this novel came from history—not only the history of my country, but of my family.

My paternal grandparents, Giuseppe and Maria Scottoline, were compelled to register as "enemy aliens" on February 27, 1942, although they had lived in Philadelphia for thirty years and violated no laws. My grandfather was a laborer and my grandmother a housewife; he was illiterate in both Italian and English, though she had been a schoolteacher in Italy and was literate in Italian. They raised four children: three girls and then a boy—my father, Frank. Ironically, at the same time that Giuseppe and Maria were being registered as enemies of the country, their son, Frank—my father—was serving in the United States Air Force. I learned their story only recently, when my father gave me their alien registration cards shortly before his death. (I include a copy of their registration cards at the end of this book.) I am forever indebted to my father, and to my grandparents, for this novel, and, of course, for much else.

By way of historical background, at the outbreak of World War II, President Roosevelt signed into law a series of presidential orders that identified all Italian-born Americans as "enemy aliens." The presidential orders compelled Italian-Americans to register as enemy aliens, and some 600,000 registered. The orders also authorized their arrest by the FBI and relocation to internment camps. As a result, more than 10,000 Italian-Americans were evacuated from their homes and places of business, and sent to internment camps around the country.

The major internment sites for Italian-Americans were Fort George Meade in

Maryland, Camp McAlester in Oklahoma, Fort Sam Houston in Texas, and Camp Forrest in Tennessee. Italian-Americans were also sent to Fort Missoula, Montana, and any one of the forty-five other internment camps used by the Immigration and Naturalization Service and the Provost Marshal General's Office.

Some of the Italians interned were visitors to the United States, such as waiters working at the World's Fair in New York or sailors on visiting cruise ships, but many were Italian-Americans who had lived in the United States for decades without violating any laws or without giving the government any factual basis for designating them as enemies. Some were editors of Italian newspapers, bankers, or other professionals. Many had adult children serving in the United States military, fighting against Axis nations, including Mussolini's Italy.

Italian-Americans on the West Coast were greatly affected, because its enforcing general, Lieutenant General John DeWitt of the Western Defense Command, was so vigorous in his enforcement of the presidential orders. In addition, the government believed that the coasts of the United States were especially vulnerable to communication with the enemy. Italian-Americans were registered as enemy aliens en masse and as many as 52,000 Italian-Americans on the West Coast had their daily travels confined to "exclusionary zones" and were subject to dusk-to-dawn curfews. For example, the father of baseball great Joe DiMaggio was not permitted to visit his son's restaurant on Fisherman's Wharf because it lay outside his exclusionary zone. Fishermen and sailors were particularly targeted for this reason. Many were no longer allowed to work as fishermen, and in some instances had their boats seized.

Italian-American residents of the East Coast registered en masse as enemy aliens. They were not permitted to travel without their registration booklet and were subject to inspection and search on demand. Many had their homes searched for flashlights and radios, and this property was confiscated on the belief that it could be used to signal enemy submarines and warships off the East Coast. As on the West Coast, the fishing business on East Coast port cities such as Philadelphia, Boston, and Gloucester were affected. Fishermen were not permitted to fish, even if it supported their families; in Boston alone, 200 fishermen were grounded.

The status of enemy alien was eventually lifted, but the suspicion, hard feelings, and monetary losses remained. To date, no reparations have been demanded or paid to any Italian-American interned and no reimbursement has ever been made to them for any property confiscated. In 1999, as a result of lobbying by the Italian-American community, the United States Congress addressed the treatment of Italian-Americans during World War II, which resulted in House Resolution 2442, acknowledging that the United States violated the civil rights of Italian-Americans during World War II. The bill was passed in the House of Representatives in 1999, in the Senate in 2000, and signed by President Clinton in the same year.

This chapter in American history represents a turbulent confluence of war, law, and family. It wasn't the first time that civil liberties have been set aside in times of armed conflict, and it won't be the last. You don't need me to tell you that history is on a loop. More recently, the September 11 terrorist attacks and the war with Iraq have raised a number of legal issues regarding the suspension of civil liberties during wartime. This summer the Supreme Court will decide questions concerning the rights of "enemy aliens" and "enemy combatants," including the right to sue in U.S. courts for unlawful detention in internment camps. As long as there is armed conflict—whether abroad or domestic—these legal, political, and emotional issues will recur, and will shape the contours of justice.

My own awareness of the historical context for this novel was heightened greatly by the good works of the National Italian American Foundation, and they get first and deepest thanks here. For those who would like to learn more about the internment, please refer to the following materials: Lawrence DiStasi, *Una Storia Segreta: The Secret History of the Italian American Evacuation and Internment During World War II* (2001); Stephen Fox, *Uncivil Liberties: Italian Americans Under Siege During World War II* (2000); Chief Justice William H. Rehnquist, *All the Laws but One: Civil Liberties in Wartime* (1998); Carol Van Walkenburg, *An Alien Place: The Fort*

Missoula, Montana, Detention Camp, 1941–1944 (1995); Gary Glynn, *Montana's Home Front During World War II* (1994); Umberto Benedetti, *Italian Boys at Fort Missoula, Montana, 1941–1943* (1991); and *Bella Vista: An Unseen View of WWII,* a television program produced by Kathy Willows and Montanans for Quality Television.

In this regard, special thanks to Umberto Benedetti, a former internee at Fort Missoula whose many books have cast light on the subject, as well as to Alfredo Cipolato, another internee at the Fort, who has educated all of us. I would like to note that in my search for the graves of the Italian internees who died at Fort Missoula, which began at the National Archives and ended at the Catholic cemetery herein described, I discovered a secret: that the memorial markers of the three Italian internees who died at Fort Missoula were paid for not by the United States government, but personally by Mr. Benedetti and Mr. Cipolato. These two men have never been recognized or thanked for their previously anonymous act of generosity and grace. They should have been. *Grazie mille.*

Thanks to the staff at the National

Archives in College Park, Maryland, who helped me find the original files of the internees at Fort Missoula, and a huge hug to my amazing assistant, Laura Leonard, who was by my side all the way, as always. Thanks so much to Director Robert M. Brown at the Fort Missoula Museum and his wife, Claudia, and to staff members Donna McClure, Jocelyn, and most of all, to archivist and gentleman Dale Johnson and his wife, the lovely Coby, librarian and great lady. Happy Birthday, Coby!

Thanks to Jim Edgar and his great staff at the Montana Bureau of Vital Statistics, and also to the gang at Fact & Fiction Bookstore and The Books Exchange for the excellent books on Missoula and Montana history. Thanks to the legendary Tattered Cover in Denver for my cowgirl books, *Cowgirls, Women of the American West*, by Teresa Jordan, University of Nebraska Press (1992), and *Cowgirls,* Candace Savage, Ten Speed Press (1996).

Thanks to the Recorder's Office at City Hall, Philadelphia, especially Ward Childs, archivist, and Jarrance Nesbitt, Title Registration Supervisor, Department of Records, who were so kind. Thanks to the Otts at

Clews Boats in Frazer, Lisa Baute, M.D., of Penn Medicine, and Paul Davis. Thanks for all things Italian to Sebastian Pistritto of www.gustobene.com.

Huge thanks to Theodore Nacarella, Esq., for excellent legal advice and all-around intelligence and good cheer; if I say more about what vital part he helped with, you'll guess a PLOT TWIST. Thanks to my other genius lawyers, dear friend Jerome Hoffman, Esq., and now his amazing son, David Hoffman, Esq. For constitutional law assists, thanks to Professor Judy Brown, Esq., and Lisa Gleicher, Esq. Thanks to Glenn Gilman, Esq., and to Forever-Detective Art Mee, my go-to experts for everything wonderful and helpful.

Thanks to all of those generous people who donated to a worthy cause in return for their names in the novel, Bern Gibboni (American Red Cross), Marti Funnell (American Diabetes Association), Lisa Gemmill (Free Library of Philadelphia), Lorraine Pecora (Free Library of Philadelphia), Stephen Nicastro and Louis Nicastro (Friends' Select School), Gail Lasko (PAL), and Ernest and Leslie Eadeh (Pennsylvania Home of the Sparrow for abused women and children).

On the writing side, a huge and grateful hug to the best editor in New York, Carolyn Marino, with whom I have worked for eleven books. I am blessed in her and in everyone at HarperCollins: the great Jane Friedman, Cathy Hemming, Susan Weinberg, Michael Morrison, Carl Lennertz, Patti Kelly, Christine Boyd, Rockelle Henderson, Carrie Kania, Libby Jordan, Roberto De Vicq de Cumptich, Bob Spizer, and Jennifer Civiletto. And I also owe Carie Freimuth and Tara Brown. I love you all. Deepest thanks and love to everyone at the Aaron Priest Agency, mainly my terrific agent, Molly Friedrich, and the Amazing Paul Cirone, for improvements to this manuscript and guidance in all things.

Thank you to all of the hard-working book-sellers who have forever supported me and my books, and to my pal Joe Drabyak of Chester County Books & Music, who nur-tures me with all sorts of wonderful reading and even made comments on an early draft of this manuscript.

Love to my family, for their constant sup-port and love.

And to a certain man, who taught my heart to talk.

"Green cards for Giuseppe Scottoline and Maire Scottoline."

Alien Registration No. 2129 258

Name Giuseppe none Scottoline
(First name) (Middle name) (Last name)

RIGHT INDEX FINGERPRINT

(Signature of holder) Giuseppe Scottoline

Mathers Freedman
52 Arlington St. Phila. Pa.

16—26150-1

Birth date Aug 31 1881
(Month) (Day) (Year)

Born in or near Ascoli-Piceno Italy
(City) (Province) (Country)

Citizen or subject of none last of Italy
(Country)

Length of residence in United States 32 yrs., — mos.

Address of residence 4923 Thompson St
(Street address or rural route)

PHILADELPHIA, PA.
(City) (County) (State)

Height 5 ft., in.

Weight 145 lb.

Color of hair Brown

Distinctive marks scar on forehead left side

(STAMP)
PHILADELPHIA, PA.
FEB 27 1942
M.O.B.

Sadie A. Walsh
(Signature of Identification Official)

Application filed in Alien Registration Division. Copy filed with Federal Bureau of Investigation office at

PHILADELPHIA, PA.

16—26150-1

Alien Registration No. 3225477

Name Marie none Scottoline
(First name) (Middle name) (Last name)

RIGHT INDEX FINGERPRINT

Maria Scottolini

Maria NoNo

(Signature of holder) Maria Scottolini

16—26150-1

Birth date May 4 1893
(Month) (Day) (Year)

Born in or near Ascoli Piceno Italy
(City) (Province) (Country)

Citizen or subject of last of Italy
(Country)

Length of residence in United States 29 yrs., 9 mos.

Address of residence 4923 Thompson Street
(Street address or rural route)

PHILADELPHIA PA
(City) (County) (State)

Height 5 ft., 2½ in.

Weight 147 lb.

Color of hair brown

Distinctive marks none

PHILADELPHIA, PA.
FEB 27 1942
M.O.B.

Marie A. Wall
(Signature of Identification Official)

Application filed in Alien Registration Division. Copy filed with Federal Bureau of Investigation office at

PHILADELPH'A. PA.

16—26150-1